Taking the Field

TAKING THE FIELD

a marching arts novel

GEMMA LANE

Taking the Field © 2025 Gemma Lane

This is a work of fiction. Names, characters, places, and incidents are the product of the author's imagination or are used fictitiously. Any resemblance to actual persons, living or dead, events, or locales is entirely coincidental.

ISBN (Paperback): 979-8-9985732-0-0

Printed in the United States of America

First Edition

The cover and interior has been designed using resources from Flaticon.com

@gemmalanebooks
www.gemmalanebooks.com

For the misfits who found home in the band room.

For Jessica,

who, even from the other side of the field,
was my first supporter.
You gave me the courage to keep sharing my stories.
Thank you, and rest easy, friend.

01 Lost & Found

Jessica

The guy in the black BMW honked, swerved into my lane, and flipped me off. Welcome to Southern California.

I gripped the steering wheel of my beat-up Corolla, knuckles white as I dodged another lane changer who didn't believe in turn signals. Every mile felt like a new level of a video game—except instead of racking up points, I was racking up anxiety. Back in Riverview, the only traffic jam I'd ever seen involved a tractor and a stray cow. Here? It was like *The Hunger Games*, but with Teslas and luxury SUVs.

"I hate cities," I muttered, glancing at my phone mounted to the AC vents, barely holding on. Thirty minutes to go. Thirty more minutes of palm trees, bumper-to-bumper traffic, and the blaring soundtrack of impatient horns.

The heat didn't help. Even with the AC blasting, it felt like the sun had decided to sit shotgun. I adjusted the vents, aimed them at my face, and took a sip from my water bottle—only to remember it had been sitting in the cupholder long enough to double as tea.

Another car zipped past. I glanced at the driver: perfect makeup, oversized sunglasses, phone glued to her hand as she yelled at someone through her Bluetooth. She probably ordered oat milk lattes and knew how to contour. Meanwhile, I was sweating through my tank top, trying to remember which exit I was supposed to take.

My parents and brother were probably already at the house, supervising the movers and pretending this was all normal. Like uprooting our lives and dragging us to the other side of the state wasn't a big deal.

But it was a big deal. It was huge. Back in Riverview, I'd been somebody. Drum major. Leader. The girl everyone looked to when the band hit the streets. Now, I was just another new kid trying to navigate freeways and figure out if *hella* was an insult or a compliment.

I rolled into the neighborhood, my Corolla rattling like it might fall apart. The houses all looked the same—stuccoed clones with identical lawns and spotless driveways. The place screamed *I have money, but I shop at Target for the vibe.*

It didn't feel like home. It didn't feel like anything.

I parked behind the moving truck and killed the engine. For a moment, I just sat there, staring at the place where my life was supposed to restart. It was too clean, too perfect, like a set for a TV show about a family who had their lives together.

With a deep breath, I grabbed my trumpet case from the passenger seat and my parade mace from the back. I stepped out into the relentless sun.

Dad waved from the porch, his grin too wide—like he was trying to convince himself this was a good idea. Mom stood nearby, fanning herself with a clipboard, already slipping into her role as commander-in-chief, micromanaging every box coming off the truck.

I followed them up the steps and into the house. My sneakers squeaked on the spotless tile. The place was enormous, dwarfing our old one, but it felt... sterile. The walls were painted in neutral tones, the shade of beige you'd see in a furniture showroom. The air smelled faintly of fresh paint and lemon cleaner. Sunlight poured through oversized windows, bouncing off the polished floors and making everything look bright and staged. It was grand, sure, but also hollow—like it was trying too hard to impress. A house that didn't know how to feel like a home.

"Aiden?" I called, heading toward the noise coming from the back. Rapid clicks and digital explosions grew louder. I peeked into what was supposed to be the den and found my brother exactly where I expected—slumped in his wheelchair, face glued to his phone, fingers furiously tapping.

"Hey," I said, leaning against the doorway. "You settling in?"

He didn't look up. "Define 'settling.'"

I stepped closer, peering over his shoulder. Some kind of first-person shooter played on the screen, his character darting around corners and blasting enemies. Typical Aiden. His dark hair stuck out in every direction, and his pale skin practically glowed in the dim light. He was thin—too thin—but his sharp features and steady hands gave him an intensity that could either intimidate or charm, depending on his mood.

The wheelchair, sleek and matte black, was tucked close to the desk. It was as much a part of him as his sarcasm, though neither of us talked about it much. We didn't need to. It was just there—like gravity. Inescapable and ever-present.

"You could at least pretend to be excited about the new house," I teased, plopping down on the desk's edge. "This place is massive. You could probably do donuts in here."

"Yeah, great," he muttered, glancing up with a smirk. "A whole new layout to memorize and another set of narrow doorways to squeeze through. Living the dream."

Guilt prickled. Aiden always knew how to weaponize humor when he felt out of control.

"I'm sure Dad will make adjustments if you need them," I offered, though I wasn't sure I believed it.

He rolled his eyes. "Whatever. I've got bigger things to worry about, like not getting sniped by a twelve-year-old right now."

I laughed—more out of habit than amusement. "Fine. Be a hermit. I'm gonna get some practice in."

I'd been obsessing over this ever since we left Riverview. The night Dad announced the move, I stayed up until midnight drafting an email to Mr. Trust, Arcana High's band director, introducing myself. It wasn't just about joining the band—I asked if I could try out for drum major.

Mr. Trust replied the next day. His response was surprisingly warm. He welcomed me, attached information about the leadership tryouts, and wished me luck. I should've felt relieved. Instead, it just lit a fire under me.

Arcana's band was massive, award-winning, intimidatingly perfect. If I was going to prove I belonged, I couldn't just be good—I had to be flawless.

As I headed into the hall, already feeling the weight of it all, Aiden called out. "Hey, Jess?"

"Yeah?" I paused, glancing over my shoulder.

"Don't overthink it," he said. "The whole band thing. You're good at what you do."

I managed a small smile. "I'm not overthinking it."

Lie. I was always overthinking it.

Aiden smirked knowingly and turned back to his game.

Upstairs, I lugged my trumpet case and mace in one hand, a bag of essentials in the other. The staircase was wide, the steps polished and silent. Everything about this house felt shiny and new—which only made me miss Riverview more. At least there, every squeaky floorboard and chipped banister had history.

The second floor opened to a long hallway with evenly spaced doors. Mom had texted which room was mine. I made my way to the one at the end and kicked it open.

It was massive—twice the size of my old room. Plush carpet, a lazy ceiling fan, a wide bay window pouring in afternoon light. I stood there a moment, just taking it in. It was beautiful, but distant. Polished to the point of being untouchable.

My eyes caught on the full-length mirror mounted to the closet. I lingered, studying my reflection—the way I stood so still, hands at my sides, like I was afraid to disturb anything.

I set the trumpet case and mace down on the built-in desk beneath the window. The soft thud broke the silence. I ran a finger along the desk's edge, already imagining late nights practicing or hunched over my computer.

Outside, a large oak swayed just beyond the window. Its branches brushed the glass, like they were testing the barrier. The trunk was thick, the lower branches sturdy. The kind of tree I might've climbed as a kid.

I pressed my palm to the glass and stared a little longer than I meant to. It was comforting—like maybe this house wouldn't always feel so foreign. Not yet, but maybe someday.

I turned to my instrument, unlatching the case, checking valves, polishing the mouthpiece. My mace came next. I picked it up, twirled it once—the weight grounding and familiar. The metallic shine caught the sunlight, and for the first time since we arrived, I felt a little more like myself.

"Jessica," Mom's sharp voice cut through the hallway.

She said my name like a reprimand. Clipped. Just enough edge to make it sound like I'd already done something wrong.

I froze, mid-spin, gripping the mace like I'd been caught holding a weapon.

"Don't spin that thing in the house," she called again, voice trailing down the hallway. Equal parts disapproval and an unspoken *you should know better.*

"I'm not going to break anything!" I shouted back.

Her tone wasn't just a warning—it was a verdict.

"You'll break the ceiling fan," she said, passing the doorway with a box. "Or a window. Or yourself. Take it outside."

There was always something in the way she talked to me—like she was keeping score. I wanted to tell her I wasn't that clumsy kid anymore. But the words never came out right.

So I did what I always did. I stayed quiet. I obeyed.

I glanced back at the window, sunlight bouncing off the mace. Probably best not to test her patience today.

As I headed downstairs, her voice followed, lighter but still sharp. "Dinner's at six. No getting lost in whatever you're doing."

I sighed, gripping the mace tighter. She always said it like that—like I might spiral out of control if she didn't set the timer on my life.

"Got it," I muttered, halfway out the door.

The backyard was quiet. Untouched.

I stood in the center, gripping the mace like an extension of my arm. The weight was steady. Familiar. I closed my eyes. The movements came back instinctively—fast, clean, grounded in muscle memory. I could almost hear Riverview's Main Street, the band echoing off brick buildings, reminding me of who I was. Who I still wanted to be.

I spun again. Faster this time. Sharp, deliberate. Every toss and snap helped quiet the noise in my head. When I was focused—when I was perfect—there was no room for anything else. No past. No cracks. No doubt.

It's why I'd been a great drum major. Not just because I had talent, but because I worked. I stayed late, ran every sequence until I couldn't get it wrong. And maybe I got lost in it sometimes—but it was better than getting lost in everything else.

I tossed the mace higher, caught it mid-spin. The sunlight glinted off the silver finish like a spark.

Arcana didn't know me yet.

But they would.

Christian

"Tell me you're joking."

I blinked at Mr. Trust, sure I'd misheard him.

He leaned back in his chair, folding his arms with the kind of calm that only made me more tense. "I'm not joking, Christian. We have a new senior transferring in. She wants to join the band—and try out for drum major."

Drum Major? My drum major position?

The words rang in my ears like a badly tuned trumpet: off-key, obnoxious, and impossible to ignore.

I stared at him, trying to process. "You're seriously telling me someone's going to audition… against me?"

Mr. Trust raised an eyebrow, clearly amused. How could he be so calm?

"You've never had competition before. Maybe it's time you did."

"That's because no one else can do what I do," I shot back, heat rising in my chest. That—and maybe everyone else was too intimidated to try.

He chuckled, like I'd just proven his point.

"I've been drum major for the last two years. I know this band. What does she know?"

"Her name's Jessica Welling," Mr. Trust said, ignoring my outburst. "She's coming from a small town in Northern California—Riverview. Drum major since her sophomore year. Just like you. She emailed last week asking about leadership tryouts."

The name meant nothing to me, yet something inside me twisted all the same.

"Look," he said, leaning forward, his tone softer now. "You're good, Christian. You've proven that time and time again. But being a leader isn't just about being good—it's about handling challenges with grace. This is a chance for you to grow. Don't waste it."

I crossed my arms, jaw tight. "I don't need to grow, Mr. Trust. I've earned this."

His gaze stayed steady, unshaken. "Then earn it again. Tryouts are in a few weeks. Show me why you deserve to stay on the podium."

I didn't answer. There wasn't anything I could say that wouldn't sound defensive or desperate. Instead, I gave a stiff nod and turned back to the drumline equipment I'd been organizing before this whole conversation wrecked my focus.

The first time I stepped onto the podium, I nearly threw up.

It was freshman year, mid-season. Our drum major came down with strep the morning of the biggest football game of the year. Mr. Trust scanned the field during rehearsal, his expression calm but searching—until his eyes landed on me.

"Gutierrez," he said, jerking his head toward the podium. "You're up."

I froze, snare sticks clutched so tight I could feel the wood pressing into my palms. "Me?"

"Yes, you. You've been watching the formations and calling cues all season. You know the music better than anyone."

"But—"

"Go," he said, and that one word carried enough authority to get my legs moving before my brain caught up.

The podium felt higher than it looked from the field. A hundred eyes were on me, and my knees locked. I gripped the railing so tightly my knuckles went white, my heart pounding too loud to hear the tuning below me.

Then Mr. Trust called out from the field, calm and clear. "Take a deep breath, Christian. You're the leader now—show them where to go."

That was all it took. One line. I felt my pulse slow just enough to remember why I loved this. My hands raised, tempo steady, and the band followed without hesitation. By the time the last note rang out, I didn't want to come down.

Afterward, Mr. Trust clapped a hand on my shoulder as I stepped down. "Good job, Gutierrez. You've got the instincts of a leader. Don't let me down."

I never forgot that moment. It wasn't just that he believed in me—it was the way he handed me responsibility like he already knew I could handle it, even before I did.

The band room was where I spent most of my summer. While everyone else posted beach selfies and *lived their best lives*, I was here, checking inventory, labeling uniforms, making sure every last cymbal and mallet was accounted for. Someone had to keep this place running—and it might as well be me.

At least here, everything made sense. There was structure. Rules. Order. Things didn't bend, no matter how much chaos waited outside these walls.

Unlike home.

I grabbed a clipboard off the nearest chair and started checking snares, marking each one. The rhythm of it helped steady me, though the Jessica Welling bombshell still hadn't left my chest.

"You know," Mr. Trust said from behind his desk, "most students spend their summer doing something a little more relaxing than inventory."

I glanced over my shoulder, keeping it cool. "Yeah, well... most students aren't me."

His mouth twitched into the faintest smile. "True enough."

He didn't press. I was grateful. Mr. Trust wasn't the prying type, but he always noticed more than I wanted him to—like the fact that I wasn't here just to prep for camp.

I was here because the band room felt more like home than my actual house ever had.

At home, everything was breaking—not in a crash, but slowly, like a piano slipping out of tune. No matter how hard I tried to play, the melody came out wrong. Offbeat. Off-key. I could pound the keys, adjust the bench, even try humming the harmony—but the song was lost. The more I tried to fix it, the worse it sounded.

Dad was always working. Late nights, early calls. The man could draft a hundred-page contract in his sleep, but he couldn't make it to a single performance. Every time I thought *maybe this time*, there was always a last-minute excuse.

"You understand, don't you?"

And Mom? Mom was worse. At least Dad pretended to care.

Her affair wasn't even subtle. The way she disappeared for whole weekends. The soft, playful voice on late-night calls. The "friend" she saw twice a week but never brought home.

They thought I didn't notice. Like I was too wrapped up in band to see the truth.

But I saw everything. Every strained glance. Every door that didn't quite close. They were holding on by a thread, waiting for me to graduate so they could finally let it snap—like timing would make it hurt less.

It didn't. It just made everything quieter.

That's why I stayed here.

Here, there were no whispered fights behind walls. No fake smiles over silent dinners. Just music. And order.

I exhaled and checked off the last snare. The drums were ready. The uniforms were ready. The band was ready.

I was ready.

"I'm gonna head out, Mr. T," I said, dropping the clipboard on the table with a soft clatter. The tubas gleamed under fluorescent lights, lined up like soldiers.

Mr. Trust looked up from his desk and waved. "Thanks for your help. I'll see you at tryouts."

I grabbed my bag and headed for the door. The room was quiet now—just the hum of the AC and the sound of my footsteps on tile.

This wasn't just about keeping my title.

This was about proving no one else deserved it as much as I did.

Jessica could try.

But she wouldn't outwork me. Or outsmart me. Or out-lead me.

This was my band.

✗ ✗ ✗ ✗ ✗

The house was dark when I got home, save for the blue flicker of the TV in the living room. Mom lay stretched on the couch, wrapped in a blanket, eyes glued to her phone. She didn't even look up.

"Hey," I said, not expecting much.

"Dinner's in the fridge," she muttered, still scrolling. Probably texting him.

I dropped my bag by the door and kicked off my sneakers. The thunk echoed through the hollow space.

The house looked like a catalog page. Glossy surfaces. Perfect furniture. Pictures on the wall that looked more like decorations than memories.

I opened the fridge, pulled out a plastic container of pasta, and ate it standing up. Straight from the container.

Dad wasn't home. No note. No call. Just the usual: late meeting, last-minute trip, work came up.

Even when he was here, it wasn't like he *was*.

I tossed the container into the sink and climbed the stairs.

My room was the same as always—functional, slightly messy. A stack of sheet music on the desk. My laptop. An empty coffee mug I kept forgetting to take down.

I dropped into my chair and opened the laptop, not sure what I was looking for.

Something. Anything.

Jessica Welling Riverview High, I typed.

Nothing. Just old articles about Riverview. One headline mentioned a car accident, but it was buried. No photos. No videos. No sign of who she was or why Mr. Trust thought she could challenge me.

Maybe I'd misspelled it. I tried again, slower: *Riverview High School Marching Band*.

A few blurry photos loaded. Forty kids, max. Local parade energy. No real website. No accolades.

It was almost laughable.

What was Mr. Trust thinking?

But still—he'd *named* her. That meant something.

I tried one more search: *Riverview High marching band scores.*

The page shifted. Northern California competition results. Riverview wasn't on the radar—until I scrolled to the parade drum major section.

Riverview High: **1st place**.

Every. Single. Competition.

Two years straight.

I stared, the tightness in my chest creeping higher.

Parade scores weren't the same as field shows. Everyone knew that. But still—first place *every time*?

That wasn't luck.

I leaned back in my chair.

So she wasn't a nobody.

Fine. She was good at parades.

But Arcana? Arcana was another level.

Whatever trophies she had didn't matter here.

Not in my band.

Not on my podium.

Jessica

Morning light spilled through the blinds, striping my room in pale gold. Sleep had been elusive. I spent the night practicing my conducting, repeating each motion until they felt both natural and precise. I'd perfected each flick of my wrist, each shift of my stance, until every move felt correct. Yet, no matter how many times I rehearsed, something felt off—some intangible detail slipping just out of reach. If I couldn't get it exactly right here, alone in my room, how could I expect to stand out at tryouts?

I dragged myself out of bed, the excitement from yesterday replaced with a heavy, nervous energy. Today was the day. Today, everything could change.

In the kitchen, the smell of freshly brewed coffee and toast filled the air. Mom was at the stove, humming softly as she flipped pancakes. Aiden was at the counter, halfway through a stack of pancakes, his face animated as he talked about some new video game release. Mom listened, nodding with soft, unwavering attention, completely absorbed in his every word.

I hovered by the doorway for a moment, feeling like an outsider in my own kitchen. Finally, I cleared my throat and stepped in, pulling a chair out from under the table.

"Morning."

She looked up, her smile shifting just slightly as she turned her attention to me. "Good morning, Jessica," she replied. She placed a plate in front of me, setting it down with a practiced care that felt almost rehearsed.

"Thanks," I said as I picked up my fork, forcing a small smile, even though my stomach twisted in knots. The tryouts were going to be tough, and I knew I needed the fuel, but somehow, even eating felt like a chore under her gaze.

Sitting down across from me, she took a sip of her coffee, her eyes sliding back to Aiden, who was engrossed in his food. "You know, Arcana's a big school with plenty of talented students. Just make sure you're at your best—first impressions are everything. And if it doesn't go how you want... well, not everyone's strengths are in the same place."

I paused, the fork halfway to my mouth. It was just a small comment, just a little reminder—but it stung. It always did. Like she'd already written me off, quietly preparing me for failure before I'd even had the chance to prove myself.

Aiden glanced up, frowning slightly as he looked between the two of us. "She'll do great. She's been practicing for weeks," he said, his tone casual but with a hint of defensiveness.

Mom's face softened immediately as she turned to him. "I know, honey. You're so supportive." She reached over and placed a gentle hand on his shoulder. The gesture filled with a warmth that felt like it had no place in my direction.

I squeezed my fork a little tighter, forcing myself to smile at Aiden. "Thanks," I murmured.

He shrugged, flashing me a small, supportive smile before turning back to his plate. "You'll be fine, Jess."

My mom took another sip of her coffee, still watching Aiden with that proud, almost doting expression. It was as if she couldn't help but see him as the perfect son—the one she needed to protect, the one who could do no wrong. And I was the one she was always preparing for disappointment, the one who needed her "reminders" not to aim too high.

The pancakes tasted like sawdust as I forced them down, each bite grainier than the last. After breakfast, I retreated to my room to get ready, trying to push her words—and the look on her face—out of my mind. Today was too important to let anything, or anyone, shake me.

The drive to Arcana High felt uneasy. My fingers mindlessly tapped against the steering wheel, as I silently rehearsed and practiced in my head. My mom's words would always cut into my thoughts, looping with an edge that refused to dull. I reached for the volume knob, desperate to drown out the echo with static or music or anything, but even the radio couldn't replace the noise in my head.

My fingers drifted to my lips, a habit I didn't even realize I'd fallen back into until I felt the familiar sting of a nail bitten too short. I dropped my hand to the steering wheel, but the urge lingered. I needed to focus on something else—anything else—but the anxiety kept crawling under my skin.

I'd left early, maybe too early. I needed the extra time to find the right building—or so I told myself. Really, I just needed to be moving, to be doing something, anything, so I wouldn't get swallowed whole by my own thoughts.

When I finally pulled into the parking lot, the school loomed ahead, sprawling and pristine, with wide lawns and sleek glass windows that reflected the early morning sun. It looked polished, like a campus plucked straight from a college brochure—the kind you'd keep on your dresser as a daily reminder of what you were working toward. The buildings itself seemed to stretch on endlessly, with wings branching off in every direction and an athletic complex that looked bigger than Riverview's entire school grounds.

I took a deep breath, trying to steady the nerves buzzing just beneath my skin. The place felt massive, buzzing with a kind of energy that was almost overwhelming. The students here would be talented, polished, the kind who were used to winning and who expected nothing less. I felt the weight of being just one person— one small fish in a vast, well-funded pond.

You've got this, I told myself, gripping the steering wheel until my knuckles turned white. *You've practiced. You're ready.* But as I looked at the imposing campus ahead, I couldn't help but feel unprepared.

Stepping out of the car, I slung my bag over my shoulder with my parade mace in hand and headed towards what I hoped was the music building. The campus was eerily quiet, the only sound my footsteps echoing off the pavement. But as I got closer, faint strains of music reached my ears. The sound bounced off the buildings, growing louder and clearer with each step, guiding me like a beacon.

I followed the music down a pathway and around a corner, where it intensified, leading me to a large building with double doors. This had to be it. The band room.

Taking a deep breath, I pushed open the door, and a wall of sound hit me—a vibrant, layered cacophony of instruments tuning, voices laughing, and drums pounding. The room was large. Tall ceilings arched overhead, gleaming floors reflected rows of meticulously organized equipment, and polished instruments and framed awards lined the walls—a testament to the band's legacy.

The moment I stepped inside, everything stopped. The noise, the music, the commotion—it all came to an abrupt halt as dozens of eyes turned to stare at me. I felt their gaze linger, assessing, curious, and I suddenly noticed every detail, from my posture to the weight of my bag slung over my shoulder. This was their territory, their home, and I was the outsider standing in the doorway, just one unfamiliar face in a room filled with talent and tradition.

A prickling heat crept up my neck, but I straightened, shoulders back, chin up, holding steady against the dozens of eyes fixed on me. My fingers curled around my mace, holding it tightly. Every instinct screamed to step back, to disappear into the floor, but I held my ground.

"Hi," I said, my voice steady despite the nerves twisting in my gut.

A few whispers broke out among the students, and I caught a few skeptical glances. They were sizing me up, judging me before I even had a chance to show what I could do.

I just had to make it through this.

"Jessica Welling, I take it?" A middle-aged man near the front spoke up, his steady voice slicing through the tense silence. I nodded, and he smiled warmly, waving me over to him. "It's nice to meet you, Jessica. I'm Mr. Trust, the band director here."

As I made my way to the front, I tried to focus on his welcoming expression rather than the eyes still trained on me. My heart pounded in my chest, a mix of excitement and dread. Was I really cut out for this level of marching?

I forced myself to shove those voices down, refusing to let them take hold. I was here for a reason, and I wasn't about to let self-doubt ruin it. After a silent breath, I reached out and shook Mr. Trust's hand, hoping he couldn't feel the slight tremor in mine.

"Welcome to Arcana," he said, his grip firm and reassuring. "I'm looking forward to seeing what you can do."

He intended his words to be encouraging, but they only made the weight on my shoulders heavier. I managed a small smile, trying to push the anxiety out of my mind. "Thank you," I replied, my voice steady despite the storm inside. "I, uh... I'm ready to give it my best."

"That's all we ask for here—your best." Mr. Trust nodded, his eyes kind but discerning. "Now, I think I forgot to mention in my email that you'll have to play a little something on your instrument."

My heart stopped, an icy shock rippling through my chest. I hadn't prepared for this. My mind scrambled, searching for any solution, any way I could fix this oversight. How could I have missed this? How could I be so careless? I didn't even think about bringing my instrument. My stomach twisted, the familiar pang of panic clawing its way up. I prided myself on being ready for everything, rehearsing every worst-case scenario. But this—this was a complete blind spot.

I forced myself to breathe, but the thought kept echoing, relentless: *I didn't practice for this.*

"What is it you play?" he asked.

"Trumpet?" The word slipped out, weak and wavering, barely resembling an answer. My voice betrayed me, cracking under the weight of his gaze.

A sharp intake of breath rippled through the room, followed by a few stifled laughs that prickled at the edges of my hearing. My cheeks burned, and I glanced toward the director. He was watching me, an amused smirk tugging at the corner of his mouth, as if he knew something I didn't. My pulse quickened, confusion tightening in my chest. What was I missing?

"Ignore them," Mr. Trust said. "We just didn't realize that you and Christian, the other drum major candidate, both play the same thing. It'll be an interesting day, for sure."

A weight settled in my chest, pressing down hard. Christian. The name echoed in my mind, sharp and unwelcome. So he was my competition—and we played the same instrument? I forced a neutral expression, but the edges of my nerves frayed. This wasn't how I'd pictured walking into this audition, not at all.

"I didn't prepare anything for trumpet," I mumbled, trying to cover up my mild panic. My mind was racing, trying to come up with a plan, anything that would get me through this without embarrassing myself.

Mr. Trust waved a hand dismissively. "No worries, Jessica. We just need to see a snapshot of your musicality—it doesn't need to be a whole piece. You can borrow a trumpet from the school's inventory. You'll be fine."

Fine. The word echoed in my mind, sharp and biting. Fine wasn't good enough—it was barely scraping by. Fine was what you said when you settled, when you didn't care enough to push yourself to be better. I didn't do *fine.* I did perfect. And perfect took preparation. Perfect took practice. And I didn't practice.

My chest tightened, the weight of my own expectations pressing harder with every second. My mind clawed for a piece to play, something, *anything* that could salvage this, but my thoughts blurred like static. It was like flipping through a filing cabinet in the dark—scales, fragments of old concertos, disjointed runs of arpeggios, all just out of reach. Every piece I'd ever learned was stacked somewhere in my memory, but now it felt like the entire stack was toppling over.

Of all things, *Hot Cross Buns* sprang to mind—loud, relentless, and mocking, like a cruel joke my subconscious had decided to play. Heat crept up my cheeks. *Absolutely not.* I hadn't spent years drilling scales and memorizing concertos to squeak out a tune every fifth grader could play with their eyes closed. My brain must've been short-circuiting because, for the life of me, I couldn't dredge up anything better.

I sifted through my mental archive of music, flipping through dusty file after dusty file, but all I got was a blank wall and that relentless three-note taunt. *Hot. Cross. Buns.* It wouldn't go away. My confidence crumbled a little more with every passing second, the surrounding silence stretching thin.

I forced myself to nod, keeping my face as calm as I could, even though I was anything but. "I'll figure something out."

Mr. Trust offered a reassuring smile and motioned for one student to bring me a trumpet. I could feel the weight of everyone's expectations as they handed it over, a suffocating pressure building with each hesitant touch and murmured word.

I took the instrument and found a seat. My hands felt unsteady, but I couldn't let that show. It was a good thing I came early. I'd have some time to practice... something. I pushed on the three pistons, hoping something would pop into my head just from muscle memory.

Thank goodness.

The moment my fingers found the valves, a flood of muscle memory took over, guiding me before I could second-guess myself. My mind latched onto *Flight of the Bumblebee*, the rapid, intricate piece I'd drilled endlessly last year to keep myself grounded, to drown out everything else. The relentless pace, the challenge of each twisting note—it demanded all my focus, leaving no room for anything else to creep in.

The sound of a baton hitting a music stand brought me out of my focus. "Alright, settle down everybody. We're going to get started pretty soon," Mr. Trust's voice carried through the room. There were a few other adults standing with him at the podium, to which I assumed were the section staff. "We'll start off with the woodwinds section leader candidates."

I scanned the room, spotting clusters of flutes, clarinets, and saxophones—a dozen or so players, already warming up with scales and arpeggios that floated through the air. Laughter bubbled from one corner, casual chatter from another, their voices blending into a low hum that seemed to pulse around me. They moved easily, falling into conversations as if they'd known each other forever. Meanwhile, I stood there, my trumpet cold and heavy in my hand, my presence barely noticed in the blur of woodwinds.

Their effortless smiles and easy camaraderie felt like an invisible wall, pushing me further to the edges.

Mr. Trust cleared his throat, and the room fell into a hushed anticipation. "Next, we'll have the brass section leader candidates, Jessica and Christian too, since you're both on trumpet."

The transition to the brass section was a welcomed change. I gathered my trumpet and stepped forward with determination, trying to shake off the lingering feeling of being out of place.

"Speaking of which," Mr. Trust said, looking at his watch and then scanning the room. "Where's Christian?"

Someone holding a trumpet spoke up. "He's on his way. His truck's got a flat."

"Thanks, Alex," the band director said, looking down at his clipboard. "Well, we should keep the party rolling. Why don't you go first?"

Alex groaned as he shuffled some sheet music out of a folder and placed it on the music stand beside Mr. Trust. He blew the condensation out of his trumpet, took a breath, and filled the room with the bright, bold opening of Hummel's *Trumpet Concerto in E-flat Major*. The familiar notes rang out, crisp and confident, and I felt a pang of irritation at myself.

Of course. I'd played Hummel's concerto before—I knew it well enough to have brought it to mind before even thinking about *Hot Cross Buns*. As I listened, I pushed aside the frustration and let myself focus, mentally running through the opening measures, each note and rhythm flooding back like second nature.

When he finished, he bowed as a few girls in the back clapped for him. "Welling, you're up," Mr. Trust announced.

I got up from my seat and made my way to the front, pushing the music stand aside as I had to do this all from memory. I warmed up, playing the scales and arpeggios that led into the piece, letting the familiar melody guide me through the nerves. The quick tempo and challenging passages were actually a relief—they gave me a focus, a purpose. I could see Mr. Trust watching me with an amused yet thoughtful expression, and the murmurs from the students had quieted down as they turned their attention toward me.

I played through the piece with a mix of determination and urgency, feeling the notes come alive under my fingers. As I finished, I glanced up, hoping my performance had been enough to impress or at least to mitigate my earlier anxiety.

Mr. Trust's eyes sparkled with approval. "Well done, Jessica. That was impressive—especially on such short notice. You've clearly put in the work, and it shows. Thank you for taking on that challenge."

I let out a slow, shaky breath, the tension easing from my shoulders. My fingers tingled, still buzzing from the final note, but this time with something closer to pride than panic. Against all odds, I'd pulled it off. My lips curled into a slight smile as I replayed the performance in my mind, each measure steady and controlled. The weight that had been pressing down on me lifted, replaced by a small spark of confidence that warmed me from the inside.

As I stepped back, I caught sight of Alex's narrowed eyes fixed on me, his gaze sharp and assessing. He was sizing me up, like I'd crossed some invisible line I didn't even know existed. It wasn't like I was competing for the trumpet section lead, but something in his look made me feel distinctly unwelcome. Or maybe I was imagining it. Still, I couldn't ignore the weight of his stare, a reminder that I had more than just my own expectations to live up to here.

I took a step toward my seat, but a sudden bang shattered the hum of the room. The door slammed open, the echo ricocheting off the walls as every head whipped toward the entrance. Conversations died mid-sentence, instruments paused in mid-tune, and a heavy, stunned silence settled over us all, like the air itself was holding its breath.

Slowly, the room seemed to shift—students sitting a little straighter, adjusting their posture like they'd been caught slouching. A few exchanged quick, wide-eyed glances, but most just stared at the door where he stood. This must be *him*.

My competition.

Christian stormed in, his dark hair a disheveled tangle, grease streaking his forehead and hands like battle scars from a car engine. He looked clearly frustrated. Even with grease smudges on his skin and a shirt that looked like it had been thrown on in a hurry, he carried an intensity—a presence that commanded the room without effort. Every eye followed him, drawn to the unapologetic authority radiating off him like heat from asphalt on a summer day.

Christian

The morning was already unraveling. I'd barely rolled out of bed, my brain foggy and weighed down by today's tryouts, when I stumbled outside to find my truck leaning awkwardly to one side. Crouching down, I squinted at the tire—deflated and sagging against the asphalt. Not a small leak. Done for.

"Seriously?" I muttered, dragging a hand through my tangled hair. The flat stared back at me like it had chosen this moment just to spite me. I could almost hear the seconds slipping away, ticking down my chances to make it on time.

"Of course this happens today. Of all days!" I snapped, kicking the tire lightly, knowing full well it wouldn't fix anything. "Screw you, universe. Real helpful."

For a second, I thought about calling for help. But Uncle Jacob's voice echoed in my head, *"Come on, Christian. You've got this. Be prepared for whatever life throws at you."* The memory was crystal clear—him crouching next to me by the truck, guiding me as he showed me how to change a tire. *"One of those skills every guy should have in his back pocket,"* he'd said, clapping me on the shoulder with that affable grin of his.

Grabbing the tools from the back of my truck, I got to work. Sweat rolled down my face as I cranked the jack and loosened the lug nuts, grime caking my hands. Every second felt heavier than the last, the minutes slipping away no matter how fast I worked. "Come on, come on, you stupid piece of—" I muttered, gritting my teeth as the wrench slipped. "Why now?"

By the time I tightened the last bolt, I was already running late. Tossing the tools into the truck bed, I tried to shove down the frustration simmering in my chest. I was halfway down the road before it hit me—I'd left my trumpet at home.

"Are you kidding me?!" I smacked the steering wheel, unleashing a string of expletives at the universe as I pulled a sharp U-turn and gunned it back to the house.

By the time I'd grabbed the trumpet and got back on the road, my shirt was damp with sweat, grease smudged across the front, and my knuckles tight around the wheel. So much for showing up confident and collected. Instead, I was about to storm in looking like a mechanic who'd just lost a fistfight with a carburetor.

Tearing down the road toward Arcana High, the truck rattled over the uneven streets. The morning had already sabotaged me. Of all days, it had to be today—*my* day. The flat wasn't just an inconvenience; it was a crack in the image I'd built of showing up, owning the room, and leaving no doubt that I was the only choice for drum major. And now? I was starting on someone else's terms. The thought burned like acid. *F-you, universe.*

As the school came into view, I shoved the frustration down, forcing my focus back where it belonged. The second I walked through that door, the chaos of the morning would be behind me.

The sound of a trumpet cut through the air as I approached the band room. Crisp, confident notes rang out, sharp enough to stop me in my tracks. My brow furrowed. It wasn't Alex—I knew his playing like the back of my hand. This was someone else. Someone better.

My grip on the door handle tightened as irritation prickled under my skin. Was this *her*? The supposed drum major prodigy from the middle of nowhere?

I pushed the door open harder than necessary, the loud bang reverberating off the walls. Conversations and music came to an abrupt halt as dozens of heads turned to look at me. The weight of their stares pressed down, but I kept my expression neutral, shoving my frustration deep.

Scanning the room, my gaze locked onto Mr. Trust. He raised an eyebrow, a flicker of amusement tugging at the corner of his mouth. The look said everything: *Late on tryout day? Really?*

"Sorry I'm late," I said, voice clipped. My hands found my pockets as I forced a casual shrug. "Had some car trouble."

Mr. Trust nodded, his way of saying that he accepted the apology—but barely. His gaze flicked to the front of the room, landing on a girl I didn't recognize. She stood tall; her trumpet still in hand, her expression calm and composed. Something about the way she carried herself grated on me—too steady, too assured.

I sized her up, taking in the straight posture and the way she carried herself. Her sun-kissed skin had a warm glow, and her brown hair was pulled back into a clean ponytail—not a strand out of place, like she had it all together. Then there were her eyes, green and sharp, locking onto mine with a look I couldn't quite decipher. Was it indifference? A challenge? Either way, it sparked something in me—an irritation I couldn't shake.

"You must have perfect timing," Mr. Trust said. "Because you're up next."

Perfect timing, after the morning I'd just had? I yanked my case open and grabbed my trumpet, ignoring the stares from the room as I brought it to my lips. No warm-up. No prep. Fine. I'd play through it.

I launched into *Autumn Leaves*, letting muscle memory take over. The first notes carried the weight of my frustration, raw and sharp, but the melody soon smoothed out, taking on a life of its own. By the time I hit the final phrase, the room had shifted. Silence hung in the air as I lowered the trumpet, my pulse thrumming in my ears.

Mr. Trust nodded, the faintest hint of approval in his expression. Without a word, I turned and made my way to an empty seat near the back. My gaze stayed forward, ignoring the lingering stares—or the girl sitting just a few feet away.

Mr. Trust continued with the rest of the brass section leader auditions as I sat back, trying to cool myself down from the mess of this morning. Once he finished going through the percussion candidates, he dismissed everyone for a break.

As soon as Mr. Trust announced the break, the room buzzed with quiet conversations and the sound of chairs scraping against the floor. I kept to myself, still trying to shake off the frustration of the morning, when I noticed the competition making her way toward me.

It was clear she was trying to bridge the gap, to make some sort of connection. Part of me knew I should at least acknowledge her effort, but the stubborn part of me—the part still pissed off at how the morning had gone—wouldn't let me.

"Hi, I'm Jessica," she said, her voice steady. She held out her hand, offering a polite smile.

My eyes flicked down and then back to her eyes, ignoring her hand. Instead, I gave her a nod, barely making eye contact. "Christian," I said shortly, my tone cool. Then I turned away, making it clear the conversation was over before it even began.

Out of the corner of my eye, I saw her hesitation, the way her hand dropped back to her side. She looked like she was about to say something else, but thought better of it. After a moment, she just gave a small nod, her polite smile fading, and walked back to her spot.

I could feel a twinge of guilt—maybe I should have handled that better—but I pushed it aside. I had more important things to focus on. Like making sure I didn't mess up the rest of the tryouts.

As the break ended and Mr. Trust called us back, I shoved the interaction out of my mind, focusing instead on the next phase of the auditions. But I couldn't help but notice the way Jessica held herself as she prepared for the next round—determined, focused, and unfazed. It was irritating how she didn't seem rattled by anything.

"Alright, drum major candidates outside for parade!" Mr. Trust called. "I'm not letting you two spin those things in here. Last time we did this, an entire row of trophies got knocked down. I'm looking at you, Christian."

Heat climbed up my neck as a few chuckles rippled through the room, all eyes flicking to me like I'd declared war on Arcana's trophy case. "That was one time," I muttered under my breath, shoving my hands into my pockets. The memory of that day—the loud crash, Mr. Trust's exasperated groan, and the silent, horrified stares from my peers—flashed in my mind like an awful movie. Sure, it had been an accident, but apparently, no one was letting me live it down.

Jessica and I followed our band director outside, and so did the rest of the room. I guess they all wanted to watch me wipe the floor with her.

"Who's first?" Mr. Trust asked, clipboard in hand. His eyes flicked between me and Jessica.

"Ladies first," I said, trying to sound casual, like I wasn't already dreading this part of the audition. I needed a second to steady my nerves, anyway.

Jessica rolled her eyes but stepped forward, clutching her mace with practiced ease. The chrome head caught the sunlight as she settled into position, her stance calm and deliberate. A whistle blast cut through the air, sharp and commanding, and then she was off.

The mace spun in tight, controlled arcs, her movements fluid and precise. No drops, no hesitation. She caught it clean every time, transitioning effortlessly into the next routine. Watching her was like seeing my own intensity reflected back at me—every movement purposeful, every beat saying, *I'm supposed to be here.*

I hated how good she was.

When she finished, she cast a quick glance in my direction. Not smug, just assessing. Like she was measuring my reaction. I met her gaze with a tight nod, refusing to let anything show. She wasn't getting under my skin.

Mr. Trust scribbled something on his clipboard, then turned to me. "Your turn, Christian."

I stepped forward, holding my military baton. It felt small and flimsy compared to her mace. I knew the routine; it was a simple parade sequence I'd performed a hundred times before. Clean. Simple. No room for mistakes.

I moved through the motions, the baton light in my hands as I spun and tossed, each move landing exactly where it needed to. When I finished, I glanced at Mr. Trust, expecting a nod of approval.

Instead, he raised an eyebrow. "Same routine as last year. Very original."

The words hit like a sour note in the middle of a perfect melody, but I kept my face blank, jaw tight. Fine. I'd prove myself in the conducting round. No one could touch me there.

"Alright, back inside." Mr. Trust said, his eyes sweeping over both of us. "We're going to conduct the *Star-Spangled Banner*. Christian, why don't you go first?"

Finally, my strong suit.

I stepped forward, already feeling the rhythm pulsing in my head, steady and sure. The second the first note rang out, everything else vanished—the room, the faces, even Jessica. My hands moved with precision, sweeping through each phrase, guiding an invisible band through crescendos and subtle shifts, every beat under my control. This was where I belonged, where every movement was mine to command. The chaos of this morning, the sting of Mr. Trust's comments, the weight of Jessica standing beside me—all of it faded, disappearing into the background.

As the last note lingered, I lowered my hands, allowing myself a quiet, steady breath. I caught Mr. Trust's approving nod, a small glint in his eyes that told me I'd nailed it. And right then, that was all I needed—proof that no one could come close with conducting.

"Jessica, you're up," Mr. Trust said.

I stepped back, my pulse still thrumming from the rush of the performance, barely taking a breath before Jessica moved forward. She raised her hands, settling into her stance, but even from where I stood, I could see the slight tightness in her shoulders, the trembling in her hands. Her movements were careful, almost too careful, each beat precise but missing that spark, like she was holding something back. She was good, but there was a crack in her confidence—a hairline fracture I could almost see splintering further with each bar she conducted.

The room stayed silent, every set of eyes locked on her, following her every move. When she lowered her hands, her gaze flickered, a shadow of doubt flashing behind her steady expression. Satisfaction twisted in my chest, a small jolt of triumph I couldn't ignore. But it mixed with another, more uncertain feeling. I knew exactly what it felt like to stand there, wide open for everyone to judge. Still, this was a competition, and I couldn't afford to let sympathy trip me up.

Mr. Trust nodded again, though his expression was more neutral this time. "Thank you both," he said. "I'll need a moment to confer with the staff. We'll be back shortly."

As Mr. Trust and the other staff members retreated to his office, the tension in the room thickened. Everyone mingled, the low hum of conversation filling the space, but I stayed where I was, letting the adrenaline ebb away. Jessica stood off to the side, a bit out of place, keeping her expression flat.

I clenched my fists, my focus narrowing to a single thought: this had to be mine. Whatever she felt—whatever anyone else thought—it didn't matter.

I wasn't leaving without that podium.

Jessica

My heartbeat pounded in my chest—relentless, heavy— each beat echoing in the silence. Voices buzzed in the background, faint and blurred, like I was underwater. The rush from the audition had drained away, leaving behind a restless energy that had me tapping my foot and tugging at the hem of my shirt.

My thoughts looped over every detail—the spins, the salutes, each lift and drop of the mace. I couldn't shake the memory of how stiff I'd felt, how deliberate my movements had been, like I was forcing myself into a rhythm that never quite landed. Field conducting never felt natural to me, and I was sure it had shown. And then there was Christian—calm, poised, every flick of his hands fluid and instinctual. His confidence lingered in my mind, sharp and unshakable.

I scanned the room, hoping to catch a read on anyone else's reactions. Most looked relaxed, like this was just another day. But for me? Everything was on the line. I needed this—not just the title, but the validation. I wanted to be seen. Respected.

My gaze drifted to Christian. He hadn't looked at me once; his focus locked somewhere else. Not that I expected him to say anything—he'd made it clear he wasn't here to make friends—but the silence between us still felt loaded. Like it carried all the judgment he hadn't spoken out loud.

Mr. Trust's office door stayed shut. The staff were still deliberating, every second dragging like an eternity. My stomach twisted tighter with every tick of the clock.

I took a deep breath. *Whatever happens, I did my best.* But no matter how many times I repeated it, the fear of falling short wouldn't go away.

I didn't even notice someone approaching until they spoke.

"Hey. Jessica, right?"

I looked up to see a girl with short, dark hair and a bright smile. She held a pair of mallets, tapping them rhythmically against her thigh like there was always a beat in her head.

"Yeah," I said, offering a small smile despite the nerves buzzing under my skin.

"I'm Tracy," she said, leaning against the wall. "Your mace routine was insane. Seriously—I was half expecting you to light it on fire or something."

I blinked. "Oh. Um—thanks. It took a lot of practice."

"It shows." She nodded. "You had everyone's attention. Even Christian's. You should've seen his face—his jaw practically hit the floor. Best part of the day. No contest."

The tension in my chest eased slightly. "Thanks," I murmured, caught off guard by the kindness.

Tracy tilted her head.

"Has he always been...?" I hesitated, looking for the right word.

"A dick?" she offered with a laugh.

I couldn't help laughing too. "Yeah. That."

"Classic Christian," she said with a shrug. "He's been the big shot forever. He's good—can't deny that—but sometimes I think he forgets other people exist."

"Tell me about it," I said, thinking back to when I'd introduced myself and he completely blew me off. "I tried to introduce myself to him earlier and he didn't even shake my hand."

Tracy rolled her eyes. "He probably panicked the second he

realized you weren't just another face in the crowd. He's used to being untouchable."

I shook my head. "I didn't think he'd be so competitive."

She grinned. "Welcome to Arcana. Nothing's casual here— especially not with Christian. But don't let him get in your head. He's all bark. Deep down, there's a soft side… Way, way deep down. Like, buried-under-cement deep."

"I'll believe it when I see it."

Tracy nudged my shoulder, friendly and reassuring. "Don't let him make you doubt yourself. You're good. *Really good*. I don't think he was ready for someone who could match him. Maybe even outshine him."

My gaze flicked to Christian again. He stood off to the side, his arm slung around the waist of one of the color guard girls, laughing like he didn't have a care in the world. That calm confidence radiated off him, and my fingers twitched at the sight.

Back at Riverview, I'd been the best, hands down. No one had challenged me like this before. It felt like I was playing an entirely new game, with rules I didn't know.

The door to Mr. Trust's office opened, and the room immediately fell silent. My heart, which had calmed during my chat with Tracy, began hammering again. She gave me a quick pat on the shoulder as everyone turned to face the front.

Mr. Trust stood with a stack of papers, his expression calm and unreadable. "First, I want to thank everyone for your effort and dedication today. The amount of talent in this room is remarkable. You should all be proud, no matter the outcome."

I nodded, trying to absorb his words, but my stomach was in knots. My eyes darted to Christian. He was leaning against a desk, looking impossibly relaxed, like the decision was already a foregone conclusion. His gaze flicked to mine briefly before I looked away, pretending to focus on Mr. Trust.

"This year's show will be *Romeo & Juliet*," Mr. Trust continued, his voice tinged with excitement. "It's a story of passion, rivalry, and ultimately, tragedy. It will push us artistically and emotionally, and I have no doubt it will be a season to remember."

A murmur of excitement rippled through the room. *Romeo & Juliet* was ambitious, demanding both technical precision and emotional depth. But I couldn't let myself focus on the show yet—not until I knew if I'd even be a part of it.

"And now, the announcements you've all been waiting for," Mr. Trust said, glancing down at his list.

My breath caught.

The section leader names rolled by in a blur—Tracy for pit percussion, Alex for high brass. My pulse quickened as each name brought us closer to the drum major announcement.

"For drum major…" Mr. Trust paused, his gaze sweeping the room. "Christian Gutierrez."

Applause broke out, but I barely heard it. My chest tightened as I watched Christian stand, his expression flickering between pride and smug satisfaction. Of course, he'd expected this.

But then Mr. Trust raised a hand, signaling for quiet.

"And," he added, his voice steady, "for the first time in Arcana's history, we'll have a second drum major—co-drum majors. Jessica Welling."

Silence, thick and shocked.

Then: whispers.

Skeptical. Surprised. Some outright stunned.

My breath caught in my throat.

Christian turned slowly, jaw clenched, eyes like daggers. That stare held fire—sharp, furious, disbelieving.

Mr. Trust didn't flinch.

"You both bring unique strengths to the table," he said. "Together, I believe you'll lead this band to incredible success."

The applause started hesitantly. One clap. Then another. Scattered, uneven, awkward.

This wasn't how I imagined this moment.

Sharing the title?

With *him*?

Christian's jaw tightened. His nostrils flared. His shoulders rose in a sharp inhale. For half a second, I thought he'd let it go. But as the applause died off, I heard–

"What the fu—"

Christian

I paced the length of Mr. Trust's cramped office, the walls feeling closer with every step. My footsteps thudded against the tile, sharp and restless, as if I could stomp the anger out of my system.

Two years. Two whole years I'd poured into this band as a drum major. Every rehearsal, every blister from hours spent perfecting that damn military baton, every second spent learning how to lead from the top of that podium—and now it was being split. Like the title meant nothing. Like my work could be halved and handed off without a second thought.

My jaw clenched. I dragged a hand through my hair, fingers catching in the mess. The image of Jessica standing there, just as stunned as I was, refused to leave my mind. And somehow, that only made the fire burn hotter.

She didn't get it. She had no idea what it meant to lead here. This wasn't a role you stepped into just because you knew how to spin a stick and keep tempo. This was my turf. My responsibility. And now I was supposed to share it?

The door creaked open. Mr. Trust walked in and closed it softly behind him. He didn't say anything, just moved behind his desk and looked at me—waiting.

"So, are you going to explain this?" I demanded, unable to hold it in. "Because right now, none of this makes sense."

"Sit down, Christian."

"I don't want to sit down. I want to know why—"

"Sit. Down."

His tone left no room for argument. I dropped into the chair, my knees bouncing, fists clenched just tight enough to keep the frustration from spilling over.

He took a seat across from me, folding his hands calmly. "I understand you're upset."

"Upset?" I scoffed. "I'm pissed off. Why are we doing this now, of all times? Two drum majors? This isn't fair."

"We didn't make this decision lightly," he said. "Jessica earned her place. Just like you did."

"Earned?" I barked a laugh. "She's been here for five minutes. So what if she can throw a mace around? She doesn't know this band. She doesn't know what it takes."

"And you do?" Mr. Trust's eyes narrowed. "You think you're the only one who understands what this role demands?"

"I've been doing it for two years," I snapped. "Yeah, I think I've got it figured out."

"That's exactly why I made this decision," he said, voice cool but sharp. "You're a strong leader, Christian—but you've grown comfortable. Jessica will challenge you. And I think that's exactly what you need."

I bit down on the inside of my cheek. "So this is what, a lesson? Some character-building exercise?"

"It's not a punishment," he said. "It's an opportunity. For both of you. The band gains two strong leaders, and you gain someone who'll push you to be better."

An opportunity. All I saw was a threat. Still, his gaze was steady—unshaken.

"Fine," I muttered, pushing out of the chair. "But don't expect me to like it."

"I'm not asking you to like it," he said. "I'm asking you to make it work."

I was halfway to the door when he stopped me.

"Wait a moment." His tone softened slightly. "It's time we bring Jessica in."

I froze, hand still on the doorknob. Of course. He wanted to talk to her too. And I had to sit here through it? My stomach twisted, but I stepped back, folding my arms.

Mr. Trust opened the door and called into the hallway. "Jessica, can you come in for a moment?"

Footsteps. Then she appeared in the doorway, hesitating just slightly before stepping inside. Her posture straightened when she saw me—like she braced for something. Good. She should be nervous.

"Come in," Mr. Trust said, gesturing toward the seat I'd just vacated. "We need to talk about how this is going to work."

She nodded once and took the seat, her hands folded in her lap, jaw tight. I stayed against the wall, arms crossed.

Mr. Trust leaned on the edge of his desk. "First, congratulations to you both. You each bring something different, and I believe together, you'll raise this band to a new level."

Jessica sat quiet, but her fingers fidgeted slightly in her lap. I noticed, even if no one else did.

"I know this isn't the outcome either of you expected," Mr. Trust continued. "But this was the best decision for the band."

She nodded.

I stayed silent.

"This won't be easy," he said. "There will be disagreements. But I chose both of you because you balance each other. You challenge each other. You have what it takes—to lead together."

He turned to me. "Christian, you've been a steady hand for this band, but you've plateaued. Jessica brings a perspective we haven't had before."

Then to her: "And Jessica, you're stepping into unfamiliar territory. Christian's experience will help guide you."

She nodded again, more confidently this time.

"I expect both of you to lead—and to teach. Not just the band, but each other. This year's show will be demanding, and it will take everything you've got."

He glanced between us. "You can see each other as competition—or as partners. The choice is yours."

Silence settled over the room. Jessica stared at the floor, brow furrowed. I watched her closely. I couldn't read her thoughts, but I knew mine: she wasn't taking this from me. I wouldn't let her.

Mr. Trust stood and gathered his clipboard. "Take some time to think it over. We'll regroup before band camp."

He looked at us both. "This is a test of leadership. Of trust. You can either grow together or fall apart. That's up to you."

He left, and the door clicked shut behind him.

The room was silent.

Jessica broke it first. "You didn't have to react like that."

"React like what?" I turned to her, eyes narrowed.

"Like a child throwing a tantrum," she said, arms crossing. "You're still drum major."

"Co-drum major," I said, the word sour on my tongue. "And if you think I'm stepping aside—"

"I'm not asking you to." Her tone sharpened. "I'm a senior, too, okay? He made *both* of us drum major. Whether or not you like it."

"Just stay out of my way," I spat, stepping closer. "This is my band."

Her eyes flared. She tilted her head, voice low and edged with mockery. "Funny. I thought it said 'Arcana' on the uniforms, not 'Christian Gutierrez.' Guess I'll have to get mine reprinted."

"You don't belong here."

She stood her ground, eyes steady. "And maybe you should stop acting like you're the only one who does."

The air between us buzzed. Her stare didn't flinch, didn't soften. She met me beat for beat.

"Fine," I said. "Prove it. Prove you belong here."

"I will."

We held each other's gaze, unmoving, unblinking. My pulse thundered. Hers didn't waver. Two wills, two sparks, locked in place—daring the other to flinch.

Jessica

The late afternoon sun filtered through the parking lot's trees, stretching long shadows across the pavement. Mr. Trust's conversation replayed in loops—followed by that confrontation with Christian. I felt frustrated, angry, and—though I didn't want to admit it—a slight sense of failure.

"Jessica!" a voice called.

I looked up to see Tracy jogging toward me as I walked through the parking lot, mallets tapping rhythmically against her thigh. Her bright smile and windswept hair felt at odds with the storm still clinging to me.

"Heading out already?" she asked, falling into step beside me.

I shrugged. "Yeah. It's been a day."

"Come with us," she said, like it was the most obvious thing in the world. "Section leader tradition. Milkshakes. Post-tryout decompression. You'll love it."

I hesitated, glancing back toward the school. Company wasn't exactly on my wishlist, but Tracy's warmth softened something in me.

"I don't know... it's just been weird."

"All the more reason." She grinned, bumping her shoulder into mine. "You're one of us now. And don't worry, Christian's not coming."

That last part shouldn't have been the deciding factor. But it was.

Before I could fully agree, Tracy had already looped her arm through mine and steered me toward a small group near the side entrance.

Alex was there, standing beside a tall guy casually twirling drumsticks. Alex's smirk was in place, but it didn't quite reach his eyes.

"Look who Tracy dragged in," he said, eyeing me like a wild card he wasn't sure how to play. "Jessica Welling, co-drum major."

His loyalty to Christian hung in the air between us, unspoken but obvious.

"Jessica, meet Marcus," Tracy said, nodding toward the guy with the sticks. "Drumline captain."

Marcus grinned. "What's up? You crushed it with that mace."

"Thanks," I said, bumping his fist, still feeling a little off-balance from the day.

Alex raised a brow. "Not every day someone stuns Christian into silence. That earned you some points."

I tried not to flinch. "He didn't seem thrilled about the co-drum major thing."

Tracy snorted. "That's just Christian. He's intense about everything. Band, gas station slushie rankings, you name it."

Marcus nodded. "He goes all in. Always has. But he's solid. Once he sees you're serious, he'll come around."

Alex's arms were still crossed, but his tone softened. "It's not personal. He's just proud of what he's built here. You being new, it's... different."

"I get it," I said. "It's not how I pictured things either."

He studied me for a second, then gave a small shrug. "Well, you're stuck with us now."

Their banter drifted around me, and bit by bit, the image I had of Christian—arrogant, territorial, untouchable—started to chip. These people respected him. Liked him, even. They'd seen parts of him I hadn't.

"Does he ever... lighten up?" I asked.

Marcus laughed. "Not about band. But last year, after we lost regionals, he organized a whole pep rally out of nowhere. Lights, music, speeches. It actually helped."

Tracy nodded. "He's not easy. But he's loyal. Pushes people hard because he thinks they can take it."

That surprised me. Loyalty wasn't the word I'd have used an hour ago.

The diner was just down the street—neon sign flickering, scent of grease and vanilla hanging in the air. We crammed into a worn booth near the back, Tracy and Alex arguing over shake flavors like siblings. It was chaotic and loud and easy in a way I hadn't expected.

"So, Riverview mystery girl," Tracy said, leaning in. "What's your deal? Why Arcana?"

"My dad got a new job," I replied with a careful smile. "It was a last-minute move."

Not a lie. Just not the whole story.

Aiden's face surfaced in my thoughts—his tired smile, the way he brushed off whispers and stares like they didn't sting. Moving here had been for him, even if no one else saw it.

Alex stirred his milkshake. "Tough switch senior year. Must've been hard to leave your old band."

"Yeah," I said. "It was a smaller group. More like a family. Arcana's... different."

"Different how?" Alex asked. "Like, too intense?"

"Just... bigger. More pride, more pressure. At Riverview, we had to beg people to show up. Here, it's like people actually care."

Marcus nodded. "You've got the chops. And you're here, which means you can handle it."

I smiled faintly. "I'm trying."

"You'll fit in," Tracy said. "Just give it time."

Conversation turned lighter—rehearsal disasters, section jokes, the time someone used a sousaphone as a popcorn bowl during band camp. And then...

"So," Tracy asked, leaning in conspiratorially, "has anyone warned you about Kingston yet?"

"Should I be worried?"

Alex chuckled. "They're our rival. Like, actual blood feud level. Arcana vs. Kingston is legend."

Marcus nodded. "Their guard once dumped glitter in our uniforms."

"Arcana may or may not have unplugged their sound system during warm-up once," Tracy added innocently.

My eyebrows rose. "This sounds... normal."

"For here? It is," Alex said. "This year, the big face-off lands on homecoming night."

"Let me guess—Christian lives for this rivalry?"

"Lives, breathes, and would probably tattoo 'Beat Kingston' on his forehead if we let him," Marcus said. "It gets personal. Especially for him."

It made sense. Christian didn't just lead the band—he carried its pride. No wonder he saw me as a threat.

Still, as their stories painted a fuller picture, I couldn't shake the feeling that maybe, just maybe, I'd misjudged him.

I glanced at Tracy, Marcus, and Alex, their faces full of pride and determination. I was still an outsider, but standing here, sharing in Arcana's legacy, it felt like they'd cracked the door open—just enough for me to decide if I was ready to step through.

✗ ✗ ✗ ✗ ✗

When I made it back home that evening, I walked into the living room, where my mom sat on the couch with a book in her lap. She looked up as I entered, her expression indecipherable as she closed the book.

"Well?" she asked, her tone casual, almost too casual. "Did you get drum major?"

"Co-drum major," I said, swallowing back the familiar sting of disappointment. "I'll be sharing the role with someone else."

Her lips curved in a small smile, but it didn't reach her eyes. "Co-drum major," she echoed, letting the word burn like a live wire, sparking and crackling in the space between us. "Well, I suppose that's... something."

Her voice laced with an edge that it made my stomach tighten. It wasn't outright criticism, but I could feel the weight of her judgment in those few words. Better than nothing, she basically said.

I wanted her to be proud, to say that it was enough, that I was enough. But instead, all I heard was what I was lacking.

I forced a smile. "I'm going to take a shower," I said, eager to escape the room. "It's been a long day, so I'll probably head to bed early."

She nodded, her gaze lingering on me for just a moment longer, as if assessing, then returned to her book with a quiet hum. "Goodnight, Jessica."

I stood there for a moment, waiting for something more—a word of encouragement, a sign of approval. But there was nothing. Just the soft rustle of her turning the page, her attention already drifting away.

I let out a silent breath and headed upstairs, each step heavier than the last.

Christian

The day before band camp, Mr. Trust scheduled a workshopping session for Jessica and me—a few hours designed to "find common ground," as he put it. I showed up early, hoping for a moment of silence to get my head right before having to deal with her.

But there she was.

Jessica stood with her back to me, adjusting her mace in slow, deliberate motions. She glanced over her shoulder when I walked in, gave a curt nod, and turned away without a word. No smile. No hello. Just stiff acknowledgment, like I was some *rando* on the street.

Mr. Trust handed us a single stack of sheet music—the score for *Romeo & Juliet*. Both of us reached for it at the same time, our hands colliding. Neither of us let go. I looked up, met her glare. Her grip tightened.

Mr. Trust sighed audibly, dragging the moment out with an exaggerated eye roll. "There's a copy machine in the office."

I shot Jessica a quick glare, releasing my grip just enough to let her know I wasn't about to get into a wrestling match in front of Mr. Trust. Without another word, I strode toward the office, not bothering to look back. I could hear her footsteps falling in line behind me.

In the office, I jabbed at the copier buttons harder than necessary, the beeping the only sound filling the space. She crossed her arms, her eyes boring into me, sharp and calculating. The whir and clatter of the machine continued, each thud of paper falling into the tray louder than usual.

As we waited for the copies to finish, Jessica broke the silence. "We're going to have to figure out how to work together," she said. "This isn't a solo act."

I didn't look at her, focusing on the copier instead. "I've managed just fine on my own for the past two years. Thank you very much."

"Right," she said, her tone neutral but firm. "But this time, you've got a co-drum major. So we might as well try to make it work."

I let out a short, derisive laugh. "We'll see about that."

The copier beeped, and I grabbed the stack of papers, thrusting her share toward her without meeting her eyes. My hand lingered a moment too long, though. It was strange how easily she got under my skin. Most people folded under pressure, but not Jessica—she pushed right back. She yanked the papers out of my hand with more force than necessary, and we both walked out of the office like nothing had happened.

Mr. Trust and Luna, the color guard instructor, waited for us on the podium. Jessica and I took seats at the front, our music stands holding the freshly printed copies of the score. As my eyes scanned the pages, the intricate passages leapt off the paper, promising hours of grueling practice for the band.

"We're scrapping the guard-centered concept," Mr. Trust said, finally cutting through the awkward silence. "With a male and female drum major, we've got a unique opportunity here. You're going to be the central storyline. Total crowd-pleaser potential."

"What does that mean, exactly?" she asked, her voice tight but even bracing for the answer.

Mr. Trust glanced at me, a sly grin tugging at his lips. "Well, here's the plan…" He paused, clearly enjoying the suspense. His gaze shifted to me. "Christian, you'll be Romeo."

Then, turning slowly toward Jessica, he let the weight of the moment settle. Her shoulders straightened, though I could see her stiffening with realization.

"And you," he continued, barely suppressing his amusement, "will be—"

"Juliet," we all chimed in unison, our voices colliding in a perfectly timed chorus.

Mr. Trust and the guard instructor exchanged a knowing smile, clearly entertained by our synchronized response. Meanwhile, I caught Jessica's gaze. Her eyes flickered nervously between me and the instructors, wide and pleading, as if searching for escape. Her face paled slightly, betraying a flash of anxiety, before she straightened, her shoulders stiffening in a display of forced composure.

Juliet. *Of course*. Jessica didn't strike me as a Juliet type. Too stubborn. Too guarded. And definitely not the *swoon-and-die-for-love* variety.

Still, watching her shift uncomfortably in her seat, her composure slipping just a little, gave me a strange, petty sense of satisfaction. At least I wasn't the only one hating this.

Luna chimed in, her grin wide and brimming with excitement. "Jessica, your mace spinning at tryouts was incredible. We'd love to incorporate that—maybe have you spin a flag in one of the key scenes. Everyone will expect Juliet to be from the color guard, but imagine their surprise when it's the drum major."

"Exactly," Mr. Trust agreed, his nod enthusiastic. "This dynamic between the two of you has so much potential to heighten the drama and excitement of the show."

Her face flushed crimson as she struggled to regain control. "Isn't Juliet traditionally a color guard role?"

"Which is exactly why this twist works," Luna said, practically glowing.

Jessica's lips pressed into a thin line. "Is there any room for negotiation?"

Mr. Trust chuckled and shook his head. "Not unless you can pitch a more dramatic storyline right now."

Her gaze darted toward me, narrowing briefly before she sighed, her tone resigned. "Well, at least Romeo dies in the end."

I smirked, meeting her glare. "So does Juliet. Because she fell in love with Romeo. You ready for that kind of commitment?"

Her eyebrow arched, her expression unflinching. "I don't fall, Christian. Especially not in love. But if you're so eager to drink poison and play the tragic hero, be my guest. Just don't expect me to go down with you."

The bite in her words caught me off guard, pulling me out of my smugness. I studied her face, searching for any cracks in that unshakable front. "So you don't believe in love?" I asked, ready to peel back another layer of her defenses.

She shrugged. Her teeth caught on her bottom lip, worrying the skin raw.

"Why would I?" she said, eyes flicking away. "Love just gives people ammunition to hurt each other. Romeo and Juliet? They die, and for what?" She dug her thumb along the edge of her nail, slow and absentminded. The skin there was already red.

Her words landed heavier than I expected, leaving me momentarily stunned. I'd been bracing for sarcasm or a clever jab, but not... *this*. She wasn't joking—she was dead serious. I tried to keep my expression neutral, but curiosity prickled at the edges of my thoughts. What could make someone feel this way?

Jessica caught my lingering look and rolled her eyes. "Oh, please. Don't go all Dr. Phil on me. Whether or not I believe in it doesn't matter."

Her voice had a hardness to it, laced with a bitterness that didn't match the sharp confidence she usually carried. Suddenly, her guarded exterior started making more sense. There was a story here, one I wasn't sure I'd ever get to hear. There was a hardness in her voice, a layer of bitterness I hadn't expected. Suddenly, her cool exterior made more sense, and I realized there was a lot about Jessica I didn't know—layers she kept hidden under that sharp, confident front.

I forced a smirk, hoping to steer the conversation back to lighter territory, though her words stuck with me. "So, what I'm hearing is that you're not cut out to play Juliet?"

Jessica shot me a withering glare, crossing her arms. "I never said that. Just because I don't buy into the 'love conquers all' nonsense doesn't mean I can't play the part. Don't think for a second I'm backing out."

I raised an eyebrow, my grin threatening to break through. "So, Juliet, without the whole 'falling in love' thing? Sounds like a challenge."

She huffed, rolling her eyes. "I can act, Christian. I can make people believe whatever I want them to see. I don't need to believe in the whole tragic romance to pull it off. Besides, Juliet's more than just some lovesick girl. She's determined, stubborn, and willing to fight for what she wants. I can get behind that." Jessica smirked, leaning in slightly. "The real question is, can you handle playing Romeo?"

Her eyes lit up with defiance, a spark that was almost—almost—impressive. I leaned back, crossing my arms with a smirk. "Don't worry about me. I can keep the audience awake. Wouldn't want them drifting off during Juliet's big flag moment."

Her smile sharpened, but there was a glint of challenge in her gaze. "Oh, I'm not worried about the audience. I'm worried about the podium—poor thing might collapse under the weight of your ego."

I snorted, shaking my head. "At least my ego knows how to hit its marks. You sure you can keep that flag under control without decapitating the brass section?"

Jessica raised an eyebrow, her smirk widening. "At least I'll leave a mark. Romeo stumbling through his big moment because he's too busy basking in his own spotlight? Now that's a tragedy Shakespeare never wrote."

Before I could retort, Mr. Trust cleared his throat, his amusement barely disguised. "Alright, let's leave the theatrics for the field. The audience came for a show, not a comedy routine."

Jessica and I exchanged a look, the tension between us palpable. Neither of us would back down. One thing was certain—this year was shaping up to be a battle, on and off the field.

Mr. Trust then played the music for us on the overhead speakers in the room and we followed along in the score.

The opening was soft—delicate even—like a whisper of something just out of reach. Then the winds swelled, the melody rising with urgency. It was beautiful, but it carried tension beneath the surface. A warning. A storm brewing.

As the music reached its climax, the percussion section roared to life, driving the tempo faster, harder. It was chaotic, almost frantic, like the world was unraveling around us. The battery returned with a vengeance, their rhythm sharp and jagged, clashing with the brass in a way that made my heart race. It was a battle—a fight to the finish—and I could feel the intensity, the desperation in every note.

And then, just when it felt like the music was about to tear itself apart, it all stopped. A single, solitary note clung to the silence. It was the end, but it wasn't peaceful. It was tragic, final. The silence that leaves you questioning everything that came before.

"This is going to be a memorable year," Mr. Trust said.

I caught Jessica's eye. For just a second, something passed between us—a mutual understanding, maybe, of the weight this performance would carry through its music. I thought I saw the tiniest hint of a smile tugging at the corner of her mouth, but she glanced away, crossing her arms like the music hadn't affected her at all.

09 The Blood Oath

Christian

A re we really doing this?" Alex leaned against the brick wall outside the band room, twirling a stolen drumstick between his fingers. "What if she doesn't show? Kind of a waste if she bails."

"She'll show," Tracy said, tapping at her phone. "She texted like ten minutes ago—she's on her way."

"Yeah, but what if she chickens out?" Marcus added from the pavement, sitting cross-legged and flipping a drumstick like a baton. "No offense, but she doesn't exactly scream 'I bleed green for Arcana.'"

"She's not a coward," Tracy snapped, shooting him a look.

"Unlike someone's girlfriend," Alex muttered, elbowing me.

I rolled my eyes at him. Courtney had made her thoughts on this whole initiation thing very clear: *stupid, reckless, and not worth the risk of getting grounded.* She wasn't wrong, technically. She'd called it the moment Alex and I had brought up the blood oath idea. *"Have fun with your dumb little cult,"* she'd said with a scoff before making it clear she wouldn't be sneaking out to participate.

Not that I blamed her. I warned Courtney about Mr. Trust's vision for the show earlier. She wasn't exactly happy about it—went off on a thirty-minute rant about how unfair it was for him to hand the Juliet part to Jessica, especially since that role traditionally went to the guard captain. Honestly, I wasn't sure what was bothering her more—the fact that she lost the part, or that Jessica had walked in and taken it without even trying.

As we waited for Jessica to show up, I flipped the keycard in my pocket, the motion automatic, rhythmic, like tapping out a cadence on a drumline. The others were cracking jokes, debating whether or not she'd actually show, but my thoughts were stuck in the past—on my own so-called "initiation" when I was named the new drum major at the end of my freshman year.

I hadn't asked for it. The upperclassmen leaders had cornered me after the last day of freshman year, grinning like hyenas as they dragged me to the parking lot. "Welcome to the podium," Marcus' older brother had said, clapping me on the shoulder with way too much enthusiasm. "But before you take your place as King of the Field, there's a little tradition you have to survive."

The "tradition" turned out to be a kiddie pool filled with what I can only describe as pudding, glitter, and regret. My job? Dig through it blindfolded to find the "key" to the band room. The kicker? There was no key. It was a prank, and a stupid one at that. I'd spent the rest of the night picking glitter out of my hair and rethinking my life choices.

But it was tradition. And at Arcana, tradition mattered. It wasn't just about the music or the scores—it was about the shared experiences, the ridiculous rites of passage that turned a group of strangers into something closer to family. That night, for all its stupidity, had been a turning point. It proved I could handle being the butt of a joke, roll with the punches, and laugh about it afterward.

Now, standing outside the band room with Jessica on her way, I wasn't thinking about bonding or camaraderie. This wasn't about welcoming her into the fold. This was just about tradition—and maybe psyching her out just a little. I wasn't going to make this easy for her. She'd already taken half my podium; the least she could do was sweat a little for it.

I leaned against the cold, graffiti-covered door frame of the side entrance, arms crossed, letting their chatter roll over me without comment. My fingers played with the keycard in my pocket, flipping it between my fingers like a coin. The whole thing—standing here waiting for *Jessica Welling*—felt ridiculous.

I shifted my weight, resisting the urge to check my phone for the time. "If she doesn't show in five minutes, we're calling it. I'm not wasting my night on this."

"You're the one who brought the knife," Marcus said, smirking. He pointed at my pocket with the drumstick. "Don't act like you're not secretly enjoying this."

"Shut up," I said, but my lips twitched.

Truth was, I wasn't sure why I'd agreed to this. Maybe it was curiosity. Maybe it was wanting to see if Jessica really had the guts to follow through with something as stupid as a late-night hazing ritual. Or maybe it was because some part of me still didn't think she belonged here, and this was my way of testing her. She'd wormed her way into my band, taken my podium, and every instinct I had was screaming to make her prove she was worth it.

"She's here!" Tracy suddenly exclaimed, pointing toward the far side of the lot.

Sure enough, there she was, emerging from the shadows like some kind of ninja. She had pulled her hair into a messy ponytail. She looked more irritated than intimidated; her strides were long and purposeful as she crossed the lot toward us.

"Told you," Tracy said smugly, elbowing Marcus.

Jessica stopped a few feet away, raising an eyebrow as she looked at all of us. "So," she said, voice flat. "What's this 'emergency band meeting' about? Please tell me it's not as weird as it sounds."

"Oh, it's weirder," Alex said, grinning as we started walking.

She sighed, crossing her arms as she glanced around the dimly lit campus. "I had to sneak out of my house for this. It better be good."

Tracy smirked, nudging me with her elbow. "Oh, it's good. Trust me."

"Yeah," Marcus added with a grin. "Good enough to risk getting grounded for."

I pulled the keycard out of my pocket and holding it up with a casual flick of his wrist. "Relax, Welling. You're about to witness one of Arcana's finest traditions. And, by the way, you're welcome for the after-hours access."

Jessica raised an eyebrow, her gaze shifting to the keycard in his hand. "You have a keycard? Of course you do."

I shrugged, sliding it through the reader on the door. The lock clicked, and I pushed it open, motioning for everyone to follow. "Perks of being drum major. You think the band room just magically opens itself?"

"More like perks of being the teacher's pet," she muttered under her breath, but just enough for me to hear. There was a faint smirk tugging at the corner of her lips.

I glanced back, matching her smirk. "Jealousy isn't a good look, Welling. Don't worry—you might get a keycard someday. Maybe."

Her eyes narrowed, but the smirk stayed firmly in place. "Please. The day I'm jealous of you is the day you actually deserve half the praise you give yourself."

The group entered the band room, our footsteps tapping softly against the polished tile. Dim emergency lights traced faint glows along the walls, just enough to reveal the familiar shapes of the space. The familiar scent of brass polish and old sheet music greeted me—a grounding, steady presence. Front ensemble equipment stood neatly in its usual rows, their surfaces catching the faint light.

I leaned against the whiteboard, watching Marcus, as usual, turn the simplest moment into a grand spectacle. He spread his arms wide, his voice booming like he was addressing an arena instead of a half-empty band room. "Ladies and gentlemen, welcome to the hallowed halls of Arcana! Tonight, we don't just rehearse—we etch our names into history!"

Jessica glanced around, her eyes sweeping over the rows of trophies and framed photographs lining the walls. For a split second, her expression softened—almost reverent, like she was realizing just how much history lived in this room. But then she turned back to us, her face calm, her voice steady. "Alright," she said, crossing her arms. "What's the deal? Why are we here?"

Tracy leaned casually against a music stand, her grin wide and mischievous. "Oh, you'll see," she said, her tone teasing. "It's a rite of passage. Every leader has to do it."

Jessica raised an eyebrow, unimpressed. "And by 'it,' you mean…?"

I stepped forward, flipping the knife open with a smooth, deliberate motion. The blade caught the faint light, gleaming as I held it up between us. "A blood oath," I said. "To prove your loyalty to Arcana."

Her eyes flicked to the knife, then back to me. She didn't flinch—just stared at it. "You've got to be kidding me."

"Do we look like we're kidding?" Marcus chimed in, keeping his tone serious, even as I could see him trying not to laugh.

Jessica snorted, crossing her arms. "A blood oath? What is this, the Stone Age? Are we about to sacrifice a goat too?"

Tracy smirked, but there was a flicker of hesitation in her eyes. "Come on, Jessica. It's tradition. Everyone does it."

"Yeah?" Jessica shot back, her voice sharper now. "Everyone, huh? Did you do it, Tracy? Or was this conveniently left out of your hazing?"

"Okay, I didn't do the blood part. But we all had our own version of this." Tracy held up her hands defensively, her grin faltering. "It's symbolic! A bonding thing."

Jessica's gaze swung back to me, sharp as a blade. "And what about you, Mr. Tradition? You've done this?"

My jaw tightened, but I didn't look away. "It's not about me. It's about you proving you belong here."

She let out a short, humorless laugh. "Oh, I see how it is. You've all magically decided I need to 'prove' something. Let me guess—this has nothing to do with tradition and everything to do with seeing if I'll make a fool of myself. You all want a good laugh, is that it?"

"No one's forcing you," I said, my voice cool. "You can walk out that door anytime you want."

Her lips pressed into a thin line, and for a moment, I thought she might actually leave. But then she squared her shoulders, her gaze locking onto mine with a stubborn, unflinching intensity.

"Fine," she said, her tone dripping with defiance. "If this is what it takes to join your little cult, let's get it over with."

The air shifted. I glanced over to the others, worry creeping up my legs. Tracy bit her lip, her gaze flickering to the knife. Her hands twitched, poised like a coiled spring, ready to step in if Jessica actually took this prank seriously.

I handed Jessica the knife, my movements slow and deliberate. She took it with a steady grip, her fingers curling around the handle like it belonged to her. No hesitation. No pause. Just calm and measured.

She wouldn't. *Would she?*

The thought lodged in my chest like a stone. I expected her to hesitate, at least. To freak out and give in. But instead, she turned the knife over in her hand, inspecting it like it was some dull trinket.

Her eyes lifted to mine, unblinking, and for a second, I swore the knife wasn't what held the room's attention—she was. Tracy took a half-step forward, her mouth opening, but Jessica moved first.

Fast.

In one swift motion, she positioned the blade against her palm.

"Wait—" Tracy started, but it was already too late.

Jessica's lips curved into a slow, defiant smile, her voice cutting through the tension like the edge of the knife she held. "Here goes nothing."

And then, before anyone could stop her, the blade sliced across her palm.

The room froze, every breath suspended in disbelief. No grimace. No hesitation. Just a steady, unwavering gaze locked onto mine, daring me to flinch. My thoughts scrambled, disbelief washing over me in crashing waves. She didn't—she couldn't have actually—

For a moment, no one moved. No one breathed. The room felt like it was holding its collective breath. Tracy let out a strangled noise, her hands flying to her head. "What in the holy mother of John Philip Sousa—"

Marcus's mouth fell open, his drumstick hitting the floor with a hollow clatter. Alex physically recoiled, stumbling back into a chair. "Oh my God, she actually did it!" he said, his voice cracking. "I'm gonna throw up."

My mind scrambled. *No way.*

Tracy lunged forward like she was about to wrestle the knife away, but Jessica let out an exaggerated sigh, holding up her hand. "Relax," she said, her tone dripping with sarcasm. She opened her palm, showing perfectly unscathed skin. "No offense, but you guys are the worst cult I've ever been part of."

The apprehension in the room snapped like a rubber band. Tracy slumped against a chair, dragging her hands down her face. "I hate you so much right now," she groaned. "I swear to God, Jessica, my life just flashed before my eyes."

Alex blinked, staring at Jessica like he didn't know whether to laugh or run. "I—what just happened?"

Jessica smirked, twirling the knife in her hand like she was bored. "You guys are terrible at hazing," she said, flipping the blade shut and handing it back to me. "Is that it? Am I officially part of your little club now, or do I have to jump through more hoops?"

For a moment, I couldn't move. Couldn't speak. My heart pounded in my chest as I placed the knife back in my pocket. I'd just been played.

"Hey, nice effort. You guys almost got me," she said.

Marcus clutched his chest like he was recovering from a heart attack. "I thought she actually—what even just happened?!"

Alex blinked, looking between Jessica and me like he couldn't process it. "Okay, but that was… That was terrifying. And amazing."

She turned to me. "What? Isn't this what you wanted? Proof of my undying loyalty to Arcana?"

She'd not only called my bluff—she'd completely flipped the script. And she'd done it with a smile, like she owned the whole damn room. For once, I didn't have a snarky comeback. Not immediately, anyway.

Tracy groaned again, pointing at me accusingly. "This is your fault, Christian. All of it. Next time, no knives. We're sticking to pizza parties."

Marcus nodded, still dazed. "She's nuts. Respect, but nuts."

Alex gave Jessica a long, appraising look, his brows furrowed like he was still trying to figure her out. "Yeah, alright. She's got guts. I'll give her that."

I leaned back against the whiteboard, watching Jessica as she basked in the chaos she'd created. For a brief moment, I saw it— why she'd made it this far, why she'd been chosen to stand on the podium next to me. She was fearless, or at least good at pretending she was. And that? That was dangerous.

I'm not impressed. Just… annoyed that she pulled it off.

Jessica

The early morning sun cast long, thin shadows across the damp grass as I set a foot on the field. The air was cool now, but I knew the relief wouldn't last. By midday, the heat would be merciless, smothering us as we drilled formation after formation into the ground.

Band camp wasn't just a test of skill—it was a trial of endurance. It was the one week every summer when the entire marching band came together, grinding through endless hours of practice to transform chaos into precision. Sweat, blisters, sunburns—they all disappeared when the music and movement finally clicked.

My thoughts flickered briefly to the night before, to the lingering laughter over milkshakes and fries at the diner. The chaos of the so-called blood oath had faded into something lighter, easier—a sense of camaraderie I wasn't sure I'd ever find here. But for the moment, I didn't feel like the outsider, standing on the edges of a picture I wasn't meant to be part of; instead, it felt like I'd stepped into the frame.

Mr. Trust's whistle sliced through the morning air, commanding attention. Conversations fell away as the sections snapped into formation, each led by their section leaders. Clusters of wide-eyed freshmen huddled together, their nerves palpable. I remembered that feeling—the mix of excitement and fear that came with stepping into this world for the first time. Today's focus was marching basics, the backbone of everything we'd build over the coming season.

I stood at the front, clipboard in hand, trying to seem confident as I could. But inside, the pressure was mounting. Not just to lead, but to live up to the expectations that came with this new role. I knew today would be the first real test of whether I could handle it or if I would crack under the weight.

"Before we begin," Mr. Trust's voice rang out across the field, steady and commanding, "welcome to another year with the Arcana Marching Eagles. For those of you who are new, I'm Mr. Trust, your band director. I couldn't be more excited to kick off this season with all of you."

He paused, his gaze sweeping the crowd. "You'll be spending a lot of time with me and our incredible staff this season." He gestured to the adults standing beside him, but I tuned out the introductions after the first name. The details blurred together—guard instructor, percussion expert, drill writer—each of them polished and professional, with years of experience to back them up.

The idea of having specialized staff for each section was completely foreign to me. Back at Riverview, our band barely had enough members to fill the field, let alone a team of experts. The closest we got to professional help was the occasional volunteer who'd stop by with advice.

Here, it was a different world. A well-oiled machine. It wasn't just practice—it was preparation for something serious, something real.

Mr. Trust turned back to the band, his expression shifting to one of determination. "Now, I want to talk to you about what this week is going to be. Band camp is tough—there's no sugarcoating it. You'll be out here in the heat, working harder than you ever have before. Your muscles will ache, your feet will blister, and there will be moments when you'll wonder if it's worth it."

His gaze was intense, locking onto the eyes of various students as he spoke. "But I promise you this—if you give it everything you've got, if you push through the sweat and the fatigue, you'll come out of this stronger, not just as individuals, but as a band. You'll learn to move as one, to breathe as one, to play as one. And when you step onto that field for your first performance, all the pain, all the effort—it'll be worth it. Because you'll know you've done something extraordinary."

A murmur of agreement rippled through the crowd, the weight of his words settling in.

"Remember," Mr. Trust continued, his tone softening just a bit, "this isn't just about moving your feet and playing music. It's about being part of something bigger than yourself. It's about trust, teamwork, and pushing each other to be the best we can be. So, take care of each other, support each other, and let's make this season unforgettable."

He let the silence hang for a moment, the gravity of his speech still resonating in the cool morning air.

"Alright," he finally said, clapping his hands together, "let's get to work. We've got a lot to cover today, and I know we're going to make every second count."

The band erupted into applause, the energy contagious as everyone prepared to dive into the day's activities. As I glanced around, I could see it in their faces—the determination, the excitement, and yes, even the nerves. This was it. Band camp had officially begun.

The day dissolved into a relentless cycle of drills, rehearsals, and team-building exercises, each more grueling than the last. As the sun climbed higher, the heat turned the field into a furnace. For hours, we marched in precise rows, Mr. Trust and the section leaders barking commands with sharp precision. I moved through the formations, correcting shoulders, adjusting posture, and fine-tuning every detail. Sweat trickled down my back, but I ignored it, zeroing in on each step, each angle, each note with single-minded determination.

By midday, we'd retreated to the band room, though the stifling heat followed us inside. The space buzzed with activity, a jumble of brass, woodwinds, and percussion as everyone unpacked their instruments and tuned up for the next rehearsal. The chaotic mix of sounds filled the room, echoing off the walls like a prelude to the day's next challenge.

Mr. Trust made his way through the crowd and spotted Christian and me. With a wave, he beckoned us to come forward. I pushed my way through the throng of musicians, feeling the sweat on my back begin to cool in the brief respite from the sun.

"Christian," Mr. Trust said, his voice carrying over the din, "why don't you run the band through warm-ups? Jessica, I think Luna wants you outside with the rest of the color guard."

Christian's face lit up as if he had just won a victory. I tried to ignore the satisfaction in his eyes, focusing instead on Mr. Trust's words. The idea of going back outside was almost enough to make me collapse on the spot. I was already heat-exhausted, and the thought of stepping back into the blistering sun made me shudder. But more than that, I didn't want to give Christian the satisfaction of being the only one in charge of the band's conducting.

I took a deep breath and mustered my courage. "Wouldn't it be more beneficial for me to stay and learn some conducting in here?" I asked, trying to keep my tone as professional as possible.

Mr. Trust's gaze softened, but his resolve didn't waver. "As our Juliet," he said, a hint of a smile playing at his lips, "we need you to catch up on flag basics."

The mention of my role as Juliet seemed like a small jab, reminding me of the expectations that came with it. I bit back a groan and nodded, forcing a smile. "Got it."

I turned to exit the band room, the heat from outside hitting me like a wall. Stepping onto the field was like walking into an oven. The sun bore down mercilessly, and the heat radiating off the ground was almost enough to make me turn back. The color guard was already spread out in formation, their flags catching in the faint breeze as they moved through their routines with practiced precision.

Luna greeted me with her usual warm smile, though even she looked wilted under the blazing sun. "Hey, Jessica. Ready to jump back in?"

I nodded, wiping the sweat from my forehead. "As ready as I'll ever be."

I slipped into the lineup, the hum of activity around me almost masking the oppressive heat. Luna was midway through demonstrating a flag toss, her energy as boundless as ever, despite the relentless sun. I tried to focus on the arc of her movements, but a prickling sensation along my spine told me I was being watched.

A quick glance confirmed what I already suspected—Courtney, the color guard captain, was glaring at me from down the line. Her narrowed eyes and the disdainful once-over she gave me made it clear: I wasn't just new. I was an intruder.

I could practically feel the judgment rolling off her. I forced myself to focus on Luna's demo, doing my best to ignore that annoying, uncomfortable feeling like everyone was watching, waiting for me to mess up.

Luna guided us through a series of foundational flag movements, her instructions clear and encouraging. Each flick of her wrist looked effortless, but mimicking it was anything but. Frustration built with every fumbled catch, but I bit down on it, forcing myself to push through. The mechanics were foreign and awkward, nothing like spinning a mace.

Courtney sauntered over, her flag balanced casually on her shoulder, the picture of effortless confidence. Her gaze was cool, assessing, and edged with unmistakable annoyance. "So, they really went with you for Juliet, huh?" she said, not even attempting to soften the sting in her words.

I nodded, my shoulders stiffening under the weight of her stare. "Yeah. Still learning. This whole flag thing is new for me," I said, keeping my tone even.

Courtney's laugh was sharp, humorless. "That much is obvious," she said, twirling her flag with ease. The fabric sliced cleanly through the air, the motion so fluid it almost looked rehearsed. "This is a basic toss," she added, her tone condescending, like she was speaking to a child struggling with crayons. She flicked her wrist, sending the flag into a graceful arc before catching it with practiced precision. "Think you can manage?"

My grasp tightened on the flag as I tried to mimic her toss. The flag wobbled midair, and my awkward catch sent it tipping dangerously close to the ground. Courtney's exaggerated sigh was almost louder than the snap of the fabric. She crossed her arms, her expression teetering between disdain and amusement.

"Okay, not terrible… for a rookie. But if you don't want to knock someone's teeth out on the field, you're going to need a little finesse. You're supposed to make it look like you actually know what you're doing, not like it's your first day with a flag."

I swallowed, trying to ignore the sting of her words. "It *is* my first day with a flag."

Courtney smirked, stepping closer, her voice dropping to a softer, but no less cutting tone. "You do know that being Juliet isn't just about hitting every step or following choreo, right? It's about looking graceful, like you belong there. And I hate to break it to you, but right now, you look like you'd rather be anywhere else."

My grip tightened on the flag, heat rising in my face. "I just need to practice."

Her eyebrow shot up, her expression barely hiding the skepticism. "Good. Because everyone out here is going to be watching your every move. And they're expecting Juliet to look… well, let's just say better than what I'm seeing right now." She flicked her eyes over me with an annoyed look before adding, "No pressure or anything."

I forced a smile, ignoring the burn of irritation in my chest. "Right. Thanks for the… encouragement."

She shook her head, giving me a look that was equal parts annoyance and pity. "Sure thing. Just don't embarrass us." She tossed her flag again, catching it in one flawless motion, and then turned her back, joining the rest of the color guard without another glance in my direction, leaving me with my flag and a fierce resolve not to let her doubts be right.

As Courtney walked away, her words still stinging in my ears, I felt a familiar knot of frustration and determination settle in my chest. It wasn't just her dismissive attitude that got under my skin—it was the way she'd looked at me, like I was a trespasser stomping through hallowed ground, unwelcome and out of place. I knew I was a little rough around the edges, that I didn't have her level of polish, but the way she made it so obvious I didn't know what I was doing only made me more determined. I'd work twice as hard—not just to prove her wrong, but to prove to myself that I could own this despite being completely out of my element.

Under the blazing afternoon sun, with the heat at its peak, practice finally wrapped up. I was drenched in sweat and utterly drained. I headed back to the band room, where Christian was conducting a passage from the show with an air of practiced ease. He caught my eye as I entered with that same smug smile on his face.

"Enjoy your time outside?" he asked.

I gritted my teeth and forced a smile. "Oh, it was magical. I highly recommend it."

Christian's grin widened, but he said nothing more. I walked past him, heading for a quieter corner of the room where I could finally catch my breath. The first day of band camp was over, but the battle lines were already drawn, and the real fight was just beginning.

X X X X X X

Dinner was quiet. The clinking of silverware against plates echoed louder than it should have in the stillness. I nudged the last bits of food around my plate, trying to avoid eye contact, praying the conversation would stay neutral long enough for me to escape upstairs. Band camp had wrung me out, and the thought of my blankets and the refuge of my bed was the only thing keeping me upright.

"Jessica," my mom said abruptly, cutting through the silence like a blade. "Have you started looking at college applications yet?"

I froze mid-movement, keeping my expression carefully blank. "Not yet," I said, aiming for casual. "It's still early."

"It's not as early as you think. Deadlines will sneak up on you faster than you realize. You can't afford to leave this until the last minute."

"I know," I muttered, barely swallowing the sigh that threatened to creep into my voice.

Her eyes narrowed slightly, like she could sense my reluctance. "Do you? Because you're going to need to take this seriously, Jessica. With your record…" she trailed off, the implication hanging heavily in the air. "You're going to have to work harder than most to stand out. Colleges don't ignore red flags."

Red flags. A nice way of saying, *You have to convince them you're more than your mistakes*. I focused on my plate, willing her to stop, to move on.

My dad interjected gently, his tone calm, but felt more like he was trying to defuse a bomb. "Maybe now isn't the best time."

"It's important," she shot back, giving him a quick look before her eyes locked on me again. "Jessica, you'll need strong essays. Essays that show growth and resilience—why you're worth taking a chance on."

My throat tightened, but I nodded again.

"And don't forget recommendations," she added, her tone brisk, efficient, as though she were checking off items on a list. "From someone who can vouch for your character. A teacher, a coach—someone who can explain why they trust you and why you're worth taking a chance on."

I bit the inside of my cheek, her words pressing down like a weight I couldn't shake. *Worth taking a chance on*. That's what it always came down to, didn't it? No matter how much I'd tried to move forward, the scar of my mistakes was the first thing people saw. I wasn't a person to them—I was a risk.

"You shouldn't waste your time," she continued, her eyes flicking back to me like a spotlight. "You should start drafting essays now. The more time you have to revise, the better they'll be. These essays aren't just important, they could make or break your application. You can't afford to take them lightly."

"The school year hasn't even started," I muttered before I could stop myself. The sharp look on her face made me regret it instantly. I quickly backtracked. "I'll take a look. Soon."

Her skeptical gaze lingered, weighing me down like she was already finding flaws in my resolve. Finally, she relented. "Good. We'll go over some prompts tomorrow after band camp."

I nodded quickly, standing before the conversation could continue. "I'm going to shower," I said, my voice barely above a mumble as I retreated away, hurrying upstairs.

Upstairs, I closed my bedroom door with a soft click and leaned against it, letting out a shaky breath. The conversation looped in my mind, every word burrowing deeper under my skin. *Red flags*. *Resilience*. *Worth taking a chance on*. Each phrase felt like a reminder that no matter how much I tried to move forward, my past still defined me.

I pulled out my phone, staring at the home screen for a moment before typing out a quick text to Cassie—my old friend from Riverview. I hadn't heard from her since the move, but it's not like I reached out either.

Band camp was brutal. Hope your week is better than mine.

I hovered over the send button, hesitating. I wasn't sure what I wanted from her—maybe just a reminder that someone out there saw me for more than my mistakes, that someone still knew the version of me before all of this. With a small sigh, I hit send.

The message delivered, but it didn't take the ache in my chest with it. Tomorrow would come fast, dragging with it another day of marching, scrutiny, and pretending I had it all figured out. For now, I let the stillness of my room settle around me, even as my thoughts spun endlessly, refusing to let me rest.

Christian

The sun was relentless, beating down on the practice field's astroturf and turning it into a makeshift frying pan. Sweat trickled down my back as I paced along the line, watching the brass section attempt—*and fail*—to keep their intervals straight.

"Reset!" Jessica's voice rang out, sharp and commanding, cutting through the chatter and grumbles of the trumpets. "Dressing the line means *actually* looking to your left. Use your peripherals, people. Not guessing. Not hoping. Look. To. Your. Left."

The trumpets shuffled back to their dots, groaning under their breath. A few glanced at each other, smirking like they thought this was all some kind of joke. I bit back a laugh, shaking my head. Typical. Jessica probably thought she was nailing the whole "strict leader" vibe, but from where I was standing, it looked more like overkill.

She'd been acting like this all day—snapping at sections, pacing the sidelines like she was waiting for something to explode, and carrying that tightly wound energy that made everyone, even the confident seniors, tread carefully around her. Every comment she gave felt sharper than usual, like she was daring someone to challenge her. Even the freshmen, who usually got a softer side of her, weren't immune to her short temper today. It was like she'd woken up on a mission to steamroll the entire band, and no one was safe from the fallout.

I leaned against one marimba, casually sipping from my water bottle. Out of the corner of her eye, she must've caught me smiling, because her head jerked in my direction. "Something funny, Christian?"

I lowered the bottle, raising my hands in mock surrender. "Not funny. Just... entertaining," I said, letting the grin spread wider. "Watching you bark at the trumpets like a military drill instructor when half the guard can't even march in time."

Her glare could've melted steel. "The guard isn't the problem here," she shot back, voice clipped. "Your drumline, on the other hand, keeps blowing their downbeats."

"Oh, so now it's the drumline's fault?" I stepped closer, my voice just loud enough to draw the attention of the nearby flutes. "Maybe if you weren't so obsessed with *perfectly* straight lines, you'd realize the trumpets can't keep eight-to-five to save their lives."

Jessica stiffened, her eyes narrowing. "Are you serious right now? You think straight lines *don't* matter? Maybe if you focused on basic fundamentals of marching band instead of messing around with the snare drums, we wouldn't have this problem."

A ripple of stifled laughter came from the clarinet section. I shrugged, enjoying the way her irritation flared hotter. "Oh, I'm sorry. I didn't realize this entire rehearsal was about you," I said, letting the sarcasm drip from my voice.

"At least I'm trying to fix things!" she fired back, gesturing toward the field where the trumpets stood frozen, clearly eavesdropping on us now. "What are you doing? Standing there looking smug and waiting for someone else to do all the work?"

I let out a short laugh, shaking my head. "Fix things? All you're doing is yelling. Newsflash, Jessica: nobody wants to follow a leader who makes them feel like shit."

Her jaw tightened, and for a second, I thought she might actually lose it. "Newsflash, Christian," she shot back, her voice rising, "leadership isn't about being everyone's buddy. It's about setting a standard and holding people accountable."

"And how's that working out for you?" I said, stepping closer, lowering my voice to just above a growl. "Because from where I'm standing, it looks like the only thing you're holding is everyone's patience."

Her fists clenched at her sides, and I could see the fire in her eyes as she opened her mouth to respond—but before she could, Mr. Trust's voice boomed across the field.

"Jessica! Christian! My office. Now."

The entire band froze, their attention whipping to the sideline where Mr. Trust stood with his arms crossed, his expression a mix of frustration and disbelief. The trumpets exchanged wide-eyed glances, and the flutes quickly buried their faces in their drill sheets, suddenly very interested in their marks.

Jessica turned sharply, her steps quick and rigid as she marched toward the sideline. I followed a beat later, my smirk dropping as the weight of Mr. Trust's tone settled over me.

The band stayed frozen, whispers trailing behind us as we made our way off the field. Even the drumline, usually so loud and animated, kept their sticks hovering above their snares, silent. Whatever this was about, it wasn't going to be pretty.

As I walked behind Jessica, something about her posture caught my attention. Her shoulders were stiff, her steps a little too quick, like she was trying to get away from more than just me. It didn't seem like she was just mad—I couldn't put my finger on it, but something felt... off. I couldn't help but wonder if maybe I'd pushed her a little too far.

Not that I'd ever admit it. Not yet, anyway.

The door clicked shut behind us, sealing the two of us in the still, stifling air of Mr. Trust's office. The muffled sounds of rehearsal drifted faintly through the walls—a distant reminder that the band was out there, probably whispering about what had just happened. Jessica stood stiffly beside me, shoulders squared and fists tight at her sides, like she was ready to spar round two.

I wasn't far off. My arms crossed over my chest, my jaw tight. Whatever speech Mr. Trust had lined up, I wasn't about to take the full blame for this mess. She'd been pushing too hard all afternoon, and everyone on that field could see it.

Mr. Trust's chair creaked as he settled behind his desk, folding his arms across his chest in that quiet, controlled way that was somehow worse than yelling. The silence stretched long enough to make me glance at Jessica. She hadn't moved a muscle, her eyes locked on some invisible point ahead of her.

Finally, he spoke. "Do either of you care to explain what the hell happened out there?"

Jessica's head turned slightly, but I beat her to it. "We were just trying to fix some things," I said, keeping my tone calm. "The band's timing was off—"

"And yelling at each other in front of the entire band was your solution?" Mr. Trust cut me off, his voice sharper than I expected. The words made my shoulders stiffen, and I pressed my lips together.

"It wasn't... intentional," Jessica muttered, her voice tight and quiet, like she was trying to hold back her frustration.

Mr. Trust exhaled loudly, dragging his hand down his face. "I don't care if it was intentional or not. What I care about is the fact that the two of you—the drum majors, the people this band is supposed to look up to—just gave them a front-row seat to your petty argument."

"It wasn't petty," Jessica defended, her voice rising a notch. "We were trying to get them to improve. Christian wasn't taking things seriously, and—"

"Oh, I wasn't taking things seriously?" I shot back, the words spilling out before I could stop them. I turned toward her, my voice sharp. "You were the one barking orders instead of actually helping anyone."

"That's enough!" Mr. Trust's voice boomed, slicing through the room like a whip. Both of us clamped our mouths shut, glaring at the floor like scolded kids.

He leaned forward, planting his hands on the desk as he fixed us with a hard stare. "This isn't about who's right or wrong. This is about leadership."

The word dug under my skin like a splinter. I shifted my weight, glancing briefly at Jessica. She remained as rigid as a statue, but I detected the tension in the set of her jaw.

"Jessica," Mr. Trust said, his tone softening but still firm. "I know you push this band harder than anyone because you want them to succeed. But leadership isn't about perfection. It's not about control. It's about connection. Making people want to follow you—not because they're afraid of disappointing you, but because they believe in you."

I glanced at her, half expecting her to argue, but she looked down at her shoes. The words clearly hit home.

"And Christian," he said, turning his gaze to me. My stomach twisted under the weight of his attention. "You've got a natural way with people—a way of making them feel supported. But leadership also means holding yourself and others accountable. It's not enough to stand back and let someone else carry the weight when things get hard."

I nodded, my arms tightening across my chest. I didn't want to admit it, but he was right. I'd let her take the brunt of today's rehearsal. Even if she'd made it impossible to step in, I hadn't tried hard to meet her halfway.

"You two need to step up," Mr. Trust continued, his voice steady. "If you can't figure out how to work together, you're going to tear this band apart."

The weight of his words settled heavily over the room. For the first time, I couldn't even muster the energy to glare at Jessica. I felt exhausted, the frustration that had fueled me earlier burning low now. She looked just as tired, her shoulders sagging ever so slightly.

"Do you understand me?" Mr. Trust asked, his voice leaving no room for argument.

"Yes, sir," we muttered in unison.

"Good," he said, leaning back in his chair. "Now, go back out there and fix this. Together. And if I see even a hint of another argument, you'll both be running laps until you can't stand."

We left the office in silence, the door clicking shut behind us. The muffled sound of the band rehearsing outside filled the air, but the tension between us was thick, suffocating. I ran a hand through my hair, exhaling slowly as we reached the edge of the field.

Jessica broke the silence first, her voice tight with leftover anger. "Well? You gonna 'step up,' or are you just here to watch me bulldoze my way through the rest of rehearsal?"

I stopped walking, her words sparking the irritation still simmering under my skin. "You know what? Maybe I will," I said, my voice sharp. "At least I won't treat everyone like they're robots who need to be programmed."

"Oh, please," she spun to face me. "You barely even try! You're so busy playing the 'fun leader' that you're completely useless when it actually matters."

I clenched my fists, my chest heaving as I tried to keep my voice level. "And you're so busy being in control that you don't even realize you're crushing everyone under the pressure." I gestured toward the field, where the band stood stiffly, avoiding eye contact. "It's only the second day of band camp. You're going to scare the freshmen into quitting."

I could see the frustration coiled tight beneath her expression, her lips pressing into a thin line like she was biting back another sharp retort. For a moment, I thought she might snap again, but instead, she let out a sharp exhale and looked away. Her voice softened, but it carried an extra edge. "Look, I don't care what you think of me. But if we don't figure this out, we're going to let the whole band down. And I can't let that happen."

The shift in her tone caught me off guard, like she was trying to meet me halfway. I hesitated, the fight draining from my shoulders. "Yeah," I said, my voice quieter. "I won't let it happen either."

She glanced at me, and for the first time all day, there wasn't pure frustration in her eyes. Just exhaustion. "So… are we doing this or not?" she asked, her tone wary but less combative.

I nodded slowly, the knot in my chest loosening just slightly. "Alright. Let's get through this rehearsal without killing each other."

Jessica arched an eyebrow, her lips twitching like she wanted to say something sarcastic, but decided against it. "Good. Because I'm not running laps because of you."

"Likewise," I muttered.

As we headed back toward the band, the tension between us didn't disappear, but it shifted—less like a battle line and more like an uneasy truce. I didn't know if this would last, but for now, it was enough to get us through the rest of the day.

Once we returned to the field, I caught myself watching her more closely than I meant to. At first, I thought I was waiting for her to blow up again, to go back to barking orders and grinding everyone down. But… she didn't.

Instead of shouting at the trumpets for messing up their diagonals, she stopped and walked down the line, adjusting one person's foot placement with a quick correction and nodding in approval when they reset correctly. "That's it. Keep your toes up on the roll step," she said, her voice firm but less cutting. The clarinet player straightened under her gaze, looking like he'd just passed some sort of test.

Later, when the mellophones missed their cue during a drill, she didn't sigh dramatically or make a snide remark like I'd half expected. Instead, she waited, reset the group with a calm "Let's try it again," and nodded when they got it right on the second try. "There you go. Much better."

It was subtle, but it was there—the patience, the effort to meet people halfway instead of steamrolling them. She even tossed out a few words of encouragement, which had to be hard for her, given how tightly she usually held onto control. "Nice work, clarinets," she called after one set. "You're locking in the spacing. Let's keep it consistent."

I blinked, surprised by the shift. This wasn't the Jessica who'd stormed into camp with something to prove, who seemed determined to bulldoze everyone into perfection. It was like Mr. Trust's words had actually gotten through to her, like she was trying to be… better.

And it was working. The tension in the band felt lighter somehow, the chatter between sets more relaxed. Even the freshmen, who usually looked like they were one wrong move away from fainting, seemed less panicked under her gaze.

It was weird seeing this side of her, but it wasn't bad. If anything, it made me realize maybe she could do this.

I didn't say anything, though. It wasn't like I was going to pat her on the back for doing what we'd both been told to do. Still, as I called out to the drumline to reset for another run, I found myself glancing her way more often than I intended, watching as she took those first, tentative steps toward being the kind of leader Mr. Trust had told her she could be.

Christian

It's completely unfair," Courtney crossed her arms tightly as she stared out the window of my truck. We were on our way to the last day of camp, and she hadn't stopped complaining since I picked her up. "I'm a senior. I'm the guard captain. I've earned my spot. And now Mr. Trust hands the Juliet role to Jessica? It's ridiculous."

I kept my eyes on the road. "I get it, Court. But Mr. Trust has a vision for the show. It's not about playing favorites."

"Vision?" she scoffed, turning to glare at me. "What about my vision? What about everything I've worked for? Jessica shows up from Cow Town, California, and suddenly she's the centerpiece? Meanwhile, I'm picking up the slack for the rest of the guard while she gets all the attention."

"She's just doing what she's asked to do, like the rest of us."

Courtney let out a sharp exhale, her gaze flicking back to the window. "It's easy for her. She hasn't had to prove herself like I have. She hasn't had to work half as hard."

I sighed, my patience wearing thin. "Court, I know this sucks. But you're still the one leading the guard. People look up to you. That doesn't change just because Jessica's playing Juliet."

She shook her head, her voice quieter now but no less bitter. "It's not about being captain, Christian. This was supposed to be my year. My moment. And now it's just… gone."

I pulled into the school parking lot, cutting the engine as I turned to her. "It's not gone. You're still making an impact, and everyone sees that. You're the reason the guard's as good as it is. That doesn't just disappear because of one role."

She glanced at me, her expression softening for a moment before the frustration crept back in. "It'd be nice if you actually had my back for once. Instead, you just defend Mr. Trust like he's some kind of genius."

"It's not about defending him. It's about trusting the process. He's trying to push all of us to be better."

"Easy for you to say," she said, opening the door. "You're still drum major. You wouldn't know what it's like to feel invisible."

I didn't respond right away, but her words lingered. She was wrong—but how could I tell her that? How could I explain what it felt like to stand in the middle of my own house and feel like a ghost? To sit across the table from my parents, trying to hold a conversation while they barely looked up from their phones or each other's arguments?

The truth burned in my chest, but I swallowed it down. This wasn't the time, and Courtney wasn't the person who'd understood things like this. She wanted me to have her back, not unload my own baggage. So I stayed quiet, gripping the wheel a little tighter.

I parked the truck and turned to Courtney. "Look, it's our senior year. Last chance to make our mark. Let's just go out there and do what we do best. We can't control every decision Mr. Trust makes, but we can show everyone what we're made of."

She gave a resigned nod.

We stepped out of the truck and made our way to the field, the sun already high and relentless. The band was busy with final preparations, and the color guard was spread out, practicing their routines with renewed focus. The culmination of a week's worth of effort was about to be tested, and everyone was ready to give it their all.

Jessica was off to one side of the field, surrounded by a cluster of freshmen who looked both relieved and overwhelmed. Her presence was a stark contrast to the intensity of the rest of the band. She was patiently demonstrating the 8-to-5 sizing step (probably for the hundredth time), her voice soft but firm as she corrected their mistakes. The freshmen seemed more at ease, their anxiety eased by her supportive presence.

As she moved among the freshmen, her voice steady but gentle, I watched them gravitate toward her, their anxious faces relaxing with each nod and smile she gave. I caught one kid, one of the freshman contra tuba players, looking at her like she'd just saved his life, his shoulders dropping from a rigid line into something almost comfortable.

When lunch rolled around, the parent board had splurged on food to celebrate the last day of camp. They had hired a Mexican food truck to come out and feed our 160-plus band members. Everyone was ecstatic to take a break and enjoy the delicious spread.

As the line formed in front of the truck, Mr. Trust grabbed a drumstick and banged it against a cowbell, immediately capturing everyone's attention.

"Listen up, everyone!" Mr. Trust called out. "I want to take a moment to recognize how far we've come in just one week. Your hard work, dedication, and teamwork have been nothing short of amazing. This is just the beginning of what we can achieve together."

He paused for a moment, letting his words sink in. "After lunch, we'll be calling you up in small groups for uniform fittings. It's a chance to see how we're all coming together in our new gear. Let's keep this momentum going and finish strong. Enjoy your break, and let's make the most of the rest of the day!"

With that, he stepped back, and the chatter of excited band members and the clatter of the food truck continued as everyone eagerly lined up for their meals. I made sure everyone had their food before grabbing a plate of tacos and sitting next to Alex in the shade.

Alex took a big bite of his taco and grinned. "Man, this food is awesome. Way better than the usual ham sandwich."

"Agreed," I said, digging into my plate. "It's nice to have a change of pace. And I think everyone's earned it after this week."

Alex nodded, his eyes scanning the field. "Hey, you know, I've been meaning to ask—what's up with Jessica?"

I raised an eyebrow. "What do you mean?"

He shrugged. "Just, I don't know. She's been kind of impressive this week, even after that rough start, and I guess I can see why you've been so worked up about her. She's got a… presence."

"A presence?" I said, skepticism clear in my tone.

Alex chuckled. "Yeah, like a certain kind of charm or something." He paused, grinning like he was about to push a button. "Okay, fine—she's hot."

I rolled my eyes, shaking my head. "You think everyone's hot, Alex."

He smirked, unfazed. "Maybe. But that doesn't mean I'm wrong."

I shot him a look. "Trust me, you are."

"Sure, sure," Alex said, clearly enjoying himself. "But you've got to admit, she's got something… Call it confidence, call it whatever you want—but it's there."

"Yeah, an annoying attitude," I said, rolling my eyes. The thought of anyone—even Alex, who flirts with anything that breathes—finding Jessica attractive literally made me want to throw up. So what if she happened to look good while spinning a flag? It doesn't dismiss the disruption she's caused.

"Don't tell me you haven't noticed."

"Noticed what?" Courtney's voice popped up out of nowhere. She sat down beside me on the grass.

Alex's grin faltered as Courtney joined us. I tensed, trying to figure out how much she'd overheard. "Uh, nothing important," Alex said quickly, shoving the last of his taco into his mouth, but his eyes darted between me and Courtney, clearly nervous.

Courtney narrowed her eyes at him, then turned to me. "Christian, what's he talking about?"

I shot Alex a glare, then forced a casual shrug. "Just band stuff."

Alex nodded enthusiastically, swallowing his food with a loud gulp. "Yeah, you know, how everyone's really stepped up, including the new folks." Courtney and I both saw Alex's eyes drift over to Jessica for a few seconds.

We both flipped our heads to see Jessica laughing as she sat with Tracy. "You're joking." Courtney rolled her eyes so hard I thought she might strain something

"What?" Alex asked with a shrug. "I think she's pretty…" There was a slight pause as Courtney narrowed her eyes at Alex. "—good. I think she's pretty good. You know, at drum majoring and the flag spinning thing." His vocabulary dwindled.

Courtney didn't look convinced. Her gaze flicked to Alex, then back to me. "Right. Well, I hope you two are keeping your focus where it belongs. We can't afford any distractions or slip-ups this season."

"No distractions here," I said, resting my arm around her shoulders and pecking her cheek.

Alex gagged at the sight of our PDA. "Well, that's my sign to leave." He got up with his half eaten plate and made his way across the field towards Tracy and Jessica.

Courtney narrowed her eyes, lowering her voice. "I've been thinking. I might have a way to get Jessica out of the picture."

"What kind of way?"

She leaned closer, her voice dropping conspiratorially. "When school starts, I could… borrow my mom's office keys." Her mom was part of the administration at Arcana.

"Just a quick look around," she continued, her tone light, as if this was no big deal. "If there's anything buried in Jessica's file—something personal, something she wouldn't want getting out—well, it might be enough to make her rethink her place here."

I paused, the weight of her words settling in. Something about this felt… wrong. But the idea of solving all the Jessica-related problems in one clean sweep was tempting.

Courtney leaned in closer, her voice soft and coaxing. "Come on, Christian. If we find anything that casts a shadow over her, she might just leave on her own. No drama, no confrontation. You'd have your drum major spot back. We'd all have our season back."

I hesitated, glancing across the field where Jessica was laughing with Tracy. She seemed oblivious to everything—but that only made her intrusion harder to ignore. Courtney's plan was risky, sure, but wasn't it worth it to protect what we'd built?

Courtney nudged me, her voice dropping lower. "Think about it. She's already taken Juliet. She's sharing your podium now. What's next? Solos? Mr. Trust's entire focus? She's not stopping, Christian.

She's just going to keep pushing until there's no space left for the rest of us."

I looked at her, seeing the fire in her eyes. She believed this was the right move. And maybe she was right. Maybe Jessica didn't belong here. Maybe we needed to show her that.

I sighed, keeping my voice low. "If you can get the file, we'll see if there's anything we can use. Just don't get caught, okay?"

Courtney smiled, satisfied. "Don't worry. I'll handle everything."

She leaned in to kiss me, and I returned it, but my thoughts swirled. This wasn't just about Jessica anymore—it was about how far I was willing to go. I told myself it was just a strategy, a way to fix the chaos she'd brought. But deep down, I couldn't shake the feeling that this might be crossing a line I couldn't come back from.

13 A Fitting Role

Jessica

The afternoon sun beat down on us as the freshmen finished up their uniform fittings, their nervous excitement infectious as they emerged from the fitting room, some tugging at stiff collars or smoothing out freshly pressed jackets. The entire process felt like a rite of passage—everyone eager to don the official colors of Arcana High, to feel like a genuine part of the team.

"Jessica, your turn," a voice called, breaking me out of my thoughts.

I headed toward the fitting area, mentally preparing myself for a standard drum major uniform. An all-white uniform with accents of gold and green—I'd seen it before when I was researching all about Arcana before I had moved down here. But as soon as I stepped into the room, I realized how wrong I was.

Instead of the familiar jacket and pants, the uniform assistants handed me a garment bag. It was much larger than I expected, and when I unzipped it, my heart sank.

Inside was a dress.

I stared at it, my mind racing. The dress was beautiful, I couldn't deny that—deep crimson with intricate gold embroidery that shimmered as it caught the light. The designer clearly intended the dress to stand out and catch the audience's attention, but that's what made it worse. It was a dress meant for Juliet, not for me.

"Is there some mistake?" I asked, my voice wavering. "I'm a drum major, not a member of the guard."

The assistant shook her head, her smile polite but firm. "No mistake. Mr. Trust wants you to wear this as part of the show's theme. You're playing Juliet, after all."

My heart pounded. I'd spent my entire time here working hard to prove myself as a leader, to be seen as equal to Christian. The idea of being on that podium, leading the band, while wearing a dress that screamed 'damsel-in-distress' made my skin crawl. It felt like a step back, like all the progress I'd made was being overshadowed by this role I hadn't asked for.

"But… I've never worn anything like this for conducting," I stammered. "I need to move freely, to lead the band."

"It's designed to be functional," the assistant assured me. "There's plenty of room for movement, and it's lightweight. You'll be fine."

Fine? Ugh. Every fiber of my being wanted to push back, to refuse, but what could I do? This was Mr. Trust's vision, and if I protested, it would only make me seem difficult—or worse, weak. And I couldn't afford that.

Reluctantly, I nodded and took the dress to a changing room. As I slipped it on, the unfamiliar fabric swished around my legs, feeling both foreign and constricting. I stared at my reflection. This girl in the mirror looked… exposed.

It made me feel bare, defenseless in a way that set my teeth on edge. I fought hard to avoid being perceived as delicate. It shrank me, reduced me to something fragile, something soft. And I refused to be breakable.

My chest tightened, unease coiling like a spring. Juliet wasn't the role I wanted. I wanted to lead—to stand equal, unshaken, untouchable. But this dress, this role, asked for softness. For grace. For a surrender I didn't know how to give.

A shaky breath escaped me, and I clenched my fists, the fabric bunching beneath my fingers. No. I wouldn't let this break me.

Somehow, I'd make it work. I'd find a way to stand strong—even if it meant playing a part I didn't believe in.

I slipped the dress back off, feeling discouraged, and placed it back into the garment bag. I handed the bag to the assistant. "How'd it fit?"

As much as I hated that it did indeed fit perfectly, I answered, "Like a glove."

I returned to the classroom, where the band was already rehearsing the opener. Sliding into a seat beside Alex and the other trumpets, I grabbed my instrument and joined in, even though I wouldn't be playing it during the show. I needed something to make me feel like I was part of the band.

"You alright?" Alex leaned in and whispered, his voice tinged with curiosity. "You've got that 'I just walked through a haunted house' vibe going on. How was the fitting?"

I forced a half-hearted smile, still feeling the constricting fabric I'd just tried on. "They want to put me in a dress."

Alex's eyebrows shot up, and he let out a low whistle. "A *dress*? Wow. That's… bold. Very Victorian drama queen. Did they give you one of those parasols, too? Maybe a tiara?"

I couldn't help the faint chuckle that escaped me. "No parasol, but they definitely nailed the damsel-in-distress aesthetic."

"Missed opportunity," he said, shaking his head. "If you're gonna go full theater kid, might as well commit to the bit."

Despite myself, I smiled, but it faltered as I murmured, "I thought I'd be wearing the same uniform as Christian. I thought I'd be… equal."

Alex softened as he leaned closer. "Jessica, you are equal. The uniform's just cloth and buttons. You've been absolutely crushing it this week. Trust me, everyone knows you deserve to be up there."

His words should've been comforting, and part of me wanted to believe him, but a nagging voice twisted in the back of my mind.

"Thanks, Alex," I said, my voice faltering despite myself. "I just… I don't want to be seen as the girl who got handed a role because it fit the theme. I want to earn it, just like everyone else."

He clicked his tongue, tilting his head like I'd just told him the sky wasn't blue. "You think they handed it to you? Believe me, Mr.

Trust doesn't 'hand out' anything. If you're wearing that dress, it's because you've already earned it. End of story."

He put an arm on the back of my chair. Instinctively, I sat forward. "Besides, think of it this way: you're gonna look epic up there. Like you just stepped out of a movie poster. Honestly, I don't think even Christian could pull off leading a band while wearing a dress."

That pulled a laugh out of me. "I would pay good money to see that," I said, shaking my head.

"Same," he said, grinning. "He'd hate every second, too, which makes it even better."

His goofiness made it easier to push the doubts aside, but they didn't disappear completely. As I turned back to my sheet music, his words lingered, tempting me to believe them.

Mr. Trust stood at the front, conducting with his usual intensity. He hadn't yet figured out how Christian and I would split the show, and I couldn't help but notice Christian leaning against the wall at the front, arms crossed, watching everything with that familiar look of superiority. He hadn't picked up his trumpet all week, preferring instead to hover near the front, as if trying to remind everyone who was really in charge.

The final note of the opener rang throughout the band room, and Mr. Trust lowered his hands, a satisfied smile on his face. "Nice work, everyone. That's how you end band camp."

There was a smattering of applause and a few whoops from the band, and I couldn't help but smile, too. We had made it through the week, and the music was starting to feel real, like something we could actually pull off.

✗ ✗ ✗ ✗ ✗ ✗

The neon sign outside the diner flickered faintly as we pushed through the doors, the jangle of the bell announcing our arrival. The place buzzed with laughter and the clatter of plates, leaving only a cramped two-seat booth at the far end of the room. Tracy slid into the booth first, claiming her spot by the window, while Marcus and Alex argued over who would sit on the edge.

"Rock-paper-scissors for it?" Marcus offered, already holding his fist out.

"Please, I'm not wasting strategy on you," Alex shot back, tossing a triumphant grin.

"Where's Christian and Courtney?" Tracy asked casually. "They're going to have to stand if they don't get here soon."

"Nah, they're not coming." Alex smirked, sliding into the booth across from Tracy. "They're probably too busy making out to remember we exist."

I stiffened, my smile faltering for a split second before I forced it back. Of course, they weren't coming. Because I was invited.

They invited me to their little group hang after camp had ended—an apparent tradition after surviving the week-long gauntlet of drills and sunburns. I'd hesitated at first, nerves pricking at the edges of my mind. Was this just another hazing ritual masked as a casual hangout? Another way to test me or make me the butt of some inside joke I hadn't been let in on? But Tracy's calm reassurance and the sheer exhaustion of the day had worn down my resistance, and I found myself agreeing.

Still, as they joked and laughed, their dynamic so seamless and familiar, I lingered by the door, wondering if I'd made the right choice. Maybe this wasn't my space to fill.

I hesitated, hanging back for a moment before Tracy waved me over. "C'mon, Jess. We're not going to bite."

"Speak for yourself," Alex quipped, shooting me a grin. "I make no promises."

I rolled my eyes but managed a small smile, sliding into the booth beside Alex.

"What are we ordering?" Marcus asked, flipping the menu open as if he didn't already know exactly what he wanted.

"Milkshakes," Alex said immediately. "Obviously. And fries. Lots of fries."

"And mozzarella sticks," Tracy added, leaning over to peek at Marcus's menu. "You're paying, right?"

Alex feigned offense, clutching his chest. "What do I look like, a millionaire?"

Marcus and Tracy looked at each other and then back at him. "Uh, yes, *Mr. I-drive-a-convertible*," Tracy tagged on.

The light banter swirled around me, and for a moment, I felt almost... normal. Like I belonged here, with them. Almost.

As we waited for the food to arrive, Alex leaned forward, propping his chin on his hand as he grinned at me. "So, Jessica, what's your milkshake flavor of choice? This is important. Your answer will determine whether or not we can remain friends."

I gave him a flat look. "Strawberry."

Alex gasped, clutching his chest again like I'd personally offended him. "Wrong answer. It's chocolate or nothing."

"Vanilla is superior," Marcus chimed in, earning a chorus of groans from both Tracy and Alex.

"Vanilla is not a flavor; it's a default," Alex argued, leaning back and draping an arm across the back of the booth. His hand brushed against my shoulder, and I stiffened immediately, the contact sending a jolt of discomfort through me.

Alex didn't seem to notice, continuing his animated debate with Marcus, but Tracy shot me a quick glance, her brows knitting together in concern. I shifted slightly, leaning forward to put some distance between us, but Alex's arm stayed where it was, his presence a little too close, a little too casual.

"You okay?" Tracy murmured under her breath, her voice low enough that only I could hear.

I nodded quickly, forcing a smile. "Mm-hmm."

But I wasn't. I hated how my body betrayed me in moments like this—how something as innocent as Alex's arm brushing against me could send me spiraling. I knew he didn't mean anything by it, that he was just being his usual, oblivious self, but that didn't make it easier.

The food arrived soon after, and the conversation shifted to band camp, with Marcus recounting every mistake Alex had made during the final run-through. Alex, of course, defended himself with flair, turning even the most embarrassing moments into exaggerated stories that had Tracy laughing so hard she nearly spit out her drink.

I tried to relax, to let myself laugh with them, but the tension in my shoulders never fully eased. Every time Alex leaned forward or gestured wildly, his arm would graze mine, and I'd have to fight the instinct to pull away completely.

Alex's arm brushed against mine again, and my stomach twisted. Across the table, Tracy cackled so loudly, she knocked over her drink. They were all so at ease, so unbothered. *Why couldn't I be the same?*

By the time we left the diner, my chest felt tight, like I'd been holding my breath the entire time. As we walked out into the cool night air, Alex slung an arm around my shoulder, his weight leaning into me as he grinned down at me. "This was fun, wasn't it?"

I froze, my muscles locking up as the familiar discomfort surged back. Tracy, walking beside us, stepped in without hesitation, smoothly inserting herself between us. She looped an arm through Alex's, guiding him forward with a laugh like nothing was out of the ordinary.

Alex laughed, completely unfazed, and I managed a weak smile, grateful for Tracy's intervention. But the unease lingered, a reminder that no matter how much I wanted to belong, there were still parts of me that couldn't fully let go.

As we reached the parking lot, Alex called out, "Next week is our last first day of secondary education. The end of an era."

Marcus groaned dramatically, tossing his drumsticks into the passenger seat of his car. "Thanks for the reminder, man. Way to ruin a perfectly good evening."

Tracy rolled her eyes, pulling her keys from her pocket. "He's not wrong, though. Senior year. It's going to be weird not spending every waking moment in rehearsals with you guys after this."

I lingered by my car, watching as the group dissolved into lighthearted banter about the upcoming school year. Tracy leaned against her door, laughing at one of Marcus's exaggerated impressions of Mr. Trust, while Alex leaned over the hood of his car, tossing in quips that had them doubled over. It was effortless— the way they clicked, the way their jokes bounced off each other like they'd been doing this forever.

There was a rhythm to their dynamic, one I hadn't quite learned yet, like stepping into the middle of a song you didn't know the words to. No matter how much I tried to keep up, I couldn't shake the feeling that I was an echo in a room full of melodies—present, but never quite part of the harmony.

Tracy glanced my way mid-laugh, catching the half-smile I hadn't realized I was faking. Her grin softened, and she tilted her head slightly, like she could see straight through me. She didn't say anything, though, just gave me a look that said she understood—more than I probably wanted her to.

The lot grew quieter as engines rumbled to life, headlights cutting through the dusk. One by one, they drove off, their laughter and teasing fading into the still night air. I stood there for a moment, letting the silence settle over me.

I wanted to be here. I wanted to feel like I belonged, like I was part of this—like Alex's arm on the back of the booth was nothing more than a casual gesture. But I couldn't stop the way my body locked up, the way my mind spiraled.

Belonging wasn't supposed to feel like this.

14 The Dirt

Christian

The door creaked open as I pushed it with my shoulder, juggling my bag and the fatigue that clung to me after a grueling day at band camp. An unsettling quiet hung in the house. It was the sort of silence that settled in places where people were meant to be close but weren't. I wanted nothing more than to disappear into my room and forget about the world for a while.

Just as I reached the hall, voices drifted from the kitchen, low but sharp. My parents' voices, as familiar as they were exhausting. Arguments had become their language, their way of filling the silence, and I'd learned to block it out like white noise.

I debated slipping up the stairs unnoticed, but as I took my first step, my mother's voice sliced through the air. "Christian! Is that you?"

I winced. So much for sneaking by. I turned to find her standing in the kitchen doorway, her face partially hidden in shadows, a glass of wine dangling from her hand. She was trying to look concerned, but the glossiness in her eyes and the faint smell of liquor told me this wasn't about me. She was simply looking for a distraction from whatever argument was brewing.

My father stood behind her, barely acknowledging my presence, his gaze fixed on something beyond us all. He held his own glass, the subtle clinking of ice the only sign that he was alive. They both looked worn, not just from each other, but from whatever they'd stopped pretending to care about years ago.

"I was just heading upstairs," I said, hoping to just avoid all of this.

My mother's eyes softened in a way that felt empty, as if she were playing the role of a concerned mom rather than actually being one. "How was your... band thing?" she asked, her tone overly bright, too forced, like she was grasping at a semblance of maternal interest.

"It was fine." I tried to keep my response short and noncommittal. There was no point in giving her more than that; I'd learned by now that anything I said would only be fuel for whatever was on her mind, twisted to fit her narrative.

As I turned to make my escape, I heard my father mutter, "Let him run off and hide." The words weren't loud, but they were pointed, slipping under my skin like needles.

I stopped, turning back to him. "I'm not hiding," I said. "I just don't want to be in the middle of—whatever it is you two call... *this*."

He scoffed, taking a long sip from his glass, clearly done with the conversation. My mom put her glass down, taking a step toward me as if she could bridge the distance between us by crossing a few feet. Her lips pressed into a thin line, her brow furrowing just enough to mimic concern. But the hesitation in her gaze gave her away, like she was reaching for a thread of empathy she no longer knew how to weave.

"Christian, I just..." she began, her voice softer, almost pleading. But it was the same hollow tone she'd used a hundred times before. It was a voice that pretended to care but was always quick to shift back to criticism, to disinterest.

I swallowed, not wanting to give her the satisfaction of seeing how exhausted I was. "Look, I get it. You have your... stuff going on." I tried to keep my voice steady and neutral. "But don't make me a part of it. I don't want to witness whatever this is."

Her eyes flickered, as if she might say something, but the moment passed, and she picked up her glass again, clutching it like a lifeline. My father hadn't moved, his attention already drifting, as if the conversation itself was beneath him.

Without waiting for another word, I turned and walked toward the stairs, each step feeling heavier than the last. I was nearly at the top when I heard her voice, softer now. "Christian, please…"

I paused, but only for a moment. I knew that tone; it was the one she used when she wanted me to take her side, to be her support. But I couldn't keep doing that—I was done filling in the gaps, done pretending we were something we weren't.

I pushed forward, making my way down the hall and into my room. Once inside, I shut the door with a quiet click, letting out a breath I hadn't realized I was holding. The silence in my room felt different—heavier, but safer somehow. I slumped against the door, closing my eyes as the weight of everything settled over me.

I moved over to my bed, sitting down and staring at the walls. The room was a sanctuary of sorts, but it felt like it was closing in on me. I needed something to distract myself, something to pull me away from the constant noise and conflict that seemed to follow me wherever I went.

I reached for my phone, scrolling through messages and social media posts, clinging to the distraction like a lifeline. It was a temporary escape, just pixels on a screen, but it was something—anything to take my mind off the relentless cycle of anger and disappointment at home. As I skimmed through old photos of band competitions, I focused on the snapshots of a life that felt worlds apart from the chaos downstairs.

Band was a sanctuary, a place where I could lose myself in the rhythm and the discipline, where every beat, every formation felt like a step toward freedom. On the field, the noise at home faded, replaced by something more powerful: purpose, unity, the kind of camaraderie I couldn't find anywhere else. Band was a place where I didn't have to question my worth or worry about disappointing anyone. For those few hours each day, I didn't have to be the son caught in the crossfire of his parents' battles—I could just be Christian, the drum major, leading a team that believed in me. There, I knew who I was and without it… I wasn't sure who I'd be.

As I scrolled through memories, I reminded myself that there was more to me, to life, than the shouting and resentment that filled

GEMMA LANE

my house. Band was my way out, my way forward—a place that hadn't been wrecked by the lies and betrayals that seemed to infect everything else in my life.

I froze mid-scroll when a new photo from Alex popped up on my feed. There they were—Alex, Marcus, Tracy, and… Jessica, all grinning like they'd been friends for years, each of them holding a milkshake. They looked like the perfect quartet, laughing and carefree, like nothing I'd been dealing with even existed. My jaw clenched, the bitterness rising. Alex was supposed to be my best friend. And here he was, buddy-ing up with the very person who'd thrown everything off balance.

Traitor.

I closed the app in frustration and tossed the phone on my bed.

✗ ✗ ✗ ✗ ✗ ✗

The first day of senior year arrived like a breath of fresh air, and I couldn't have been more relieved. During summer, home had felt like a cage—a place filled with anxiety and arguments that I couldn't escape. But today, the campus was my refuge.

I stepped out of my truck, feeling the warmth of the sun on my face and the cool breeze that signaled the start of a new year. My backpack was slung over one shoulder, and I could already feel the familiar buzz of excitement that came with the beginning of a new school year. The campus was alive with activity, students milling about, catching up with friends, and exchanging summer stories.

I headed to my locker, navigating through the sea of students with practiced ease. There was something comforting about the routine of it all—the way the lockers clicked open, the way I could line up my books and supplies just so. It was a small but a significant part of the day that grounded me, and I savored the simplicity of it.

As I organized my locker, I caught sight of a familiar face across the hall. It was Courtney, looking amazing as usual. She spotted me and waved, an almost-evil grin spreading across her face. I gave a nod and made my way over, pressing her up against the lockers and kissing her.

When I pulled back, she smiled up at me. "I have something for you," she said, placing a yellow folder on my chest.

I stared at the bold letters at the top of the page—Welling, Jessica. This was it. This was the dirt we'd been hoping for, something to take her down a notch. I felt a surge of satisfaction as I began flipping through the pages, Courtney peeking over my shoulder.

"You got it already?" I asked, glancing at her.

She shrugged, a sly smile playing on her lips. "I have my ways. Figured we could use it."

As I skimmed the document, I found the usual stuff—address, previous schools, grades. Nothing too exciting, but nothing bad, either. She was a good student, straight A's and AP classes. My eyes narrowed as I looked for something—anything—that could give me an edge. Jessica had been a thorn in my side since she showed up at tryouts.

Courtney nudged me, pointing to a section near the bottom of the last page. "Look at this."

There it was, in bold letters: **DUI**. The letters seemed to leap off the page, and for a moment, my stomach dropped. My breath hitched, and a faint prickling sensation crept up my spine. I blinked, rereading it over just to make sure.

Jessica Welling, Little Miss Perfect, had a DUI on her record.

"This is exactly what we needed," Courtney said, her voice cutting through the haze, but I barely heard her. My mind raced, trying to reconcile the confident girl I'd seen leading on the podium with the harsh reality printed on that page.

I closed the folder slowly, my fingers trembling slightly as I tucked it under my arm. The weight of it felt different now, heavier somehow, like it wasn't just paper but something much more dangerous.

"She won't see it coming."

"I don't know," I hesitated. "This is kind of serious. We don't know the entire story. Court, I don't think we should use this."

She scoffed. "Seriously? You've been complaining ever since she arrived. We have the dirt—let's use it."

I rubbed the back of my neck, feeling the tension knotting up my muscles. My eyes darted to the side, unable to meet hers. "Look, I get that this is a big deal, but… This… this might be too much."

Courtney's voice hardened, her arms crossing over her chest. "Too much? You're overthinking it. We're just leveling the playing field."

I shook my head, feeling the conflict twist in my gut. "I'm not saying she doesn't deserve to be knocked down a peg, but this? It's too much. What if there's more to it?"

She narrowed her eyes at me, her voice dripping with frustration. "You're going soft, Christian. This is your chance to get back at her, to show everyone that she's not as perfect as she pretends to be."

I sighed, the tension in my chest tightening like a vise. "I just need to think about it, okay? Before we do anything, let me figure out if this is really something we should do."

Courtney stared at me for a long moment, her jaw clenched. I could see the irritation flashing in her eyes, but finally, she let out a huff and stepped back.

"Fine," she said, her tone begrudging. She gave me a tight-lipped smile, though it didn't reach her eyes. "And Christian... we might not know the whole story here, but she's still the enemy."

As she walked away, I stood there in the crowded hallway, the folder feeling heavier in my hand than it had before. The excitement I'd felt earlier had drained away, leaving behind a gnawing sense of doubt. I glanced down at the folder once more, the bold letters staring back at me. **DUI**.

I shoved the folder into my backpack, trying to ignore the tightness in my chest. This wasn't just about Jessica anymore—it was about the kind of leader I wanted to be. And right now, I wasn't sure I liked the answer.

My thoughts were still tangled when movement near the entrance caught my eye. Jessica walked through the front doors, a backpack slung over her shoulder, pushing a guy in a wheelchair. There was a warmth in their interaction that suggested familiarity, a shared history, even if they didn't look exactly alike. At first, I only noticed their easy rapport, the way they moved in sync, but then something else caught my attention.

There was a care in the way she pushed the wheelchair, each movement slow and deliberate, like she was trying to shield him from something I couldn't see. She glanced down at him every few steps, her expression tight, like she was bracing herself for something. And the way he looked up at her—it wasn't trust exactly. It was something heavier, like he was searching for reassurance he wasn't sure he'd get. I didn't know what kind of weight he was carrying, but it was there, plain as day, in the way his shoulders hunched and his hands fidgeted with the edge of his lap.

The questions, the doubts, the plans I'd been turning over in my head—they all blurred as I watched them. Jessica's face, stripped of its usual walls, showed something real. I was trying to piece her together from that file, turning facts into stories that fit what I wanted to believe. But seeing her now, like this, made all of it feel hollow. The DUI, the secrets, all the assumptions I'd made—they were puzzle pieces that didn't quite fit.

For the first time, I didn't want to assume or guess. I wanted the truth. Her truth. Not the pieces she let people see, not the lies I'd told myself about her. The version she kept hidden, even when she thought no one was looking.

15 First Day Blues

Jessica

T he morning sun was just starting to peek over the horizon as I rolled the wheelchair to the back of the car. The metal frame clanked softly against the pavement, a familiar sound that usually faded into the background of my daily routine. But today, it felt louder, more pronounced, like it was echoing off the walls of my mind, reminding me of everything that was about to change.

I popped the trunk and hefted the wheelchair inside, careful not to scratch the car. Aiden leaned against the passenger door, holding to the top with both hands for balance, his gaze fixed on something far off in the distance. It always threw me how much taller he actually was compared to me.

After securing the wheelchair, I walked over to him, fixing a smile as I opened the passenger door. "Ready?"

He glanced at me, his expression blank. "Yeah."

I helped him into the seat, and he adjusted the seat belt until it clicked into place. We'd done this a thousand times before, but today it felt different. The weight of the new school year, of starting over in a place where no one knew us, hung heavy in the air between us.

Sliding into the driver's seat, I took a deep breath and started the engine. The car hummed to life, and I started our drive to Arcana High. Once we arrived, I parked the car in the vacant handicapped spot. I shut the engine off, but neither of us moved. We just sat there, staring at the massive school buildings in front of us, as if waiting for something—*anything*—to happen.

The silence stretched out, long and uncomfortable. I could feel the tension in my chest, the fear that I was trying so hard to push down. I didn't want him to see it, to know how much this day was affecting me. He had his own things to deal with.

Finally, I broke the silence, my voice barely above a whisper. "We're going to be okay, right?"

Aiden looked at me, his eyes searching mine. For a moment, I thought he might say something reassuring, something that would make everything feel a little less overwhelming. But his gaze held that same flicker of worry, the one I'd seen too many times before. He was just as terrified as I was.

"We'll be fine," I answered myself.

I nodded, forcing myself to believe it. We didn't have a choice.

With one last deep breath, I unclicked the seat belt and popped the trunk open. The click of the latch felt like a starting gun, signaling that it was time to move. I stepped out of the car, walking around to Aiden's side, and helped him out of the seat. His grip tightened on my arm as I lowered him into his chair, his fingers ice-cold despite the warmth of the morning sun.

As I straightened up, pushing a strand of hair behind my ear, the school loomed ahead of us—tall, unwelcoming, the same kind of place where whispers had once chased us down hallways. I could feel Aiden's tension through the metal of the chair. He didn't have to say anything; I already knew the memories he was carrying in with him.

As we rolled forward, memories of our last school drifted into my mind uninvited—the taunts, the sidelong glances, the way Aiden's face would freeze whenever he caught someone staring at him for a little too long. They'd started out as whispers, low enough that he'd pretend not to hear, but the words only got louder as the months went on. I remember finding him in the library one afternoon, hiding behind a row of shelves with his fists clenched and his head down, as if he could disappear into himself.

They'd call him names, and more than once, someone "accidentally" knocked into his chair, like it was just in their way. I could only do so much—stand up for him, glare at anyone who dared to look our way, be the sister ready to throw herself between him and every cruel word. But no matter what I did, the words found their way in. They always did.

This was supposed to be our fresh start, but I could see the past still clinging to Aiden, weighing him down. And as I gripped the handles of his chair a little tighter, I made a promise to myself: *I wasn't going to let anyone here hurt him like that again.*

We reached the entrance, and I pushed the door open with my shoulder, guiding Aiden inside. The hallways were mostly empty, just a few students milling about, their voices echoing off the walls. I held a printout of Aiden's schedule and locker information in my hand; the paper crumpling slightly under my grasp as I tried to focus on what needed to be done. We arrived early just to have time to help him find his way around before the crowds filled the hallways.

"Let's find your locker first," I said, more to fill the silence than anything else.

Aiden nodded, and I led him down the corridor, counting the locker numbers until we found his. My heart eased slightly when I saw it was a lower locker, one that he'd be able to reach without a problem. At least something was going right.

I knelt beside him, the cold floor pressing against my knees as I helped him with the combination. The numbers on the lock blurred for a moment, and I had to blink a few times to clear my vision. My hands were shaking, and I willed them to be steady. This was straightforward. Why was I so nervous?

"Okay, it's 14… 28… and then 4." I turned the lock.

It clicked open, and I let out a breath I hadn't realized I was holding. I pulled the door open, revealing the empty metal interior. "There you go. You should be all set."

Aiden gave me a small smile, one that didn't quite reach his eyes. "Thanks, Jess."

Before I could respond, I heard footsteps behind me, slow and deliberate. The hairs on the back of my neck prickled, and I straightened up, turning around to see Christian standing there, watching us. His eyes flickered between Aiden and me, something unreadable in his expression.

"Helping your... brother, I'm assuming?" There was a subtle tension underlying his words that made me wary.

I felt my muscles tense, my protective instincts kicking in. "Yeah. So what?"

Christian shrugged, a smirk tugging at the corner of his mouth. "Nothing. Just didn't know you had a brother."

I narrowed my eyes. "Well, now you do."

For a moment, we just stared at each other, challenging the other to speak first. I could feel Aiden watching us, his silence urging me to keep things civil, but I couldn't shake the anxiety that crept up my back.

He finally broke eye contact, glancing down at the locker. His smirk was infuriating, like he'd already won some unspoken battle. "Need any help?" he asked, but the way he said it, like he was offering out of pity, made my skin crawl.

"We're fine," I snapped, but the words felt hollow. Christian didn't move, his gaze locking with mine. He wasn't just standing there; he was testing me, waiting for me to flinch.

Christian was too close, his presence suffocating, like a dark cloud settling over my morning. I could feel his eyes on me, prying, judging, and it made me want to lash out, to shove him back into whatever hole he'd crawled out of. But I couldn't—not in front of Aiden, not on his first day. I had to hold it together. For him.

"Actually," my brother said. "I could use some help to find my homeroom."

Christian's smile widened as he maneuvered his way behind Aiden's chair, a casual confidence that made my stomach twist. I felt a surge of resistance, the cold metal of the handles digging into my palms as my grasp tightened instinctively. But then Aiden glanced up at me, a quiet plea in his eyes that cut through my reluctance. I saw it—the hope, the need for just a little space, a chance to face this new world without me constantly by his side.

Slowly, I released my hold, my fingers lingering on the handles before I let them drop. Stepping back, I crossed my arms over my chest, but the tension in my body wouldn't dissipate. My shoulders were rigid, and I had to remind myself to breathe, each exhale sharp and unsteady, as if I could push away the nerves clawing at me.

Christian glanced over his shoulder, his face laced with something that set my nerves on edge—satisfaction, amusement, maybe both. It made me want to lunge forward and throttle him— just enough to wipe off that smug look without ending up on the evening news.

As they started moving, I stayed frozen, my arms falling uselessly to my sides. I tried to look calm, like I had it together, but every muscle in my body was strung tight, unwilling to let him go just yet. My feet twitched like they wanted to follow, every instinct screaming to stay close. But I knew better. Aiden needed this—to find his way without me hovering like some overbearing shadow.

Still, as I turned to leave, I couldn't stop myself from stealing a glance over my shoulder. Christian was already guiding Aiden down the hall, leaning down to say something I couldn't hear. Aiden tilted his head, listening like he actually cared what Christian had to say, and it made my stomach twist. How did he slip into this so easily, like he'd been waiting for the chance to take over?

I shook off the thought and quickened my pace, focusing on finding my own locker and homeroom. The hallways were starting to fill, students laughing and weaving around each other like they didn't have a care in the world. The noise grated against my nerves, and when I finally spotted my locker number, I made a beeline for it, desperate for a moment to collect myself.

My fingers fumbled with the lock, the stupid combination slipping out of my head twice before I got it right. When the lock finally gave, I yanked the door open harder than I meant to. The loud clang of metal on metal made a few heads turn, but I didn't care. I shoved my backpack inside and stared at the empty space for a moment, trying to shake the nagging unease that clung to me like static.

I took a deep breath, smoothing down my hair and adjusting my shirt, trying to convince myself that everything was under control. But the knot in my stomach didn't loosen, and I couldn't shake the feeling that I'd just made a mistake by letting Christian take Aiden.

"Get it together, Jess," I muttered under my breath, slamming the locker shut. I had my own first day to survive. Aiden was fine. *He'll be fine.*

I straightened my shoulders, trying to project confidence as I turned and headed toward my homeroom. The crowd in the hallway seemed to press in on me, but I pushed through, my mind racing with thoughts of Aiden, Christian, and the day ahead.

When I finally reached my homeroom, I paused outside the door, taking one last deep breath to steady myself. I stepped inside, trying to leave my worries behind me as I walked to the first empty seat I saw. Someone had scribbled "AP Calculus" on the whiteboard ahead. It was too early for math to be the first class in the morning. I dropped my head down on the desk and waited for the first bell to ring.

The cold surface of the desk felt oddly comforting against my forehead, grounding me in the midst of the whirlwind that was my first day. The classroom was starting to fill up, the quiet murmur of conversations swirling around me, but I kept my head down, trying to block it all out.

My brain already felt scrambled from everything that had happened so far, and the thought of diving into complex equations made me want to crawl back into bed. I let out a quiet sigh, closing my eyes briefly, wishing the first bell would just ring already so I could get this over with.

Footsteps shuffled closer, followed by the scrape of a chair sliding out from behind the desk in front of me. Without lifting my gaze, I kept my focus elsewhere—small talk with a random classmate was the last thing I wanted.

But then I heard that familiar voice, low and smug. "Is this seat taken?"

For the love of—

My eyes shot open, and I stared in disbelief as he dropped into the seat like he owned the place. Christian. Of course it was Christian. Why wouldn't it be Christian? His stupid, infuriatingly confident smirk might as well have been a flashing neon sign announcing my bad luck.

Of all the seats in the room, he had to choose the one right in front of mine. I stared at him for a moment, trying to process why he was here, why he wasn't off helping Aiden, why he seemed so damn pleased with himself.

"Seriously?" I muttered under my breath, half hoping he wouldn't hear me, but of course, he did.

"What can I say? I like to keep my friends close," he replied, leaning back in his chair and folding his arms behind his head as if he didn't have a care in the world.

"Friends?" I echoed, raising an eyebrow. "We're not friends."

"You seem to forget there's a second part to that expression." Christian shrugged, still grinning. "We're going to be spending a lot of time together this year, Welling. Might as well get used to it."

I rolled my eyes, leaning back in my chair with a huff. "Does that include you shadowing me to every class?"

"That depends, I guess, on if you have all AP classes. And don't give me that look, Welling. I'm not the idiot you paint me out to be." I could sense him smiling, though I could only see the back of his head. "If it bothers you that much, I can move," he offered, though his tone suggested he had no intention of actually doing so.

I glared at the back of his head. Of course, Christian Gutierrez had decided that today—the day I was barely holding it together—was the perfect time to play smug and irritating. I shouldn't have cared where he sat, shouldn't have even cared that he was here at all, but somehow, his presence always felt bigger than it should.

"Whatever." I needed to pick my battles, and this one wasn't worth it. "Just don't expect me to help you if you get stuck on derivatives."

Christian chuckled, glancing over his shoulder at me. "I wouldn't dream of it. But maybe you'll be the one needing help. Calculus can be tricky."

The bell finally rang, signaling the start of class. I straightened up in my seat, trying to focus as the teacher spoke, but it was hard to ignore the feeling of Christian's presence just inches away. I crossed my arms, settling back in my chair, trying to put as much distance between us as I could without moving. It wasn't much, but it made me feel a little more in control.

As I half-listened to the teacher explain the day's lesson, my pen drifted to the corner of my notebook, where I began absentmindedly sketching a tiny trumpet. I'd drawn the same shape so many times that my hand moved without thinking, tracing the outline over and over until it was almost perfect. It was just a small habit, something I did when my mind wandered, but the shape felt comforting, like a piece of me that I carried wherever I went.

Christian glanced back, his eyes flicking down at my notebook for a split second before meeting mine. "You keeping up okay back there? Or should I start taking notes for you?"

I raised an eyebrow, not missing a beat. "I think I'll manage, but it's sweet of you to worry," I replied, adding another small curve to the trumpet doodle in the corner of my page.

He smirked, leaning back in his seat. "Just checking. Hate to see you struggle on the first day."

I rolled my eyes. "Trust me, I'm doing just fine without your help."

He shrugged, his smirk still in place. "If you say so, Picasso."

I gritted my teeth, refusing to give him the satisfaction of a reaction. Instead, I focused on the doodle, tracing over the lines with a little more emphasis, letting it ground me as I ignored him.

Christian

The final bell had rung, signaling the end of the school day. I walked into the band room, feeling the familiar buzz of excitement and anticipation that always accompanied our practices. The room was already bustling with the sound of instruments being unpacked and students chatting, but I could feel my focus zeroing in on one person.

I slouched into my seat among the trumpeters, tuning out the chatter around me. My focus was on Jessica at the front of the room, her voice cutting through the noise with an edge that demanded attention. She looked confident, sure of herself, but there was a stiffness in her shoulders.

The way she conducted was sharp, precise, like every motion had been drilled into her. It wasn't just about getting the job done; you could tell she cared—maybe too much. But there was a distance to her, too, like she was keeping everyone at arm's length, even as she pushed them to be better.

There was more to her than I'd initially seen—something intense, driven, and unexpectedly vulnerable. Even as she dismissed the group to head outside, a flicker of relief softened her features, hinting at the person beneath the polished facade.

Out on the field, the band took their places as marked in the drill book. They had learned about a third of the show's drill, but had not put the music to it yet. Today was the first day of attempting to piece it together.

Jessica was sitting at the top with her feet dangling off the podium while the staff got the band into their next positions. I climbed up and took my place next to her and kicked her shoe playfully.

"I talked to my brother," she said to me quietly, like she wanted absolutely no one to hear it. "Thanks for showing him around today. I'm not sure what your angle is, but... it was decent of you."

"Decent? Hmm." I rubbed my chin and smiled. "I think that's the nicest thing I've ever heard you say, Welling."

Jessica rolled her eyes, unimpressed. "I'm just trying to be polite, not make you think you're Superman."

"Aw, come on," I said, leaning in. "I'm just trying to understand why someone like you would say something nice. Doesn't seem like your style."

"It's not," she shot back. "But I'm also not an asshole. I'm just keeping things civil."

I chuckled, enjoying the banter. "Civil, huh? That's one way to put it."

"Look, I don't know what you're trying to accomplish," she said, her tone firm but tinged with a hint of frustration. "But don't expect me to suddenly warm up to you just because you're being nice to my brother. I still don't trust you."

With that, she hopped off the tall podium and walked towards Mr. Trust, showing some freshman their drill spots. I watched her for a moment longer, noting the way she balanced authority with her approachable nature. I couldn't help but feel intrigued and challenged to know her better.

The few minutes I spent with her brother that morning, he seemed anxious as I pushed him toward his classroom. At one point, he glanced up at me and asked, "Are you the asshole who's been harassing my sister?" I couldn't help but smirk—I knew right then I liked him.

There was something about him that caught my attention right away—maybe it was the bluntness, or the way he didn't shy away from calling me out. He had this quiet confidence, even behind the nerves, that made me think he was a lot tougher than he let on. It was clear he cared about his sister, enough to confront someone who stood twice his height without hesitation. I respected that. In a weird way, it made me want to know more about the both of them—what their story was, and how the DUI fit into their history.

"That was some pretty pathetic flirting," Tracy said, leaning against her marimba with a knowing smirk. "If you can even call it that."

"I wasn't flirting," I shot back, rolling my eyes. Tracy always had a way of making everything sound like a joke at my expense.

"Sure," she sang, her grin widening. "You're totally not into her. You're just watching her every move for fun."

"She's easy to provoke," I said, shrugging. "That's all there is to it."

Tracy arched an eyebrow, her expression sharp but not unkind. "Uh-huh. And why do you care so much about provoking her?"

"I don't care," I said quickly, a little too defensively. "It's just... interesting, that's all."

"Interesting," Tracy repeated, her tone skeptical as she adjusted her mallets. "Right. Well, just remember, Jessica's not some puzzle for you to solve. She's her own person, and maybe you should think about what she's dealing with before you start pushing her buttons for fun."

I blinked at her, surprised. "What's that supposed to mean?"

Tracy shrugged, her voice softening slightly. "Look, I don't know her that well either, but she's new here. She's got a lot on her plate, and not everyone wears their problems out in the open. If you keep poking at her, don't be surprised if you hit something you didn't mean to."

I frowned, the weight of her words sinking in. "You think she's hiding something?"

"Don't know, and it's not my business," Tracy said with a pointed look. "But people build walls for a reason, Christian. If you're gonna mess with them, maybe think about what it's gonna mean—for her, and for you."

She gave me a light shove—not playful, but firm, like she

wanted to make sure her words stuck. "Just… don't be an idiot, okay?"

With that, she walked off, her words trailing behind her and lodging themselves in the back of my mind. Maybe she was right—I didn't know Jessica, not really. But something about her kept pulling me in, and for better or worse, I wasn't ready to let it go.

X X X X X X

As the last echoes of rehearsal faded into the night, Courtney and I drifted out toward the parking lot, the hum of the fluorescent lights casting a soft glow over rows of cars. The familiar scent of damp grass and cooling asphalt filled the air, grounding me after hours spent under the stadium lights. Just ahead, I spotted Alex, Tracy, and Marcus, huddled by Tracy's old Jeep, their laughter carrying on the breeze.

Courtney nudged my arm, a grin tugging at the corner of her mouth. "Looks like the gang's all here."

We stepped up to join them, a sense of ease settling over me as we exchanged nods and smirks. They'd already loaded Tracy's Jeep with bags of snacks and an old blanket.

"Ready to hit the woods?" Tracy asked, jingling her keys with a mischievous sparkle in her eyes.

This little trip had become a ritual, one we'd created back in freshman year on the first day of school. It had started as an escape, a way to shake off nerves and celebrate the fact that, against all odds, we were navigating high school together. Now, it was tradition—a rite of passage we returned to year after year. We never missed it.

Marcus clapped Alex on the shoulder. "Last one to the clearing has to start the fire!"

Alex rolled his eyes, chuckling. "As if I'd trust any of you with that responsibility."

Tracy laughed, hopping into the driver's seat. "We'll see who's laughing when I crank this baby into gear."

We piled into Tracy's Jeep, the kind of old, battered vehicle that somehow still roared to life every time she turned the key. The drive was filled with laughter, the windows down as we blasted music and yelled over the rush of air. Tracy pulled the Jeep to a stop in our usual spot, an open clearing surrounded by thick woods where the night sky stretched wide above us.

We climbed out, grabbing the snacks, blankets, and an old metal lantern that flickered weakly to life after a few taps. Alex, as promised, took charge of the fire, expertly arranging the kindling and logs until a steady flame crackled to life. The warmth pushed back the night's chill, casting long shadows that danced around the clearing. We settled in a loose circle on the ground, backs to the trees, the fire crackling between us.

"Alright," Tracy said, dusting her hands off. "Who's kicking us off? Dreams, fears, the whole 'this is our last year' spiel."

We all exchanged glances, waiting for someone to bite first. Marcus leaned forward, a crooked grin on his face. "Guess I'll start. Y'all know college isn't exactly in my plan. It's the band or bust. Me and the guys? We're tight. We've been working on some tracks, got a couple of gigs lined up. It feels real, you know? Like it could actually happen."

Courtney tilted her head. "So... no backup plan?"

Marcus shrugged, unbothered. "Not yet. I figure if it flops, I'll regroup. But I can't not try. I don't wanna look back and wonder what if."

"That's brave," Tracy said, her voice soft. "Risky, but brave."

"Easy for him," Alex cut in, shaking his head. "My dad would have a stroke if I even suggested not going to college."

We all turned to him, waiting for more, but he just sighed. "Family business. You guys know the drill. Business school, internships, working my way up the ladder. It's... fine, I guess."

"Just fine?" I asked, raising an eyebrow.

He hesitated, staring into the fire like it held the answers. "I don't hate it. But sometimes I think about what else I could do, you know? Something less... predictable."

The firelight caught Courtney's frown as she picked at the edge of her drink can. "Predictable isn't always bad."

Alex glanced at her, something unspoken passing between them, but he didn't push.

Tracy went next, her voice steady but her hands fidgeting with the edge of the blanket she'd spread across her lap. "I'm applying to music schools. Berklee's the dream."

"You'll get in," I said, the conviction in my voice surprising even me. "You're a better musician than all of us put together."

She gave me a small smile. "Thanks, Gutierrez."

Courtney straightened, her expression sharpening as if she couldn't let the moment linger too long. "Well, I know what I want," she said, her voice firm but a little too casual. "Medical science. I'm aiming for UCLA or Berkeley. Research is the goal—finding cures, making a real difference—changing people's lives. *Yadda-yadda.*"

Medical science? Berkeley? This was the first I was hearing about it. We'd only ever talked about going to UCLA together, and I couldn't remember a single time she'd mentioned being interested in science.

"Does that mean we have to call you Dr. Courtney in the future?" Tracy teased.

"Of course not," Court laughed. "It's Dr. Sullivan to all of you losers."

The group laughed, but then all looked my way. "So, Mr. Drum Major?" Marcus asked, breaking the silence. "What about you? Got any big plans?"

"Honestly?" I said, staring into the fire. "I have no clue what I want to do after this year. UCLA, I guess. I know I'm supposed to have it figured out by now. And you guys probably think I do, but…" I paused, looking at the group, each eye on me. "If I'm being real, I just want this year to feel… different. I want to feel like people actually see me for once."

The fire crackled softly, filling the silence that followed. The words hung in the air, raw and exposed, like I'd taken something from inside me and laid it out for everyone to see. But no one jumped in. No quick reassurances, no immediate jokes—just the quiet shuffle of Marcus poking at the edge of the fire with a stick, Tracy fiddling with the hem of the blanket across her lap, Alex leaning back like he hadn't really heard me. Even Courtney didn't say anything, her drink crumpling slightly in her grip as she stared at the flames.

Finally, Alex broke the silence, his tone half-teasing but not as sharp as usual. "You? Invisible? From the guy everyone looks at first? You literally have a spotlight on you for 12 minutes during a field show."

Tracy laughed softly, a sound that didn't quite reach her eyes. "He's not wrong," she said, her voice careful. "You're the one everyone follows out there, Christian. People see you."

"Yeah," Marcus added, his voice a little too casual, "you've got, like, the most visible role in the band. Kinda hard to miss."

I nodded along, forcing a smile as their words bounced off me, missing the point entirely. They were trying, I guess, but it felt like we were speaking two different languages. They saw the drum major, the leader, the guy with the confident grin and the steady hands. But that wasn't what I meant—not even close.

Courtney shifted beside me, her voice quiet but firm. "I don't think that's what he meant."

Everyone turned to her, surprised, but she didn't elaborate, her gaze fixed on the fire. I wanted to thank her, to say *yes, exactly*, but the moment passed too quickly.

"Well," Alex said, trying to lighten the mood. "At least you've got time to figure it out. Maybe senior year will do its thing, and you'll find your big epiphany or whatever."

"Yeah. Maybe." I took a sip of my drink, letting the warmth of the fire mask the weight that was still pressing on my chest. They were my friends, the people I'd practically grown up with, but in that moment, I'd never felt more alone.

Courtney's smile faltered for a second, her hand pausing on her drink. I caught a flicker of hurt in her eyes before she masked it with a soft smile, her fingers tightening around her cup.

"Christian..." she started, her voice quiet as she leaned in so the others wouldn't hear. "You know I see you, right? I mean, I've known you since we were kids."

I glanced at her, a soft pang of guilt settling in. I knew Courtney meant it; we'd been close for years. She was always there, knew my routines, my quirks, the things that ticked me off. But there was still this part of me that felt... out of reach, even to her. Like she saw the person I tried to be, but not the person I was when no one else was looking.

"I know, Court," I said, trying to keep my tone gentle. "I don't mean it like that. It's just... I don't know, it's hard to explain."

Her expression softened, but that flicker of disappointment lingered. "You're not invisible to me, Christian."

Alex leaned forward, breaking the tension with a loud exhale. "So, the great Christian Gutierrez actually wants something he doesn't know how to get." He smirked, the usual easygoing humor in his eyes, but there was an edge to it. "Guess you're just like the rest of us, after all."

"Yeah, maybe I am," I muttered, giving him a slight grin. He was trying to keep it light, but I could see him watching me, maybe realizing for the first time that there were pieces of me he'd never really noticed.

Finally, Tracy nudged me. "Hey, do you think we should've invited Jessica? She *is* part of the team now."

Courtney's head popped up, her eyebrows furrowing. "Jessica doesn't belong here," she said flatly. "She's only here because Mr. Trust decided to play favorites. She hasn't earned this."

The group fell silent, the crackle of the fire snapping too loud. Tracy looked uncomfortable, but Courtney wasn't done. "And let's not pretend she's some innocent transfer. People don't just switch schools for no reason."

"Courtney," I said, trying to cut her off. She ignored me, her voice rising.

"She's just... I don't trust her, okay? All she cares about is herself. And if you can't see that, then—"

"That's enough," I said, sharper this time. Her mouth clamped shut, her cheeks flushing as she realized everyone was staring.

"Wow, Courtney," Marcus muttered. "Tell us how you really feel."

Tracy cleared her throat, doing her best not to ruffle feathers. "Jessica's been working hard. Maybe give her a chance."

From across the fire, Alex snickered. "It sounds like someone is jealous."

Courtney shot him a glare, her eyes narrowing. "Jealous? Please. I just don't like... change."

Marcus chuckled, trying to lighten the tension. "Court, for real. Why all the hate? She hasn't done anything to you."

Courtney folded her arms, her gaze flicking to me as if she expected backup. "Christian, you can't seriously be okay with her swooping in like this," Courtney pressed, her voice sharp. "This is supposed to be our year." I hesitated, the weight of her words pressing down on me. She wasn't wrong—Jessica's arrival had changed everything. But it wasn't as simple as Courtney made it sound.

I hesitated, the weight of her words pressing down on me. "She's working hard. Maybe we should focus on that instead of how she got here." *Let it go*, I wanted to say to her.

Courtney's lips pressed into a thin line, but she didn't respond. Instead, she leaned back, her drink crumpling slightly under her grip. The firelight danced across her face, illuminating the frustration and something else—hurt, maybe—that she wasn't saying aloud.

"Alright, enough drama. Let's enjoy the campfire before Courtney roasts us all." Alex raised his hands in mock surrender. "It's our last year out here. Let's just, I don't know, appreciate it, I guess."

The group chuckled softly, the mood easing as Marcus tossed a marshmallow across the fire, narrowly missing Alex's head. "Yeah, because nothing says senior year like flaming marshmallows and cheap blankets," Marcus said, his grin wide. "Classic us."

"Classic us," Tracy echoed, her voice quieter, almost wistful. She pulled the blanket tighter around her shoulders, her eyes flicking to the fire. "Feels weird, doesn't it? Knowing this is the last time we'll do this?"

For a moment, no one spoke. The fire crackled, its warmth chasing away the cool night air, but the weight of her words settled over the group like the smoke curling into the trees.

"We can always come back here," I said after a moment, the words slipping out before I could second-guess them. "Before the start of every school year. We'll come here, sit around the fire, and catch up. It doesn't have to end just because we graduate."

The group exchanged glances, the flickering firelight casting soft shadows across their faces. For a second, I thought they'd laugh it off, but instead, a quiet kind of agreement settled over us.

"I'm in," Alex said, extending his hand like he was sealing a business transaction. "I'll be stuck in Arcana forever anyways."

"I'm in, too," Marcus echoed, his tone softer as he nudged a stray ember back into the flames.

Tracy nodded, her lips curving into a small smile. "I'll hold you all to it."

Courtney didn't say anything at first, just stared into the fire with a look I couldn't quite place. Finally, she glanced up and shrugged, her usual edge softened just enough. "Fine. But someone better bring a decent playlist next time."

The fire crackled as the group fell quiet again, the weight of what we'd promised hanging in the air. It wasn't just about coming back here. It was about holding onto something—this moment, this group, this version of us—knowing that time would eventually try to take it away.

For now, though, we were still here. Together.

As the flames burned lower, the laughter faded into quiet conversations, and one by one, the group began to drift off. Tracy pulled her blanket tighter, leaning her head on Courtney's shoulder, and Alex stretched out on his back, pointing out constellations Marcus swore didn't exist.

I stayed where I was, staring at the fire as it dwindled, the embers glowing faintly against the dark. The fire wasn't roaring anymore, but it was still there—burning low, steady, and alive. Like us. Like all the changes we didn't understand yet but knew were coming.

Maybe change wasn't something to fear. Maybe, like the fire, it was something we could feed, nurture, and let light the way forward.

Jessica

A t the end of rehearsal the following week, Mr. Trust asked Christian and me to stay behind. The band room, usually buzzing with chatter and the clatter of instruments, had grown quiet as the last of the students filed out. I sat near Mr. Trust's desk, poring over the score in front of me, committing every tempo shift and key change to memory. It was how I always worked—methodical, precise, determined to know the music inside out.

Christian stood a few feet away, leaning casually against the wall with his arms crossed, the faintest smirk tugging at the corner of his mouth. He wasn't looking at the music, didn't even seem concerned. Instead, his eyes flicked toward me now and then, as if daring me to react. I kept my focus on the score, refusing to give him the satisfaction.

The door opened, and Mr. Trust entered, balancing a stack of drill sheets and a steaming cup of coffee that smelled faintly of hazelnut. "Thanks for waiting, you two," he said, setting everything down on his desk. He looked between us, his grin wide, his eyes bright with the kind of excitement that usually meant he'd come up with something ambitious.

"I've got an idea," he began, leaning back in his chair. "I'm hoping it'll take our show up a notch."

Christian straightened slightly, interest sparking in his eyes. I shifted in my seat, my heart picking up its pace in anticipation.

Mr. Trust unfolded a large sheet of paper—a field map—and spread it out across the desk. He tapped two spots marked with X's at the front and backfield 50s. "Two podiums," he said, looking up at us. "One for each of you. We will split the band into two sides—Montagues and Capulets. The tension between the two families will drive our opener."

My eyes traced the lines of the map, the clear division between the two sides of the band. The idea was bold, theatrical. It would grab attention. But it also meant constant, direct comparison between Christian and me. Every movement, every cue, every downbeat would be measured against his.

"The opener will highlight the rivalry," Mr. Trust continued, his voice gaining momentum. "But as the show progresses, there'll be moments where you'll need to come together—symbolically, of course. The audience should feel the tension between you both in every moment of the performance."

Christian's gaze flicked toward me, his smirk widening just enough to be annoying. I kept my expression blank, though my stomach twisted at the thought of being under that kind of scrutiny.

"And then there's Juliet's ballad," Mr. Trust said, turning to me. "We're featuring a flag solo during that moment—just like the balcony scene in the play. It's going to be emotional, visually stunning, and entirely yours, Jessica."

The weight of his words settled heavily on my shoulders. I'd been working with Luna, the guard instructor, but I still felt woefully unprepared. My mind raced with images of all the ways this could go wrong—an awkward spin, a mistimed toss, an audience of thousands watching me stumble through something I wasn't even sure I could pull off.

I glanced toward the guard closet, where Courtney was tidying up the flags. She caught my eye, her expression sharpening into a glare so icy it sent a chill down my spine. If I'd ever considered asking her for help, that thought dissolved the moment she narrowed her eyes. *Grace and finesse*, she'd said that first day of band camp. Something I didn't have.

"There'll also be a pivotal podium switch," Mr. Trust added, breaking into my spiraling thoughts. "It's timed with a big musical shift in the opener. It'll be a key moment—a chance for both of you to shine."

Christian leaned forward, resting his hands on the desk. "If we time the switch right," he said, his tone thoughtful, "it could really emphasize the shift in the story. We'll play up the conflict between the two families, and then the switch could mark the moment Romeo falls for Juliet."

His confidence grated on me. The way he so easily jumped into the planning, as if he'd already envisioned himself commanding the front 50-yard line, made my jaw tighten. I watched him carefully, trying to gauge whether he was genuinely invested in the show or just making a play for the spotlight.

Mr. Trust beamed, clearly pleased. "Exactly. That's the kind of energy we need. The audience should feel the stakes in every beat."

I nodded, swallowing hard as the conversation moved on. Mr. Trust handed us each a stack of drill sheets, along with a breakdown of the show's structure. "You both need to think about how you're going to approach your roles," he said. "This isn't just about conducting. It's about embodying these characters, bringing them to life through your movements. You're not just drum majors—you're Romeo and Juliet."

The words pressed down on me, heavy with implication. My fingers twitched instinctively, the urge to bite my nails rising like a reflex I couldn't shake. I caught myself just in time, clasping my hands together in my lap, willing them to stay still. My leg started bouncing instead, the nervous energy finding a new outlet.

Christian glanced at me then, his smirk softening into something more thoughtful. His gaze lingered a little too long, a strange intensity in his eyes that made me feel exposed and uncertain, as if he could see right through me. The weight of his attention prickled along my skin, and I forced my leg to stop, my posture stiffening as if sheer willpower could keep me from unraveling.

"Alright," Mr. Trust said with a smile. "That's all for today. We'll start working out the logistics during the next rehearsal."

Christian and I gathered our things in silence. The rest of the band had already dispersed, leaving the room eerily quiet. I slid the score carefully into my bag, replaying Mr. Trust's instructions in my head, when Christian's voice cut through the stillness.

"Looks like this show is going to be intense," he said, his tone unusually neutral.

I glanced over at him, instantly on guard. "Mm-hmm." His sudden attempt at politeness or normalcy was throwing me off. I tightened my grip on the strap of my bag.

"For what it's worth," he continued, his voice quieter, "I think you'll do fine with that flag solo. It's probably just nerves."

I froze for a beat, his words lodging like a thorn. "Nerves?" I echoed, the sharpness in my tone undeniable. "You don't think I can do it, do you?"

His brow furrowed, clearly surprised. "Wait, hold up." He raised his hands, palms out. "I said you'd do fine. I'm not doubting you."

But his words only fueled my suspicion. "Right," I said, voice flat. "Because you've always been so supportive."

Christian let out a short, hollow laugh. "I get it. I'm not exactly your favorite person. But I'm serious—you've got this. Everyone gets a little nervous when they're doing something they've never done before. Even me."

The casual way he said it, like we were suddenly equals, sent a ripple of doubt in me. "You? Nervous? Yeah, right," I scoffed.

"Why do you look so surprised?"

"Because ever since I met you, you've acted like nerves are beneath you. Like the rest of us are just peasants panicking in the mud while you stride by on your golden chariot."

Christian gave me a faint smile, but it didn't quite reach his eyes. For a second, I thought he might shoot back with something equally sarcastic, but he didn't. Instead, he glanced away, his jaw tightening like he was weighing his next words. "Not always," he said finally. His voice was softer now, almost doubtful. "Just... don't psych yourself out before you even get started."

The shift in his tone caught me off guard, stealing the smugness from my chest. I expected him to play along, to fire back with some overconfident remark.

I could almost believe him. Almost. But letting him see that would feel like handing him the upper hand. "I'll be fine," I said. "You should work on your pep talks."

"And you should work on letting people have your back," he shot back, his smirk resurfacing but less cutting this time. "Once in a while wouldn't kill you."

I narrowed my eyes at him, walking just a little bit slower. "Letting people have my back? Sounds like a trust fall fail waiting to happen. And I'm not into falling."

His smirk deepened, the corners of his mouth quirking up like he knew exactly what I was doing. "You keep saying that, Welling, but it sounds like you're just scared someone might actually catch you."

I stopped walking now and waited for him to turn around to face me. "Or maybe I just don't trust people not to drop me on purpose."

For a moment, we just stared at each other, the banter fading into something quieter, more pointed. His expression softened, like he was seeing me through a window of a wall I'd thrown up, and that was enough to make me shift uncomfortably.

"Or maybe, I'll surprise you." He said this like he was certain.

"Maybe," I finally said after a beat. "Or maybe not."

The uneasy silence stretched between us as we reached the parking lot. Christian stopped by his car, resting his hand on the door handle, before turning back to me. His smirk softened into something warmer—something unexpected.

"See you tomorrow, Juliet," he said, his voice teasing but with an undercurrent of sincerity that sent a ripple through me.

I rolled my eyes, but the heat creeping up my neck betrayed me. "Okay, Romeo."

Then it happened—a flicker, a tightening in my chest, like an ember catching where I'd thought nothing could burn. It wasn't just his voice or the way he smirked, though those didn't help. It was something else.

Moments like this felt risky.

The way he looked at me, like he wasn't distracted by my walls but saw straight through them. Like he'd noticed the things I tried to keep hidden—the nervous habits, the flicker of doubt I couldn't always suppress—and decided not to call them out, but to meet them with something close to encouragement instead.

The flutter in my chest felt foreign, unwelcome. It made me want to retreat. I hadn't let myself feel anything like this in so long, hadn't dared to thaw the frozen layers I'd built to keep myself safe. I shook my head sharply, as if I could dismiss the feeling before it grew into something I couldn't handle.

This was just Christian being Christian, I told myself. Nothing more. Nothing deeper. And definitely nothing dangerous.

X X X X X X

When I stepped through the door, the house greeted me with a silence so sharp it felt intentional, as if the walls themselves were holding their breath. The usual warmth of home was absent, replaced by an unsettling stillness. The faint scent of dinner had long faded, like it had been cleared away hours before.

From the kitchen, I heard my mother's voice, low and laced with barely contained frustration. "Jessica. You're late."

Her tone sliced through the quiet, harsher than usual, thick with a disapproval that sank straight into my chest. I took a steadying breath, feeling the familiar weight settle over me as I slipped off my shoes, the soft thud swallowed up by the tension in the air. "Rehearsal ran long. Mr. Trust wanted to talk afterwards," I murmured, keeping my eyes down.

I started toward the stairs, hoping to avoid what I could already sense was coming, but she stepped into the doorway, blocking my escape. She crossed her arms tightly, set her mouth in a thin, unforgiving line, and swept her gaze over me; it felt less like a mother's concern and more like scrutiny.

Her voice was low, brittle, barely hiding the resentment underneath. "You could've called, but I suppose that's asking too much these days."

A flash of anger flickered in my chest, but I held it back, swallowing down the words I wanted to say. "I didn't realize the time," I said, my voice small, hating how weak it sounded. It was a flimsy excuse, one that neither of us believed.

Her eyes narrowed, a hint of something colder crossing her face. "Jessica, do you think this house revolves around your schedule? Around your rehearsals?" The word came out sharp, almost like an accusation. "You've already put us through enough. The least you could do is show a little respect."

"I'm sorry," I said quietly, trying to push down the simmering frustration. She was the one who couldn't let go, couldn't move past it, even though every day I felt the weight of it on my shoulders.

She sighed, a harsh, disappointed sound that felt more like judgment than forgiveness. "I worry about you, Jessica," she said, but her words were laced with something colder, an edge that made it clear this wasn't just about concern. "You may not realize it, but what you do affects everyone in this family."

There it was—*everyone in this family.* As if you could even call us a family anymore. My dad was still here, technically, but his presence had hollowed us out long ago, leaving behind a silence that pressed down on everything. He was always "working," always somewhere else, even when he was right in front of us. Maybe that was his excuse—a way to avoid dealing with this mess, this life he'd left us to manage without him truly being part of it.

And she carried it like a weapon, her disappointment cutting deeper in his absence, her words heavier without someone there to soften them. A subtle reminder that my actions were somehow more of a burden, that Aiden's well-being was always at the forefront of her mind, as if he were fragile glass and I was a shard of ice, sharp and inevitable, ready to crack him apart.

It didn't matter what I did or how hard I tried to move forward. In her eyes, I was the one who threatened the delicate balance of this family, who had already "done enough damage."

I bit back the urge to point out the hypocrisy, to remind her that I wasn't the only one in this house making mistakes. But we all pretended, didn't we? Pretended not to notice the unspoken cracks, the secrets we swept under the rug so we could blame everything else on me.

"I understand," I replied, my voice barely above a whisper, feeling her eyes on me, as if she were searching for some sign of rebellion, some excuse to keep this going.

Her gaze softened with pity, as though she saw me as something broken, something that needed constant monitoring. "I just want to make sure you're staying on the right path," she said.

The right path. Like Dad's silence was an example I should follow. Like she hadn't been the one to push me farther off course. But I nodded anyway, giving her the response she wanted, and turned toward the stairs, forcing my legs to move despite the weight pushing down on me. I couldn't help but wonder if this was just what families like ours did—let the silence speak for everything we couldn't.

Aiden's door was slightly ajar as I passed, the faint sound of a video game humming in the background. I hesitated, the soft light spilling into the hallway, a stark contrast to the darkness that had settled inside me. I knocked lightly on the door frame, hoping for a distraction.

"Hey, can I come in?"

Aiden glanced up from his game, his face lighting up. "Yeah. Just finishing up a level."

I stepped into his room, taking in the familiar posters and game consoles that lined the walls. His little world felt like a refuge— untouched by the tension that seemed to cling to everything else. "How's school going?" I asked, leaning against the door frame, trying to sound casual.

"It was alright," he said, pausing the game. "Teachers seem cool, but I don't really know anyone yet."

I nodded. "You'll get to know people soon enough," I said, though the words felt hollow. "Did anything interesting happen this week?"

Aiden hesitated, his fingers hovering over the controller. "Uh, no, not really."

I studied him for a moment, the way his shoulders tensed just slightly, his fingers gripping the controller like it might shield him from the conversation. Something was off. Aiden wasn't the type to pause a game mid-round unless he had something on his mind.

I stepped further into the room, crossing my arms as I leaned against the desk. "Aiden," I said, soft but firm. "Come on. What happened?"

"Nothing." He shrugged, his eyes darting back to the screen. "I said it was fine."

His nonchalance might've worked on someone else, but not me. I tilted my head, narrowing my eyes. "You're a terrible liar, you know that?"

He sighed, his shoulders slumping. "It's not a big deal, okay?"

"Aiden," I pressed, my tone leaving no room for argument.

He hesitated, his fingers fidgeting with the joystick. "Some guys… knocked my books out of my hands."

I froze, my chest tightening. "What? When?" My voice came out sharper than I intended, but I couldn't help it.

"It doesn't matter," he muttered, still avoiding my gaze. "It's not like it hasn't happened before. I just picked them up and moved on."

My fists clenched at my sides. "Did a teacher see? Did you tell anyone?"

"It's not a big deal, Jess," he blurted hoping to pacify me. "Seriously, it's not worth the trouble."

I swallowed my frustration, forcing myself to exhale slowly. The thought of anyone mistreating Aiden made my blood boil, but I had to stay calm for his sake. "If it happens again, you tell me. Got it?"

Aiden gave me a resigned sigh. "I got it."

I nodded but couldn't shake the anger. He shouldn't have to get used to something like that. I paced the room for a moment, looking for a way to change the subject and release the tension simmering inside me.

"Your friend, Christian…" Aiden said suddenly, his voice cutting through my thoughts like a record scratch.

I froze. "What about him?"

"I like him," Aiden said, pausing his game to look at me. "He's nice."

My jaw dropped. "Christian? My friend? Yeah, no," I said, the words sharper than I intended. "And he's definitely not nice. You barely know the guy."

Aiden didn't seem fazed by my reaction. "He sits with me at lunch when you're not there."

I blinked, trying to process that. "He—wait, what?"

"We just talk," Aiden said, his tone steady. "Games, sports, random stuff. Oh, and he asks about you sometimes."

"He—what?" A mix of disbelief and suspicion surged through me. "Are we talking about the same Christian? Tall, dark hair, smug face that makes you want to punch it?"

Aiden chuckled. "Yeah, that Christian. He's not *that* bad."

I folded my arms, narrowing my eyes. "Why would he be nice to you when he's been nothing but an ass to me?"

"It's not like you've been nice to him either."

I opened my mouth to argue, but the words stuck in my throat. Aiden raised an eyebrow, clearly enjoying the rare moment where he had the upper hand in a conversation with me.

"That's different," I said finally, my tone defensive. "I... we... It's just different. Complicated."

"Right," he said, dragging out the word like he didn't believe me for a second. "Because sitting with me at lunch and asking about you totally screams 'not complicated.'"

I pointed a finger at him. "Don't start."

He raised his hands in mock surrender, a smirk tugging at the corners of his mouth. "I'm just saying, maybe he's not as bad as you think. Or maybe he is, and he's just really good at pretending he's not."

I snorted. "Trust me, he's definitely as bad as *I* think."

Aiden leaned back in his chair, his smirk widening. "If you say so. But for what it's worth, he's been cool to me. And if he's asking about you, maybe you're not as bad as he thinks either."

I frowned, unsure how to respond to that. Christian wasn't supposed to care—not about me, not about Aiden, not about anything beyond his own reflection in the mirror. And yet... here was Aiden, casually dropping the bomb that Christian had been sitting with him at lunch, like it was the most normal thing in the world.

I crossed my arms, my voice quieter now. "What does he even ask?"

Aiden shrugged, his tone light but his expression thoughtful. "Stuff. How you're doing, if you're still mad at him... that kind of thing. He doesn't talk about himself as much as you make it seem he does."

My stomach twisted, and I hated that I couldn't tell if it was from annoyance or something else. "He's probably just trying to score points or something."

"Maybe," Aiden said, his smirk softening. "But I think he just cares."

I scoffed, turning toward the door. *Cares,* my ass. "Don't get used to it. That guy is demon spawn."

Aiden studied me for a moment, his calm gaze steady. "Or maybe you need to give him a chance. I know you have a hard time trusting people, but not everyone's out to get you, Jess."

His words left me momentarily speechless. I shifted uncomfortably, unwilling to meet his eyes. "Yeah, well..." I was out of words. "I'm gonna get ready for bed."

Aiden chuckled softly, picking up his controller again. "Okay. Whatever you say."

I turned to leave, but his words lingered, sinking in deeper than I wanted them to. *Not everyone's out to get you.*

As I closed the door behind me, the truth of his observation settled. I was good at assuming the worst, at building walls so high and thick they kept everyone out. Trust wasn't something I could just give freely—not anymore. Not after being betrayed by someone who had once made me feel safe.

Whatever Christian's deal was with Aiden, it didn't erase the smugness or those endless power plays with me. Still, the thought of him—his voice, his teasing, those rare moments of unexpected sincerity—clung to me.

Christian

The late summer sun was dipping low, its warmth giving way to the coolness of evening. From my spot on the podium, I took in the final design for our show, everyone spread out in perfect formation. Weeks of grueling rehearsals had finally paid off. The show was complete. We'd nailed that last set, and for the first time, I could feel the entire ensemble moving in sync, the music filling the air with this incredible sense of purpose.

My eyes drifted across the field to the other podium, where Jessica stood. Her face set in that familiar determined expression—brow furrowed, eyes narrowed, like she was daring the universe to find a flaw in her performance. I've seen that look a hundred times, but lately, I've noticed something else too, something just beneath the surface. It's like there's a layer of doubt hiding behind all that confidence. Maybe it's nothing. Or maybe it's because our conversations have been… different lately. Less sharp-tongued jabs, but something softer.

"Reset from Set 32," Mr. Trust's voice rang out over the field.

As the band members scrambled back to their places, my gaze landed on Emily in the pit. She was helping Tracy adjust a keyboard stand, her movements quick and precise. Emily was new to Arcana, a transfer who had joined just last week, and already was an anomaly. Auxiliary percussionists were usually in the background, focused solely on their music, but Emily was different. She had this habit of hovering at the edge of the field during breaks, watching the formations like she was trying to commit the drill to memory.

"You're staring," Alex said, his voice teasing as he passed by the backfield podium. "What's the verdict, Gutierrez? You think Emily's got a secret agenda too?"

I rolled my eyes but didn't respond. Something about Emily felt... off. Maybe it was how quickly she'd adapted to our routines or how easily she navigated the social dynamics of the band. Or maybe it was just that I didn't trust people who showed up and blended in too fast.

As the band played through the closing bars, adrenaline surged through me. This was it—the culmination of all our hard work. I could see it in the musicians' faces too, the pride, the way they stood a little taller, played a little stronger. I felt it too, that mix of relief and excitement when something tough finally comes together. But even as the last note hung in the air, my gaze found its way back to Jessica.

She remained focused and intense, guiding the band with her usual exacting precision. But this time, when she caught me watching, there was a flash in her eyes—something like acknowledgment, maybe even understanding. It wasn't much, just a small nod in my direction, but it felt like a silent agreement, a signal that we were on the same wavelength, that we were clicking.

For the first time, it felt like we were in sync, both of us moving toward the same goal, no longer pulling against each other but leaning into the rhythm of our roles. Each cue she gave to the band flowed seamlessly with mine, her movements confident and precise, like a language only the two of us understood. It wasn't a truce exactly—there was still a challenge in her gaze, but it was enough to make me think maybe we could actually make this work.

✗ ✗ ✗ ✗ ✗ ✗

The days blurred together in a haze of rehearsals, the rhythm of the season becoming second nature. The first football game was tonight, and with it, our first chance to put everything on the line in front of a crowd. It wasn't just any audience—it was our home crowd, the people who knew us, expected us to be great. And that added pressure.

The band room buzzed with a mix of nervous energy and excitement. I could hear the brass section warming up outside, their notes sharp and clear in the evening air. The color guard was already out by the field, running through their routines one last time. As I adjusted my uniform in the mirror, focusing on the details that would reflect our collective effort tonight, I felt the weight of the performance ahead.

Emily caught my eye across the room, standing near Marcus as they debated the best way to stack the percussion equipment on the cart. She wasn't saying much, just nodding occasionally and fidgeting with her mallets. Then, without warning, she broke away and wandered toward the back of the room, her gaze scanning the drill charts pinned to the wall.

"What's up with her?" I muttered to Tracy as she walked by, rolling a timpani.

Tracy shrugged. "She's quirky, but she's good. I mean, she plays like she's been here for years."

"That's what bothers me," I said under my breath.

"Relax, Gutierrez. Not everyone's out to steal your thunder," Tracy teased, giving me a nudge. "Besides, you've got bigger things to worry about tonight. Like not messing up the podium switch with Jessica."

I snorted, but my eyes lingered on Emily as she quickly returned to the percussion section, her movements calm and deliberate. There was something calculated about her, but I couldn't put my finger on it.

Just as the final pre-show jitters settled in, Jessica's voice cut through the noise, pulling me away from the sea of anticipation.

"Christian, could you help me?" Jessica's voice, soft but clear, sliced through the noise. I turned, surprised, to see her head peeking out of one of the practice rooms.

I walked over, expecting some last-minute music issue or maybe a question about the podium switch. But as I stepped into the room, my breath caught in my throat. Jessica stood there in her performance dress, the deep red fabric hugging her form. The dress didn't just cling to her—it reframed her, set her apart with a kind of boldness I wasn't used to seeing. The color seemed to set her apart from the uniformity of our usual routine, a splash of boldness in a sea of sameness.

"Can you help with the zipper? It's stuck," she said, turning slightly so I could see where the zipper had caught about halfway up her back. I snapped back into attention.

I hesitated for a split second, still processing how different she looked, then moved to help her. My fingers brushed against the fabric as I gently tugged at the zipper.

"There." The zipper finally gave way and slid smoothly into place. My voice sounded strangely distant, even to my own ears.

"Thanks," she said, turning back around and smoothing out the dress with a quick, practiced motion. For a moment, our eyes met, and I realized I was still staring and standing way too close. I glanced away, feeling something unfamiliar pulling at the corners of my thoughts—things I shouldn't be thinking, especially *with a girlfriend*.

"No problem," I muttered, attempting to dispel the thought. "You, uh, look ready."

Jessica gave a small nod, her usually guarded expression slipping back into place. "Yeah. You too."

Before she could leave, I cleared my throat, forcing myself to meet her eyes again. "Hey, are you… ready? For the flag solo, I mean."

Her hand lingered on the doorframe, and for a second, I thought she might brush it off. But then her shoulders dropped just slightly, the tension in her posture giving her away. "I think so," she said, her voice quieter than usual. "I mean, I've practiced it a million times, but…" She hesitated, her fingers brushing the edge of the frame. "It's different when everyone's watching."

I nodded, stepping a little closer. "Yeah, I know what you mean. But… you'll be fine."

"Just fine?" she asked, a faint smirk tugging at the corner of her mouth.

"Well, no. Better than fine. You know what I mean." I took another step forward, meeting her gaze head-on. "What I mean is, the audience will be impressed. You're going to make it look easy."

She smiled then, small but genuine, her guard slipping for just a moment. "Thanks," she murmured. Her fingers curled tighter around the frame, like she was grounding herself.

But then her eyes flicked past me, her expression shifting, more guarded again. "Courtney won't be impressed, though," she said with a dry laugh. "Pretty sure she's still hoping I'll drop the flag right on my face."

The mention of Courtney was like a bucket of cold water. I stepped back instinctively, the distance between us growing again. I awkwardly crossed my arms across my chest, forcing a casual shrug. "Courtney's... Courtney. She'll be fine."

Jessica's smile faded just slightly, but she nodded, the moment slipping through our fingers as quickly as it had come. "Yeah. See you out there," she said, before finally stepping out of the room.

Trying to shake off the distraction, I headed outside, where Mr. Trust had formed the band into a block. The sky was deepening into twilight, and the outdoor lights flickered on, casting long shadows over the campus. The distant cheers of the football crowd filled the air, a reminder of the excitement awaiting us. Jessica and I marched side-by-side, leading the block towards the stands.

Once we reached the bleachers, the band settled into position, and the familiar buzz of excitement crackled through the air. The first half of the game was our time to shine with pep band music. We took turns choosing the tunes, trying to keep the energy high. I couldn't help but steal glances at Jessica as the band played. She was in her element, her movements fluid and confident. Each time she turned to give me a nod or a quick smile, it was like a jolt of energy.

A few steps away, Courtney stiffened, her shoulders snapping straight and her jaw tightening as her eyes locked on Jessica. She crossed her arms, fingers digging into her sides, her foot tapping against the floor in quick, impatient bursts. Even from here, the tension rolling off her was impossible to miss.

Minutes before halftime, the band gathered on the far side of the field, anticipation crackling in the cool night air. The sky was a deep navy, dotted with the first twinkling stars as the stadium lights cast their bright glow across the turf. I could feel the energy build as we prepared for our moment in the spotlight.

The announcer's voice boomed over the PA system, introducing us with that familiar mixture of excitement and reverence. I took a deep breath, channeling all the rehearsals and all the energy of the past weeks into this one moment. The center snare tapped out the rhythm, sharp and assertive, and I called the command with a decisive, "Band, forward, march!"

The band moved as one, a seamless wave of color and sound, making its way to the center of the field. Jessica and I took our positions on opposite podiums, facing each other across the sea of musicians. Our eyes met briefly, a quick nod of mutual acknowledgment passing between us. I raised my hands and gave the count-off, the rhythm of our opening number beginning to pulse through the field.

The show unfolded with practiced precision, each movement and note seamlessly weaving the story into the air. As the tempo softened into the ballad, Jessica stepped forward, flag in hand, her crimson dress catching the light. The stadium seemed to hold its breath as she began her solo, each motion precise and seamless, the flag slicing through the air with mesmerizing grace.

From my podium, I couldn't look away. She wasn't just performing; she was commanding the moment, every sweep and toss radiating strength and fire.

She was Juliet.

And *Juliet is the sun.*

The narrator's voice echoed over the field.

"Did my heart love till now? Forswear it, sight! For I never saw true beauty till this night."

The words struck like lightning, weaving themselves into the moment as if they had been meant for her. My chest tightened, the world around us narrowing to the rhythm of the music and the energy she carried. I didn't want to look away.

The ballad ended in a thunderous crescendo, but the image of her remained etched in my mind, lingering long after the final note faded. It wasn't just beauty—it was power, resilience and something I hadn't dared to notice before. Something I couldn't ignore now.

As the final echoes of the ballad faded, I snapped back to reality just in time to see Jessica climb onto the podium. Her movements were purposeful and fluid, a stark contrast to the disarray of thoughts swirling in my mind. She counted off with a commanding precision, her hands slicing through the air as the band prepared for the closer.

The ballad flowed effortlessly into the closer. The band launched into the rhythm with renewed vigor, and the color guard's flags shimmered as they twirled and snapped in synchronization. Despite the vibrant performance unfolding before me, I felt strangely detached, as if I were watching the scene through a foggy lens. The melody was exhilarating, the energy remarkable, but my focus remained on Jessica. Her solo flag work from earlier had left an imprint, and the way she carried herself now—poised and confident—was etched into my thoughts.

As the closer built to its final, triumphant chords, I managed to push aside the distracting thoughts, channeling all my energy into leading the band with the same intensity that had marked the beginning of the show. Yet, even as I conducted, a part of me remained caught in that moment of revelation, wondering how it had shifted everything I thought I knew about Jessica—and about myself.

After the football game, which Arcana's football team had won, everyone piled back into the band room across the campus. Mr. Trust was smiling at the front of the classroom making one of his motivational speeches. The crowd loved the show. There were a few details that needed to be ironed out, but everyone knew we had something special.

Then we were dismissed.

I shrugged off my drum major uniform, letting the cool evening air brush against my skin. The adrenaline from the show was still coursing through me, but there was a strange, lingering sense of disquiet that I couldn't quite shake. I tried to ignore it, focusing instead on the camaraderie of the band members, who were chattering about the performance and making plans for the weekend.

As I finished changing, I grabbed my keys and headed toward the parking lot, scanning for my truck. The night offered a cool breeze, a welcome change from the performance's heat. That's when I saw Courtney leaning against my truck, her arms crossed and her expression tight.

"Hey," I called out, keeping my voice neutral.

Courtney's eyes were blazing with frustration as she pushed off the truck and squared up to me. "Hey? That's all you've got after practically drooling over Jessica all night?"

I blinked, caught off guard. "What are you talking about?"

"Don't play dumb," she snapped. "You couldn't stop staring at her, Christian. It was like you forgot the rest of us existed."

I tried to keep my voice steady. "I wasn't staring at her. I was focused on the show. We're drum majors; we need to watch everything, including each other."

Courtney's glare didn't waver. "Oh, cut the crap. It wasn't just tonight. It's like you've got this fixation on her."

I felt a flash of irritation. "Fixation? Come on, Court, you know that's not fair."

"Don't." Her voice slightly trembled. "I've seen the way you look at her. It's not just tonight."

My frustration bubbled over. "What the hell are you trying to say?"

Courtney's face flushed with anger.

I took a deep breath, trying to regain my composure. "Look, if you're implying there's something more going on, you're wrong. I'm focused on the show and making it the best it can be. I'm just playing the part of Romeo, okay?"

Courtney's shoulders relaxed slightly, but her tone remained sharp. "Fine. Whatever."

"Look, if you're so concerned, why don't you just talk to me instead of making accusations?"

I opened the door to my truck and slammed it back closed, the sound echoing in the quiet parking lot. Frustration bubbled up with words on the tip of my tongue, but before I could let them spill out, I heard footsteps behind me—soft but purposeful. I turned, and there she was, standing just a few feet away, her expression unreadable in the dim light.

Jessica. Her presence silenced the chaos in my head, and for a second, I forgot why I'd been so worked up in the first place.

Jessica

The band room cleared out; the echoes of laughter and the thrill of our first performance still hanging in the air. I was just finishing up helping Tracy and the new senior, Emily, with the last of the pit equipment. We wheeled the timpani back toward the storage closet, each of us tired but satisfied.

As we reached the closet, Tracy shot me a grateful smile. "Thanks for the help, Jessica. I'll catch up with you both later—I promised Marcus I'd help him track down some missing mallets."

She darted off, leaving me alone with Emily. It felt a little strange, this new girl who had slipped into our routine so seamlessly, yet still felt like a bit of a mystery. She'd barely been here a week, but she moved like she knew her way around, like she'd been part of our world for longer than she actually had.

As we maneuvered the last piece of equipment into place, Emily turned to me, her gaze soft and oddly thoughtful. "You were really impressive out there tonight," she said, her voice carrying a warmth that caught me off guard.

"Oh," I managed, surprised. "Thank you."

Emily's smile widened, and she nodded toward the field outside. "You bring this… intensity to your performance. It's like you're not just conducting; you're telling the story. You make it feel personal."

My hand rubbed at the back of my neck. "I just practice a lot. I'm a little obsessive about making things perfect."

Emily nodded, her gaze never wavering. "I can tell. Honestly, the show's concept, the energy—you make it look effortless. I'd bet people around here don't know how lucky they are to have you leading."

I felt a small warmth spread at her words, even if something about her intense gaze felt… a little too sharp, like she was absorbing every detail. "That's nice of you to say," I replied, trying to keep things casual as I put a cymbal in its case. "It's all a team effort, though."

"True." She nodded, then glanced over at me, a glint of curiosity in her eyes. "Leadership like that doesn't go unnoticed. I'm sure other band programs would kill for someone like you. Like Kingston."

"Kingston?" I stiffened, caught off-guard. The name carried a weight I didn't entirely understand, but it was impossible to ignore. Everyone here talked about Kingston like it was the enemy, a constant shadow hanging over our rehearsals. Even the freshmen, who'd barely stepped onto the field, adopted the same wary, almost combative attitude toward their band. It was an unspoken rule: we were Arcana, they were Kingston, and that was all that mattered.

I hesitated, suddenly hyper-aware of Emily's expectant gaze. There was a certain ease in her expression, too easy, like she was waiting to see how I'd react. "Where did you say you transferred from?" I asked, trying to keep my tone casual, even as a flicker of suspicion took hold.

She gave a small shrug, her smile never wavering, but her eyes held a flicker of something unreadable. She was already halfway to the door when she looked back over her shoulder. "I didn't," she said softly, her voice barely above a murmur. "See you around, Jessica."

The words hung like a blade, heavy and unsettling, echoing in the quiet space of the percussion closet. And just like that, she slipped out, leaving me alone with a creeping chill spreading through my chest.

X X X X X X

As I walked to the parking lot that evening, I saw Christian and Courtney arguing loudly by his truck. Their voices carried through the cool night air, a jarring contrast to the post-game buzz of excitement. I was heading towards my car, determined to avoid getting involved, when I heard my name pierced through the cacophony.

"—why are you always watching her?" Courtney's voice was sharp and cutting.

I stopped in my tracks, my heart skipping a beat. Her words stung more than I expected. I hesitated, torn between walking away and confronting whatever this was. The last thing I wanted was more drama, but something in the way Courtney was speaking, that mix of anger and bitterness, made me stop and listen.

Christian's response was muffled but unmistakably defensive. "I'm just playing the part of Romeo—"

I could feel the heat rise in my cheeks. I wanted to stay out of it, but the way they were talking about me made it impossible to ignore. The mention of my name, especially in such a charged context, twisted something inside me.

I took a deep breath, trying to steady my nerves, and walked closer to my car, my footsteps deliberate and measured. The argument continued to escalate, but I didn't need to hear any more of this.

As I rounded the corner of a vehicle, Christian's voice cut through the night again. "Look, if you're so concerned, why don't you just talk to me instead of making accusations?"

Just then, I fumbled with my keys, dropping them on the pavement with a clatter. The sound was louder than I expected, and both Christian and Courtney turned toward me, their argument halting abruptly.

Courtney's eyes locked on mine, her expression a mix of frustration and something like pity. She shot Christian one last glare before storming off, her shoes clicking angrily against the asphalt.

Christian and I found ourselves in an uneasy silence. He shifted his weight from one foot to the other, looking more uncomfortable than I'd ever seen him. I bent down to retrieve my keys, avoiding eye contact as I tried to regain my composure.

Christian started, his voice hesitant. "I'm sorry you had to hear that."

With the keys gripped tightly in my hand, I straightened up. "I don't need to get involved in whatever's going on between you two. I heard enough to know that this—" I gestured vaguely toward the empty space Courtney had left, "—is above my pay grade."

I heard Courtney's accusation loud and clear—that maybe there was something stirring in Christian for me. It's absolute nonsense. But looking at him now, with that vague sadness hovering over him, it almost felt true.

Christian's eyes met mine, and for a moment, the facade of arrogance and irritation was gone. He looked tired, almost vulnerable, his shoulders slumped in a way I hadn't seen before. "Look, I know what that sounded like. But I want you to know that what she said—it's not true. There's nothing to worry about."

I pressed my lips together, unsure of what to say to that. I mean, good. He shouldn't be feeling anything close to what Courtney was accusing him of. There wasn't anything to worry about, because there's nothing going on. Right?

Still, the way my chest tightened at his words made me wonder if I was trying a little too hard to believe that.

Our dynamic had changed over the past few weeks. We were no longer in constant fight mode; instead, there was a strange, tentative truce between us. My brother seemed to trust him, and that trust had made me reconsider my own assumptions.

I took a steadying breath, trying to maintain my casual tone, even though doubt was twisting in my stomach. "Look, I don't really know what's going on between you two. But if you think it'd help, I could try talking to her?"

He looked genuinely surprised, a flicker of appreciation in his eyes and a small laugh escaping. "I didn't expect you to say that."

"Let's just say I'm willing to take one for the team."

Christian shook his head, a slight smile tugging at the corners of his mouth. "No, it's okay. I'm sure she'll come around."

I nodded, but skepticism still lingered. The tension between them was obvious, and I doubted it was as easy as he was making it sound. "Well, if you're sure," I said, feeling awkward but trying to keep the conversation moving. "Not that it matters, but... I don't think she likes me very much, anyway."

"That's okay." His expression softened. "I don't think she likes me very much right now, either."

I snorted. "I should probably head home. My mom hates it when I'm a minute late. Goodnight."

He smiled, and we both got in our vehicles, rolling down our windows. Christian dawdled for a moment, fiddling with his phone or adjusting the radio. As I attempted to start my car, it sputtered and died. My heart raced as I glanced at the clock on the dashboard. I was already cutting it close to curfew, and I couldn't deal with another lecture from my mother.

Christian, who had been lingering in his truck, noticed my trouble. He approached, a look of concern on his face. "Everything okay?"

I forced a smile, trying to hide my growing frustration. "Not really. It's not turning over. I need to get home before..." I let my words die out; he didn't need to know my mother's incessant need to have me home by a certain time.

He looked at me with a mix of sympathy and determination. "I can give you a ride if you want."

I hesitated for a moment, considering my options. The idea of accepting his help wasn't exactly appealing, but being late was worse—facing my mother after curfew was worse. "Actually, that would be really helpful."

Christian nodded, and we both climbed into his truck. As we drove away, I couldn't help but notice the subtle change in the atmosphere between us. It was quiet, but not uncomfortable. Christian glanced over occasionally, as if checking to make sure I was alright.

"So," he said after a few moments, "where to?"

I gave him the address, settling back into my seat as the car pulled onto the main road. Outside, the passing scenery blurred in soft streaks of gold and green, and I tried to lose myself in the steady hum of the engine, in the gentle rhythm of the drive. But my thoughts kept circling back to Christian.

He was being unusually thoughtful, the kind of considerate I hadn't expected from him. The Christian I'd known before this—

confident, cocky, and constantly challenging—wasn't exactly the picture of reliability. And yet, here he was, quietly steering us toward my house, no jokes, no sarcastic comments, just this unspoken understanding filling the space between us. It was… surprisingly comforting.

I glanced over at him, watching as he focused on the road, his expression unreadable but calm. He looked like he had done this a hundred times, like he knew exactly what to do. A tiny part of me wondered if I'd misjudged him all along—that the way his friends described him was actually accurate. Maybe there was more to him than I'd let myself see, something beyond the competition, beyond all the moments that had driven me up the wall. The idea settled somewhere between uneasy and curious, lingering even as I tried to push it away.

"So, is your mom strict?" he asked, keeping his eyes forward.

I sighed. "That's one word for it." Sensing my avoidance of that conversation, he asked nothing more.

As we neared my house, I felt a mix of relief and lingering tension. We pulled up in front of my yard, and I turned to him, a touch of awkwardness in the air.

"Thanks again, Christian," I said, opening the door. "I owe you one."

He smiled, that familiar flicker of confidence back in his eyes. "No problem. I'll see you at practice tomorrow."

I felt the heaviness of the evening's events lift a bit. "Got it. See you tomorrow."

He did a two-finger salute as I stepped out of the truck and headed towards my front door.

But as soon as I shut the truck's door, I remembered I had no way of getting back to school in the morning for Saturday's rehearsal. I turned, and his passenger window was already down. "I'll pick you up tomorrow," he said, reading my thoughts.

I let out a breath of relief, the corners of my mouth tugging into a smile. "Thanks."

"A thousand times goodnight, Juliet." He flashed me a smile, and something in my chest warmed—like a spark igniting.

Not this again.

Something lit up inside of me as I met his unwavering gaze, the intensity of his earnestness rattling. This wasn't his usual challenging smirk. His smile was different this time—softer, like sunlight slipping through the cracks in a fortress I'd spent years building. It was the kind of look I hadn't seen in a long time, like he wasn't seeing the version of me I showed everyone, but something underneath, something I barely even let myself acknowledge.

For a moment, I felt exposed, my defenses thinning. The warmth in his eyes stirred something I'd buried—a quiet, unfamiliar kind of hope—and it unsettled me. I tried to step back, to put distance between us, but the emotions swirled too close, too strong. It was a reminder of the part of me I'd locked away, a part I thought I'd outgrown.

I took a shaky breath, trying to ground myself. I'd always been good at staying guarded, keeping things detached and safe, especially around Christian. But his kindness lingered, and I couldn't ignore the flicker in my chest, a soft ache that made it harder than usual to turn and walk away.

For just a second, I wondered—*what if I didn't?* What if I let him see more, let him see me?

The thought burned like a match, bright and dangerous, snuffed out as quickly as it came.

I watched as his truck pulled away, the night air feeling suddenly colder as it turned the corner. As I turned to head inside, the weight of the evening's events settled heavily on me.

As I closed the front door behind me, the clatter of silverware and the murmur of conversation from the dining room reached my ears. I took a deep breath, steeling myself for the inevitable interrogation that awaited me.

I walked into the kitchen, where the smell of a hastily prepared dinner wafted through. My mom sat at the table, her expression a mix of irritation and concern. Aiden sat at the table, already engrossed in his phone. My dad also doing the same.

"Who was that?" my mother's accusatory voice rang out.

A brief hesitation gripped me, the familiar edge in my mom's tone signaling her quiet judgment. Glancing toward Aiden, I caught him deliberately avoiding my gaze, his eyes fixed elsewhere, leaving me to turn back and face her directly.

"Just a classmate. My car wouldn't start, so he offered me a ride home."

"Why didn't you just call us?" she pressed. "You know better than to get in a car with someone we don't know."

"His name's Christian," I responded carefully. "And it's not like he's a stranger. He's in band with me. I didn't want to trouble you, and I thought it would be easier to just get a ride."

She crossed her arms, clearly agitated. My mom opened her mouth, but Aiden cut her off. "Mom, can we just eat? Jessica's here now. Let's not make a big deal out of it."

I could feel my mom's disappointment and frustration simmering. I knew it wasn't just about Christian or the car; it was about her concerns for me, wrapped in layers of judgment.

She sighed, but finally relented. "Fine. You need to know how to handle these situations better in the future."

I nodded, feeling a mix of relief and frustration as we ate in silence, the conversation shifting to more mundane topics. But the tension lingered, thick and unyielding. My mom's concern hovered like a shadow, a silent reminder that she wasn't letting go of her suspicions anytime soon. And there was my dad beside her, his gaze fixed somewhere far beyond the table, as if the conversation didn't even exist.

Each glance she cast in my direction felt heavy, weighted with all the judgment I expected. The entire act of sitting here, pretending things were normal, was exhausting. I knew she cared, but her brand of "concern" always left me feeling guilty, as if I constantly needed to prove myself to avoid disappointing her. The more time I spent in this house, the more suffocated I felt.

One day, I'd be free of this—free to breathe, to make my own choices without the shadow of her disapproval looming over every step. Just a few more months, I reminded myself. Once I graduated, I wouldn't have to explain, wouldn't have to apologize, wouldn't have to feel like every decision I made was wrong in her eyes.

Once I get my hands on that diploma, I'm never looking back.

Christian

I couldn't quite pinpoint why I was so caught up in how I looked today, but there was this nagging need to make a good impression for Jessica's mom—even if I didn't fully understand why.

As I finally headed out the door, I found myself driving with a heightened sense of anticipation. The drive to Jessica's house felt longer than usual, my thoughts buzzing with a mix of excitement and nerves. I parked in front of her house, took a deep breath, and tried to steady my racing heart.

When I got out of the truck, I saw Jessica standing on the porch with her mom. Jessica's posture was stiff, her hands gripping the straps of her backpack, and her mom's expression was just as tight, her eyes scanning me like I was something she needed to figure out.

"Hi, I'm Christian," I said, extending a hand toward her mom. "Thanks for letting me pick Jessica up this morning."

Her handshake was firm, her gaze sharp as it flickered between me and Jessica. "Christian," she repeated, like she was measuring him up. "Jessica mentioned you're her drum major partner."

"Yes, ma'am," I replied, nodding. "We've been working together a lot lately for the show."

Her lips pressed into a thin line, and I could feel the weight of her assessment, like she was trying to decide whether I was trustworthy enough. "I appreciate you helping her out last night," she said finally, though her tone carried an edge. "I assume you've been driving for a while? No accidents?"

"Yes, ma'am," I said again, keeping my voice calm. "I've had my license for over two years. I drive to and from school and rehearsal every day."

Jessica shifted slightly, and her mom's eyes flicked to her before returning to me. "Well," she said after a pause, "we'd like to have you over for dinner tonight. It's important to us to know the people Jessica spends time with."

"Uh…" Jessica's voice cut in, a mix of discomfort and surprise, but her mom didn't so much as glance at her.

I hesitated, caught off guard by the invitation. "That's very kind of you," I said carefully. "I'd be happy to join." Jessica stared at me in shock, a look that shouted, *You have no idea what you're getting yourself into.*

Her mom nodded, her expression softening just slightly. "Good. We'll see you tonight, then."

Jessica gave me a quick, almost pleading look as her mom turned back toward the house. "Come on," she muttered, already heading toward the truck. "We're going to be late."

I felt the tension radiating off her as we made our way to the truck. As soon as the doors shut, she let out a sharp breath. "I'm sorry about that," she said, her voice clipped. "She's just… like that."

"It's fine," I said, glancing at her as I pulled away from the curb. "I get it. She's just looking out for you."

As we drove off, I couldn't help but notice the tension in the air. The usual silence between us felt heavier today. I glanced over at Jessica, who was staring out the window, biting at her fingernails.

"Are you okay?" I asked, breaking the silence. "You seem… I don't know, kind of tense."

Jessica shifted in her seat, her arms crossed, her gaze fixed on the window. "It's nothing."

I glanced at her, unconvinced. "You don't have to tell me if you don't want to, but I can sense something's up. Call it 'drum major's intuition.'"

Her eyes flicked toward me for a second, like she was debating whether to say anything. Finally, she sighed, her voice quiet. "It's my mom... I feel like I can't breathe around her."

I stayed quiet, giving her space to continue. "Did something happen after I dropped you off?" I asked.

"No... Okay, yes," she groaned, leaning her head against the window. "It's always something with her. Like last night—she didn't like that I let you drive me home, but what was I supposed to do? Wait in an empty parking lot by myself for who knows how long? Wait for a tow truck—who'd also be a stranger?"

I frowned, her words sinking in.

She let out a bitter laugh. "No matter what I do or say, it's always wrong. I can't win."

Her voice cracked slightly, and I could hear the exhaustion under the frustration. It wasn't just about last night; this was something deeper, something she'd been carrying for a long time.

"I get that. Maybe it's not about winning." I paused, choosing my words carefully. "Maybe it's about surviving. Doing what you can to hold it together, even when it feels like the people who should have your back are the ones making it harder."

Jessica turned to look at me, and for a split second, I saw something unguarded in her expression—vulnerable in a way that caught me off guard. "Exactly," she whispered, her voice cracking just enough to betray the emotion she was trying to hold back. "Even becoming drum major—wasn't enough. Killing myself over AP classes—still not enough... Keeping it together at school, making sure Aiden's okay—none of it is enough for her. It never is."

I nodded slowly, choosing my words carefully. "Sometimes it's not even about meeting their expectations. It's like... no matter what you do, it's never enough because they've already decided it won't be. Like they're not even looking at you."

Jessica's gaze flicked to me, and something shifted. The walls she kept so carefully guarded didn't crumble, but I felt the door crack open—just enough to let me see inside. It wasn't much, but it was enough. And as her expression softened, I saw it—something familiar, something that mirrored my own. The weight, the frustration, the feeling of never being enough. It was there, written in her eyes, and for a second, it knocked the air out of me.

I wasn't sure if she saw the same thing in me, but it felt like she did. Like we'd both been carrying the same invisible burden, too heavy to share with anyone else. The space between us felt fragile, tentative—one wrong word and the door would slam shut again. But right now, in this moment, it was open. And somehow, that made the weight a little easier to hold.

"And the worst part?" I added, keeping my voice steady. "You start wondering if it's even worth trying. Like, if nothing's ever going to be enough for them, then why keep breaking yourself to prove something they'll never see?"

Jessica's gaze dropped to her hands, her fingers curling slightly. The silence felt heavier than before, like she was wrestling with something I couldn't see.

Finally, her shoulders eased slightly, and she leaned back against the seat. For a moment, her lips parted like she wanted to say something, but instead, she just nodded, a quiet understanding settling between us. "Yeah," she said, her words floating between us. "Exactly."

It was strange—the way hearing her agreement made something in my chest loosen.

We drove the rest of the way in a more comfortable silence, the air between us less charged than before. I could tell that talking about her mom had lightened her burden, even if just a little. The school came into view, and for once, it didn't just feel like another day. Today was about stepping up for the band, even if their so-called leaders were a little broken themselves.

"By the way," I said, hoping a change of topic would ease her mind a little more. "I brought some jumper cables. Your battery probably died."

She turned to me, and a small smile formed on her lips. "Thanks."

✗ ✗ ✗ ✗ ✗ ✗

By the end of rehearsal, everything clicked—the percussion's tight rhythms, the brass's powerful fanfares, and the woodwinds weaving it all together seamlessly. Even the staff, usually so critical, were nodding with satisfaction, their excitement unmistakable. This wasn't just practice anymore; it was a glimpse of the show we'd been building toward, and the energy on the field crackled with possibility.

From my vantage point, I could see how every section, every individual, was contributing to something greater than themselves. The percussion's driving cadences provided the heartbeat of the show, while the brass section's soaring fanfares sent shivers down my spine. Even the smallest details, like the way the guard caught their flags in perfect sync or how the flutes hit that high note just right, were falling into place. It was like watching a masterpiece being painted in real time, each stroke adding depth and emotion.

During the last full run of the day, everything fell into place. The transitions were smooth, the dynamics spot on, and the intensity was exactly where it needed to be. As I conducted from the podium, I could feel the connection between us all—the musicians, the guard, the staff, and the drum majors. We weren't just a band anymore—we were a force, breathing life into the show with every note, every movement.

By the time we finished rehearsal, there was a sense of exhilaration in the air. The kind that only comes after a truly great rehearsal. The staff broke into applause, and I could hear some of the other students whooping and cheering, their pride and excitement bubbling over.

I looked over at Jessica perched on her podium across the field. Her eyes were scanning the group, taking in the same scene I was. When our eyes met, there was a brief, unspoken acknowledgment—a shared understanding that what we had just experienced was special. This was the show that could take us to the next level, and we both knew it.

As I walked off the field, the high from the rehearsal still lingering, I spotted Courtney near the band room. She was leaning against the wall, arms crossed, her face set in a stony expression. The second our eyes met, she looked away, her lips pressed into a thin line. She'd seen me arrive with Jessica that morning, and since then, she hadn't spoken a word to me.

I sighed inwardly, knowing this wasn't going to be easy. Courtney's silent treatment was her way of punishing me, but I wasn't in the mood to play her games. I still hadn't figured out how to smooth things over with her, or if I even wanted to. A part of me felt guilty, but another part—one I wasn't ready to admit even to myself—was relieved. Things had been off with us for a while now, and her jealousy over Jessica was only making it worse.

Before I could even think about approaching Courtney, Alex sidled up next to me. He had a grin on his face, probably still buzzing from the great rehearsal. "Hey man, that was killer out there! Did you hear that high E I hit?"

"Yeah, it's really coming together," I replied, trying to match his enthusiasm, though my mind was elsewhere.

"Dude," Alex threw his arm around my shoulder, leaning in and speaking low. "Did you hear about Kingston High's field show?" Now my mind was captivated.

Honestly, I hadn't heard much about our crosstown rival this year. Kingston High was usually the talk of the marching band circuit, their reputation as the "top-dogs" of the scene preceding them. People knew their field shows for being loud, aggressive, and chaotic. They prided themselves on being the rebels, always pushing the boundaries just to get under everyone's skin. Even their band director leaned into the *"us-against-the-world"* vibe, fueling their arrogance.

For years, Arcana and Kingston had been at each other's throats. It wasn't just about the music; it was about pride. The rivalry ran deep, from the taunts and pranks during competitions to the not-so-subtle jabs on social media. Arcana was known for its precision and discipline, the kind of band that emphasized technical excellence and showmanship. Kingston, on the other hand, thrived on chaos and energy, always aiming to shock the audience with something unexpected.

So the fact that Kingston had been keeping quiet this season was surprising, almost unsettling. It wasn't like them to lie low. Normally, by this point, they'd have made some big, bold move, like unveiling a show with a controversial theme or trash-talking our band on social media. But this year?

Radio silence.

"They're up to something," I muttered, narrowing my eyes. "They always are."

Alex nodded, his grin widening. "Oh, they definitely are. Word is, they've got something huge planned. They're so hush-hush this year. I heard they're doing something Shakespearean too."

If Kingston was doing something Shakespearean too—especially if it was *Romeo and Juliet*—then this wasn't just competition. It was war. "Great," I sighed, already feeling the pressure mount. "Just what we need—a surprise from Kingston."

"Hey, man," Alex shrugged. "Wouldn't be a marching season without them trying to steal something from us, right?"

The rivalry between Arcana and Kingston was the stuff of legends. No matter how well we did, they were always there, nipping at our heels, trying to prove that chaos could beat out discipline. And this year, with everything already hanging by a thread, the last thing we needed was for Kingston to pull some stunt that would throw us off our game.

"Hey, are you doing anything tonight?" Alex asked, nudging me with a grin. "My parents just installed this insane new sound system in the theater room. I've been trying to get you to come over forever, man. Thought we could finally break it in—watch a movie, crank up the volume till the walls shake or something. Bring Courtney."

I hesitated. Normally, I'd be all in for something like that—to escape my parents bickering at home—but tonight was different. I had dinner at Jessica's place, and I wasn't sure how long that would take or what exactly was going to happen. Plus, there was no way I wanted to bring up the whole situation with Courtney right now.

"Nah, I've got plans tonight," I said, keeping it vague.

Alex raised an eyebrow. "Plans? With who?"

I shrugged, trying to play it off casually. "Just something I need to take care of. Maybe another time."

Alex seemed to buy it, but there was a flicker of curiosity in his eyes. "Alright, man," he said, backing off. "Another time then."

In the parking lot, Jessica was waiting by her car with the hood popped up. I walked over, toolbox in hand, and she stepped aside, giving me a sheepish look. "Guess it really was the battery," she said, crossing her arms.

"Good thing I brought the jumper cables," I replied, setting to work. She stood nearby, silent but watchful, as I connected the cables and got her engine running again.

When the car roared to life, she let out a relieved breath, her posture relaxing. "Thanks. I seriously owe you."

"Don't worry about it," I said, brushing my hands on my jeans. "Happy to help."

She hesitated, her fingers drumming lightly against the car door. Then she looked up at me, her expression shifting to something a little more uncertain. "Um... could you give me a fifteen-minute head start?"

I raised an eyebrow. "Head start?"

Jessica glanced away, clearly embarrassed. "Yeah, just... so I can, you know, warm up my mom before you show up."

I smirked, unable to resist a little teasing. "You mean I didn't win her over this morning with my sparkling charm?"

"More like she's suspicious of it," Jessica said, shooting me a dry look. "You're not exactly off the hook yet. So, head start?"

"Alright, fifteen minutes," I agreed, still grinning. "But only because you asked nicely."

She rolled her eyes, but there was a flicker of a smile on her lips. "Thanks. I'll see you in a bit."

I watched her pull out of the lot, the tension in her shoulders still visible even as her car disappeared around the corner. Despite her nerves, there was something about the way she'd asked—like she was letting me in, even if just a little. It was a small gesture, but it felt significant.

As I walked back to my truck, the weight of Courtney's judgment from earlier lingered in the back of my mind. She'd barely said two words to me all day, but her pointed glances had spoken volumes. I knew I couldn't avoid dealing with her forever, but right now, my focus was elsewhere.

I leaned against the door of my truck, letting out a slow breath. The memory of Jessica in the car earlier, opening up about her mom, replayed in my mind. It wasn't like her to let her guard down, but today had felt different.

Something was shifting between us, and even though I didn't fully understand what it was, I couldn't stop thinking about it.

Christian

The landscaping was clean and well-kept, the kind of place that didn't draw much attention but exuded a sense of strict order. Jessica was already waiting outside when I arrived, standing by the front steps like she had been there for a while.

As I got out of the truck, I took a deep breath, trying to shake off the unease that had been building up ever since she mentioned her mom earlier in the car. There was something about the way she'd said it—the tension in her voice, the way she'd pressed her forehead against the window like she was trying to escape. I couldn't shake the feeling that tonight was going to be uncomfortable.

I grabbed the bouquet of flowers I'd picked up on the way, hoping it would make a good impression. Jessica eyed the flowers with a raised brow, looking almost… puzzled, like she thought they might be for her.

Before she could say anything, I held them up a little awkwardly. "They're for your mom."

"Oh, I didn't realize we were kissing ass tonight," she muttered, a dry smile tugging at her mouth.

I shrugged with a grin, trying to keep it light. "Moms love this sort of thing. You show up with flowers, and suddenly you're a saint." I leaned in slightly, lowering my voice with a smirk. "Besides, I gotta stay on her good side if I'm going to keep dragging you to band practice."

Jessica raised an eyebrow, giving me a look that was half-amused, half-dismissive. "That was a one-time thing, Christian."

A flicker of disappointment must have crossed my face before I could mask it. "Right. Yeah, sure," I said quickly, trying to shrug it off with another grin. But Tracy's voice echoed in my head, teasing: *"That's some pretty pathetic flirting."*

Her smirk lingered as we headed toward the door, but there was a hint of something softer in her gaze, like maybe she appreciated the effort—even if she'd never say it out loud.

"Hi, Mrs. Welling," I said with a smile as we stepped inside, handing her the flowers.

She took them with a practiced smile, her grip firm as she shook my hand. "Thank you, Christian. And for driving Jessica home last night and fixing up her car this morning. We really appreciate it."

"No problem. It just needed a jump," I said, glancing at Jessica, who was standing off to the side, her shoulders tense. I couldn't tell if she was more nervous or annoyed. Maybe both.

"Why don't you come in?" her mom continued, still holding that same smile. "Dinner is almost ready."

I hesitated, but Jessica gave me a quick, almost imperceptible nod. "Sure, I'd love to," I replied. If Jessica needed me here, then here I'd be.

Inside, the house was just as orderly as I imagined it would be. Everything was in its place, from the neatly arranged photos on the walls to the perfectly aligned furniture. Jessica's mom led us into the dining room, where the table was already set, the smell of dinner wafting through the air.

Aiden was at the table, fiddling with his phone on his lap. He gave me a quick nod before returning to whatever game he was playing. "Jessica's dad is still working, so he won't be joining us tonight," her mom said. I took a seat next to Jessica.

Dinner began with the usual small talk—questions about school, my plans after graduation, safe topics that required little thought. Jessica's mom led the conversation, directing most of her questions at me, her tone overly polite, almost performative. She asked about my classes, my interests, my plans for the future. I answered, keeping my responses light, but I couldn't ignore Jessica's growing silence beside me, like she was retreating inward with every word her mom directed at me.

"It's nice to see someone so focused," her mom said, her smile tight, her voice sugary. "You've always had such big dreams, Jessica. I just wish you'd focus on something concrete, like Christian here." She turned to face me again, talking about her daughter like she wasn't in the room. "She has no idea where she wants to go to college—I don't even know if she wants to go."

Aiden was lost in his own world, chewing quietly, silent in the tension building in the room. He seemed uncomfortable, as if speaking up would just charge the room more. Jessica's free hand drifted toward her mouth, her thumbnail pressing against her teeth. I'd noticed her do that once or twice before, but now it clicked—it wasn't random. It was a nervous habit, something she did when her anxiety got the better of her.

"Jessica, stop that." Her mom's voice snapped like a whip, her eyes narrowing. "You're not a child."

Jessica flinched, her hand dropping instantly to her lap as a flush crept up her neck. "Sorry," she muttered, barely audible, her eyes glued to her plate.

It was as if Jessica was completely alone at this table, surrounded by her own family but unseen, unheard. Her mom's words were like little daggers, each one sharpened with a subtle, practiced precision that only Jessica seemed to notice. The worst part was, no one else was stepping in. No one was coming to her defense.

I cleared my throat, trying to break the tension. "With all due respect, Mrs. Welling, Jessica's one of the hardest-working people I know. She's been a huge part of why our band is where it is this year. Honestly, I've seen her push through things that most people would quit over."

The room went dead silent after I spoke up, and for a moment, I thought maybe I'd crossed some invisible line. Jessica's mom's eyes narrowed slightly, her smile remaining intact but her gaze cooling, like she wasn't used to anyone pushing back. I felt Jessica shift slightly next to me, her foot brushing mine under the table, as if to say, *Don't bother.* But I wasn't going to let her sit there and take it.

"Well, that's very kind of you, Christian," she said, her smile remaining fixed but her tone taking on a sharper edge. "But ambition isn't just about working hard. It's about having a clear direction, knowing where you're going. And unfortunately, that's where some people seem to lose their way."

My jaw tightened, but I kept my expression calm. I didn't want to make things worse for Jessica. But from the corner of my eye, I caught her looking at me, her gaze softer than usual, like she was... surprised. Grateful, even. I wasn't sure I'd ever seen her look at me that way before.

Jessica looked back at her mom, her expression unreadable, but I could feel the tension in the room thickening. Maybe I'd only made a dent in her mom's perfect armor, but if it meant that Jessica felt even a little bit seen, it was worth it.

"So, Christian," her mom said, her attention swiveling to me like Jessica wasn't even at the table. "Your parents must be proud of the work ethic you've developed. What do they do? I imagine they've set a strong example for you."

Proud? I couldn't even remember the last time they'd come to one of my performances or talked to me about... anything. "My dad's some business executive, and my mom's a doctor. They're busy."

Another way of saying, *they're never home.* It was an understatement, but I wasn't about to get into the details here. Besides, this wasn't really about me, was it?

"Well, they must be doing something right," her mom replied with a sugary smile. "You're such a well-mannered young man." The unspoken comparison landed hard. Jessica didn't flinch, but I *felt* it for her.

Her mom's gaze drifted to Aiden, her tone softening like she was sharing a bittersweet memory. "Jessica used to be so full of life—always laughing, always bright. But after Aiden's accident... and that boy she was seeing..." She paused, giving a long sigh, just long enough to let the implication sink in, her eyes flicking to me briefly before landing back on Jessica. "She withdrew from all of us.

Locked herself away in her room for days, barely spoke to anyone, barely got out of bed. It was like she wasn't even there anymore."

Her voice turned wistful, as though she were recounting a tragedy, like she was talking about someone already dead. "It's hard to see someone with so much potential waste it like that. I just hope one day she'll start taking responsibility for herself again."

Jessica's hand froze mid-cut, the knife poised over her plate like she'd forgotten it was there. Slowly, her fingers tightened around the handle, her knuckles blanching as if holding on to the only thing grounding her. Her chest rose sharply, just once, as though she were trying to steady her breathing. Then, with deliberate precision, she set the knife down, the faint clink of metal against porcelain cutting through the tense silence.

Her face was a careful mask, but I caught it—the way her nostrils flared, the slight tremor in her jaw as she clenched it tight. Her eyes stayed fixed on her plate, unblinking, her focus so sharp it was almost unnerving, like she was trying to retreat into herself, to escape the weight of her mother's words. It wasn't just composure she was fighting for—it was control, a desperate attempt to keep from unraveling right there at the table.

The air grew heavier, thick with the unspoken accusations that hung between them. Her mother's disappointment was unmistakable, a resentment that seeped out in these carefully chosen phrases that seemed harmless on the surface but cut deep beneath. I could see it now—the gulf between them, the resentment Jessica carried, the bitterness in her voice whenever she mentioned her mom. She wasn't just dealing with disapproval; she was bearing the weight of her family's expectations and unspoken blame, carrying a burden that was never fully acknowledged but always there.

Her mom turned to Jessica, her voice heavy with that practiced mix of sweetness and reproach. "Aiden's had to adjust so much since. We all have. But I suppose that's just life, isn't it? Learning to live with the choices we make."

Jessica's face went rigid, and I could feel the hurt beneath her defiant gaze as she lifted her eyes to her mother, a bitterness sparking in their depths. "I think you've made your point, Mom."

She was holding on by a thread, her composure like armor she'd pieced together to survive these moments. In that instant, I wanted to pull her out of that room, away from these wounds her family kept reopening, away from the guilt and blame they piled onto her shoulders.

Her mom feigned innocence, tilting her head with a small, patronizing smile. "I wasn't trying to upset you, sweetie. It's just important to learn from mistakes. Isn't that what maturity's about, Christian?"

The words had barely left her mouth before Jessica pushed her chair back with a force that made it wobble. The raw defiance in her eyes was like nothing I'd ever seen before, daring anyone at the table to stop her. The calm, composed mask she wore had shattered, and for a moment, she was exposed, furious, and hurt.

Her voice was low, steady, but each word carried the weight of restrained fury, honed sharp and deliberate. "If you want to blame me, fine. But let's not pretend this is about 'helping.' You just want someone to point fingers at." Her eyes snapped up, locking with her mother's in a challenge so fierce, it left no room for misunderstanding.

Without waiting for a response, Jessica turned on her heel and strode out of the dining room, her footsteps echoing through the house. Her mom's carefully crafted smile slipped, a flash of shock and irritation crossing her face before she quickly recovered, straightening herself as if nothing had happened.

I didn't hesitate. I shot a quick, apologetic glance at her mom, then excused myself and following Jessica out of the room.

"Jessica," I called out, but she didn't stop. I followed her outside, catching up to her as she made her way to my truck. She reached for the passenger door, gripping the handle, only to find it locked. She let out a frustrated breath, her shoulders slumping as she turned to me.

For a moment, we just stood there, her hand resting on the door handle, her expression caught somewhere between anger and something more vulnerable, something that made my chest tighten.

"Can we get out of here?" she asked, her voice quieter, almost pleading. "Please?"

I nodded, fishing the keys from my pocket. The click of the lock sounded louder than usual in the silence between us. She didn't move right away, just glanced at the door and then at me, as if that small gesture—letting her in—meant more than just leaving her house.

Finally, she opened the door and slid into the seat, letting out a shaky breath. I walked around and got in on the driver's side, starting the engine without saying a word. The quiet stretched between us, comfortable and charged all at once, and out of the corner of my eye, I saw her shoulders begin to relax, the tension easing just a bit.

As I pulled away, I couldn't help but feel that this wasn't just about leaving her house—it was about giving her space to breathe, a chance to let someone else in, even if only for a drive.

I knew exactly where to take her—a place where she could let it all out without anyone judging her. I took her to the patch of secluded woods near the high school, the special place where my friends and I would escape to. We passed by a No Trespassing sign, but being here so many times before, there never was anyone to enforce it. My truck vibrated as we went off the asphalt onto the pebbly path between the trees.

Finally, we pulled up to my spot in the woods, the place I went to when I needed to get away from everything. It was quiet here, peaceful, with nothing but the sound of the wind in the trees.

Jessica climbed out of the truck, her shoes crunching against the gravel as she stepped onto the narrow path. I stayed back for a moment, watching as she took in the woods, the stillness, the way the trees stretched up into the night sky like they were holding the stars in place.

She paused, her gaze landing on the fire pit a few feet away. The ashes from last time were still there, scattered in the ring of stones we'd always used. It wasn't much—just a spot we'd cleared out years ago—but the sight of her standing there, staring at it, made my chest tighten.

"This is your spot, isn't it?" she asked softly, her voice almost too quiet for the space around us.

I nodded, stepping closer. "Yeah. A few of us come here sometimes. It's… where we go to talk, get things off our chest. Dream a little, I guess."

Jessica didn't say anything, just crouched near the fire pit, her fingers brushing lightly over one of the stones. I stayed back, watching her, unsure if she wanted space or needed me to fill the silence. She seemed lost in thought, her movements deliberate, like she was trying to puzzle out some unspoken truth.

"It must be nice to dream," she said quietly, her fingers brushing the edge of a stone. "For me, it's not like that. Every day feels like… just getting through it. Surviving."

I opened my mouth to say something, anything, but nothing felt right. The weight in her voice, the rawness of it, left no room for easy responses.

"Jess," I said finally, my voice quiet, careful. "What happened?"

She froze, her hand hovering over the stone. For a long moment, she didn't move, didn't look at me. Then, slowly, she turned her head, her eyes meeting mine. They were unguarded now, stripped of the sharp edges and deflections she usually used to keep people away.

What I saw there instead was… exhaustion.

"You don't have to tell me," I said, stepping closer, my voice steady but soft. "But I'm here… if you need someone to listen."

Her breath hitched, and for a second, I saw the moment she almost retreated—but didn't. But then her shoulders sagged, and she let out a shuddering breath, the kind that sounded like it had been trapped inside for too long.

And then, Jessica started to talk.

The next chapter will deal with sensitive subjects, including themes of emotional trauma, sexual assault, and mental health struggles. These topics are depicted to reflect the characters' experiences, but reader discretion is advised.

Please take care while reading.

Jessica

The summer before Junior year

"Jessica," Cassie said, trying to grab my attention as I studied. "There's a college party tonight—come with me. You need a break."

I shut the textbook with a forceful snap, the sound echoing in the quiet room. My fingers trembled slightly as I rubbed my temples, trying to push away the growing anxiety. "I don't know, Cassie. I have so much studying left for this English test, and I promised Aiden we'd have a game night. I just—" My voice wavered, and I glanced at the clock, my chest tightening with every tick. "I feel like I'm drowning in it all."

"That's exactly why you need a break!"

It was the middle of summer, but my mom had signed me up for courses at the community college. She wanted me to have a leg up, but it just felt like I was drowning.

"Just bring Aiden along. Bring your boyfriend too."

I sighed, feeling the weight of my mom's expectations pressing down on me. She was always on my case about studying, about being perfect, about not wasting time on "frivolous" things. But the thought of a night out, a break from all the pressure, was tempting. Plus, Cassie was right—Aiden loved hanging out with us, and my boyfriend had been nagging me to spend more time together.

"Okay, fine," I relented, closing my textbook with a thud. "But just for a little while. I can't stay out too late."

Cassie grinned, her eyes lighting up with excitement. "You won't regret it, Jess. It'll be fun, I promise. You deserve a break."

Although I wasn't entirely convinced, I nodded anyway, forcing a smile. "Let me go talk to Aiden."

As I walked down the hallway to my brother's room, I tried to shake off the unease gnawing at me. My mom wouldn't approve if she knew, but maybe that was part of the appeal. Just for one night, I wanted to forget about the constant pressure, the need to be perfect.

I knocked lightly on Aiden's door before pushing it open. He was sitting on his bed, controller in hand, engrossed in a video game. His face lit up when he saw me.

"Hey, you ready to get your butt kicked in Smash Bros.?" he teased, a playful glint in his eye.

I chuckled, shaking my head. "Actually, change of plans. How would you feel about coming with me and Cassie to a party tonight?"

Aiden's eyebrows shot up in surprise. "A party? Like, a real one? With people?"

"Yeah, a real one," I said, rolling my eyes. "And don't worry, it'll be fun. You'll get to hang out with us and maybe meet some new people."

Aiden hesitated for a moment, then shrugged. "Sure, why not? It's not like I have anything better to do." He jumped up from the bed and walked over to his dresser.

"Great. I'll let you know when we're leaving."

As I walked back to my room, I grabbed my phone and sent a quick text to my boyfriend, letting him know about the change of plans. I could almost hear the excitement in his reply. This was going to be good for us. A night to relax, to just be normal teenagers for once.

But even as I got ready, picking out a simple outfit that wouldn't draw too much attention, a part of me couldn't shake the feeling that I was doing something wrong. The anxiety I was trying to escape kept bubbling beneath the surface, but I pushed it down, reminding myself that I deserved to have fun.

After all, what's the worst that could happen?

The drive to the party was filled with the usual banter between Cassie and Aiden, but I couldn't fully immerse myself in the conversation. My mind kept wandering back to the nagging voice in my head—my mom's voice—telling me I was making a mistake. But I pushed it aside, determined to have a good time. I deserved a break, I told myself again.

We arrived at the house, which was already buzzing with music and laughter. It was bigger than I expected, with lights strung across the front yard and people spilling out onto the lawn. Cassie led the way, her confidence contagious as she pulled us inside.

"Come on, Jess, let's grab a drink!" she called over her shoulder.

I hesitated for a moment. I wasn't much of a drinker. And by not much, I meant not at all. But tonight was about loosening up, about letting go of the stress and the endless pressure. I followed Cassie into the kitchen, where a makeshift bar was set up. Bottles of every kind of alcohol were scattered across the counter, and a guy I didn't recognize was mixing drinks for a small crowd.

Cassie handed me a cup, already filled with something fruity. "Here, try this. It's good."

I took a sip, the sweet taste masking the burn of the alcohol. It wasn't bad. I took another, longer drink, feeling the warmth spread through me. One drink won't hurt, I told myself, taking a tentative sip. The alcohol burned a little, unexpected beneath the sugary taste, but I forced it down, ignoring the knot of discomfort in my stomach. This wasn't me. This wasn't who I was supposed to be. But I wanted to let go—to not think about what I should be doing, who I should be.

Just for tonight, I thought, ignoring the twinge of guilt tightening in my chest. *Just this once.*

As the night wore on, the drink in my hand kept getting refilled. At first, it was a conscious choice—a way to keep the anxiety at bay, to fit in with the others. But as the alcohol started to take effect, the edges of my worries blurred, and I found myself laughing more, dancing with Cassie, and even letting my boyfriend pull me into a slow, lazy kiss in the middle of the living room.

Finally, I wasn't thinking about the English test, or my mom's disapproving glare, or even the fact that I'd promised Aiden I'd play video games with him tonight. I was just… there, in the moment, having fun.

But as the night continued, I started to lose track of time—and of myself. My boyfriend's grip on me tightened as he led me away from the noise, his voice a low murmur in my ear that I couldn't quite make out. I was too far gone, my mind foggy from the drinks, my limbs heavy.

He guided me up the stairs, his hand firm on my arm, each step feeling unsteady beneath me. The hallway stretched endlessly, the dim light blurring at the edges of my vision. When we reached the bedroom, he shut the door behind us with a quiet click that echoed too loudly in my ears.

I stumbled as he led me forward, his control tightening. For a second, I thought he might help me sit down, but instead, his hands pushed me onto the bed. My body felt like it sank into the mattress too quickly, like the room itself was tilting. I tried to protest, but the words came out thick and slurred, sticking to my tongue.

Nothing made sense, but a quiet panic began to claw at the edges of my mind. His weight pressed down—heavy, unrelenting. My limbs refused to cooperate. I tried to push him back, but my arms felt like they belonged to someone else, sluggish and disconnected. His hands roamed, rough and insistent, and I could hear my own voice, small and trembling, begging him to stop.

But it wasn't my voice—not really. It was someone else's, faint and hollow, like it was coming from somewhere far away. The world around me blurred and dimmed, the edges of the room smearing together into a shapeless void. The walls weren't walls anymore; they were shadows, stretching and twisting, swallowing the space whole.

I stared at the ceiling, the light flickering overhead like it was struggling to stay on. My heart thudded in slow, heavy beats, the sound deafening in the stillness. Each one echoed, dragging me deeper into the void. I tried to move, to escape, but my body wouldn't listen. The panic clawing at me dulled into something quieter, heavier, like my mind had wrapped itself in layers of cotton to muffle the terror.

The further I slipped, the harder he pulled me down, his weight suffocating me, my consciousness drifting into oblivion. Everything felt unreal, detached, like I wasn't in my own body anymore. I was somewhere else, anywhere else. My mind spiraled away, but the faint pull of pain somewhere below lingered like a distant echo. The pressure pushed harder, rough hands tugging at fabric, and then...

Nothing.

My ears rang a deafening pitch. Tears welled up, sliding from the corners of my eyes as I squeezed them closed. *Keep your eyes shut, Jess. Don't look. Don't feel. When you open them again, this will all be over.* The thought whispered through my mind, weak and trembling, both a prayer and a lie.

I let myself drift, fading into the space between moments until I was nothing more than a ghost.

Then, the pressure lifted—yanked away with violent force. The room filled with a roar, Aiden's voice cutting through the haze. "What the hell are you doing? Get off her!" The words trembled with fury and panic. Air rushed back into my lungs as I gasped, trembling, and when I opened my eyes, the nightmare fractured, my brother at its center.

He stumbled back, cursing, but Aiden shoved him out of the room with a ferocity that made my chest ache. The door slammed, and suddenly it was just us. Aiden turned to me, his eyes wide, his face pale as though he didn't recognize what he was seeing.

I reached to adjust my skirt, but my hand froze. There it was—a smear of red against my leg, sharp and undeniable. The air fled my lungs as shame tore through my chest, fierce and all-consuming.

Aiden saw it too. His voice dropped to a whisper. "You're... bleeding."

I turned away, grabbing the pillowcase off one of the pillows. My fingers trembled as I pressed it to my leg, the stain disappearing into the fabric. But its weight stayed—vivid, permanent, scorched into my chest like a branding iron.

He just wanted to play video games. The bitter thought twisted through me. We could've stayed home, laughed, fought over controllers, stayed safe in that bubble we always had.

I failed him.

This is my fault.

I didn't dare look back at Aiden. If I met his eyes, I might shatter completely. My movements became mechanical, like cleaning up the evidence was the only thing holding me together. The pillowcase in my hands, the pressure against my leg—they were something to focus on. Anything but the rest.

"Let's just… go," I whispered.

Without another word, Aiden wrapped his arm tightly around my waist, practically carrying me down the stairs. The party continued around us, laughter and music filling the air, oblivious to the devastation that had just unraveled. But I couldn't focus on anything, couldn't hear anything, except the pounding need to escape.

As we walked out of that house, I felt like I was leaving a part of myself behind—a part I'd never get back.

We made it to my car, and I fumbled for the keys, my hands shaking so badly I could hardly hold onto them. I knew I couldn't drive—not like this. My chest heaved, the air feeling sharp and thin in my lungs, and the thought of sitting behind the wheel made my vision blur. Without a word, I handed the keys to Aiden. He hesitated for a split second, his eyes wide with uncertainty, but then he nodded, taking them from me.

"I'll get us home," he said, his voice steadier than I would've expected. "Just… try to breathe, okay?"

I nodded, sinking into the passenger seat as he started the car. I closed my eyes, willing myself to calm down, but the panic was still there, clawing at me from the inside.

The drive was a blur. I remember the headlights streaking past us, the hum of the engine, and Aiden's white-knuckled grip on the steering wheel. The adrenaline that had been holding me together was fading fast, leaving exhaustion and dread in its place. I tried to stay awake, to stay focused, but my body felt hollow, like the night had gouged me out from the inside, leaving nothing but a fragile shell behind.

Then, suddenly, everything went wrong.

There was a flash of light, a screech of tires, and the car jolted violently. The world spun around me, and then everything went dark.

When I came to, I was lying on the asphalt, the cool night air biting into my skin. I could hear sirens in the distance, growing louder with each passing second. I tried to move, but my body wouldn't respond. Panic flooded through me as I turned my head, searching for Aiden.

He was sprawled out a few feet away, motionless, his body twisted at an unnatural angle that made my stomach churn. His face was pale, ghostly under the harsh glare of the streetlights, and a dark pool of blood spread beneath him, seeping into the cracks in the asphalt.

"No, no, no," I whimpered, clawing at the ground to crawl toward him, but my arms wouldn't cooperate. "Aiden, please…"

A figure loomed over me, and the moment hands clamped down on my shoulders, my entire body recoiled. I flinched hard, a raw, instinctive panic tightening every muscle. "Miss, are you okay? Can you hear me?"

A flashlight pierced my vision, blinding me as it flicked from eye to eye.

I blinked up at the blurry face of a police officer, his voice distant, muffled under the pounding in my ears. "My brother…" I choked out, barely forming the words. "Is he… is he okay?"

The officer glanced toward Aiden, his expression grim. "Paramedics are on their way. Can you tell me what happened? Who was driving?"

The question sliced through the fog clouding my mind, and I froze. Aiden had been driving. He didn't have a license. He was hurt because of me—because I let myself be weak.

Guilt crashed over me, suffocating, relentless. My eyes locked on Aiden, his body broken and still, and I knew: if I didn't protect him now, I'd lose him completely.

"I was," I whispered, my voice shaking, barely audible. "I was driving."

The officer nodded, scribbling on a notepad, but his voice faded into static. My focus stayed on Aiden—on the rise and fall of his shallow breaths, the blood pooling beneath him, and the cold stillness of the ground beneath my knees.

The world blurred into a haze of flashing lights and urgent voices, but none of it mattered. I wanted to rewind time, to go back to the moment before it all went wrong, back to a time when I could still protect my brother.

But it was too late.

X X X X X X

Now

My heart raced as I looked up at Christian, bracing myself for some kind of reaction—judgment, disgust, anything to confirm the shame that had been suffocating me. The silence stretched unbearably, my chest tightening with each passing second.

Christian's eyes stayed locked on mine, his expression unreadable. I couldn't look away, even as every instinct screamed at me to retreat, to put up my walls again. Then he stepped closer, his movements slow and deliberate, his gaze softening in a way that felt both comforting and terrifying. My muscles tensed, a flicker of panic sparking before I could force it down.

He stopped just shy of touching me, his hand twitching at his side. His voice was careful, unsure. "Can I... can I hold you?"

The question caught me off guard, so unexpected that it took a moment to sink in—for my body to process his words. I stared at him, and for the first time, I felt like I was seeing the real Christian— the one hidden behind all the arrogance and sharp edges. After a moment, I gave the faintest nod, unable to trust my voice.

He stepped closer, his arms opening hesitantly, and for a second, I froze. I'd spent so long pretending I was fine, holding everything together so tightly, that letting someone in felt impossible. Slowly, I leaned into him, letting his arms wrap around me. His warmth slipped past the walls I'd built around myself, settling deep in the spaces I'd kept hollow, anchoring me in a way I hadn't realized I craved.

I buried my face in his shirt, my hands clutching at the fabric as if it were the only thing keeping me upright. His hand moved in slow, steady circles on my back, and I felt my walls begin to crumble, piece by piece.

The words came before I could stop them, raw and jagged, slicing through the quiet night. "It should've been me," I whispered, my voice cracking. "I should've been the one in that wheelchair, not Aiden." My throat tightened, but the confession kept pouring out. "It's my fault. I let him drive. I let it happen."

Christian's hold tightened, steadying me as I unraveled. "Jessica," he murmured, his voice gentle but firm. "You didn't—"

"They pushed him around, made fun of him, and he never said a word. He just... took it. And I couldn't stop it. I couldn't fix it."

The words spilled out faster now, each one dragging a weight I'd carried for too long. "I kept telling myself I was fine," I said, my voice trembling. "That I could handle it, that if I just smiled enough, laughed enough, no one would notice. No one would see how much I was falling apart—how every day felt harder, like I was barely holding it together." I let out a shaky breath, the words spilling out before I could stop them.

"And the worst part?" My voice cracked as I forced the words out. "I don't remember what it's like to feel anything but this—like the hurt isn't just inside me anymore, but *me*. That's all there is now."

I clung to Christian, my breath hitching as the tears I'd fought so hard to suppress finally broke free. He held me tighter, his silence steady, like he understood there was nothing he could say to make it better—but that didn't stop him from being there.

After a moment, he pulled back slightly, just enough so he could meet my eyes. His hands stayed on my shoulders, his touch grounding me, steadying me. "Jess," he said softly, his voice thick with emotion. "Look at me."

The words caught me off guard, familiar in a way that made my chest tighten. I froze, my instincts screaming to retreat—to shut down, to close my eyes and block everything out. "I can't," I whispered, my voice trembling.

"Yes, you can," he said, firmer this time, his hold grounding me. "You've spent so long trying to shut it all out, but you don't have to do that anymore. Not with me. Look at me, Jess. Please."

Slowly, hesitantly, I opened my eyes. My vision blurred with tears, but I locked onto his face—his own eyes glistening, his jaw tight, his expression raw and unguarded.

For a moment, the old instinct reared up again—the urge to disappear, to drift into that space where nothing could hurt me. But Christian's gaze held me there, steady and unrelenting, pulling me back into myself.

"It's not your fault," he said, his voice low but unwavering. The words came out like a promise, like he needed me to believe them as much as he did. "Not Aiden, not what happened, not your mom. None of it's your fault."

"You don't have to keep shutting your eyes and pretending it'll all go away," he said, his voice low but unwavering. "You're stronger than that. And you're not alone anymore."

I shook my head slightly, the guilt pressing harder against my chest, but Christian didn't look away. "Jess," he said again, making sure I'd heard it. "It's not your fault."

Something inside me cracked, the words breaking through the walls I'd spent so long building. My sobs came harder, wracking my body as the weight of everything I'd been carrying poured out in waves. Christian's arms were around me again, pulling me back into his embrace, and this time, I didn't hold back.

I didn't try to fix it. I didn't try to stop it. I let myself feel every single piece of it—the anger, the grief, the guilt, and the fragile, aching relief of not having to face it all...

Because I didn't have to do it alone anymore.

Christian

I'd only ever read about this kind of thing. Stories in books or articles that seemed distant, unreal, the kind of thing that happened to someone else, somewhere else. I could never imagine what it would be like to be in her shoes.

I looked over at her, her face relaxed in sleep, her cheeks still blotchy from crying. The streaks of tears on her skin had dried. She was curled slightly toward the window, her knees tucked up under her chin and arms wrapped around herself, like she was trying to hold herself together.

It was still dark out, the faintest hint of light peeking up from behind the hills. The truck somehow felt smaller, like last night had sucked up all the air leaving us suspended in time.

I'd always thought of her as strong, someone who never let anyone in, someone who had walls I could only ever tap at. But now I realized it wasn't strength that kept her locked away. It was this—this unbearable secret she'd been carrying on her own. And she let me see it. She let me hold it, even if just for a moment.

The thing that hit me hardest wasn't the car accident or even the assault—it was the way she'd looked at me afterwards. Like she was waiting for me to turn away, to judge her, to tell her she was broken. But I hadn't. I couldn't.

Because all I could see was her. Not her mistakes, not her past. Just her.

I wondered if she felt safe now. Safe enough to rest, to let go for a little while. Safe with me?

I leaned my head back against the seat. I hated feeling like this. Like there was nothing I could do to help. Like I was useless. There was a frustration simmering just below my skin, heating me from the inside out.

I wanted to do something—anything. If I could, I'd drive up to Riverview right now and beat the shit out of this guy. I could picture it so clearly—his face, his smugness, the way he thought he could just take something from her and walk away? My hands tightened into fists at the thought.

But what would that change? It wouldn't erase what happened. It wouldn't make her pain disappear. It wouldn't fix any of it.

And that was the worst part. Knowing that no matter how much I wanted to, I couldn't protect her from what was already done.

Jessica stirred beside me, her head shifting slightly against the window. Her eyes fluttered open, unfocused for a moment as if caught between a dream and waking. When her gaze landed on me, she smiled.

And just like that, the simmering anger inside me dissolved.

But then the moment cracked. The smile faltered, reality rushing in as her eyes widened. She sat up quickly, brushing her hair back with shaky fingers, glancing around the truck like she'd just remembered where she was—and why.

"Shit," she whispered, her voice hoarse. "What time is it? Did we stay out all night?"

I straightened, guilt creeping in at how peaceful she'd looked just seconds ago. "Yeah," I whispered. "You fell asleep."

Her hands fidgeted in her lap, twisting the hem of her sweatshirt. "I—" She paused, her throat working as she tried to find the words. "I didn't mean to—"

"It's okay," I cut in gently. "You needed it."

Her gaze snapped to me, and I could see the fear and frustration swirling in her eyes. "You don't understand. My mom…

she's going to lose it. After everything last night…" She bit her lip, a flash of bitterness in her tone.

I gave her a reassuring smile, trying to ease the tension. "I'll talk to her, explain what happened. You can blame it all on me."

Jessica's hands were trembling as she pulled her phone from her pocket, her fingers flying over the screen to check the time. "No. I just—I need to get home," she whispered, her voice tight with worry but edged with something else—a weariness, maybe. "She's going to think something happened to me."

I could see the panic settling in, and I knew she needed more than just words right now. "Okay."

Jessica gave a small nod, the tension in her shoulders slowly easing. She took a deep breath, trying to steady herself. "Thank you," she breathed.

I started the truck, the engine's low hum filling the space between us as we pulled onto the road. Jessica stared out the window, her face thoughtful, shadows flickering over her as the early morning light crept through the trees. Neither of us spoke, but it felt like words hung unspoken in the air, hovering just beneath the surface. My mind churned with questions, a current of curiosity and confusion rippling beneath the steady rhythm of the drive, yet something kept me silent, letting the weight of the night linger between us.

When we reached the front of her house, I reached for my door handle, but she stopped me. "It's probably better if she doesn't see you."

I nodded and let her exit my truck. As Jessica disappeared into her house, a part of me felt like I was abandoning her. The thought of her facing that house—facing her mom—alone, gnawed at me. She shouldn't have to go through this, not after everything she's been through.

I fought the urge to follow her inside and stand by her side. There was something in me that wanted to shield her from every ounce of pain she'd endured, something that went beyond just feeling sorry for her.

I couldn't say when it happened—when Jessica stopped being a rival and became someone I genuinely cared about. Her struggles weren't just background noise anymore; they stayed with me, an ache

I couldn't ignore. I wanted her to feel free, to finally breathe, to be okay. And the pull to stand by her, to be something steady in her life, ran deeper than I'd ever expected.

As I drove away, the image of her sleeping stayed with me. The fierce, determined girl I thought I knew had let her walls crumble, and for the first time, I saw her—really saw her.

Human. Struggling. Surviving. And somehow stronger because of all of it.

She'd trusted me with her secrets, looked at me like I was the only person she could rely on in that moment. And that was enough to make me realize something I hadn't expected. I wasn't just respecting her or admiring her anymore—I was falling for her.

Everything became crystal clear. I couldn't pretend anymore, couldn't keep dragging this out with Courtney when my head—and heart—were somewhere else. She didn't deserve that. She deserved someone who could give her everything, the way I couldn't.

The drive to Courtney's place felt like a journey in itself, the familiar streets suddenly foreign under the weight of what I was about to do. Every corner I turned, I couldn't shake the image of Jessica's face, the look in her eyes when she'd opened up to me. I'd been fooling myself, trying to act like nothing had shifted between us. But something had and I didn't want to hold on anymore.

When I arrived, I sat in the truck for a moment, trying to gather my thoughts. Courtney was still probably asleep, and part of me wished I could just leave things as they were. But I knew that was a coward's way out. I owed her honesty, even if it would hurt.

I knocked on her door, and after a few moments, her mom answered, still in her pajamas and robe, rubbing sleep from her eyes. "Christian, honey, what brings you by so early? Everything okay?"

Courtney's mom had always been kind to me, the kind of person who made you feel welcome just by the way she smiled. She'd treated me like family since the start, always quick with a warm hug or a plate of food whenever I visited. Her voice was gentle now, a small comfort in the middle of what I knew would be a rough morning.

"Yes, everything's fine," I told her as she let me into her house. "I just wanted to talk to Court real quick. Is she home?"

"Yep, she's probably still in bed. You can go ahead upstairs and wake her up for me."

"Thanks, Mrs. Sullivan," I said as I stepped inside, trying to keep my voice steady. My heart was already pounding in my chest, but I knew I had to do this. No more putting it off.

I headed up the familiar staircase, each step feeling heavier than the last. I paused outside Courtney's bedroom door, took a deep breath, and knocked gently.

"Courtney? It's me," I called softly.

There was a brief rustling from inside before I heard her voice, still groggy with sleep. "Come in."

I pushed the door open and stepped inside. Courtney was sitting up in bed, her hair tousled and her eyes half-open. When she saw me, a small smile tugged at the corners of her mouth, and she immediately pushed the covers off herself.

"Christian," she said, her voice softening. "Hey. Everything okay?" She rubbed her eyes, trying to fully wake up.

I stood by the door, unsure of how to start this conversation. Seeing her like this, still waking up, made what I had to do even harder. She swung her legs over the side of the bed and stood up, crossing the room to me. She reached out, placing her hand on my arm. Her touch was warm and familiar, but it didn't bring the comfort it once did. Instead, it only made the knot in my stomach tighten.

"Courtney," I began, but she cut me off before I could say more.

"Listen for a second," she said, her tone pleading. "I know things haven't been great between us lately, and I'm sorry for that. I've been so caught up in everything that I didn't stop to think about how you might be feeling." She stepped closer, her eyes searching mine. "We've been together for so long, Christian. We can get through anything."

Her words were laced with desperation, and it broke my heart to hear it. I took a breath and decided to try one last thing—one thing to see if she truly saw me. "Courtney, can I ask you something?"

She blinked, surprised. "Of course. Anything."

"Why do you think band is so important to me?"

The question caught her off guard, and she looked at me, clearly confused. "Band?" She hesitated. "Well… it's your thing. You're good at it, and it's what you love, right?"

I waited, holding onto the hope that she might say something more. Anything. But her silence filled the space between us, and I felt a pang in my chest. Anyone could have given that answer. My head dropped, a heaviness settling over me. "It's not just that, Court. There's so much shit going on at home and my parents rarely look up. It's like I'm a ghost. At least with band, people see me." I watched her, hoping for some flicker of understanding, some sign that she could see past the surface. "But you haven't noticed, have you?"

Her expression wavered, but there was no recognition, no depth to her response. She just looked at me, deer in the headlights, like she hadn't truly heard what I was saying. It hit me hard. She hadn't even noticed the strain I'd been under, the nights I stayed late at rehearsals just to avoid going home. This was supposed to be someone who knew me inside and out, but in that moment, I realized—maybe she never really had.

The realization hit me then, as hard as the words I knew I had to say. "Courtney," I said, stepping back. I took a deep breath, forcing myself to say the words I'd been dreading. "I think we need to break up."

The room fell silent. Courtney stared at me, her expression a mix of shock and disbelief. "Break up?" she echoed, as if she couldn't believe what she was hearing. "Christian, you don't mean that."

"I do," I said, hating the pain in her eyes. "I care about you, Courtney. I always will. But I can't pretend that things are the same between us. We've grown apart, and it's not fair to keep pretending."

Tears welled up in her eyes, and she shook her head, refusing to accept what I was saying. "No. We can work it out. Don't throw this away."

Her words tore at me, but I knew I had to stay strong. "I'm not throwing anything away. I just think it's time for us to move on."

Courtney's tears spilled over, and she reached out to grab my hand, holding on like it was her lifeline. "Please, Christian. Don't do this. We've been together for so long. You can't just end it like this."

I could feel the desperation in her grip, the weight of her words pulling at me, but I gently pulled my hand away. "I'm sorry, Court. I really am." My voice cracked on the apology, the ache in my chest growing sharper with every second that passed.

The silence stretched painfully between us, heavy with everything we weren't saying. Courtney's gaze searched mine, her tears shimmering under the soft morning light. For a moment, I thought she might say something else—beg, argue, anything to change my mind. Instead, her voice dropped to barely a whisper. "This isn't just about us, is it?"

Her eyes narrowed slightly, a mix of hurt and accusation flickering in her expression. "It's about her, isn't it? Jessica."

Her name hit me like a jolt, and for a second, I couldn't respond. The truth felt like it was written across my face, betraying every emotion I'd been trying to keep buried. But it wasn't as simple as Courtney thought. Jessica wasn't the reason I was ending things, not entirely. She was just... the mirror that made me see how far apart we'd grown.

Courtney let out a bitter laugh, wiping her tears angrily. "You're ending four years for someone you barely know. You're going to regret this, Christian. I promise you."

Her words stung, digging into me with more force than I'd expected, but I held my ground. "I'm sorry," I said again, hating how hollow it sounded, knowing it wouldn't ease the ache in her voice. But I couldn't bring myself to take it back.

She looked at me, and for the first time, there was no softness in her eyes—only betrayal and heartbreak. She seemed to search my face, maybe for a sign of regret or doubt. But whatever she saw must have confirmed her fears, because her gaze hardened, and she took a shaky breath. "Just go," she whispered, the finality in her voice slamming the door shut between us.

I hesitated for a moment, hoping for something, anything that might make this easier, but there was nothing. Turning, I walked out, the sound of her quiet sobs trailing behind me, echoing in the silence. And as I stepped out of her room, I felt the weight of what I'd just lost, even though a part of me knew it had been gone for a long time.

As I walked down the stairs and out of the house, Mrs. Sullivan called after me, "Everything alright, Christian?"

I paused at the door, turning back to her with a forced smile. "Yeah, everything's fine. Thank you, Mrs. Sullivan."

But as I stepped outside into the morning air, the weight of what I'd just done settled heavily on my shoulders. The early morning sun, usually a sign of a fresh start, felt almost mocking in its brightness. I took a deep breath, trying to shake the lingering ache in my chest, but it was no use. I knew nothing would be fine for a long time.

I couldn't help but think of Courtney, alone in her room, crying because of me. We had been together for so long that she had become a part of me—a part that I was now tearing away. The guilt gnawed at me, making me question if I'd made the right decision.

Courtney was my first love, the person who knew my quirks, my habits, the person I had shared so many memories with. She'd been there through my awkward high school moments, my wins, my losses, and now, here I was, walking away from all of it. Ending things with her felt like cutting off a piece of my own history, a part of me that had once felt like home.

But then Jessica's face flashed in my mind, the vulnerability she'd shown me, the way she'd trusted me with her pain. I couldn't ignore what I felt for her, this strange mix of protectiveness and something deeper that I couldn't quite define. It was like Jessica had opened a door to a part of me I didn't even know existed—a part that was willing to take risks, even if it meant breaking someone else's heart.

And yet, the uncertainty of what came next loomed over me. I didn't know where things would go with Jessica, or if she even felt the same way. All I knew was that the safety and familiarity I'd had with Courtney were gone, and I was stepping into uncharted territory.

I shoved my hands into my pockets, staring at the pavement as I walked to my truck. Each step felt like it was carrying me further away from the life I'd known. As much as I tried to reassure myself that this was the right thing to do, the emptiness that followed me out of Courtney's house told me otherwise.

As I sat there, staring at the dashboard, I realized that this wasn't just about breaking up with Courtney. It was about changing, about growing up, and about facing the uncomfortable truth that nothing in life was as simple as it used to be.

With a deep breath, I started the truck and pulled away from the curb. As I drove off, the weight on my chest didn't lift, but I didn't expect it to. Some wounds needed time to heal, and I knew I'd just opened one that would take some time to close.

Jessica

The dull hum of my homeroom class buzzed around me as I sat with my head resting on the cool surface of the desk, trying to drown out everything that had happened over the weekend. Memories I desperately wanted to forget kept looping in my head.

I just wanted to get through the day. Maybe if I kept my head down, everyone would leave me alone, and I could pretend that none of it ever happened. I glanced up at the clock and realized that there was still a quarter of an hour until class started, and the teacher wasn't even in the classroom.

The door was right there. I could just get up and leave; no one would even notice I was gone. Just for a few hours, I needed an escape.

The decision was almost instinctual. I began gathering my things, shoving my notebooks into my bag with a quiet urgency. The room was still mostly empty, just a few early risers lost in their own world. My heart pounded in my chest as I made my way to the door, my mind racing with the need to get out, to just breathe somewhere far away from here.

But as soon as I rounded the corner, I collided with a solid chest, sending my notebooks scattering across the floor. I stumbled back, my breath catching in surprise.

"Whoa, easy there," Christian's familiar voice reached my ears as he quickly knelt down to gather my fallen things.

"Sorry," I mumbled, trying to catch my breath. Of course, it had to be him.

He handed me my notebooks, his brow furrowing as he studied my face. "You okay, Welling? You look like you're about to make a run for it."

I straightened up, trying to hold on to some shred of composure. "I might be," I admitted, stuffing the notebooks back into my bag. "My mom already grounded me for staying out all night, so… what more can she do?"

Christian's eyes widened slightly in surprise, but then a slow smile tugged at the corners of his mouth. "Skipping school? Didn't think you had it in you."

"Yeah, well, maybe you don't know everything about me," I muttered, brushing past him and heading for the door. Just as I reached the front doors of the building, I stopped, a pull I couldn't explain making me turn back. Christian was still there, watching me with that familiar curiosity.

"Do you want to come with me?" The words slipped out before I could second-guess them. I half-expected him to laugh it off or come up with some excuse. Instead, his smile grew wider, his eyes bright with that spark of mischief.

A grin flashed across his face, and without a word, he stepped forward, catching up to my side. He reached over, smoothly pulling my backpack from my shoulder and slinging it over his own with a casual confidence. "Alright, let's blow this place," he murmured, nodding toward the parking lot.

Christian glanced at me as we reached his truck, keys already in hand. "Want me to drive?" I nodded, not trusting myself to speak. "I'm starving," he said as he pulled out of the school parking lot. "Let's grab some breakfast."

He leaned back in his seat as he drove, one hand loosely grasping the wheel while the other rested on the edge of the window. He tapped his fingers against the door in time with the beat of the music playing from the speakers, his head bobbing slightly to the rhythm. Every now and then, he glanced over with a relaxed smile.

We pulled up to a charming, old-school diner with a neon sign that read "Sunny Side Up Café." A place that looked like it hadn't changed since the 70s. Christian parked the truck and held the door open for me as we walked inside.

The diner had an old-school charm—checkered floors, red vinyl booths, and the rich scent of bacon and coffee filling the air. Sliding into a booth, Christian sat across from me, his smile easy and unguarded.

As we waited for our food, conversation flowed naturally. Christian lit up talking about jazz and how it had inspired him to pick up the trumpet, while I confessed my quirky obsession with collecting marching band pins at competitions. It felt effortless, like peeling back layers we didn't realize were there.

When the food arrived—fluffy pancakes for me and a loaded plate of bacon, eggs, and hash browns for him—we dug in, the world outside fading into the background.

Between bites, the talk deepened. Christian shared pieces of his strained relationship with his dad, how work always came first, and the way Mr. Trust had become something of a surrogate father figure. I watched his walls lower, his usual confident air softening into something more vulnerable.

"Honestly," I said, sipping my coffee, trying to keep it light, "I used to think you were such a kiss-ass to Mr. Trust. I didn't realize he meant so much to you." I smiled, but Christian's steady gaze held mine, like he could tell there was more I wasn't saying. I hesitated, glancing down at my coffee cup.

"I get it, though. It's... hard when you're looking for something that isn't there, you know? Someone who's supposed to see you, really see you, and they don't." Christian's gaze softened. "I keep bending over backward, trying to get her approval. And it's like, no matter what I do, it's never enough."

"Maybe we're more alike than we thought," Christian murmured, a slight smile touching his lips. A flicker of understanding passed between us, a mutual recognition of the weight we each carried, shaped by expectations and disappointments. It didn't need to be said outright, but in that moment, we saw each other more clearly than anyone else ever had.

For just a split second, I saw a serious tone in his eyes, like he wanted to say something deeper. But he quickly shook his head. "Where are you thinking of applying to college?"

I sighed, the knot in my chest tightening. "I really haven't thought about it much. My mom keeps bringing up the essays, like every day, but it's hard to focus with everything else going on. I guess I should start soon, though."

Christian tilted his head, studying me. "You don't sound too convinced."

I hesitated, my fingers fidgeting with the hem of my sleeve. The words hovered at the edge of my tongue, and before I could stop myself, they tumbled out. "Sometimes I wonder if it's even worth it, you know? The whole college thing. What if I don't get in anywhere? Guess I'll just live in a practice room somewhere and haunt the place."

He frowned. "Why wouldn't you?"

I gave him a pointed look, my voice quieter now. "Come on, Christian. You know why. Colleges don't exactly love a DUI on a transcript."

The softness in his gaze caught me off guard. "That's not who you are, Jess. It's something that happened, yeah, but it doesn't define you. And if they can't see that, then they don't deserve you."

I swallowed hard, his words settling in places I hadn't let myself acknowledge before. "Maybe. But it still feels like something I can't outrun. Like no matter what I do, it's always going to be there. I'm basically a walking red flag."

Christian pressed his lips together sympathetically, his gaze steady. "Yeah, I get that. But once you start, it'll come together. You're good at this kind of thing."

I rolled my eyes. "Fine. How about you?"

He shifted slightly in his seat when I turned the question back to him. "UCLA, probably. Music education. I'd love to teach high school music."

I couldn't help but smile. "I can really see you doing that," I said, meaning it. "You'd be great at it."

His grin widened, a flicker of pride lighting up his face. "Yeah, it's one of the few things that really gets me going. Teaching and making music—that's where I see myself. It's one reason I love being drum major."

With our plates cleared and the check paid, Christian stood up and stretched. "Ready for our next adventure?"

I nodded, feeling a lightness in my chest that had been missing for days. "Definitely. What did you have in mind?"

Christian's eyes twinkled with mischief as he said, "How about a drive to the beach?"

I blinked, feeling a rush of excitement I hadn't expected. The thought of seeing the ocean stretched out endlessly before me, feeling the warm sand between my toes, and breathing in that salty air for the first time made my pulse race. "Let's go," I said, unable to hide my eagerness.

The drive to the beach felt like a slice of freedom I hadn't known I needed. The world outside blurred into a wash of palm trees and sunlight, a carefree rhythm pulsing through every mile. Christian's playlist of swingy jazz and upbeat pop set the perfect backdrop, like a soundtrack for a day that was all ours. We sang along to the familiar tunes, our voices clashing and blending in a way that felt perfectly imperfect. Laughter spilled out of me without restraint, filling the car, mingling with the music.

When we arrived at the beach, the vast expanse of sand and the gentle roar of the ocean were a stark contrast to the confined space of the diner. We stepped out of the truck, the salt air filling our lungs and the warmth of the sun on our skin. We strolled along the shoreline, our feet sinking into the cool sand. The waves lapped gently at our toes, and for a while, the world felt like a distant, hazy dream.

Maybe if we'd met a few years ago, before that summer, things would've been different. Back when I wasn't so guarded, before everything shifted, we might've skipped the rivalry, the bickering, the walls I built to keep people out. We could've gone straight to this— two teenagers ditching class, shedding expectations, and savoring the rare freedom of an afternoon where everything felt easy and uncomplicated.

The sand cooled beneath us as we settled in, the only sounds the gentle crash of waves and the occasional cry of a seagull. The horizon stretched endlessly ahead, and for a moment, it felt like we were cut off from the rest of the world, the chaos and noise left behind. Christian picked up a stray shell and turned it over in his hands, the edges catching the sunlight.

"My parents are getting a divorce," he said suddenly, his voice low, almost swallowed by the steady rhythm of the waves.

I froze, the words breaking through the stillness like a crack in glass. I turned to him, my chest tightening at the raw edge in his tone. He wasn't looking at me—his eyes were fixed on the ocean, his fingers absently rolling the shell back and forth.

His jaw was set, but his shoulders slumped just enough to betray the weight he was carrying. I wanted to reach out, to offer the same comfort he'd given me that night when I'd fallen apart. But something in the way he gripped that shell, like it was the only thing keeping him tethered, told me he needed the space to let it out first.

He continued, his gaze fixed on the horizon. "It's been rough. My dad's always been so focused on work, and now, with the divorce, it's like he's a ghost in our own house."

He hesitated, his jaw tightening as he looked down at the sand. "And my mom... she's been having an affair. For a while now. I found out months ago, but I never said anything." A bitter chuckle escaped him. "Guess it wouldn't have mattered anyway. She pretends like we don't know, like she's still this perfect wife and mom, but I see right through it."

There was a pause, and I noticed the raw hurt in his eyes, a look that made my chest ache. "It's like they've both checked out," he continued, his voice barely above a whisper. "My dad's always at the office, and my mom's out with... whoever. And I'm just there, caught in the middle, pretending it doesn't bother me, like I'm fine with it all falling apart."

The weight of his words settled around us, mixing with the quiet crash of the waves. I could feel the anger and loneliness radiating off him, the unspoken pain of feeling abandoned by the people who were supposed to be there for him. The hurt behind his guarded expression was palpable, and I realized how much he'd been holding in, how deeply he'd been affected by the secrets and lies unraveling his family.

"That's why I spend so much time at school and band practice," he continued. "Anything to not be home, you know?"

A pang of recognition surged within me. I knew exactly what he meant—the way he buried himself in band, in the one place that felt steady, familiar, safe. I'd done the same, finding refuge in routines, in the spaces where I could forget everything that haunted me. "It makes sense," I said, my voice soft but sure. "It's like band is your anchor. A way to shut out the chaos. Something solid to hold onto when everything else feels... out of control."

Christian turned to look at me, his gaze holding mine with an intensity that made my chest tighten. For a split second, his eyes went soft, vulnerable, and I saw it—a flicker of relief, like he'd finally been seen after hiding in plain sight for so long. There was an unguarded rawness there, a look that said, You see me.

He chuckled, the sound a mix of disbelief and something heavier, tinged with a hint of bitterness. "Yeah, I guess you could say that. It's a good way to keep everything... manageable." He paused, studying my face as if he was searching for a part of himself there. "I'm assuming it's the same for you?"

I nodded, feeling a subtle shift between us, like we'd crossed an invisible line. "Yeah... it is. More than I'd like to admit."

We both drifted into silence, letting the steady pulse of the waves fill the space between us. Christian finally broke the silence, his tone lighter but still thoughtful. "Thanks for listening. It's nice to talk about it with someone who gets it."

"What? You don't talk about this kind of stuff with your girlfriend?"

He seemed to hesitate for a moment, like he wanted to tell me something, but didn't. Instead, he shook his head and just replied with a short, "We used to."

We sat together, letting the calm of the ocean and the warmth of the sun wash over us. The conversation had opened up an additional layer of our relationship, and as the day wore on, it felt like we were finding comfort in each other's company.

Christian glanced at his watch. "Alright, we still have some time. Where to next?"

I thought for a moment, a few ideas flitting through my mind. "How about we check out that music shop down the street? I saw it when we drove by."

He grinned, clearly excited about the idea. "Sounds perfect."

We arrived at the music shop and were immediately greeted by the sight of shiny brass and polished wood. The store was lined with an impressive array of instruments, each one more expensive than the last. I found myself gravitating towards the wall of trumpets, my eyes widening at the sight of several thousand-dollar pieces.

Christian joined me, his gaze appreciative. "You really know your stuff, don't you?"

I nodded, tracing a finger along the sleek, gleaming surface of one particularly beautiful trumpet. "I've always dreamed of owning one of these. But they're way out of my budget."

As I picked up a trumpet mouthpiece, I felt a wave of dorky enthusiasm wash over me. It was ridiculous, really, to admire something so small, but it felt good to indulge in my passion without the usual judgment. "This one," I said, holding it up proudly, "is the exact model I've been wanting to get. Feel it." I passed the mouthpiece to Christian.

"It's heavy," he said, examining it with genuine interest, not a hint of ridicule in his expression. He flipped the tag around to see the price and let out a low whistle. "Holy shit, that's expensive. It's beautiful; I can see why you'd want it."

After a few more minutes of admiring the instruments, we decided to split up for a bit. Christian headed towards the back of the store while I slipped next door into a record shop.

As soon as I stepped inside, I was greeted by the soothing strains of jazz wafting through the air. I browsed the vinyl records, my eyes scanning the racks for something special. My heart skipped a beat when I spotted a record featuring Chet Baker, one of Christian's favorite jazz trumpeters. The album cover was iconic, and I knew it would be the perfect gift for him.

I carefully picked up the vinyl, cradling it as if it were a treasured find. The thought of surprising him filled me with warmth, and I couldn't help but smile at the idea of giving him something that would resonate with his passion. With a sense of excitement bubbling inside me, I headed back to the music shop to find Christian.

He was by the front counter, engaged in conversation with the worker, his enthusiasm evident. I approached him quietly, giddy with the secret gift tucked safely in my backpack, knowing he was someone who would appreciate the thought behind it just as much as I appreciated him.

As we drove back towards the school, I couldn't help but feel a sense of contentment. The day had been unexpected but perfect in its own way. It was nice to have these moments with Christian, to connect and share our passions.

We parked in the lot, waiting for the final bell to ring, sharing a bag of M&M's we'd gotten on the way back. The school was gradually emptying, and the shrieking sound of the end of the day echoed through the hallways. Streams of students began flooding through the exit, their chatter and laughter filling the air.

"Thanks for today," I told Christian sincerely. I didn't want our adventure to end quite yet. "I really needed this."

Christian gave a slight nod, his expression thoughtful. "I'm glad you enjoyed it. I had a great time too."

He hesitated for a moment, as if deciding whether to broach a sensitive subject. "There's something I've been meaning to ask you. You don't have to answer if it's crossing a line," he said, finally. "But what do the doctors say about Aiden's condition? Is he permanently in the chair?"

The question hung between us, and I could see the genuine concern in his eyes. I took a deep breath, gathering my thoughts. "His doctors said he can learn to walk again, but it's more about his own motivation. Aiden hasn't really shown much interest in physical therapy. It's like he's given up."

Christian's brow furrowed in sympathy. "I want to help… I mean, if you'll let me. My uncle, Jacob, he owns a gym in town that's specifically caters to people with disabilities. He was a physical therapist and an orthopedic doctor before he opened the gym. He's incredible at what he does."

My eyes widened in surprise. It sounded amazing, but getting Aiden to agree was another thing.

Christian nodded, a hopeful look in his eyes. "Yeah, he's great. I think he could make a real difference to Aiden. Maybe if you and Aiden are interested, you could come by and meet him. He might provide some new insights or motivation?"

I felt a spark of hope at his offer. "You'll have to ask him. I've tried to get him out of the house. Trust me, it won't be easy."

"Okay, let's go."

"Wait, right now?"

"Yes!" Christian exclaimed, already hopping out of the truck. His enthusiasm was almost infectious. "Let's go find your brother."

We hurried across the parking lot and onto the campus, Christian leading the way with a determined stride. The once-bustling area was quieting down as students dispersed. I scanned the surroundings, searching for Aiden.

We rounded the corner by the gym, and my heart dropped like a stone. Aiden was there, backed against the wall, his wheelchair pinned by a group of boys. Their voices were loud, taunting, filled with a cruel edge that made my stomach twist. I could see it in Aiden's face—his wide eyes, the way his hands squeezed the armrests—he was scared.

I froze. My breath caught, my legs locking beneath me as if they'd forgotten how to move. I wanted to rush in, to yell at them, to do something, but all I could do was stand there, my fists clenching uselessly at my sides. A flood of memories rushed in, my mind spiraling back to moments when I'd felt this same helplessness. My pulse roared in my ears, drowning out everything else.

And then Christian was moving.

"Hey!" His voice cut through the air like a whip, sharp and commanding. It snapped me out of my daze, and I watched as he strode toward the group, anger radiating off him like a storm. He shoved one of the boys hard, his movements quick and deliberate.

The group turned toward him, startled. "Who the hell are you?" one of them sneered, but Christian didn't hesitate. His fist connected with one of the boys' faces with a loud, sickening thud, the force of it jolting me into action.

I stepped forward, my legs finally cooperating, but I didn't get far before another boy swung at Christian, the punch landing squarely on his eye. Christian staggered back, gritting his teeth against the pain, but he didn't retreat.

Before the fight could escalate further, a teacher's booming voice cut through the chaos. "What's going on here?" The words rang out, freezing everyone in place.

The boys scrambled, their bravado dissolving as they darted away, their laughter hollow as they retreated. Christian slumped back against the wall, panting, his hand pressed to his swelling eye.

I ran to Aiden, dropping to my knees beside him. My hands trembled as I reached for his, my voice shaky. "Aiden, are you okay?"

He nodded slowly, though his hands still clutched the armrests tightly. "Yeah," he said, but his voice was small, shaky. "I'm fine. Can we just… go home?"

Christian approached us, his steps slower now, his face a mix of pain and defiance. "You good?" he asked Aiden, his voice gentler than I'd ever heard it. He crouched slightly, meeting Aiden's eyes. He nodded again, but Christian's gaze lingered, a fierce protectiveness in his expression.

I turned to Christian, my voice barely above a whisper. "Thank you," I said, the words heavy with a mix of gratitude and guilt. "I… I didn't know what to do."

Christian exhaled slowly, the adrenaline fading as he touched his bruised eye and winced. "It's fine," he muttered, his tone firm but gentle. "You shouldn't have to." His gaze flicked back to Aiden, his jaw tightening. "It's messed up," he said, his voice low. "People like that… deserve a fist to their face sometimes."

His knuckles were red and swollen, the fight's impact etched onto his skin. But his expression—an unyielding determination—made it clear just how far he was willing to go to protect the people he cared about, even recklessly and impulsively.

As the commotion died down, Christian walked with us to my car, his face taut with the strain of the fight. A pang of guilt hit me for freezing earlier, for not stepping in when Aiden needed me. But Christian had acted before thinking, his impulsiveness leading him into a situation I hadn't been brave enough to face.

I moved with practiced ease, gently supporting Aiden as I helped him shift from his wheelchair into the car. My hands were steady on him, careful and sure, like I'd done this a thousand times. I bent down to his level, meeting his gaze. "You sure you're okay?"

He nodded. Once he was in his seat, I double-checked his seat belt, making sure he was comfortable before I closed the door. It was second nature by now, a ritual that I took seriously every time.

But as I looked up, I noticed Christian watching. There was something in his expression I couldn't quite place—a quiet attention. He was seeing me in a way he hadn't before, witnessing this part of me I didn't always show. With Aiden, there was no pretending, no hiding. Just me, and this fierce need to make sure he was okay. And maybe Christian could see that too.

"Let me help you with that," Christian offered, his voice softer now, though there was still a hint of strain from the earlier altercation. He helped with the wheelchair, folding and gently placing it in the trunk.

Once everything was sorted, Christian turned to Aiden, who was sitting in the passenger seat, his expression a mixture of shock and grudging gratitude. "Hey, Aiden, I know this might not be the best time, but… I wanted to ask if you'd be interested in meeting my uncle."

Aiden's brow furrowed. "Your uncle?"

"Yeah, he owns a gym in town. He used to be a physical therapist and an orthopedic doctor. He's really good at what he does, and I've seen him do a lot of amazing things with people who thought they wouldn't walk again."

Aiden glanced at me, then back at Christian, his eyes thoughtful. "I don't know." There was a moment of silence, and I could see the wheels turning in Aiden's head. Finally, he let out a slow breath, his shoulders relaxing. "Alright. I guess I'm willing to give it a shot."

"Great," Christian said, a look of relief crossing his face. "We'll set something up then. I'll give my uncle a call and I'll get back to you."

As I closed the trunk, I glanced over at Christian, feeling a mix of relief and gratitude. The day had turned chaotic, but his support had been unwavering. We drove away from the school, the tension from the earlier confrontation slowly melting away.

Aiden was waiting inside the car, blasting music on the radio, leaving me a moment alone with my co-drum major. "You are full of surprises, Gutierrez."

Christian gave a lopsided grin, wincing slightly as he adjusted his position. "What can I say? I like to keep things interesting. You never know, I might have a few more tricks up my sleeve—though I'll admit, I didn't plan on getting into a fight today."

"Yeah, that wasn't exactly on my agenda either," I said, shaking my head. "You really didn't have to go all superhero on us."

He shrugged, a playful twinkle in his eye despite the pain. "I've got a soft spot for dramatic entrances, remember? Keeps life from getting boring."

As he smiled, I noticed the purple-ing around his eye, now darkening and swelling. Without thinking, I reached up, my fingers brushing the bruise softly. The moment my fingers made contact, there was an electric jolt between us, a tangible spark that made my breath catch. Christian's gaze met mine, and for a heartbeat, the world seemed to shrink down to just the two of us.

I pulled my hand back abruptly, my heart racing as I tried to make sense of the intense, unexpected feeling. Christian still had a girlfriend, and this unspoken connection felt like a line I shouldn't cross.

"Sorry," I said quickly, looking away to hide my flushed cheeks.

"No, it's okay," Christian said softly, his voice carrying a warmth that made me shiver despite myself.

"See you tomorrow," I quickly said, already retreating to the driver's side door.

I got back into the car, the music still blaring from the speakers, but the atmosphere between us had changed. I caught Aiden staring. "What?"

"Nothing," he teasingly smiled. "I haven't seen you smile that much before. You like him."

I nervously laughed. "No, I don't."

Yes, I do.

Christian

I watched Jessica's car disappear down the street, the taillights fading into the night. Aiden had barely looked at me as I helped him into the passenger seat, his shoulders hunched in silent humiliation. Jessica had murmured a quiet, "See you tomorrow," before she climbed into the driver's seat.

Now, standing alone in the empty parking lot, I couldn't move. My knuckles ached, the sting of each punch still fresh, but it was nothing compared to the mess in my head. The fight had felt justified—necessary—but as the adrenaline faded, a familiar weight pressed down on me. My dad's voice echoed in my mind, slurred and harsh, dredging up memories I couldn't escape.

I flexed my hand, staring at the dried blood on my knuckles. This wasn't who I wanted to be. Yet here I was, giving in to the same volatile anger I'd sworn to avoid.

Jessica's touch had stopped the rage cold. Her fingers had brushed the bruise near my eye with a gentleness I didn't deserve, and in that moment, the fury had melted into something quieter. She didn't look at me with judgment or fear—just concern. Like she saw someone worth saving, even when I couldn't see it myself.

And now, standing here with the memory of her touch still

fresh, I hated that she'd seen this side of me. Hated that her kindness had been wasted on someone who couldn't stop himself from falling into the patterns he despised.

I thought about my dad—the way he'd lash out, punching walls, yelling at no one. I'd told myself I'd never be like that. But wasn't this the same? Letting the anger control me instead of the other way around?

Jessica was the difference. She reminded me of who I wanted to be—not this. Not the guy throwing punches in a school hallway.

The fight was over, but the weight of it lingered, heavy and suffocating. I didn't want to carry this anger anymore. I didn't want to be my father's shadow. But I didn't know how to let it go.

x x x x x x

The week had been a whirlwind, and standing in the middle of Jacob's gym, I couldn't help but feel proud of what my uncle had built. This place was electric—the hum of energy, sleek equipment, and motivational quotes painted boldly on the walls. But it wasn't just the vibe; it was the people. Everyone here was working toward something, no matter where they were starting from. I hoped Aiden would see that.

Jacob greeted us at the door, his grin as wide as ever. He pulled me into a bear hug, his hand thudding against my back. "There's my favorite nephew."

"Pretty sure I'm your only nephew," I shot back, laughing.

"Which makes it easy," he quipped, before turning to the others. His gaze softened as he took in Jessica and her mom, and then Aiden, sitting in his wheelchair. "You must be Aiden," he said, crouching slightly to meet Aiden at eye level. "And you're Jessica. Welcome."

Jessica nodded, her smile polite but tight. Their mom stepped forward, her own posture stiff, but her voice softened when she introduced herself. "I'm Claire," she said. "Thank you for letting us come here. This means... it means a lot."

Jacob waved off her thanks with his usual ease. "No need to thank me yet. We're just getting started." He looked back at Aiden. "You ready for a tour?"

Aiden hesitated, his hands resting on his lap. Then he gave a small nod. "Yeah."

The gym was more than I could've explained when I pitched the idea to Jessica—it was a place that breathed hope into people. Jacob showed off the accessible machines first, ones modified for all abilities, and walked Aiden through how they worked. He explained every detail like it was second nature, never talking down to him or making it feel like charity. "This is about finding what works for you," Jacob said, his tone calm but full of conviction. "No pressure, no rush. Just one step at a time."

I hung back a little, watching as Aiden started asking questions—real ones. His voice wasn't hesitant anymore, and he seemed genuinely curious, even leaning forward in his chair as Jacob talked about programs he'd developed for clients who'd faced similar challenges.

Jessica's mom stayed close, her hands clasped tightly in front of her. She watched everything with an almost desperate intensity, like she was afraid this small glimmer of hope might slip away. I could see how much she wanted this for Aiden—for all of them. When Jacob demonstrated a machine that Aiden could use to work his upper body, her lips trembled slightly. She blinked fast and smiled, clinging to Jacob's every word.

But it was Jessica who caught my attention. She stayed close to Aiden, her hand brushing the back of his chair like she needed that small connection to keep herself steady. She didn't say much, but I could see her eyes shifting as Jacob spoke. That flicker of hope was there—small and cautious, but it was there. It softened her expression, loosened the tension she usually carried like armor.

Jacob led Aiden to an open space where clients worked on balance and movement. He knelt again, meeting Aiden's eyes. "You don't have to have all the answers today. Just show up, and we'll figure the rest out together. Sound fair?"

Aiden nodded, his lips twitching into a faint smile. "Yeah. Sounds fair."

The grin on Jacob's face could've lit up the whole room. "Alright then. Welcome to the team."

Jessica's mom finally let out a shaky breath, her voice cracking. "Thank you, Jacob. You have no idea what this means to us."

Jacob smiled at her.

As the tour continued, I noticed Jessica steal a glance at her mom. Maybe she wasn't used to seeing her mom so emotional—so unguarded. Whatever it was, Jessica's gaze softened briefly before she quickly looked away.

By the time we wrapped up, Aiden's whole posture had shifted. He sat taller in his chair, his grip on the armrests looser. The weight he'd been carrying didn't look so heavy anymore. And when Jacob clapped him on the shoulder, he smiled—a real, hopeful smile.

We walked back to the car in silence, but it wasn't heavy. It was… peaceful, like something had shifted. Jessica helped Aiden into the car with her usual ease, double-checking his seatbelt like she always did. I caught her brushing her hair back and glancing out at the gym one last time, that flicker of hope still lingering in her eyes.

As her mom got into the driver's seat and Aiden fiddled with the radio, Jessica lingered by the trunk with me. She glanced at me, her expression unreadable, and then, quietly, she said, "Thanks for this. For Aiden."

Her voice was soft, but there was something raw in it, something that made my chest tighten. "He's got this," I said, nodding toward the car. "And so do you."

Her lips twitched into the smallest of smiles before she turned to join her family. As they drove away, I stood there with Jacob, watching the taillights disappear.

"Wow," Jacob murmured to me once they were out of sight. His eyes twinkled with mischief. "You've been looking at her like she hung the stars."

"What?" I scoffed, my face heating up. "No, I haven't. I don't even know what that means."

"Sure, sure," Jacob said with an exaggerated shrug, but the grin on his face said he didn't believe me. "Just saying, that's not how you looked at Courtney."

I groaned. "Can we not talk about Courtney?"

"Hey, I'm just making an observation," Jacob said, holding up his hands in mock surrender. "This one's different." He gestured subtly toward Jessica. "There's something about her. I can see it."

I frowned, not sure what to say. "She's… complicated."

Jacob chuckled. "The good ones usually are."

x x x x x x

The late afternoon sun dipped low, casting long shadows over the practice field as I climbed the podium. A gentle breeze rippled through the air, taking the edge off the relentless heat we'd endured all week. It was one of those rare days where everything just *felt* right. No chaos, no tension, just an unspoken determination humming through the band like electricity.

Jessica was already on her podium across the field, her posture straight and focused as she fiddled with the megaphone in her hand. For once, there wasn't a hint of tension between us. No sharp words or sideways glares. Just two drum majors ready to lead.

"All right, everyone," I called out, my voice carrying over the quiet murmur of the band. "Let's run the opener from the top. Set yourselves. We'll try running it at tempo this time."

The musicians and guard shifted into position, their movements precise. The wind carried the faint rustle of sheet music and the metallic clink of instruments being adjusted. I looked over at Jessica, who gave a quick nod, her hand poised over the microphone button to give her own section their cue.

For a moment, I let myself take it all in—the lines of instruments catching the light, the guard's flags snapping into place, the drumline tapping out a steady cadence as everyone locked in. It was like watching the gears of a machine align, each part essential, each movement purposeful.

"Tempo's at 132," Jessica's voice came through the megaphone, steady and confident. "Let's make it sharp."

I smiled to myself. She'd come a long way since the start of camp. We both had.

Jessica raised her hands, waiting for the band to focus. The silence was almost reverent, the kind of quiet that buzzed with anticipation. We locked eyes across the field, and with a deep breath, we gave the downbeat together.

The opening notes swelled, rich and powerful, spreading out over the field like a wave. The woodwinds layered in next, their harmonies weaving effortlessly with the brass. The trumpets soared above it all, their sound bright and confident, while the drumline locked into the pulse with laser-like precision. Even the guard hit their marks with a kind of synchronized grace that seemed almost impossible a week ago.

For the first time, it wasn't just music. It was something bigger—alive, breathing, full of emotion and energy. Each note had purpose, every step landed with conviction. And Jessica and I were at the center of it, leading not as rivals but as partners.

"Great form on that arc, clarinets!" Jessica's voice rang out through the field. "Keep that alignment tight, guard—beautiful work on the flags!"

I echoed her, catching the other half of the band. "Trumpets, your release was clean—let's keep it consistent. Low brass, great power, but don't overblow. Keep it balanced."

The next transition hit perfectly. The entire ensemble moved as one, their steps crisp and the visuals seamless. Even the difficult tempo shift in the ballad came together like clockwork. I mirrored Jessica's cues for the crescendo, her timing spot-on, and I felt an odd sense of pride in how in-sync we'd become.

As the final note of the opener rang out, echoing into the stillness of the field, there was a moment where no one moved. The silence wasn't empty—it was full, charged, as if everyone on the field felt it too. This was what it was supposed to feel like.

"Reset," I called. The band was already moving back to their spots with quiet confidence, their focus unshaken.

On the sideline, Mr. Trust stood with his arms crossed, a satisfied smile tugging at the corners of his mouth. "That's what I've been waiting for," he said, loud enough for Jessica and me to hear. "You're not just conducting the music. You're *performing* it. And you're doing it together."

I glanced over at Jessica, and she was already looking at me, a rare smile on her face. It wasn't smug or competitive—just genuine, like she was finally letting herself enjoy this.

"All right, everyone," I called out, turning back to the band. "Take a ten-minute break. Then we'll run it again with the ballad and practice the podium switch. Let's keep that momentum."

As the band broke out of attention, the field scattered with water bottles and chatter. Jessica climbed back onto her podium, fiddling with her megaphone and wiping her face on the sleeve of her shirt. I jogged toward the backfield podium, already brimming with ideas for making the switch memorable.

Once I was at my podium, I grabbed the megaphone strapped to the side and raised it to my mouth. "Hey, Welling," I called across the field. My voice echoed, drawing the attention of a few band members still milling around. "You ready to see how a real drum major makes an entrance?"

Jessica's head snapped up, her eyes narrowing as she grabbed her own megaphone. "Oh, please," she said, her voice amplified and dripping with sarcasm. "You mean how a drum major sprains an ankle trying to show off?"

A ripple of laughter broke out from the band as I leaned against the railing of my podium, megaphone still in hand. "Bold words from someone whose last podium switch looked like she was descending Mount Everest."

Jessica smirked, leaning forward with her megaphone. "It's called precision, Christian. Not everyone feels the need to turn a simple move into a full Olympic event."

More laughter rolled through the field, and even the guard started turning their heads to watch the exchange. "Olympic event?" I shot back, grinning. "I'm going for gold here, Welling. Style points matter."

Jessica rolled her eyes but stayed in character, her voice coming through the megaphone loud and clear. "Well, don't let us stop you, Mr. Gold Medalist. Just make sure you don't trip and face plant—wouldn't want Romeo meeting his end before he actually meets his end."

The band roared with laughter now, and even I couldn't help but chuckle. "Hope you're ready, Welling," I called back, lowering the megaphone. "Because this is going to be legendary."

"Sure," she replied, her tone as dry as the summer heat. "Legendary in the 'how not to do a podium switch' instructional video."

"Alright, everyone," I said, raising my voice so the field could hear. "Positions for the opener. Let's make it count!"

Jessica adjusted her stance on her podium while I positioned myself at the backfield podium. The brass players whispered excitedly among themselves, clearly ready for some entertainment.

The band began the sequence, the music swelling with intensity as we conducted in tandem. I could feel the tension building, the energy coursing through the ensemble as we reached the crescendo. When the moment came, I leapt off the backfield podium, sprinting toward Jessica's.

But I couldn't resist. As I reached the edge of the podium, I ignored the ladder entirely and jumped, gripping the rail and pulling myself up in one fluid motion. A loud whoop rose from the band parents watching from the bleachers as I swung myself onto the platform. The podium wobbled slightly and Jessica adjusted her footing for balance while not missing a beat of her conducting.

The podium wasn't big enough for two, and for a moment, we stood facing each other, close enough that I could feel the warmth of her breath and see the flicker of a smile she was trying to hide.

Her gaze flicked to mine, her lips pressing into a line as she fought to maintain her composure. "Are you trying to make me fall, Romeo?" she asked, her voice low but still teasing.

"I thought you didn't fall," I returned, giving a subtle wink. I adjusted my grasp on the rail, conscious of how little space was between us. The faint scent of her shampoo lingered in the air—citrusy and subtle, almost unnoticeable, but it was there.

The band had gone still. Below us, the entire field seemed to be holding its breath. Every single eye was on us. Even the guard, usually animated during downtime, stood motionless, their flags drooping at their sides.

Jessica shifted slightly, her arm brushing against mine as she adjusted her stance. The warmth of her skin, even through the fabric of our sleeves, sent a jolt of awareness through me. I could feel her tension—not the irritated kind I'd been used to, but something softer, quieter, like she was just as aware of the closeness as I was.

"Christian," she murmured, her voice barely above a whisper, "are you going to count off the ballad, or are we just going to stand here and make everyone uncomfortable?"

Her cheeks had the faintest flush, and I could swear I saw a hint of nervousness flicker in her eyes. My own heartbeat thudded a little harder in my chest. I leaned forward, just enough to grab the megaphone resting at her feet, and let my lips curve into a smirk. "I don't know, Welling. Looks like the band's enjoying the show."

She rolled her eyes. "I need to get down and you're in the way of the ladder."

Maneuvering around, I let her pass. I raised the megaphone, turning toward the band with deliberate slowness, my grin widening as I saw the way they were all staring—some outright, others trying and failing to be subtle about it. "Alright," I said, my voice amplified across the field. "Get ready for the ballad. And for the record, no, I'm not giving anyone podium lessons after this."

That broke the tension. Laughter rippled through the ensemble, and Jessica shook her head, biting back a smile as she grabbed a flag, getting ready for the Juliet flag feature. I counted them off, my voice steady and commanding, and as the first notes of the ballad floated into the air, it felt like the moment had shifted. The energy was still there, but it was quieter now—more focused, more connected.

Jessica glanced back at me as the music swelled. There was something different in the moment, a softness in the air that hadn't been there before. The sharpness between us seemed to blur, shifting into something that felt less like rivalry and more like... something else entirely.

Jessica

The band room was buzzing with laughter when I entered after school had ended. It felt different somehow—relaxed, familiar. Most of the instruments were packed up and ready for the field, leaving behind a few random chairs and a circle of beat-up cushions that everyone had claimed as their makeshift hangout spot. I lingered by the doorway, unsure, watching Christian, Tracy, Alex, and Marcus sprawled out around the cushions, completely at ease. A part of me longed to step into that comfort, to feel like I really belonged.

"Hey, Jess!" Tracy's voice cut through my hesitation, waving me over with a grin. "Get over here—we saved you a spot."

I felt my heart do a little flip. They saved me a spot? I wasn't sure if they really had or if she was just being nice. But Christian did that head tilt, motioning me to join them. I sat down between Tracy and Christian, feeling a warmth on either side of me that I hadn't realized I was missing. Alex tossed a crumpled piece of paper at Christian, sparking a playful argument about the halftime routine, and Marcus jumped in with his usual jokes, pulling us all deeper into the conversation.

Christian leaned back, looking at me with a mock-serious expression. "Alright, real question," he said, pointing in my direction like he was about to uncover a major truth. "Best pep band song—go."

Alex didn't miss a beat. "Easy. *'Seven Nation Army,'* no question. Crowd goes wild every single time."

Tracy rolled her eyes. "Please, Alex. That's so predictable. You know nothing beats *'Sweet Caroline'*—especially at the chorus. Everyone loves a good 'bah-bah-bah!'"

Marcus snorted. "You're all wrong. It's *'Apache'*. Jump on it!" He hit the ground with his drumsticks, mimicking the cadence in the tune.

"You only think it's the best because it's drumline-heavy," Christian said. "The right answer is *'Tequila,'* but Mr. Trust doesn't let us play that anymore. Apparently, it's not 'school appropriate.'" Then all eyes turned to me. "Alright, Welling. Your turn."

I thought for a moment. "*'Final Countdown?'*"

Alex pointed at me, nodding approvingly. "Good choice. That's a classic."

"Solid pick," Marcus agreed, giving me a nod, then tapping out a quick rhythm with his sticks. "Epic intro, and it gets everyone hyped."

I laughed, feeling the warmth of their approval settle over me like a comfortable blanket.

Christian flashed me a grin, his eyes crinkling in that way that made it impossible not to smile back. "Guess we're adding *'Final Countdown'* to the list tonight," he said.

The others laughed, and Tracy threw a playful arm around my shoulders. "Welcome to the club," she said, grinning. "You officially have poor taste in pep band songs, just like the rest of us."

Just as the laughter began to die down, Courtney walked in, her gaze sweeping over us with a tight-lipped expression. Her eyes landed on Christian first, then shifted to Tracy's arm around my shoulders, and I saw a flicker of something cold in her eyes before she masked it with a smile.

"Well," she said, crossing her arms and leaning against the door frame. "Looks like I missed the exclusive invite to the 'bad taste in music' club."

There was a slightly forced brightness to her voice, her words floating into the room like a backhanded compliment wrapped in honey. I felt Tracy's arm tense slightly around my shoulder before she withdrew it, giving Courtney a brief smile.

"Oh, hey, Courtney," Tracy said. "We're just, uh, hanging out before the game, you know?"

Courtney's gaze flickered to me, then back to Christian. "Huh, weird. Didn't think I was missing out on the fun," she replied, a brittle smile tugging at her lips. There was something almost accusatory in the way her eyes narrowed, though she didn't say anything more.

Christian, though visibly uncomfortable, tried to keep things light. "Court, we were just debating the all-time best pep band song. Wanna weigh in?"

She shrugged, but her gaze didn't soften. "Nah, wouldn't want to intrude," she said lightly, her eyes lingering on Christian. "Looks like you're all having a lot of fun... without me." Her tone held a subtle edge, her words carefully chosen as her gaze flickered to me for a fraction of a second, then back to him. She offered a small, dismissive wave. "Enjoy, Christian."

A tense silence sat for a moment after she left. I shifted uncomfortably, feeling a pang of guilt, even though I wasn't sure I'd done anything wrong.

Christian's expression hardened. He stood up, brushing off the look of concern Tracy threw his way. "I'm gonna go talk to her."

I forced a nod, doing my best to sound nonchalant. "Yeah, of course. Take care of her." Of course he'd want to make sure she was okay. They were still together. Technically.

He hesitated, giving me a quick, unreadable look before he walked out. As soon as the door shut behind him, the group glanced at each other, and Tracy gave me a sympathetic look.

"Don't overthink it, Jess," she said, nudging me gently. "Don't let Courtney get to you. She can be a little... territorial, especially with Christian. But trust me, you belong here as much as anyone else."

I let Tracy's words settle, a warmth spreading through me as I looked around at the group. Alex had managed to swipe Marcus's drumsticks, grinning mischievously as he banged them against the edge of a chair in a chaotic, improvised rhythm.

"Dude, give them back," Marcus groaned, lunging to grab the sticks. Alex dodged him, holding them just out of reach.

"Catch me if you can!" Alex taunted, darting around the room with a dramatic flourish.

Tracy laughed and gave me a wink. "This is what we call 'peak band room entertainment.'"

I chuckled, feeling the last traces of tension slip away. "Guess I picked the right time to join the club."

Just then, Marcus managed to snag one of the sticks, while Alex held onto the other, tugging back and forth with exaggerated effort. Tracy clapped her hands like a referee. "Alright, alright, we've got a stalemate!"

Christian walked back in just then, glancing around at the scene with a raised brow. "Leave for two minutes, and chaos erupts."

Alex shot him a grin, finally releasing his grip on the drumstick. "Just keeping things lively."

Christian rolled his eyes, then turned to me with a subtle smile that softened his whole expression. "You survived?"

"Survived and thriving, apparently," I said, smiling back.

Tracy slung an arm over my shoulder, giving me a quick squeeze. "See? Told you—you fit right in, Welling. Now, someone hit play on 'Seven Nations Army.' I think it's time we warmed up with some unofficial pep band practice."

Alex jumped over to the speaker, scrolling through playlists until the familiar beat kicked in. Everyone grabbed their instruments, falling into sync as if it were second nature. The sound filled the room, and for the first time, I let myself fully be part of it, letting the music and laughter wrap around me.

X X X X X X

Tonight's game was a standard home game, but the atmosphere in the stadium was electric. The band's rhythms echoed through the stands, and the crowd was alive with anticipation. In the midst of the noise, Aiden was positioned in the front row of the bleachers, his wheelchair tucked comfortably against the railing. My parents had come along with him.

During the first half of the game, I caught Courtney shooting the dirtiest looks my way. That was nothing new. She'd been this way since learning about the whole Juliet ordeal, but there was something almost sinister with the way her eyes followed me tonight.

"You good?" Christian asked, standing beside me. We were stationed in front of the band in the stands. I nodded, trying to ignore the uneasy feeling settling in my stomach. I couldn't shake the sense that something was wrong.

The halftime show approached, and as we prepared for our performance, I felt a surge of nerves. The dress was beginning to feel tight around my abdomen, constricting my breathing. It wasn't just about performing well tonight; it was now about proving myself to my parents—especially my mother.

As we took the field, the stadium lights blazed down, casting long shadows that danced with our movements. The band's formation was sharp and precise, the brass section blaring confidently while the percussion drove a powerful rhythm. I could feel the beat of the drums resonating through my chest as we moved through our routine. Each step had to be perfect, each note flawless.

The music swelled, and we launched into the centerpiece of our show. The flags, twirling and spinning in synchronized arcs, created intricate choreography. The crowd's cheers and the roar of the band created a symphony of sound that wrapped around me, filling the stadium with energy. I focused on the performance, determined to keep my movements strong and my demeanor poised.

The extra pressure of having my parents watching was almost nauseating. I could see them in the stands, Mom's eyes wide with anticipation and Dad's stern gaze fixed on me. Every missed step, every wrong note felt magnified under their scrutiny. The desire to impress them, to show them that I was still capable of greatness despite everything, was a powerful motivator.

As we reached the climax of the show, I gave it everything I had. The routine was flawless, the music soared, and the crowd's reaction was electric. As the final notes rang out, I allowed myself a brief moment of relief as the cheers washed over us. The halftime show was over, and I had done my best.

With the performance behind me, I made my way over to Aiden, who was clapping enthusiastically. My parents joined us, and their smiles, though slightly strained, were encouraging. I tried to focus on the positive, on the pride I saw in their eyes.

As I walked past, I caught sight of Courtney once more. Her eyes were locked on me, a smirk playing on her lips. I forced myself to stay calm, but the unsettling feeling from earlier had returned, and I couldn't shake the sense of impending trouble.

I was pushing Aiden in his wheelchair when I heard her voice cut through the noise of the crowd. "Careful, Jessica. Wouldn't want your wheelchair driving skills to land you another DUI."

The words hit like a gunshot, sharp and unforgiving, slicing through the cheers and drumbeats around us. My heart slammed against my ribs, each beat pounding louder in my ears as the world seemed to tilt. The edges of the stadium blurred, the chaos of the halftime show fading into a distorted buzz.

The air turned heavy, suffocating, each cheer from the crowd twisting into something crueler, mocking. My grip on Aiden's wheelchair tightened, my knuckles aching as I tried to keep myself steady. But Courtney's words kept echoing, rippling outward like a wave of whispers that seemed to crawl into every corner of the band and guard.

I felt their eyes on me—sharp and cutting. Every glance was a judgment, every hushed murmur confirmation of what I already knew: they were all talking about me. The secret I'd buried, the one I fought to keep locked away, was out. Now, everyone knew.

The guard members exchanged looks, their flags forgotten in their hands, their expressions shifting between pity and something colder. Band members stood frozen, their stares darting toward me and then away, as though afraid to be caught looking too long. Alex's face hardened, his jaw tight as he shot daggers at Courtney. Tracy's mouth fell open, her eyes wide with anger, but neither of them could stop it—the quiet storm of judgment spreading like wildfire.

It was everywhere. There was no escape from it. The laughter and cheers of the crowd were nothing but noise now, blending into a suffocating hum that made the edges of my vision blur. My pulse thundered in my ears, drowning out everything else, except the weight of their stares.

Aiden's hand found my arm, steadying me. "Jessica, breathe," he said softly, his voice breaking through the chaos. "It's okay. Just ignore her."

But it wasn't okay. I couldn't ignore her. The truth was out, and there was no way to claw it back. It was all anyone would see now—the DUI, the failure, the mistake that I could never undo. My chest tightened, my breaths coming in short, panicked bursts. I couldn't stay here. Not like this. Not under their stares.

I turned abruptly, leaving Aiden in the stands as I stumbled away. My legs felt shaky, unsteady beneath me, but I didn't stop. I just needed to get away, to find somewhere—anywhere—where their eyes couldn't follow.

How did she know? Only two people in that stadium knew the full truth: Aiden, who would never tell another soul, and Christian… the guy who'd made it clear he wanted me gone from the beginning.

I felt a surge of anger. Had he really used my deepest mistake as ammunition?

"Jessica!" Christian's voice called out behind me, his footsteps following closely. His presence only heightened my anxiety. I didn't want to face him, not now, not with this swirling storm of emotions.

I was nearly at the band room, the cool air a stark contrast to the suffocating heat of the dress I'd been forced to wear. I wanted to tear it off, to disappear from this nightmare.

"Jessica!" Christian's voice was closer now, almost pleading. "I didn't tell her."

I never should have trusted him. I should have kept my secrets buried, just like I'd always done. I stopped abruptly, my hands grasping at the waist of the dress.

"How else could she have known?" I spun around to face him, my voice trembling with barely controlled anger. "Only two people knew—Aiden and you. So if you didn't tell her, who did?"

His jaw clenched, his fists hanging at his sides. "She had your school folder," he said through gritted teeth. "—your transfer papers, your grades. She showed it to me on the first day of school. I told her not to say anything, Jess."

"You knew?" My voice cracked as the words left my mouth. The weight of his confession hit me like a punch to the gut, knocking the air from my lungs. "This whole time? And you still acted like you cared? Was that all it was?" My breaths came sharp and ragged, each one harder than the last. "Is that why you sit with Aiden at lunch? Why you agreed to dinner with my family? Was it all just to dig up more about the DUI?"

Christian's eyes met mine, wide with something like desperation. "We only knew about the DUI, Jess. She doesn't know about the rest. I swear." His voice was quiet, almost pleading, but it only made the betrayal cut deeper.

"Well, congratulations," I shot back, my voice rising. "Now you have the whole story—the full, ugly truth." The anger and hurt I'd been holding in came spilling out, raw and unstoppable. "Do with it what you want. You wanted me out of your way, and now I'm giving you exactly that."

His eyes widened. "What are you talking about?"

"You heard me." I could barely keep my voice steady. "You win, Christian. I'm done. I quit."

His stunned silence was the last thing I saw before I turned back to the band room, the only place that felt like it might offer me some solace.

I quickly undressed from the tight, suffocating performance dress and stuffed it into my bag, my movements rough and impatient. I grabbed my things and stormed out of the band room, expecting to find Christian waiting for me outside.

But he wasn't there.

The night air was cool against my skin, but it did little to soothe the fiery frustration churning inside me. I trudged across the parking lot, my footsteps heavy and laden with anger. My mind was racing, a whirlwind of emotions and thoughts, and I was determined to get as far away from that stadium as possible.

When I reached my car, I stopped dead in my tracks. Leaning against the driver's side door was Emily—the new transfer student who had barely made a ripple in our otherwise chaotic world. She was already dressed out of the Arcana marching uniform into her own clothes.

"Emily?" I called out, confused.

She straightened up, her gaze meeting mine with an air of practiced ease. "I was hoping to catch you."

I frowned, the tension in my shoulders tightening. "Is something wrong?"

Emily stepped closer. "I should probably explain a bit. I'm

actually a senior at Kingston High. We've been keeping a close eye on Arcana's band, especially since we're planning to overhaul our show. Kingston's looking to shake things up for this season."

"Wait—what's going on?" I hadn't realized the extremity of the rivalry between the two schools. Was it really so competitive that they sent… spies? Even the thought of it was ridiculous.

Emily stepped forward, her expression serious. "Kingston's looking for people who stand out. I've seen you—drum major, guard, trumpet player—everything. You're a triple threat. I've already talked to the band director about you."

Her words cut through the stillness, and I could feel the sting of her offer cutting through my anger. "So, you're here to—what? Poach me?"

"I mean, after everything that happened in there," she motioned at the football stadium. "Wouldn't you want… a change of scenery?"

The idea of Kingston High actively seeking me out was both flattering and infuriating. "And you think offering me this opportunity is going to fix everything?"

Emily shrugged slightly, her gaze unwavering. "It's not just about fixing things—it's about taking a shot. I've seen what you can do, and Kingston's ready to give you a fresh start. Yeah, the rivalry's huge, but that's exactly why your talent would be a game-changer for us. We're rehearsing all weekend—why don't you come check it out and see what we're about?"

I stared at Emily, the words swirling in my mind as I tried to steady myself. Everything felt twisted after tonight. Christian's face, his excuses—they'd all left me feeling like someone had yanked the ground out from under me. Joining Kingston, leaving Arcana behind, would be the ultimate way to prove I didn't need him or anyone else. My hands tightened into fists at the thought. Christian thought he knew me so well, but maybe it was time to show him just how wrong he was.

"You don't owe them loyalty, Jessica, not after what just happened."

I stood there, the sting of Courtney's words and Christian's betrayal still fresh. Emily's offer felt like a lifeline, a way to claw back control. Maybe it was petty, maybe reckless—but it was mine.

Christian

The stadium lights dimmed as the last of the crowd trickled out, leaving the field bathed in the soft glow of the night. My heart was still pounding from the halftime show, but not for the usual reasons. Jessica's words kept echoing in my head, each one a dagger in my chest. I couldn't believe she thought I'd betray her like that. And Courtney—she had no right to throw Jessica's past in her face.

As soon as the game ended, I searched for Courtney. I found her by the concession stand, casually chatting with a couple of her cheerleader friends like she hadn't just detonated a bomb in the middle of my life.

I stormed over. "Courtney!"

She turned, her smile faltering when she saw the look on my face.

"Why the hell would you say something like that to Jessica?"

Courtney's eyes flickered with something—guilt, maybe, or just the realization that I wasn't playing around. She put on her usual innocent act, shrugging like it was no big deal. "I just made a little comment, Christian. If she can't handle that, maybe she shouldn't be drum major."

I stepped closer, lowering my voice to a dangerous growl. "You had no right, Courtney. That was none of your business."

She crossed her arms, her expression hardening. "She's hiding things, Christian. Don't you see that? She doesn't deserve to be up there with you. I was just looking out for you."

"She's not hiding anything," I shot back. "You're just pissed because I broke up with you, and now you're taking it out on her."

Her eyes flashed with anger. "This isn't about that. I'm doing what's best for the band, Christian. I'm doing what's best for us."

"There is no us." My blood boiled. "No, you crossed a line. You don't get to decide who's worthy and who isn't. And you definitely don't get to tear someone down just to make yourself feel better. You have no idea what she's been through!"

Courtney's face twisted with fury. "And you do? You're defending her now?"

I took a deep breath, trying to keep my voice steady. "This isn't about me, Courtney. This is about you being a spiteful, vindictive—"

"Don't finish that sentence," she snapped, stepping closer, her face inches from mine. "You don't know her."

"Yes, I do. Better than I knew you," I said coldly. "Leave her alone."

For a moment, we just stood there, glaring at each other, the tension crackling in the air between us. I could see the conflict in her eyes, the part of her that knew she'd gone too far, battling with the part that just couldn't admit it.

Finally, she scoffed and turned away. "Defend her all you want. But don't say I didn't warn you when it all falls apart."

I watched her walk off, the anger still burning in my veins, but underneath it was something else—something more painful. Disappointment. I'd thought Courtney was better than this, but maybe I was wrong.

Turning away from the emptying stands, I knew one thing for sure: whatever happened next, I wasn't going to let Courtney, or anyone else, tear Jessica down. Not if I could help it.

When I got home that night, I stared at my phone, the screen glowing in the dark room. I dialed Jessica's number, the familiar tones ringing in my ear, but they eventually clicked over to voicemail. I hung up, trying again, hoping—no, needing her to answer.

Nothing. I shot off a text, my thumbs tapping out a message I couldn't even find the right words for. The message sent, but the silence that followed was suffocating.

I tossed and turned in bed, the sheets tangling around me. Every time I closed my eyes, I saw her face—those green eyes, shattered and accusing.

My fault. She thinks it's all my fault. The thought twisted in my gut like a knife.

✗ ✗ ✗ ✗ ✗ ✗

Morning crept in too soon, and I dragged myself out of bed, the weight of last night still pressing down on me. At rehearsal that Saturday, I scanned the field for her. Her spot on the podium was empty, a glaring void against the backdrop of the band setting up. My stomach knotted tighter.

"Where's Jessica?" Mr. Trust's voice cut through the usual morning chatter. He frowned, his eyes scanning the group, clearly unsettled. "Anyone heard from her?"

Heads shook, mine included. The rehearsal started, but something was off, like the air was thicker, the music less vibrant. The usual energy was gone, replaced by a heaviness that clung to every note, every movement.

She had quit. She'd said she would, but I hadn't really believed it. Her absence sat like smoke or a dark cloud, a silent confirmation that she might have meant it. Mr. Trust's frown deepened with each passing minute, his worried glance at her empty spot making my heart sink further.

Monday came, the school day felt like an endless loop of empty hallways and meaningless conversations. I searched for Jessica in every corner, but she was nowhere to be found—not in our homeroom, not in any of our other shared classes. By lunch, the knot in my stomach had tightened, a persistent reminder that something was very wrong.

After school had ended, I spotted Aiden in the hallway, his wheelchair positioned by the lockers. I knew I had to talk to him, even if it meant facing the anger I could see simmering beneath the surface.

"Aiden," I called out, walking over to him. He didn't look up, but his grip on the phone tightened.

"Oh, look who it is." His voice was cold, dismissive, like he'd already decided I was the last person he wanted to see.

"How's Jessica? She didn't show up to rehearsals, and she's not here today. I'm worried."

Aiden's gaze finally met mine, his eyes blazing with accusation. "Worried after what you and your girlfriend put her through?"

I swallowed hard, the guilt crashing over me like a wave. "I didn't tell Courtney anything. I swear, I didn't know she'd—"

Aiden snapped his head at me, his voice sharp. "She trusted you, Christian. Do you know how hard that is for her? She let you in, and you let her down."

"Aiden... I didn't... I wouldn't..." I stammered, struggling to find words that didn't feel hollow. "Courtney found out from Jessica's school folder—her grades, transfer documents—everything. I never told her anything about the DUI. I didn't even know she'd use it against Jessica like that."

Aiden's glare softened, but his jaw stayed clenched, his anger replaced with a hard, calculating look. "So you really didn't tell her?" He wasn't asking, not exactly. More like he was daring me to say it wasn't true.

"No," I said, my voice firm. "I would never do that to Jessica. I care about her, Aiden. More than I've cared about anyone."

Aiden studied me for a long moment, his expression softening just enough to give me hope. "She's at home. She's fine. But she hasn't really left her room much."

"Thanks," I said, relief flooding through me. But before I could walk away, Aiden's voice stopped me.

"If you screw this up again," he said, his voice low and deadly serious, "I swear, you'll regret it."

I nodded, swallowing the lump in my throat, feeling the full weight of Aiden's warning. "I won't," I managed, steadying my voice. "I promise."

X X X X X X

That evening, I stood outside Jessica's house. The glow from the windows was warm and inviting, but I knew the reality was far from that. I didn't even think twice as I climbed the tree at the side of the house, my heart pounding as I made my way to her window. The branch was narrow, but I steadied myself, reaching out to knock gently on the glass.

For a moment, there was only silence. Then the curtain shifted, and Jessica's face appeared, her eyes widening in surprise as she saw me perched outside her window.

"Christian?" Her voice was a whisper, full of disbelief.

"Can I come in?" I asked, my breath visible in the cool night air.

She hesitated, her expression guarded, but eventually, she reached out and unlocked the window, sliding it open just enough for me to climb inside.

As I stepped into her room, the warmth of the space wrapping around me like a blanket, I knew this was my chance to make things right. And I wasn't going to waste it.

I stood in the middle of Jessica's room, the air thick with tension. She sat on the edge of her bed, arms crossed, eyes wary, like she was bracing for whatever I had to say. My heart pounded in my chest. The words tangled up inside me, but I knew I had to speak before I lost the nerve.

"Jess, please," I started, my voice low but steady. "Don't quit. The band needs you… There is no Romeo without Juliet."

She blinked, then let out a laugh—a hollow, disbelieving sound that cut through the tension between us like a blade. It wasn't the reaction I'd expected; it was bitter, almost mocking, like she couldn't quite believe I'd say something like that after everything.

"I'm serious," I continued, stepping closer. "I know I messed things up, but the band isn't the same without you. It's not the same without you there. I want you on that field with me, beside me. You belong out there with us."

Jessica's gaze hardened, her eyes narrowing as she crossed her arms. "You really expect me to believe that?" Her tone was sharp, guarded, and full of doubt. "You think I'd just… take your word for it?"

I took a slow breath, letting the silence settle between us for a moment before speaking again. "Look, I get why you don't trust me. I messed up, and I can't change that. But this isn't about me, or even what happened with Courtney. It's about you. You're a leader, Jess, whether or not you want to be. The whole band looks up to you."

She shifted, still skeptical, but I could see her walls flickering, if only for a second.

"When you're out there," I continued, keeping my voice low, "it's like the entire band is just... stronger. I'm not asking you to forgive me or even trust me right now. But don't give up on all the work you've put into this, on everything you've helped us build, just because of my mistakes. You don't deserve to walk away from something you love because of me."

Her expression softened slightly, but she still looked hesitant, like she was weighing every word. "Everyone's going to look at me differently." Her voice was soft, almost afraid.

I took a step closer, making sure she knew I was serious. "They might see things differently at first, yeah. But that doesn't define you, Jess. The band, the guard—they've seen what you're capable of. They know who you are out there on that field. Whatever Courtney tried to do, it didn't take that away. You've earned their respect."

Her eyes locked onto mine, and for a second, the guarded wall slipped, just enough for me to catch a flicker of something—hurt, maybe, or doubt. And then it was gone, replaced by a calm I knew was forced. "Fine," she said. "But we're not friends."

I nodded, swallowing the lump in my throat. "Okay," I breathed. "We're not friends."

Jessica's eyes lingered on mine for a moment longer like she was expecting a different response from me. But then she looked away, her walls back up, just like before.

At least she was coming back.

28 Castle

Jessica

I wasn't sure if I should even be here. The anger from the football game last night simmered, mixing with something darker—regret, or maybe fear. Every part of me screamed to turn back, but my pride wouldn't let me.

I could still hear Christian's voice. Part of me wanted to believe him, to trust that he meant every word. But another part of me couldn't shake the bitterness, the feeling that I was just a pawn in everyone's game.

A knock on my driver's side window jolted me out of my thoughts. I glanced over, and there was Emily, her familiar face smiling down at me. She was all enthusiasm, her blonde hair bouncing around her shoulders as she waved for me to roll down the window.

"Jessica! I'm glad to see you," she said, her voice bright as sunshine, but there was an edge to it, something eager that made my stomach twist. "Welcome to Kingston."

I forced a smile and finally killed the engine.

"Come on, Mr. Waylan's waiting for you," she urged, not even giving me a chance to hesitate before she was opening the door and pulling me out of the car.

The Kingston band room was a far cry from what I was used to. It was darker, somehow. The fluorescent lights buzzed overhead, casting harsh shadows across the tiled floor. The walls were lined with trophies and plaques, but instead of feeling like a celebration of achievement, it felt like a warning—a reminder of what this place was about. Winning, and nothing else.

Mr. Waylan was waiting for me in his office at the back of the room. He was tall and thin, with a suit that seemed just a little too tight across the shoulders, like he'd outgrown it but refused to acknowledge it. His eyes were sharp, calculating, and his smile—if you could call it that—was more like a baring of teeth. He leaned back in his chair, fingers steepled in front of him as he watched me approach.

"Jessica Welling," he said, his voice smooth but cold, like a knife's edge. "I've heard a lot about you."

There was something unsettling about the way he spoke, like he already knew everything there was to know about me. Like he'd done his research, and this was just a formality. The air in the room felt heavier with him in it, like it was pressing down on my chest, making it hard to breathe.

"Emily tells me you're interested in joining our band," he continued, his eyes never leaving mine. "As our drum major."

I held my ground with no reaction.

He pressed, "Our one and only drum major."

I nodded, though I wasn't sure if I was agreeing or just acknowledging his words.

He smiled again, that same predatory grin. "Let's get straight to it, Jessica. Kingston doesn't settle for second best, and from what I hear, you're just the edge we need. But success comes at a cost. Are you willing to pay it?"

I stiffened, the unease in my gut twisting tighter.

His gaze flicked to Emily for a brief second before settling back on me. "Arcana High has always been our biggest competition. They're good—too good. But with you on our side, I'm confident we can beat them this year. However, to secure our victory, I need you to do two things for me."

I swallowed hard, already knowing I wasn't going to like what he was about to say.

"I need you to borrow their drill book," he said, his voice low and deliberate. "It'll be easy, they trust you. With that, we'll have the advantage we need."

I stared at him, my mind racing. Steal the drill book? My stomach twisted. This wasn't just bending the rules—it was shattering them. But the weight of his stare, the subtle grin tugging at his lips, made it clear he wasn't asking. He was demanding.

"The second thing?" I asked, my voice shaking.

"We need you to continue being their drum major, take over Emily's job as a spy as we think people have started to catch onto her. Just in case Arcana throws something new into their show, we need to know about it."

I didn't trust him. There was something about him that set off every alarm in my head. But I was so angry, so fed up with how things had gone at Arcana.

I took a deep breath, trying to steady myself, and nodded. "I'll do it."

Mr. Waylan's grin widened, and he leaned forward, extending his hand. "Welcome to Kingston, Jessica."

I shook his hand, the coldness of his grip sending a shiver down my spine. I was in now, whether or not I liked it. The decision felt like a weight pressing on my chest, but there was no turning back. The day moved quickly from there, almost in a blur as if the school was sweeping me into its fold before I had time to think twice.

I was handed their musical score—a dense arrangement that looked both challenging and intricate. As I flipped through the pages, my eyes caught the title. Another Shakespeare tragedy: *Julius Caesar*. The irony wasn't lost on me. Betrayal, power struggles, and a tragic downfall—it seemed fitting for what I'd just agreed to.

Before I could dwell on it, they whisked me away to be fitted into Kingston's drum major uniform. It was all black, with sharp silver accents that gave it an edge of authority—regal and militaristic all at once. The high collar framed my shoulders, the silver buttons caught the light, and the crisp lines made it feel less like a uniform and more like armor. When I caught my reflection in the mirror, I barely recognized myself. I didn't look like someone on the edge of falling apart. I looked like someone ready for war.

I told myself it wasn't betrayal—it was survival. If Arcana wouldn't protect me, why should I protect them?

I dressed back down and followed Emily to the field, where the band has already begun running the show. They were loud and powerful, and strikingly terrifying.

X X X X X

Returning to school that Tuesday felt like walking into enemy territory. The day off had given me time to think—too much time. Christian knocking on my window the night before had rattled me in ways I didn't want to admit. I wasn't expecting to see him, and I definitely wasn't expecting him to ask me to come back.

The moment I stepped into homeroom, I could feel eyes on me, Christian's most of all. I hesitated at the doorway, and sure enough, there he was, sitting in his usual spot, his head snapping up the second I walked in. His expression was a mix of relief and something else I couldn't quite place, but I wasn't interested in deciphering it. I had a job to do, and getting close to Christian again wasn't part of the plan.

I scanned the room quickly, spotting an empty seat in the far back corner. Without looking in Christian's direction, I made my way to it, weaving between desks like I was avoiding landmines. I could feel the tension in the room, all emanating from him, but I kept my focus straight ahead. My heartbeat was louder than the surrounding whispers.

When I reached the back, I slid into the seat, dropping my bag onto the floor beside me. The cold metal of the chair against my skin was a grounding sensation, reminding me to stay focused. This was just another school day. Just another act to get through. I kept my face neutral, my expression blank—no need to give anyone more than they deserved.

As the morning announcements droned on, I pulled out a notebook, pretending to be engrossed in something, anything, other than the reality around me. But I couldn't help noticing Christian stealing glances my way. Every time I looked up, he was watching me, a flicker of concern in his eyes. It was the same look he had given me last night when he begged me to come back. But I couldn't let that get to me. Not now. Not ever.

I kept my guard up, my walls higher than ever. If I was going to survive this day—this mission—I needed to stay distant. I couldn't let anyone get close, especially not Christian. My mind was on Kingston, on Mr. Waylan's unsettling request, and on the drill book I had to steal. Every smile, every friendly gesture, every concerned look was a threat to my focus. I couldn't afford to be distracted by anything, or anyone.

The bell rang, signaling the end of homeroom, and I was the first one out of my seat. I kept my head down, slipping out of the room before Christian had a chance to catch up. I moved through the hallways like a ghost, slipping through the crowds, avoiding eye contact, and keeping to the edges. The familiar faces of my classmates blurred into a sea of indistinguishable features, all part of the background noise I was trying to ignore.

In each class, I found a seat at the back, close to the door, where I could slip out without drawing attention. My responses were clipped, my interactions minimal, a deliberate effort to blend into the background. It was easier to be the girl who was just there, not the one everyone was watching. Being a drum major again didn't hold the same weight it once did. Now, it was simply a role, a necessary step to complete the task at hand.

As I made my way to band class, I felt a hand gently grasp my arm. I turned to find Tracy standing there, her face a mix of worry and something softer—almost like regret.

"Hey," she said, her voice low, searching my face. "I just… wanted to say I'm sorry for what Courtney did. That DUI thing… it doesn't change anything. I'm still here for you, Jess. I just wanted you to know that."

Her words hung between us, warm and sincere, but I felt something cold and guarded settle over me, instinctively pushing her kindness away. A faint pang of guilt surfaced, but I forced it down, hardening myself to the moment. I couldn't afford to feel that right now. Not the sympathy, not the comfort—and definitely not the guilt. I'd spent too much time letting my guard down already.

"Thanks, Tracy," I replied quietly, a polite distance in my voice as I slid my arm out of her grasp. I gave her a small, tight smile and looked away. "I appreciate it. But I'm good, really."

Tracy's brows knit together, a flicker of hurt crossing her face, but she nodded, her grip loosening. "Alright," she murmured, almost reluctantly, as though she knew there was more I wasn't saying.

But I couldn't let her in. Not now. Not with everything so raw and unsteady inside me. I managed a small nod before turning back toward the band room, letting the space grow between us, the hollow feeling returning as I tried to numb myself from anything that felt too close.

This was the final stretch before the band's first marching competition on Saturday. Mr. Waylan had already arranged everything.

"Don't worry about the circuits," he'd said, like he'd already anticipated my question. "Arcana and Kingston aren't scheduled to compete against each other until finals. That gives us time. You lead Arcana through this weekend's comp—keep their trust, keep your cover—and by next week, you're ours. For the homecoming game and everything after."

As I stepped onto the field, the usual sounds of instruments warming up filled the air. Everyone was moving around, chatting and laughing, buzzing with energy for the upcoming competition. But I felt completely detached, going through the motions like a ghost. I climbed onto the podium, adjusting my stance out of habit more than anything else. The drill formations were all locked in my head, and I led the band with clean, sharp commands—but there was nothing behind it. No spark. No heart.

As the band ran through the show, I could feel the disconnect. The energy that usually ran through the group felt muted, like my presence had sucked the air out of the room. I caught a few people glancing up at me, their faces a mix of confusion and maybe even discomfort—but I didn't let it show. I kept my guard up, untouchable, like a wall standing between me and everyone else.

Christian was there, obviously, leading his section with that same easy confidence. I didn't let myself look at him for more than a second. Every time I caught him watching me, I snapped my focus somewhere else. I couldn't afford to let him get in my head. Not again.

Rehearsal dragged. The hours blurred together as we ran the show over and over. My face stayed blank, my voice steady, calling out counts and commands like it was just another day. The band did what they were supposed to—sharp steps, clean visuals—but something felt off. The tension was there. They could feel I wasn't the same, but no one said anything.

The switch-off between Christian and me still wasn't working. Something about it felt... off. Every time we ran it, the timing was weird, the motion awkward. It just didn't flow right, and Mr. Trust kept trying to force it into place like it was a puzzle piece that didn't quite fit. We were both hesitating—out of sync—and it showed.

After what felt like the millionth reset, I couldn't hold it in anymore. "Can you stop blocking my way off the podium?" The words came out sharper than I intended.

Christian froze, caught off guard. "I'm trying my best here, Jess," he said, voice calm. Almost apologetic. "I'm not doing it on purpose."

That threw me. I'd been ready for him to snap back, to roll his eyes or act like I was being dramatic. But he didn't. He just stood there, steady and quiet, and suddenly I felt... kind of bad. Maybe I was being too harsh.

"There's not exactly a ton of space up here," I muttered, my voice losing some of its bite. "You're jumping up too early."

He nodded. "Okay. Tell me what you need me to do."

I blinked, surprised by how serious he looked—like he actually wanted to fix it, not just for the show but for me too.

"Fine," I said, letting out a breath. "Just don't rush it. You've got four measures to get here. Use them. And if you're gonna jump up, land on this side so I can get down."

"Got it." He looked me right in the eye, like he was waiting for me to believe him.

I glanced out across the field, suddenly aware of the band watching us, the tension practically humming in the air.

"Alright, let's reset!" Mr. Trust's voice rang out, all clipped and annoyed. "And this time, let's try it without the drama. We're staging a performance, not an argument."

By the time we reached the final run-through, the sun was dipping below the horizon. The band members were tired, but they pushed through, determined to perfect the show before Saturday, our first competition. I kept my focus on the task, ignoring the weariness creeping into my own limbs. This was just another rehearsal, just another step in the plan.

When Mr. Trust finally called it a day, I stepped down from the podium without a word, gathering my things and heading toward the parking lot. The other band members lingered, chatting and laughing as they packed up, but I didn't join them.

I was still the outsider, the one who didn't belong, and that was exactly how I wanted it. How it was always supposed to be.

Christian

The morning air was crisp, biting through my jacket as I stepped onto the campus, the sky still tinged with the deep blues and purples of early dawn. Excitement and nerves mingled in the air as the band gathered, lugging instrument cases and backpacks. The first competition day always had that buzz, like everyone was a little too wound up.

I scanned the crowd, looking for her. I spotted Jessica near the back, her ponytail swaying as she walked toward the buses. She was talking to Emily, the transfer student, who had joined the band only a few weeks ago.

I wanted to sit next to her on the bus, try to bridge whatever chasm had opened up between us since she came back. But when she slipped into a seat next to Emily, I felt my chance slip away. The back of the bus was her escape today, a place I wasn't invited. I hesitated for a moment, staring at the empty aisle, before turning and finding an open seat closer to the front.

The engine rumbled to life, and soon we were on our way, the chatter and laughter of the band filling the bus. I tried to join in with the other guys, cracking jokes and talking strategy for the show, but my mind kept drifting back to Jessica. Every time I glanced over my shoulder, all I could see was the top of her head, leaning in close to Emily as they whispered to each other. It gnawed at me, how distant she was, how much I wanted to be the one sitting beside her, trying to ease whatever was still eating at her from that night.

The drive to the competition site was long, the highway stretching out endlessly in front of us. I found myself staring out the window, watching the landscape blur by, but all I could think about was Jessica. She was here, physically, but she still felt a million miles away.

When we finally pulled into the parking lot of the competition site, the bus lurched to a stop, and everyone started to gather their things. I hung back, waiting for the aisle to clear, hoping maybe I could catch her before we unloaded. But she and Emily were up and out of their seats in a flash, blending into the crowd of students spilling out of the bus. I sighed, grabbing my trumpet case and slinging my bag over my shoulder, following the others onto the pavement.

The air was filled with the sounds of other bands warming up in the distance, the occasional note from a trumpet or the beat of a drum echoing across the lot. Mr. Trust was already rounding everyone up, barking out instructions as we gathered around him.

"Alright, everyone, you know the drill. Stick together, stay focused, and let's make this one count. We've put in the work. Now it's time to show them what we've got."

Mr. Trust's words echoed through the band as we gathered for the day's first event. The parade competition was up first, and Jessica was at the helm. Her spinning skills were unmatched, and it showed as she led the band through their warm-ups with a precision that left no room for error. I kept my distance, playing trumpet among the horn line, but my eyes kept drifting toward her, watching the way she commanded attention.

The parade went off without a hitch. Jessica's leadership was flawless, and the band delivered a performance that was both impressive and precise—much like herself.

After the parade, the band had a brief break before shifting gears for the field show. Everyone was buzzing with anticipation, but a sense of unease rippled through the group. Tracy's voice, usually calm, was now fraught with panic as she spoke to Mr. Trust.

"We forgot a timpani! It's not here. I could have sworn I rolled it into the trailer myself."

Mr. Trust's face tightened with frustration, and he quickly started making calls, trying to find a solution. I could see the anxiety on Tracy's face as she frantically checked every corner of the equipment truck.

That's when I saw an opportunity. I moved closer to Tracy, trying to calm her down. "Don't worry," I said, my mind racing. "I'll handle this."

Before Tracy could protest, I headed toward the host school's band room, where I hoped they might have a spare timpani we could borrow. Jessica was nearby, her face set in concentration as she went over the field show details. I knew this was my chance to talk to her, so I didn't hesitate. I approached her with a determined stride.

"Jessica, come on," I said, grabbing her arm gently. "We need to borrow a timpani from the host school, and I could use your help."

She looked at me, clearly caught off guard. "I'm not exactly in the mood to be your assistant right now." I ignored her reluctance and pulled her toward the host band's building.

Once the door shut behind us, Jessica pulled her arm away and crossed it over her chest. Her posture was defensive, her gaze guarded. The room was still and empty, the absence of the host band director only amplifying the tension.

"What now, genius? You planning on stealing a timpani?" she asked, her tone sharp with sarcasm.

I exhaled, forcing myself to stay calm. "Look, I know you're mad. And you should be. But I need you to hear me out."

Jessica crossed her arms, her frown deepening, but she didn't move away.

"Courtney wanted you gone. After the Juliet thing, she was pissed—jealous, threatened, all of it. I should've shut it down. But I didn't. I was angry too. You came out of nowhere and took the spot I thought I deserved. It messed with my head."

Her jaw tightened, but she stayed silent. That flicker of hurt in her eyes—God, I hated that I put it there.

"Her mom works in the front office. That's how Courtney got your file. She found out about the DUI, and… she ran with it. Filled in the blanks when she saw Aiden. She made assumptions. Awful ones."

Jessica's expression shifted, just a little. I couldn't tell what she was thinking, but I kept going.

"I told her not to say anything. I didn't think she actually would." My voice faltered. "And then I got to know you. I heard what really happened that night. What it cost you. And I realized how badly I'd misjudged you."

She looked away, but not before I caught the smallest tremble in her shoulders.

"That morning—after you told me everything—I broke up with her."

Her head snapped toward me, eyes narrowing. "Why?"

I hesitated, then said the only thing that felt true. "Because I couldn't pretend anymore. I saw how much you love Aiden, how hard you fight for the people you care about. You were nothing like I thought you were. You're stronger than I ever gave you credit for. And..." I swallowed. "I was falling for you."

For a moment, Jessica just stared at me, like she was trying to decide whether I was worth listening to. Her expression shifted with every second—anger, disbelief, something close to hurt. I thought, maybe, I was getting through.

Then her arms crossed tighter, and her eyes went cold again.

"So I'm just supposed to forget that you and Courtney were digging through my past the second I showed up?" Her voice was quiet, but it hit harder than if she'd yelled. "You knew she had my file. You didn't stop her."

"Jess—" I started, but she cut me off with a shake of her head.

"You think an apology fixes this?" Her voice cracked, but she didn't back down. "You think just because you *say* you care, it erases what you did?"

"I don't," I said quickly, the words catching in my throat. "I know I can't fix this with one conversation. But I'm not walking away from it either. Let me prove it to you. Tell me what to do. I'll do it."

She looked at me for a long time, her jaw tight, her eyes unreadable. Then she exhaled, slow and tired, and gave a faint, humorless smile.

"I'm sure you'll figure something out," she said, her tone soft—but not forgiving. It felt like a door being left half-open. Before I could say anything else, the door behind us creaked open.

"Hey, I found the band director," Tracy said brightly, stepping into the room with a wide-eyed grin. Behind her was the host school's director, oblivious to the tension hanging in the air.

Jessica straightened immediately, crossing her arms again and putting the emotional distance back up like armor. The vulnerable moment between us vanished, leaving me staring after her, wondering how I could possibly climb the wall she'd built around herself.

"Yeah," I said, clearing my throat and stepping back. "We wanted to ask if you had a spare timpani we could borrow."

The band director nodded, completely unfazed by the awkwardness in the room. "Sure, I'll grab one for you. Follow me."

As they turned to leave, I glanced at Jessica, hoping for some sign that what had happened wasn't entirely in my head. But she was already pulling away, retreating behind her walls.

X X X X X X

"Now on the field from Arcana, California—the Arcana Eagles Marching Band!"

The announcement boomed across the stadium, but I barely registered it. Standing tall on the podium at the 35-yard line, I could hear the crowd's cheers morph into a high-pitched ringing in my ears. The band and guard were poised at attention, eyes locked on me, waiting for my signal. The evening air had finally cooled, a relief from the day's relentless heat. I inhaled deeply, steadying myself, and prepared for the salute.

"Drum majors… Is your band ready?"

I scanned the band, taking in each section, my gaze lingering just long enough on Jessica, who stood on the front field podium. As she stood, scanning the band and then at me, with a soft nod, she turned towards the crowd and judges, bringing her hand to her chest and snapped into a crisp salute. The crowd responded with a smatter of applause, eager to hear and see our show.

"You may now **take the field** for competition."

"1… 2… 1, 2, 3, and!"

The band sprang to life. With precision, the brass section delivered powerful notes, and the woodwinds flawlessly executed their intricate runs. The color guard moved with synchronized grace, their routines sharp and perfectly timed.

The narrator's voice played on the speaker:

Two households, both alike in dignity
(In fair Verona, where we lay our scene),
From ancient grudge break to new mutiny,
Where civil blood makes civil hands unclean.
From forth the fatal loins of these two foes
A pair of star-crossed lovers take their life;
Whose misadventured piteous overthrows
Doth with their death bury their parents' strife.
The fearful passage of their death-marked love
And the continuance of their parents' rage,
Which, but their children's end, naught could remove,
Is now the two hours' traffic of our stage;
The which, if you with patient ears attend,
What here shall miss, our toil shall strive to mend.

As the opener inched towards its dramatic close, I knew it was time to prepare for the podium switch. Mr. Trust still had no idea how to make this switch less awkward, but this time, I had a different plan. A risky one, but it was now or never.

I watched Jessica. She was conducting with such intensity it caught me off guard. Her movements were fluid, expressive—more emotion in her conducting than I'd seen before. From the backfield podium, I mirrored her arm motions, captivated by the way her hands seemed to draw the music from the band, almost as if she were weaving it from thin air. I couldn't tear my eyes away.

As the low brass signaled the impending impact point, my heart pounded harder than the bass drums. I knew my moment was coming, but I wasn't supposed to move yet. Eight more measures. Eight more measures where I was supposed to wait, let the music carry the transition like we'd rehearsed a hundred times. But I couldn't wait.

Jessica was there on the podium, commanding the moment like she always did—focused, powerful, untouchable. But something in her gaze was different today, sharper, heavier, like she was carrying the weight of the entire show alone. She didn't trust me. And maybe she had every reason not to. I'd spent so long holding back, pretending my feelings didn't matter, keeping my distance because I was afraid of what breaking that line between us would mean. But all that distance, all that waiting—it wasn't working.

I was tired of waiting.

The music swelled, pushing me forward, like every note was telling me this was my chance, my moment to stop hesitating and do something real. If I didn't move now, if I didn't show her what she meant to me, I wasn't sure I'd ever get the chance again.

My legs moved before my brain could catch up. I jumped down from the step ladder and sprinted down the 50-yard line toward her podium, dodging flutes and clarinets. The band's intensity mirrored the storm in my chest, and I jumped and swung my legs over as the brass hit their peak. Jessica turned, her eyes wide with confusion, and I knew she didn't understand. Not yet. But she would.

Jessica's eyes locked on mine, wide with disbelief. Her hands faltered in mid-motion, the crispness of her conducting replaced by hesitation. She wasn't supposed to falter—not Jessica, who always carried the weight of the band like it was nothing. I thought maybe she'd push me off.

Her lips parted, like she was about to yell at me, but no words came. Her eyes narrowed, accusing, but then something flickered behind them, something softer. Hesitation turned to resolve. Her shoulders dropped just slightly, and when her hand brushed mine, tentative and deliberate, I knew I hadn't miscalculated. The distance between us disappeared in a rush of heat, and when her lips met mine, everything—every note, every beat, every step on that field— faded into the background. For the first time in weeks, the storm inside me quieted.

In the stillness, the narrator's voice sang:

Then move not while my prayer's effect I take.

Thus from my lips, by thine, my sin is purged.

When time resumed, the roar of the crowd was almost deafening. They were cheering as if this kiss had been scripted all along, a planned part of the show.

Jessica seemed dazed. Her eyes were wide as she stepped down from the podium and made her way down to the field for her flag feature—but something was off. She moved like she wasn't fully there, like she'd left part of herself behind on the podium with me. There was a stiffness to her limbs. Her grip on the flag was too tight. And for a second—just a second—she looked like she wanted to run.

I raised my arms to signal the countdown for the ballad, hoping that this impulsive, public gesture might melt the ice between us. It had to work... because she kissed me back.

The flag moved with her, slicing through the air in a way that caught the light and reflected every bit of turmoil I suspected she was feeling. Her motions were flawless—almost too perfect—each spin and toss executed with mechanical precision. But there was more beneath the surface, something raw and intense, like she was channeling all her anger, frustration, and confusion into the performance. She wasn't just going through the motions; she was using the flag to say everything she couldn't put into words.

From where I stood, I couldn't look away. Jessica moved with a kind of controlled grace, like she was holding everything in check. The flag wasn't just part of the routine—it was a shield. She kept her guard up with every toss and catch, putting space between herself and the world.

But even through the precision, I saw it—tension in her shoulders, a hesitation in her steps. She was here, going through the motions, but her mind was somewhere else.

Did she regret it? Was she angry I dragged her into this? Or just scared—of what it meant, of letting someone in? I didn't know.

But as she ended with that final, flawless flourish, I knew one thing: Jessica was still fighting.

And damn, I admired her for it—even if I had no idea where we stood.

As the final note echoed through the stadium, I signaled the cutoff and brought my arms down, steadying myself. The band was already in motion, marching off the field with precision, their movements crisp and clean.

My gaze lingered on Jessica as she stepped down from her podium. Her hand gripped the railing tightly, her knuckles white against the metal. She placed her free hand on her chest, her shoulders rising and falling with quick, shallow breaths.

Something was wrong.

Her movements were stiff as she descended, her usual fluidity replaced with a rigid, almost mechanical precision. When her foot hit the ground, it wasn't with the confidence I'd come to expect from her—it was hesitant, shaky. She pressed her hand harder against her chest, her fingers curling slightly as though trying to steady herself.

I called out, "Jessica?"

She didn't look at me. Her head was down, her eyes darting to the ground, unfocused. Each breath she took was audible, quick and uneven, like she couldn't quite get enough air.

The crowd's roar behind us only seemed to grow louder, and I saw her flinch slightly at the sound. Her shoulders tensed, drawing up toward her ears, and her hand dropped to her side, clenching into a fist.

"Jessica," I said again, louder this time, taking a step closer.

As soon as we reached the gate exit off the field, she bolted.

Jessica

I wasn't entirely sure how I ended up in the host school's percussion closet having a panic attack. The room was dim, lit only by a flickering fluorescent light that cast eerie shadows over the stacked drums and cymbals. The smell of rubber and rosin mixed with the musty odor of neglected cleaning supplies. It was stuffy and hot, the air thick with stale sweat and metal.

My breaths came in ragged bursts, shallow and uneven, like trying to breathe through a straw. Knees drawn tightly to my chest, I clutched at the fabric of my dress like it could anchor me. The flickering light blurred, the edges of my vision narrowing as the walls pressed in.

The kiss. Christian's hand on my neck, his lips on mine—it replayed in sharp, inescapable fragments. It wasn't the same. Not even close. But the suddenness, the vulnerability—it dragged up memories I'd buried so deep they barely felt like mine.

Then came the deal. The secret with Mr. Waylan. The betrayal. The weight of it all pressed down on my chest, each breath harder than the last. I could almost hear his voice, slick and smug, promising success if I sold my integrity.

The room spun. My vision blinked in and out. I pressed against the cool wall, hoping the solid surface would steady me. My hands trembled, tears slipping down my cheeks, guilt and shame crashing through me with every breath.

I tried to focus—on the clink of metal around me, on the rhythm of my breathing. Anything to anchor me to the present. I thought the panic attacks were behind me. I hadn't had one in months.

Hands fumbling, I reached for my phone and dialed a number I hadn't called since leaving for Arcana.

The ringing in the speaker stopped, followed by, "Jessica?" I could hear the familiar voice of my childhood best friend, Cassie.

"I can't... breathe," I manage through the phone.

After the accident with Aiden, panic attacks became a regular part of my life. Cassie had noticed right away and convinced me to see the school counselor, who taught me breathing techniques. Since then, Cassie had been there through every attack, guiding me through each one, holding on to me when I felt like I was slipping away.

I heard Cassie's voice through the phone, and the sound alone was a small relief. Her voice was steady, and she wasted no time getting straight to the point.

"Jessica, listen to me. You're safe. You're just having a panic attack, okay? I need you to focus on my voice and follow my instructions. Can you do that for me?"

Her calm, reassuring tone was like a lifeline pulling me back from the edge. I took a shaky breath, trying to steady myself.

"I... I'll try," I said, though it felt like my lungs were closing up.

"Good," Cassie said firmly. "First, let's focus on your breathing. I want you to take a deep breath in through your nose, slow and steady. Count to four as you breathe in. Ready?"

I nodded, even though she couldn't see me, and took a breath. My chest felt tight, but I tried to follow her instructions.

"One, two, three, four," Cassie counted softly, her voice steadying me.

"Now, exhale slowly through your mouth. Count to six as you breathe out. I'm right here with you, Jess."

I exhaled, the breath coming out in a slow, uneven stream. The air in the closet felt stifling, but Cassie's voice guided me through it. With each breath, I felt a little more grounded, a little more in control.

"That's it," Cassie encouraged. "In through your nose for four, out through your mouth for six. You're doing great. Just keep focusing on your breathing. Remember how we practiced this together? You've got this."

Her words brought me back to those countless nights when we'd sat together, working through my anxiety with these very techniques. The memory of her support, of her patience, helped me center myself. I pictured her sitting beside me, her reassuring presence calming the storm in my mind.

I focused on the rhythm of my breath, matching it with Cassie's voice. The tightness in my chest began to ease, and I could feel the panic slowly releasing its grip on me. The dizziness subsided, and I started to feel more like myself again.

"Jessica, are you there?" Cassie's voice was filled with concern. "Are you feeling better?"

I took another deep breath, managing a more even exhale this time. "Yeah, I think so," I said, my voice steadier than before. "Thank you, Cassie. I didn't think... I didn't think I'd have another one like this."

"Is everything okay?" she asked softly. Cassie knew the weight I was under—my mom's constant pressure and the car accident after the party she'd invited us to. She'd sensed that something changed in me after that night, and weeks later, when I finally confided in her about the assault, she understood why the accident wasn't the only thing haunting me.

"Did something happen to trigger the attack?" Cassie's gentle tone was like a balm to my nerves.

I hesitated, unsure if I should tell her everything. But the ache of missing her, of needing the comfort she always seemed to give so easily, finally made me open up. I shared everything—the competition, the rivalry with Christian, and the deal I'd made with Kingston's band director.

When I finished, Cassie was silent, the weight of my words settling between us.

Finally, she asked, "So, when he kissed you… was that it?"

I let out a long, shaky sigh. "Maybe? It's not just the kiss, though—it's that feeling of totally losing control, like something's happening to me, and I can't stop it or steer it." I paused, then took a deep breath, the words surprising even me. "But Cass… I think I really like him."

I could hear her thinking on the other end of the line. "I think you need to tell him the truth, Jess."

"I know," my voice cracked.

"Jessica, I'm so sorry you're going through all this. I know you've been dealing with so much, and I wish I could be there with you. It makes sense that you'd feel overwhelmed, especially with everything that's happened."

There was a pause on the other end, a thoughtful silence as Cassie processed everything. "I get why you're scared. After everything, it's hard to let your guard down. But maybe… maybe Christian isn't like the others. He might have made mistakes, but it sounds like he's really trying to make it up to you. And the fact that you're feeling something for him—it doesn't mean you're losing control. It means you're healing, that you're allowing yourself to feel again."

She hesitated for a moment, then continued, "I know it's not easy to trust, especially after what you've been through. But maybe Christian is someone worth trusting. He's put himself out there in a way that most guys wouldn't, especially in front of all those people. It might have been a little misguided, but that has to count for something, right?"

Cassie's voice softened, filled with the warmth of someone who just wanted the best for her friend. "You deserve to have someone who cares about you, Jess. And if there's even a chance that Christian could be that person, maybe it's worth seeing where it goes. It doesn't mean you have to rush into anything, but you don't have to push him away, either."

I wiped my face, took a deep breath, and tried to steady the racing thoughts in my mind. After talking to Cassie, something shifted inside me. It was time to come clean to Christian. I couldn't keep running from everything, especially not him. He deserved to know the truth, and I needed to face whatever came next.

I left the closet, the cool air of the evening hitting my face as I made my way back out to the field. My steps quickened as I approached the buses and Arcana's equipment trailer, my heart pounding with every step. But as I got closer, I saw Mr. Trust standing by the trailer, his expression calm but concerned.

"Jessica," he called out as soon as he saw me. "Can I speak with you for a moment?"

My heart skipped a beat. "Sure," I said, walking over to him, trying to keep my voice steady.

He led me a little away from the group, his demeanor gentle, almost paternal. "How are you feeling?" he asked, his eyes searching mine.

"I'm fine," I lied, but the look in his eyes told me he wasn't buying it. "I'm good. I promise."

"Did you and Christian plan that kiss ahead of time?" he asked, his tone neutral. He wasn't angry, just genuinely concerned. I hesitated, then nodded.

"Yeah," I said, trying to sound convincing. "We thought it would add something extra to the show, you know? Make it more memorable." The lie tasted bitter on my tongue, but I wasn't about to let Christian get into trouble for something that had been my fault as much as his.

Mr. Trust studied me for a moment, then nodded slowly. "Well, it certainly made an impression," he said with a small smile. "But I just wanted to make sure you were okay. You seemed... shaken afterward."

I bit my lip, my eyes darting to the ground. "I'm okay, really. Just... everything caught up with me for a moment. But I'm good now."

He nodded again, his gaze softening. "You know, Jessica, you've been through a lot, and Arcana's no walk in the park—it's highly competitive. But remember, even the best performers need to take a breath sometimes. It's okay to take your time, slow down, and figure things out. You've got the talent and the drive, but you don't have to carry it all on your shoulders. And if you ever need someone to talk to about anything—I hope you know you can talk to me.

"At the end of the day, it's only marching band. What matters most is you."

For a moment, I was speechless. I hadn't expected this kind of care from him, this kind of understanding. I could see now why Christian looked up to him so much. He wasn't just a band director; he was someone who genuinely cared about his students.

"Thank you, Mr. Trust," I said, my voice a little shaky.

He gave me a reassuring smile, then glanced at the field. "It's almost time for the awards ceremony. Are you ready? The others are already lined up by the gate waiting for you."

As we walked back toward the field, I could see the other drum majors, percussion captains, and guard captains lining up for the awards ceremony. My eyes scanned the crowd until I found him—Christian. My heart twisted with everything I needed to say but couldn't yet.

He stood with Courtney and Marcus, his posture tense, but his gaze locked onto mine the moment I spotted him. Something shifted in his expression—regret, concern, maybe even fear. Without a word, he broke away from the group and started toward me, his steps quickening with purpose.

The noise of the crowd melted away as he approached, leaving only the rapid pounding of my heart in my ears. His eyes, usually sharp and guarded, were soft now—uncertain, almost pleading. His tension was unmistakable, like he was bracing himself for whatever I might say. But words weren't what I needed right now.

"Jessica, I'm sor—" he began, his brow furrowed in regret.

I didn't let him finish. I couldn't. No apology could rewrite the past or undo the mistakes. Words wouldn't fix us. I needed something tangible.

Before I could second-guess myself, I closed the distance between us. My fingers tangled in the stiff collar of his uniform as I pulled him down, and then I was kissing him. His lips met mine with a moment of surprise, but then the shock melted away, and he responded. His arms wrapped around my waist, pulling me closer, the tension in his shoulders softening as he relaxed into the kiss.

His lips were warm and soft, his embrace grounding me as the world steadied around us. Every nerve in my body felt alive, like waking up from a long, heavy sleep.

It wasn't desperate, like the kiss during the performance. This was deeper—something that had been simmering beneath the surface for too long, finally breaking out. For the first time in weeks, the weight of my secrets, my guilt, and my fear faded into the background. For this moment, at least, I let myself be free.

When I pulled back, my fingers lingering against the rough fabric of his uniform, I saw something new in his eyes. They weren't filled with uncertainty anymore but something else—hope, understanding, affection.

"C'mon, Romeo." I slipped my hand into his and gave it a light tug, my heart finally steady. "We've got an awards ceremony to get to."

✗ ✗ ✗ ✗ ✗ ✗

The crowd erupted in cheers as Christian and I stood side by side, the weight of the trophy in my hands. I couldn't help but smile as I held it up, feeling a sense of pride that was new and exhilarating. Christian bumped me gently, a quiet affirmation that this moment was as much mine as it was his.

Our school had placed in every single category. Even when the field conductor category came up, and they called up Arcana High, Christian had nudged me forward to accept the trophy for the both of us.

The bus ride home was buzzing with the afterglow of our first win. Laughter echoed in the dimly lit bus, a mixture of exhaustion and pride. But as the night wore on and the adrenaline wore off, the chatter began to quiet. The hum of the engine became the soundtrack of the ride, mingling with the occasional rustle of jackets and muffled yawns.

I leaned my head against the cool glass of the window, my thoughts swirling with everything that had happened today: the kiss, the performance, the way Christian had looked at me during the awards ceremony. It all felt like too much and not enough all at once.

I barely noticed when he slid into the seat next to me until the dip in the cushion made me turn. Christian gave me a tired smile, his eyes heavy with sleep but still holding that spark of something unspoken. Without a word, he leaned his head against my shoulder, the warmth of him seeping through the fabric of my jacket. I stiffened, my breath catching for a moment, but then I relaxed, letting the weight of his presence ground me.

His breathing grew steady, and I realized he'd fallen asleep. There was something so vulnerable about him like this—so different from the confident, sharp-edged Christian I was used to. My hand twitched with the urge to brush his hair back, to touch the boy who had shown me kindness in ways I wasn't sure I deserved. But I didn't. Instead, I stared out the window, the passing streetlights painting fleeting patterns on his face.

I couldn't keep doing this—not with the secret I was carrying. The guilt had been eating at me all week, and tonight's win only made it worse. He didn't know the truth. None of them did. But he deserved to know. He deserved more than my silence.

I took a deep breath, summoning the courage I wasn't sure I had. "Christian," I whispered, my voice trembling slightly.

He stirred, his eyes fluttering open. He blinked at me, groggy and confused for a moment, before a soft smile crept onto his face. "Hey," he murmured, his voice thick with sleep.

"Hey," I replied, my heart pounding. "I need to tell you something."

His brows knit together, concern replacing the drowsy warmth in his gaze. "What is it?"

I hesitated, the words caught in my throat. Just as I opened my mouth to speak, a flicker of red and blue lights flashed through the bus windows, cutting through the darkness. The bus jerked to a stop, and the hum of conversation turned into hushed murmurs as everyone noticed the police cars parked in front of Arcana High.

"What's going on?" someone asked, their voice tinged with unease.

Christian sat up straighter, his hand brushing against mine as he steadied himself. "I don't know," he said, his voice low but steady.

The band members shuffled off the bus, their excitement replaced by a growing tension. The sight that greeted us as we approached the school made my stomach drop. Police officers stood near the entrance, their radios crackling softly in the still night. The front doors were propped open, and I could see the faint glow of fluorescent lights spilling into the parking lot.

The closer we got to the band room, the more the disarray became visible. Loose papers trailed into the hallway like breadcrumbs leading to disaster. I froze in the doorway, my breath catching as I took in the scene.

Inside, the band room was chaos. Sheet music was scattered across the floor, instrument cases flung open with their contents strewn about. The whiteboard, once neatly filled with notes and reminders, was wiped clean, replaced with crude drawings and slurs. My gaze darted to the front of the room, where Mr. Trust's office door was ajar, papers littering the ground like confetti.

And then I saw it—the empty spot where the drill book should've been.

My chest tightened, the weight of everything crashing down on me. This was my fault. All of it. Mr. Waylan's threats echoed in my mind, a cruel reminder that he'd warned me he could make my life hell. And now he had.

Christian's voice broke through my spiraling thoughts. "Who could've done this?" he asked, his tone laced with anger and disbelief.

I couldn't meet his eyes. My hands clenched into fists at my sides, and I forced myself to keep my expression neutral. "I don't know," I said quietly, the lie burning on my tongue.

Mr. Trust's voice cut through the room as he spoke with the officers, his tone measured but tense. "The drill book is missing," he said, and the words felt like a knife twisting in my gut.

The officers nodded, taking notes as they surveyed the damage. Around me, the band members moved in a daze, picking up scattered papers and righting overturned stands. I joined them, keeping my head down and my hands busy. The guilt was suffocating, but I couldn't let it show. Not here. Not now.

Christian knelt beside me as I gathered a pile of sheet music. His hand brushed mine, and I flinched, the contact sending a jolt through me. "Jessica," he said softly, his voice barely above a whisper. "Are you okay?"

I nodded quickly, not trusting myself to speak. If I looked at him, I knew I'd break. And if I broke, everything would come spilling out. Anger bubbled up inside me, twisting my thoughts into a mess. I wanted to scream, to punch something, but I couldn't let any of them see just how deep this cut. So, I did the only thing I could—I threw myself into helping clean up the mess, keeping my head down as the others worked around me, their spirits low.

When no one was looking, I slipped out of the band room and made my way to Kingston High. The school was dark, save for the light spilling from Mr. Waylan's office. He sat behind his desk, flipping through a stack of papers with a smug smile, as if he'd been expecting me.

"I'm done," I said, trying to keep my voice from shaking. "I'm not playing your game anymore."

He didn't look up right away, just straightened a paper. Then, finally, "Jessica. You always did have a flair for the dramatic."

"You got what you wanted—the drill book. We're finished."

"Not quite." He leaned back, steepling his fingers. "You came to me, remember? Desperate to escape Arcana. And I delivered. Drum major. Kingston. A real spotlight. Now you want to walk away because it got hard?"

"You didn't help me. You used me to get back at Arcana."

His smile barely flickered. "Maybe. But don't pretend you didn't benefit."

I took a step forward. "You don't own me."

"No," he said quietly, opening the folder. "But this story does." I froze. My record. He tapped the top sheet with a single finger.

"One DUI on your record. Add theft, vandalism, academic dishonesty? You won't even make it to the audition round at UCLA—any school for that matter. And I'll be the concerned adult who tried to give you a second chance."

My heart pounded. He saw it. He knew.

"So here's the deal," he continued. "You stay through homecoming and one competition. You show up, play your part, and this ends clean. Try to walk away?" He slid the folder toward me. "I make one call."

I stared at the file. My hands clenched at my sides.

"Fine," I said. "But after that, I'm done."

"Of course," he said smoothly, his smile triumphant. "Just remember, Jessica—if you slip up even once, I won't hesitate to keep my promise."

I turned on my heel and stormed out, the cool night air biting against my flushed skin as I walked to my car. But it did nothing to calm the storm raging inside me. How had I let it come to this? Every step deeper into his game felt like losing a piece of myself, like I was unraveling thread by thread, and Waylan held the scissors.

His threats looped in my head. He had me cornered, every exit blocked by his smug, calculated cruelty. But as fear and shame coiled tighter in my chest, a spark of defiance flared against the darkness.

I'd made mistakes. Big ones. But this? This was different. I wasn't going to let Waylan hold my future hostage. Somehow, I'd find a way to fix this.

For the band. For Christian. For myself.

Christian

The ride home felt different tonight. The usual post-competition exhaustion was there, but something had shifted. Despite the mess at the band room and the anger still simmering beneath the surface, my heart felt lighter than it had in weeks. Jessica and I were finally on the same page. That kiss on the field—the way she looked at me afterward—it felt like we'd silently agreed: *whatever this was, we were in it together.*

When I pulled up to the house, the driveway was empty. Dad must still be at work. Mom? Who knew. I stepped inside, the quiet greeting me like an old, unwelcome friend. Usually, it pressed down on me. Tonight, it was just there.

I dropped my bag and headed to the kitchen, thinking I'd grab something before crashing. But when I flicked on the light, I froze. A yellow envelope sat on the counter, my name written in Mom's neat handwriting.

My stomach dropped.

I didn't want to open it. Already knew what it was. But my hand moved anyway.

Divorce papers.

I pulled them out, my hands trembling. Two signatures. Side by side. Mom's elegant script next to Dad's blunt, blocky print. The contrast made my chest ache. I stared at the space between their names. It felt like a canyon.

The room tightened around me. I could hear them from months ago: *We won't do this until after graduation. We promise.*

Lies.

I gripped the counter, trying to stay grounded, but the anger came fast and hot, burning away the peace I'd felt earlier. How could they do this? Sign away our family like it didn't matter? Like I didn't matter?

The papers crumpled in my fist before I forced myself to let go. What good would it do? They'd already made their choice.

I leaned over the counter, head down, trying to breathe through the heaviness pressing into my chest. That high from earlier—Jessica, the kiss, the win—it felt like it had happened in another life.

How was I supposed to keep it together when everything around me was falling apart?

I couldn't stay in the house. Every inch of it reminded me of what we'd lost. So I grabbed my keys and left, the door slamming behind me.

I didn't have a plan. Just needed to move. The truck seemed to drive itself, familiar turns guiding me somewhere safe.

Jessica crossed my thoughts, but I couldn't bring myself to call or text her. Not with this mess. She didn't need to see me like this, spiraling out of control.

My truck seemed to move on autopilot, the familiar route taking me to the one place that felt like it might offer some sort of comfort. Mr. Trust's house.

I hadn't planned it, but as soon as I realized where I was headed, I felt a strange sense of relief. Maybe he'd know what to do. Maybe he'd have some advice, some words of wisdom that could help me make sense of this chaos.

When I pulled up to his house, the lights were still on inside. I sat in the car for a moment, staring at the warm glow spilling out from the windows. It looked so... normal. A cozy house with a happy family inside, sharing a late-night meal after the competition.

It was everything I didn't have. Everything I was losing.

I took a deep breath and got out of the car, my legs feeling like lead as I walked up to the front door. My hand hovered over the doorbell for a second, doubt creeping in. Was this a mistake? Was I really going to burden him with my problems at this hour? But before I could talk myself out of it, the door opened.

Mr. Trust stood there, a look of surprise quickly turning into concern when he saw me. "Christian? Is everything okay?"

"I... I didn't know where else to go," I admitted, my voice barely above a whisper. The weight of everything suddenly crashed down on me again, and I felt like I might break apart right there on his doorstep.

Without hesitation, he stepped aside and motioned for me to come in. "Come on in, Christian. We were just finishing up dinner. You hungry?"

I shook my head, though the smell of food wafting from the kitchen reminded me that I hadn't eaten since before the competition. "No, I'm... I'm fine. Thanks."

Mrs. Trust appeared in the hallway, a warm smile on her face that faltered slightly when she saw my expression. "Christian, it's good to see you. Are you sure you're not hungry? We have plenty."

"I'm okay," I said, trying to muster a smile but failing.

"Let's go talk in the living room," Mr. Trust said, guiding me gently towards the couch. "Hon, could you bring us some tea?"

Mrs. Trust nodded and disappeared into the kitchen, leaving me alone with Mr. Trust. We sat down, and he turned to me, his expression full of the kind of concern and patience I hadn't seen in my own parents in a long time.

"What's going on, Christian?" he asked softly, like he already knew something was wrong.

I stared down at my hands, the words catching in my throat. But I couldn't keep it in any longer. "They signed the papers. The divorce papers. I found them on the kitchen counter when I got home."

Mr. Trust's brow furrowed, and he nodded slowly, as if processing what I'd just told him. "I'm sorry, Christian. I know you were hoping they'd hold off until after graduation."

"They promised," I said, my voice cracking with the weight of it all. "They promised me they wouldn't do this yet. But they didn't even tell me. Just... left them there for me to find."

Mr. Trust leaned back in his chair, his eyes never leaving mine. "I can't imagine how that must feel, Christian. But I want you to know that what they did isn't a reflection of you. It's not your fault. Sometimes, people make decisions that hurt others, even when they don't mean to. It doesn't mean they don't care about you."

I wanted to believe him, but the anger and hurt still gnawed at me. "But they don't! They don't care about me. If they did, they wouldn't have done this. My family is breaking and I don't know how to fix it."

"You can't fix everything, Christian," he said gently. "Sometimes, all you can do is march forward, even when it feels like the ground is crumbling beneath you."

I nodded, not trusting myself to speak. The anger was still there, but it had dulled to a low ache. Talking to Mr. Trust, being here in this house that felt like a real home, it helped. It didn't take the pain away, but it made it a little more bearable.

Mrs. Trust returned with two mugs of tea, setting them down on the coffee table in front of us. "Stay as long as you need to, Christian. We're here for you."

"Thanks, Mrs. Trust," I said quietly, feeling a lump rise in my throat.

"You're welcome, dear. And if you need anything, don't hesitate to ask." She gave me a reassuring smile before heading upstairs, leaving us alone in the living room.

"You can crash here for the night if you need to," Mr. Trust offered. "I know it might be hard going back home right now."

I hesitated, the idea of going back to that empty house making my stomach turn. "Yeah… Okay, thanks."

He gave me a firm nod. "Get some rest, Christian. You've had a long day."

As I settled onto the couch with a blanket, Mr. Trust dimmed the lights and quietly left the room, leaving me alone with my thoughts. I stared up at the ceiling, the events of the day playing on a loop in my mind. The competition, the kiss with Jessica, the vandalized band room, and now this. It felt like too much for one day, but somehow, being here made it all feel less overwhelming.

✗ ✗ ✗ ✗ ✗ ✗

The next morning, I opened my phone and pulled up Jessica's contact, my thumb hovering over her name. We hadn't had much of a chance to talk since returning back from competition to a vandalized band room—the night still playing over in my head, especially the kiss. Part of me felt like I should give her space, let her sort through everything. But the bigger part of me just wanted to see her, to figure out where we stood. Especially since she had disappeared last night. We never got a chance to talk.

Finally, I typed out a message: *Hey, want to hang out today? Maybe grab coffee or just chill?*

I hit send and felt my pulse quicken as I waited for her response. Her reply came quicker than I expected.

Jessica: *Hey :) That sounds fun, but I'm still grounded... my mom found out about our "unplanned" day off. So I'm pretty much on lockdown until further notice.*

I couldn't help but smile, picturing her shrugging or rolling her eyes at that. Even over text, she had this way of sounding so real, like I could hear her voice in my head.

Me: *Bummer. You hanging in there?*

Jessica: *Yeah, it's not too bad. Just keeping a low profile, doing time lol.*

I laughed under my breath, shaking my head. I could practically see her expression: half-exasperated, half-amused.

Me: *Do you want me to break you out of jail?*

Jessica: *Lol, no it's okay. Thanks for checking in though. I'll see you at school on Monday.*

I tossed my phone next to me, a grin lingering on my face from Jessica's texts. She might be grounded, but knowing she was still there, still reachable, was enough to keep me in a good mood.

And since I wasn't going to be seeing her, I figured I'd head over to Alex's place. He'd been bugging me for weeks to check out his new sound system, and honestly, I needed the distraction.

The drive over took me through the nicest part of town—the kind of neighborhood where the lawns are always perfectly green and the houses look more like mini-mansions than regular homes. Alex's house sat near the end of the street, massive and sprawling with huge glass windows that reflected the trees lining the driveway. When I parked and headed up the steps, he was already waiting, his tall, wiry frame leaning against the door, a lazy grin on his face.

"Dude, took you long enough," he called, stepping aside to let me in. "I was about to fire up the system without you."

I rolled my eyes. "Right. Wouldn't want me to miss your latest playlist of jazz-funk remixes."

"You know you love it," he shot back, punching my shoulder. "Come on, I've got it set up in the theater room."

We headed through the house, passing a few rooms I was pretty sure I'd never even seen before. Alex's parents traveled a lot, and they were always adding something new to the place. Today it was a painting that took up most of one wall—a massive, modern piece that looked like a bunch of splattered paint but was probably worth more than my family's entire house.

As we reached the theater room, Alex settled in, scrolling through his playlist. But he glanced up, giving me that too-familiar smirk.

"So," he started, not even trying to be subtle, "what's the story with that kiss at the competition?"

I shrugged, trying to play it off casually. "You know, just part of the show. Mr. Trust wanted something memorable."

Alex raised an eyebrow. "Memorable. Passionate. Same thing, right?"

I felt a flush rise to my cheeks. "It wasn't—look, it wasn't planned. Not like that."

He paused, a little grin creeping up on his face. "Is that why you broke up with Courtney? Because of Jessica?"

I shifted uncomfortably, looking away. "I mean... yeah. I guess that's part of it."

Alex's eyes widened, his grin turning into a full-blown smirk. "Dude! You were with Courtney forever. And now you break it off with someone you've barely known for a few months?"

I sighed, bracing myself for whatever Alex was about to throw my way. "Look, I know how it sounds, alright? It's just... different with Jessica."

He tilted his head, eyebrows raised. "Different how? Like, 'movie moment on the field' different, or just 'rebound' different?"

I rolled my eyes, but I couldn't keep the small smile from creeping onto my face. "Not a rebound. She's just... I don't know, man. She gets me. It's like she sees through all the stuff that's just for show and gets who I am underneath it."

Alex leaned back, crossing his arms, clearly intrigued. "And what, Courtney didn't get that?"

"It's not that she didn't get it," I said slowly, trying to put my feelings into words. "With Courtney, it was always about fitting the perfect image, you know? I felt like I had to be this version of myself that looked good, sounded good—like it was all about being what everyone else expected. With Jessica, I don't feel that pressure. She knows me, flaws and all. And I like her for that."

Alex watched me for a moment, then nodded. "Alright, I'll give you that. Jessica doesn't seem like someone who would care about all that 'perfect couple' nonsense."

"Exactly," I said, feeling a weight lift just talking about it. "She just... sees me. She understands. And I can be myself with her."

Alex's smile softened, and he looked at me with an understanding that surprised me.

"You know," he said, leaning back against the couch, "this reminds me of that night at the campfire—the first one, after school started. Remember what you said?"

I nodded slowly, the memory of that night coming back. The flickering light of the fire, the quiet, honest vibe as we all shared the things we'd never say in the light of day. I'd been the last to speak, and I'd let it slip. How I just wanted someone to actually see me. Not some version of me people expected, but who I was underneath all of that.

"Yeah, I remember," I said quietly.

"Maybe that's why you're all in on her," Alex said thoughtfully. "It's like she just... clicked right into that wish, man. She sees you, flaws and all, and doesn't try to change anything."

I felt a strange sense of relief at hearing that, like he'd put into words what I'd been struggling to say. Jessica hadn't just come into my life—she'd actually heard what I needed before even I fully understood it. And I didn't have to be "on" around her. I could just be Christian.

"Guess that's why it feels different," I admitted, my voice a little rough.

Alex nodded, a real, genuine smile on his face. "Well, here's hoping you don't mess it up." He laughed, then added, "Seriously, though—sounds like you finally found what you were looking for."

32 Girlfriend

Jessica

As I walked through the doors of Arcana High, I could barely contain the flutter of nerves and excitement that danced in my stomach. The past few days had been a whirlwind—performances, secrets, and unexpected turns. But now, with the storm of competition behind us and a new chapter ahead, I was eager to face it all.

My footsteps echoed in the quiet hallway as I made my way to homeroom. It was the usual buzz of students settling in for the day. I slipped into the classroom and headed toward my seat. Christian was at his desk, head bent over a notebook. I hesitated for a moment, the awkwardness of our new dynamic settling in. How do you navigate being a couple in the middle of a school day when everything had been so tumultuous just days ago?

When he looked up and his eyes met mine, his face lit up with that familiar, warm smile. It was as if he was seeing me for the first time all over again. His smile was a beacon of joy, cutting through the lingering haze of tension from our earlier days. I felt a smile tugging at my lips; the awkwardness melting away in the warmth of his gaze.

"Morning," I said, aiming for casual as I slid into the seat behind him. The tension still lingered between us—a quiet reminder of how everything had shifted—but it was hard to feel self-conscious when his eyes lit up like that. The happiness in his gaze was infectious, tugging at something warm in my chest.

"Morning," Christian said, his voice a little too bright, carrying the same unease I felt. He glanced over his shoulder at me, and for a moment, it was like the rest of the room faded away. His gaze lingered, warm and unsure all at once, like he was trying to figure out how we fit together in this new, uncharted space we'd found ourselves in.

"So," I said, leaning into the familiar rhythm of our banter to shake off the last traces of hesitation, "is this the part where you apologize for climbing onto my podium a whole 8 bars too early?" I raised an eyebrow, letting a playful grin tug at my lips. Banter was safe, a thread we could follow back to who we were while figuring out what came next.

Christian turned to face me fully, a cheeky grin spreading across his face. "Climbing onto your podium? Please, I'd call it a bold, creative choice. It added a bit of excitement to the performance, don't you think? Speaking of which," he paused for dramatic effect. "Mr. Trust played me the judges' tapes. They loved it. The crowd loved it! I think we're going to have to do every single performance now." His grin turned sly as he leaned in just slightly, his eyes sparkling with a teasing challenge that sent a familiar warmth creeping up my neck.

"Oh, is that right?" I could feel my cheeks burning bright red. "So, you're telling me I should start preparing for an entire season of it? I'll need to start my lip balm collection right away."

Christian's grin widened, and he shook his head playfully. "Definitely, you should. I'm thinking of making it a signature move. You know, for dramatic effect." He leaned closer, lowering his voice to a mock-serious tone. "But you'll need to practice your surprised face, too. Can't have you looking too prepared."

I rolled my eyes, but couldn't suppress a smile. "Oh, I'll make sure to put that on my to-do list right between 'defeating world hunger' and 'finding a way to make you behave.'"

A textbook snapped shut, breaking us out of our world. "If you two are done," the teacher said, unamused. "Class has started."

Christian and I exchanged one last look, the teasing still hanging in the air like static. I slid into my seat behind him, pressing my lips together to keep them from smiling too big. It was weird, but in a good way. This thing between us was new, but it felt, I don't know. Nice? Nice to be thought of in this way, to be cared for. Nice to let him see all of me without him running the other direction.

X X X X X X

As I approached Aiden's table at lunch, my stomach grumbled in protest at the sight of our sad-looking trays. The pizza was as unappetizing as the carrots were mushy. We both pushed our trays away with a shared look of disappointment, and I was about to suggest we head out for something better when Christian strolled over, his face bright with a grin and a white paper bag from the diner down the street in hand.

"Guess what I've got?" Christian announced, setting the bag down on the table with a flourish.

Aiden's eyes widened, and his gaze flicked between me and Christian as he tucks a strand of hair behind my ear. Christian passed out wrapped burgers to each of us.

"So, what's this?" he asked, narrowing his eyes between us. "Bribing my sister with burgers? Is that why she's being nice to you?"

Christian laughed, his eyes twinkling with mischief. "I did. And a bag full of fries." He spills out the second takeout bag on a napkin.

Aiden raised an eyebrow at me, clearly noticing the shift in our dynamic. "Wow, you two are actually getting along. What is this?"

I glanced at Christian, my mind scrambling for the right words. "We're, um… well, I mean, it's kind of…" I trailed off, heat creeping up my neck as I fumbled for something that made sense.

Christian, ever steady, stepped in with a small, reassuring nod. "We're… together." His smile was warm, grounding me as he placed his hand gently on my back. The gesture was so casual, so simple, but it steadied my nerves in a way I didn't expect.

Aiden studied us for a moment, then shrugged with a half-smile. "Well, if this is how you're treating her and I get free food, I guess I can't complain. Thanks for the burgers, bro."

I took a sip of my drink just as Christian handed Aiden his food.

"Don't mention it," Christian said, pulling out the burgers and fries. "Just happy to make sure my *girlfriend* and her brother have something decent to eat."

The word hit me like a jolt. I choked on my drink—and immediately sprayed Christian in the face. Root beer dripped from his chin and splattered his shirt as I froze in horror, my hand flying to my mouth.

"Oh my God," I squeaked. "I am *so sorry!*"

"So that's what you think of my declaration, huh? Root beer to the face?" Christian blinked, wiping at his face with a napkin, his expression caught between disbelief and amusement. "I guess it's better than you running off in the opposite direction. Oh, wait…"

I dissolved into nervous laughter, burying my face in my hands as Aiden burst out laughing beside me. "She's marking her territory," he said, barely able to get the words out between wheezes. "Guess you're officially hers now."

Christian smirked, shaking his head as he grabbed another napkin. "I mean, it's not how I thought it'd happen, but… I'll take it," he said.

"But maybe don't call me *that* without a little warning next time."

He leaned back, his smile wide and infuriatingly charming. "Call you what?"

"You know what."

Christian's grin widens as he reached for another napkin. "Oh, you mean girlfriend? Should I try it again? Girlfriend. Girlfriend. Girlfriend."

I groaned, still half-hiding behind my hands.

"Just making sure you're used to it." He gave me a playful wink, dabbing at his shirt again. "Besides, I'm pretty sure this is the first time someone's ever baptized me with root beer. It's practically a sacred moment."

Aiden snorted, popping a fry into his mouth.

"Oh, for the love of—" I groaned louder, grabbing a napkin to help clean the mess on his shirt. "I said I was sorry! Can we move on?"

Christian leaned closer, his voice dropping just enough for only me to hear. "Sure, but only if you admit you like it when I call you my girlfriend."

I froze, my cheeks heating as his words sank in. "I—" My brain blanked, leaving me floundering for a response.

Aiden leaned forward, grinning like a Cheshire cat. "She's speechless. Mark it down. September 21st, 12:24 p.m.—Jessica rendered incapable of snark."

Christian chuckled, handing me a fry. "Guess I'll take that as a yes."

I snatched the fry out of his hand, glaring at him through my blush. "I hate you. Both of you." My face burned, the heat creeping up my neck as I fumbled to steady my drink, suddenly hyper-aware of his gaze on me. A nervous flutter stirred in my chest, and my fingers toyed with the edge of a napkin as if it could somehow ground me.

Aiden caught my reaction and laughed, clearly amused by the shift in my demeanor. "Well, that's new," he said. "Look at you guys, all cute and disgusting."

As we dug into the deliciously greasy food, I couldn't help but notice how easily Christian fit into this. It was just me and Aiden holding onto our secrets for so long. It was surreal to have someone new be a part of that, to know our past, and still want to sit and joke around with us.

"How are your appointments going with my uncle, Aiden?" Christian asked, dipping a fry in ketchup and then throwing it into his mouth.

Aiden took a sip from his soda before responding, his gaze shifting between Christian and me. "Pretty well, actually. Jacob's got me working on some new exercises. It's a lot of work, but I can feel some progress. It's slow, but it's there."

Christian nodded, his expression one of genuine interest and concern. "That's really great to hear. I'm glad you like him. He's certainly a lot better company than my dad is."

I glanced at Christian, feeling a swell of gratitude for his support. It wasn't just about the food or the public displays of affection; it was the little things that showed he genuinely cared about my family.

By the time band class came around, a group of seniors had gathered near the front door, their voices hushed but tense. As I approached, snippets of their conversation floated over, sharp and cutting. My chest tightened when I heard Emily's name.

"—definitely a spy for Kingston," Courtney said, her voice dripping with disdain. "It's too convenient. She shows up out of nowhere, and suddenly our band room gets trashed? She's feeding them information. It's obvious."

Tracy, standing beside her, nodded in agreement, her arms crossed tightly. "Courtney's right. Kingston's been playing dirty for years, and this feels like them ramping it up. We can't just let it slide."

My stomach churned. Tracy was someone I trusted, someone who'd made me feel like I belonged here. Hearing her now, caught up in Courtney's venomous theory, felt like the ground beneath me was crumbling.

"We need to figure out a way to hit back," Tracy continued, her tone sharp. "Something they'll feel. Maybe a little payback during Friday's football game. They need to know Arcana doesn't just roll over."

"I mean, do we even know for sure?" I cut in, forcing my voice to stay light. "It could've been anyone who trashed the band room. Maybe it's just some random prank, you know? It doesn't make sense to start pointing fingers without proof."

Courtney turned to me, her glare icy and dismissive. "A prank? Are you serious? You think someone just 'pranked' us by timing a vandalism for when we were at a competition? That's not a coincidence, Jessica."

Tracy hesitated, looking between Courtney and me. "Jess, I get what you're saying, but it's hard to ignore the timing. We can't just sit around and let them walk all over us."

I forced a smile, trying to mask the panic rising in my chest. "I just think we should be careful. If we start accusing people without proof, it could backfire. We're better than that, right?"

Tracy seemed to soften slightly, but Courtney wasn't letting up. She crossed her arms, her glare sharpening. "You're being naïve. Kingston plays dirty. If you've been around as long as the rest of us, you'd know that. If we don't stand up to them, they'll keep doing it."

Her gaze flicked over me like she was sizing me up. "Unless, of course, you've got a reason to defend her."

Before I could respond, Christian's arrival broke the group apart. Most of the seniors scattered, but Alex lingered to fill him in. I stayed back, my pulse pounding as I watched Christian's expression darken.

"So, Emily's being blamed for the vandalism?" Christian asked, his tone low but incredulous.

"Yeah," Alex said, running a hand through his hair. "Tracy and Courtney are fired up about it. They think she's a plant from Kingston."

Christian sighed, his jaw tightening. He looked toward the others, his voice firm. "This stops now. No more rumors until we have proof. If we're wrong—" He didn't finish, but the weight of his concern was clear.

I stood frozen, my heart racing. His words should've felt like a reprieve, a defense against Courtney's aggression. But instead, they only deepened my dread. Because if they ever found out the truth, there would be no defense for me.

The conversation lingered like a heavy fog as the group began to break apart. I wanted to catch Christian's eye, to find some assurance that everything would calm down, but his focus was locked on Alex, his jaw tense. I took a step back, my own thoughts spiraling. Should I say something? Try to deflect attention away from Emily? Or would that only make things worse? The knot in my throat tightened, choking off the words before they could form.

The weight of Courtney's glare followed me into the band room, her skepticism palpable. I sank into my chair, trying to steady my breathing as the rest of the class filtered in. A moment later, Christian joined me, sliding into the seat beside mine. His hand brushed against mine before he laced his fingers through mine, the simple gesture grounding me for a brief moment. I exhaled slowly, my heart settling just enough to remind me I wasn't alone.

From the hallway window, I caught a glimpse of Courtney standing just out of sight. Her expression wasn't sharp or cold this time but something softer—tinged with sadness. Her lips pressed together as her gaze flicked from our joined hands to my face. For a moment, she looked less like the sharp-tongued, confident girl I'd always known and more like someone who was trying—and failing—to mask the hurt she still carried.

She turned away quickly, disappearing down the hall before I could say or do anything. But the look on her face stuck with me, the way it flickered between irritation and something quieter, something heavier. It reminded me of what it feels like to lose your footing, to feel like the ground beneath you isn't solid anymore.

I couldn't shake the thought that my connection with Christian had somehow added to her pain. And even though she'd spread the DUI rumor, even though she'd made it clear how much she disliked me, there was still a part of me that wanted to reach out. To tell her that none of this was about revenge or taking something from her.

Because I'd been there—feeling unseen, pushed aside—and I hated the idea of making someone else feel that way.

33 An Honorable Handshake

Jessica

I needed an excuse. Something believable enough to skip the game, keep Mr. Trust off my back, and buy myself one more night. Just one more lie.

I knocked on the door and stepped inside. "Hey, Mr. T," I greeted him with a forced smile. "I just wanted to let you know that my family and I are heading out-of-town tonight, so I won't be able to make it to the game."

Mr. Trust's smile was warm and understanding. "Oh, that's no problem at all. Remember, there's no rehearsal tomorrow. You kids all deserve a break."

I nodded. "Thanks, Mr. Trust."

Mr. Trust gave me a nod of approval. "Alright, have a pleasant trip. See you on Monday, then."

I left his office, my shoulders slumping the moment the door clicked shut. Relief flooded in, but it was muted, dulled by the overwhelming weight of everything else. Just one football game and one competition—then I'd be free of Kingston, of Mr. Waylan, of all the lies tying me in knots. I told myself I could make it, but even the thought felt hollow. I wasn't trying to win anymore—I was just trying to survive.

When I arrived home after school, I received a text from Christian: *Wherefore art thou, Juliet? Sad you won't be at the game. What time are you getting home? Maybe we can catch a movie after or are you still grounded?*

Technically, I was still grounded. I was allowed to go to band events, and my mom thought all my Kingston activities were just extra Arcana rehearsals. The lie was becoming exhausting. I texted him back, knowing I needed the entire night clear: *Wish I could, don't know when I'll be back.*

I couldn't risk getting pulled into anything tonight. There was too much on the line.

As I walked into my room, my eyes landed on the Kingston drum major uniform lying on my bed, and the sight of it twisted my stomach. I ran my fingers over the stiff, pristine fabric, its weight heavy in more ways than one. It wasn't just a uniform—it was a symbol of the secret I was keeping and the betrayal I was about to carry out.

Sliding the jacket off the hanger, I held it up to my body, staring at the reflection in the mirror. The uniform looked perfect, but the person wearing it didn't feel like me. Instead of pride, all I felt was guilt, the kind that seeped into my skin, staining every choice I'd made since agreeing to this scheme.

Just a football game and a competition—tonight and tomorrow. That's all Mr. Waylan wanted from me. Then I'd be free. But as I laid the uniform back on the bed, the knot in my stomach tightened. Every step I took in it felt like a step further from the person I was trying to become, sealing a fate I wasn't sure I could escape.

✗ ✗ ✗ ✗ ✗

As I approached Kingston High, the sun had already dipped below the horizon, casting long shadows across the parking lot where the buses were idling. The air was thick with the hum of engines and the low chatter of band members preparing for the trip to Arcana. My heart pounded in my chest.

I spotted Mr. Waylan standing near the front of the line, his sharp eyes scanning the crowd until they landed on me. He didn't smile, but the smirk that curled at the corner of his lips was enough to make my stomach twist in knots.

"Didn't think you'd show," he said, his voice dripping with satisfaction and superiority.

I forced myself to stay calm, shutting down the swirling emotions that threatened to overwhelm me. "I keep my promises."

"Good," he replied, his eyes lingering on me a moment longer before he turned away to bark orders at the rest of the band.

As I boarded the bus, the familiar hum of voices and the rustle of uniforms filled the air, but none of it felt familiar to me. The other band members barely glanced in my direction as I passed by, their conversations flowing around me like I wasn't even there. Maybe that was better—blending in was the whole point tonight, right?

But how could I lead these people when I didn't even know their names? I was in their uniform, in their colors, but all of it was a facade. I slid into an empty seat near the back, pressing myself against the window as guilt and dread churned in my chest. For all the authority the title of drum major was supposed to carry, I felt like an imposter at the front of their ranks. A placeholder. Nothing more.

By the time we arrived at Arcana, night had fully settled in, casting the school in shadows. The buses hissed to a stop. As the band piled out, I slipped on my helmet, adjusting the feather plume to hide as much of my face as possible.

With the helmet on and my emotions firmly locked away, I felt like a different person—someone who could get through this night without crumbling under the pressure. I was no longer Jessica Welling, the girl trying to find her place at Arcana. I was the Kingston drum major, a figure of authority and discipline. And that's all I could be tonight if I wanted to make it through without falling apart.

As we marched into the stadium, the familiar sights and sounds of Arcana washed over me, but I forced myself to block them out. This wasn't my school tonight. These weren't my friends, my band. I had a job to do, and I would do it, no matter how much it tore me up inside.

I could see Arcana's band lining up on the opposite side of the field, their uniforms crisp and proud under the stadium lights. Somewhere in that sea of familiar faces was Christian, but I couldn't let myself think about that. Not now. I had to stay focused, stay in control.

As halftime approached, the tension on the field thickened. The energy from the crowd buzzed in the cool night air, the stadium lights casting a harsh glare on the two bands preparing at the same goalpost. The Arcana band stood tall and proud, their uniforms shining under the lights, while the Kingston band remained in formation, each member focused on the task ahead.

I stood at the front of the Kingston formation, a conductor's baton steady in my gloved hand. The muffled sound of my heartbeat thudded in my ears, growing louder with each passing second. Just when I thought I had myself under control, Mr. Waylan's voice cut through the noise like a blade.

"Let's have some fun, shall we?" he called out, a twisted smile on his face. "Why don't we get a little sportsmanship going? Don't you think it would be honorable to acknowledge our friends at Arcana before we show them how it's done? How about a handshake between our drum majors before we begin?"

My heart skipped a beat, then sped up, pounding against my ribs like a trapped bird. *No, no, no. This wasn't part of the plan.* I had counted on staying in the shadows, hidden behind the anonymity of the helmet and the uniform. A public handshake with Christian was the last thing I needed.

But Waylan's gaze didn't falter, his smile growing wider as if he could see the panic rising in me. "Let's set the right tone, shall we?" he added, his voice sugary sweet. "Go on, now. Show Arcana how gracious we can be."

There was no escaping now. Mr. Waylan's eyes were on me, expectant and amused, clearly relishing the discomfort he knew I'd be feeling. With no other option, I took a deep breath and started walking toward the space between the bands where Christian was already making his way toward me.

I kept my head down. *I'm going to get caught*, I thought. I was thankful for the height difference between us, hoping it would be enough to keep my identity hidden. My heart raced faster with each step, my mind spinning as I focused on controlling my breathing, on not giving anything away.

When we finally reached each other, Christian's presence loomed in front of me, familiar and yet painfully distant. I couldn't bear to look up, to see his face, to risk him seeing mine. Instead, I extended my hand, the black glove stark against the bright white of his uniform. The heat under my helmet felt suffocating, beads of sweat trickling down my temple as I struggled to steady my breathing.

He hesitated for a fraction of a second, just long enough for me to feel the weight of his gaze on me, searching, questioning. Then he took my hand, his grip warm and strong, sending a jolt of something through me—something that made it harder to keep my emotions buried. The handshake was quick, but in those few seconds, time seemed to stretch, the noise of the crowd fading into the background. It was just us, standing on opposite sides of the same battlefield, yet worlds apart.

And then he leaned down, close to my ear.

His voice was low, meant only for me, cutting through the roar of the crowd like a blade. "We know about your spy."

My breath caught as I struggled to keep my grip steady. He pulled back, his expression cool and unshaken, as if he hadn't just turned my world on its head. My stomach twisted into knots, the weight of what I was doing crashing down on me like a tidal wave. I pulled my hand back as quickly as I could.

I turned and forced myself to walk away, every step feeling heavier, my legs trembling beneath me. I had never felt more terrified.

A small, reckless voice in my head screamed to rip off the helmet, to end this twisted game and tell him everything. But the weight of Waylan's expectations held me in place, crushing that impulse before it could take root.

The announcer's voice boomed over the speakers, calling Kingston to the field. I moved on autopilot, each step blurring into the next.

I told myself I could make it through the show. Just the show. Just tonight.

But deep down, I already knew I was running out of time.

Jessica

I stood on the podium, scanning the enormous Kingston Marching Band preparing. "Performing their show, *Ides of March*, please welcome to the field, the Kingston High School Marching Band!" the announcer's amplified voice filled the overhead speakers. There was a massive wave of booing that emanated from the home field crowd.

"Drum major, is your band ready?"

Keeping my head down, I turned towards the crowd and saluted. Traditionally, I'd take the helmet off, but there was no way in hell I was doing that tonight. Just one more night, I chanted in my head. *One more night and this will be all over.*

As the show began, I moved through the motions, conducting with a sharpness that mirrored the resentment churning inside me. The music was powerful, the rhythms driving, but all I could feel was the weight of the deception I was a part of. Every downbeat felt like a blow to my conscience, every crescendo a reminder of the choices I had made to get here.

As I continued conducting, my gaze was drawn to the center of the field, where two figures emerged in stark contrast—one dressed in black, the other in white. The brass and woodwinds swelled, and in a chilling, perfectly timed motion, the figure in black thrust a color guard saber into the figure in white, who stumbled, clutching their chest before collapsing to the ground. The music echoed with dark intensity, underscoring the betrayal that played out in front of me. It was Brutus and Caesar—a friend's ultimate treachery, driven by conviction but filled with betrayal. A shiver ran through me as the narrator's strained voice came across the speakers: *Et tu, Brute?*

When we reached the third movement, I caught sight of a formation that sent a chill down my spine. It was familiar—too familiar. My eyes narrowed as I watched the brass section move into position, the drill forming precise lines and curves that I had seen before. The realization hit me like a punch to the gut: this was Arcana's drill.

Mr. Waylan hadn't just stolen the drill book; he had used it, repurposing Arcana's hard work and creativity for Kingston's gain. The audacity of it made my blood boil, but there was nothing I could do now. The show was in motion, and I had to see it through.

As we entered the last bars of the show, the music swelled, and the drill became even more intricate. The familiar patterns unfolded before me, each one a stab of guilt that cut deeper than the last. I could imagine the Arcana band members in the stands, watching in stunned silence, their anger building with every step, every note.

Christian, especially. He would be livid. I could picture the fury in his eyes, the betrayal he would feel, not just because of the stolen drill but because I was up here, conducting it.

The final chords of the closer rang out, and I brought the band to a sharp, decisive halt. The crowd erupted into applause, oblivious to the undercurrent of tension that had colored the entire performance. I stood there for a moment, chest heaving, the baton still gripped tightly in my hand.

But inside, all I felt was a hollow, aching regret. I had done what I had to do to get out of this mess, but the cost was far greater than I had anticipated. As I descended from the podium, I couldn't shake the image of Arcana's band room, vandalized and ransacked because of me. I couldn't stop thinking about the people I had hurt—people I had come to care about more than I ever wanted to admit.

And now, as I walked off the field with the Kingston band, all I could do was brace myself for the fallout. Because if there was one thing I knew for certain, it was that nothing about this night was going to be forgotten.

X X X X X X

The game was down to the wire; the score tied with only seconds left on the clock. Kingston had possession, driving down the field with the kind of determination that would either clinch the win or push the game into overtime. I silently hoped for anything but overtime— I just wanted this night to end. The uniform felt wrong on me, heavy and stifling, like it was suffocating who I really was.

The sharp blast of the referee's whistle snapped my attention back to the field. As the ball was snapped to the quarterback, Kingston's offensive line stood firm, preventing Arcana from breaking through. The quarterback wound up, launching the ball downfield towards a teammate already in full sprint toward what could be the winning touchdown.

But just as the ball seemed destined to land in his hands, an Arcana player appeared out of nowhere, intercepting it with the kind of speed and precision that drew gasps from the crowd. He pivoted and took off in the opposite direction, racing towards Arcana's end zone like his life depended on it. The stands erupted, the roar of the crowd shaking the bleachers, but I couldn't bring myself to cheer with them. My heart was with the team on the other side of the field.

The seconds ticked down—five, four, three—and the Arcana player pushed himself harder, his eyes locked on the goal line. With a final burst of speed, he crossed into the end zone just as the buzzer blared.

"Touchdown, Arcana!" the announcer's voice boomed over the speakers, electric with excitement. "That's it, folks! This year's winner of the annual cross-town rivals game is the Arcana Eagles!"

Mr. Waylan called for everyone to head back to the bus in frustration to Kingston losing the game—though it was out of his control. "I just need to grab some water," I said quickly. He nodded, already turning back toward the parking lot.

I knew the Arcana campus too well by now, especially where to find a quiet spot. The drinking fountain behind the guest bleachers was deserted, just as I'd hoped. I leaned over it, letting the cold water hit my tongue, trying to calm my racing thoughts.

"There she is!" The shout made my heart lurch. I glanced up to see Alex and two other seniors rounding the corner of the bleachers, their eyes locked on me. Panic surged through me, and I started walking the other direction, quickening my pace with each glance back. My hands tightened the strap of the helmet on my head, desperate to keep it in place.

My mind screamed at me to run, but I couldn't bring myself to do it. Running would only confirm my guilt, wouldn't it? I adjusted the helmet, pulling it down further in a futile attempt to hide my face, but I knew it was only a matter of time.

"Hey, drum major!" another voice called out, sharper this time. I glanced over my shoulder to see Courtney, resplendent in her homecoming queen dress, flanked by her posse of guard girls. They were closing in fast.

The field entrance was just ahead, but the distance seemed to stretch endlessly. *Just a few more steps*, I urged myself. *Almost there.* But before I could reach it, a strong pair of arms yanked me into the box office, slamming me against the door. My pulse pounded in my ears, drowning out the distant cheers from the field. I was trapped.

Tracy's eyes blazed with betrayal, her hold on my shoulders like iron. "Get this stupid thing off—" She stopped mid-sentence, her voice strangled as she ripped the helmet from my head. It clattered to the floor, the sound echoing in the small space like a gunshot.

Her breath hitched, disbelief and hurt flashing across her face. "Jessica?" Her voice was barely a whisper, but it carried the weight of everything breaking between us. I wanted to shrink, to disappear into the floor. How could I have done this to her?

Her grasp loosened slightly, just enough for me to breathe, but the storm in her expression only grew. She took a step back, shaking her head. "It was you," she said, her voice cracking. "This whole time, it was you."

"Tracy, just listen," I started, my voice trembling, desperation clawing at my throat. "It's not what you think—"

"Not what I think?" she cut in, her voice sharp and trembling. "How could you? I trusted you. We trusted you. You were supposed to have our backs, Jessica. And Christian…" She choked on his name, her anger flickering with something far deeper— disappointment, betrayal.

Tears stung my eyes. "I didn't want this. I didn't mean for it to go this far. Please, Tracy, just let me—"

"Let you what?" she snapped, her voice rising. "Sneak back onto their bus and pretend none of this ever happened? How long have you been lying to us? To me?" Her voice cracked, and the raw emotion in her tone made my stomach twist. "I thought we were friends."

"We are friends," I said, the words catching in my throat. "I'll tell you everything tomorrow. I swear. Just... don't tell Christian. Please."

For a moment, I thought she might hit me. Her fists clenched at her sides, and her shoulders trembled with the force of holding herself back. "You don't deserve his trust," she said finally, her voice quiet but sharp as glass. Then, with one last, searing look, she shoved past me and stormed out of the box office.

I stumbled after her, pressing my ear against the door. My heart pounded as I strained to hear what was happening outside.

"Where did she go?" Christian's voice rang out, his tone laced with concern.

"She already got on the bus," Tracy lied, her voice steady and even. But I could hear the tension beneath it, the weight of everything unsaid. She didn't linger. Her footsteps faded into the distance, leaving me standing there, frozen in guilt and shame.

My legs felt like they might give out beneath me. Tracy had just saved me, but at what cost? The realization that I had shattered any trust she had in me was like a punch to the gut. As I leaned against the door, tears welled up, but I forced them back. I didn't have time to break down. Not now. But I couldn't ignore the truth any longer—I was losing everything I cared about, and it was all my fault.

X X X X X X

I made it back home in one piece, but the bus ride back from Kingston was truly awful. Every bump and turn seemed to mock me, reminding me that Mr. Waylan was probably reveling in the fact that I was almost caught. The weight of my deception felt heavier than the marching uniform I had just shed.

I stumbled into the bathroom and took a quick shower, hoping that the hot water would wash away not just the grime of the night but also the creeping sense of guilt that clung to me. I scrubbed my skin as if trying to erase the memory of the evening, but no matter how hard I tried, I couldn't shake the feeling of betrayal.

Once out of the shower, I wrapped myself in a towel and retreated to my room. I wanted nothing more than to crawl into bed and escape into a deep, dreamless sleep. Tomorrow, I promised myself, I would come clean to Christian after the Kingston competition. I would finally set things right. With that comforting thought, I settled under the covers, allowing my tired eyes to close.

Just as I was about to drift off, my phone buzzed loudly on the nightstand. The sudden noise jolted me awake, and my heart raced as I grabbed the phone, seeing Christian's name on the screen. Panic shot through me.

Had Tracy already spilled the truth?

My hands trembled as I answered the call. "Hello?"

"*Jeessssiccaa,*" Christian's voice slurred, thick and heavy. I checked the time; it was already past midnight. "Are you home? Did you g-get back yet? Can I... can I come over?"

"Christian, it's late," I whispered, trying to keep my voice calm. "Are you okay?"

"I just... I just need to see you," he mumbled, his words barely coherent. "Please?"

The knot in my stomach tightened as I listened to him. I was already drowning in secrets, but his voice—so raw, so broken—pulled me out of my head and back into the moment. He needed me, and no matter what was hanging over me, I couldn't let him down. "Where are you?"

"I'm at home in the driveway... in my truck," he said, and I could faintly hear the rumbling hum of the engine. "Please, Jess."

"Get out of your truck," I said urgently. My heart pounded.

The thought of him drinking and driving made my chest tighten. A cold rush of fear swept through me. I couldn't bear the idea of him getting into an accident, or worse.

"Christian, please get out of your truck," I begged. "Go inside and leave the front door unlocked. I'll come to you."

For a moment, there was only silence on the other end, then a soft, "Okay." The engine noise stopped, and I exhaled. I hurried to get dressed, my mind racing.

Slipping out of my room, I tiptoed to the window, my heart pounding in my chest. The thought of my mom catching me was terrifying, but not as terrifying as the idea of Christian out there on the road. I pushed the window open and swung one leg over the sill, my pulse racing as I grabbed hold of the tree outside.

When my feet finally touched the ground, I didn't waste a second. I darted to my car, sliding into the driver's seat with trembling hands.

I drove through the empty streets, my mind a whirlwind of worry. Christian's house loomed ahead, the lights dim and inviting. I parked only seeing his truck in the driveway and quickly made my way through the front door.

The staircase creaked beneath my feet as I ascended, each step echoing my growing anxiety. At the top, I found his door slightly ajar and pushed it open, stepping into a space that was both foreign and intimate.

The room was dimly lit by a single lamp on his desk, casting a warm, golden glow across the room. Posters of bands and sports teams adorned the walls, the room filled with the faint smell of old leather and lingering cologne. A tangled mess of blankets and clothes lay strewn across the bed, and an open closet revealed neatly hung clothes, a stark contrast to the chaos of his room's surface.

Christian sat slumped on the floor, back pressed to the bedframe, fingers tangled in his hair. His knees were drawn up, elbows braced on them, and for a moment I wasn't even sure he knew I was there. His shoulders trembled—not with big, dramatic sobs, but with the quiet kind, the kind you try to bury in silence. The room felt too still, like even the air didn't want to intrude. His hands flinched, dragging down over his face like shame had slipped over him like a second skin.

I knelt beside him, my hands brushing against his arm gently. "Christian, it's me," I whispered, my voice soft and soothing.

He looked up, his eyes red and glassy. "Jessica..." His voice was a broken whisper, filled with pain. "I—I'm sorry."

I shook my head, placing a hand on his shoulder. "It's okay. Talk to me. What's going on?"

He took a shaky breath, trying to steady himself, but it came out broken. "My parents... they were fighting when I got home," he started, his voice muffled and trembling. "They signed the divorce papers, and now it's just…" He dragged his hands down his face, his fingers clutching at his jaw as if he were trying to keep it from falling apart. "They're fighting about everything. About the house, money… about me."

His voice cracked on the last word, and he turned his head, pressing it against the edge of the bedframe. Tears streaked his cheeks, falling freely, his breaths coming in uneven gasps. "They don't want me, Jess. Neither of them."

He stayed there for a moment, hunched and trembling, his words dissolving into silence. Then, in a voice so small it barely made it past his lips, he whispered, "Why don't they love me?"

The quiet broke me more than anything else. His question hung in the air, bitter and desperate. He was pleading for an answer.

My heart shattered at his words. All I wanted was to hold him forever and make this pain go away. Without thinking, I climbed onto his lap, gently taking his face in my hands. His fingers instinctively found their way to my waist, grounding him in the midst of his distress. Our eyes locked, and I could see the tears shimmering at the corners of his eyes. I pressed my forehead to his.

"I do," I breathed, the words escaping before I could second-guess them. "I do. I love you."

The room seemed to hold its breath as we stared at each other, the world outside fading into the background. Christian's hand trembled as it moved to the back of my neck, pulling me closer.

His lips met mine in a kiss that was hesitant and clumsy. The alcohol had blurred our edges, making the moment unsteady but charged with a raw need for connection. As the kiss deepened, there was an urgency in his movements—a desperation neither of us fully understood. I felt his pain in every touch, every trembling breath, and a part of me ached to give him the comfort he was seeking, to offer him something real in the middle of his unraveling. He gently guided me down, laying me flat on the floor as he hovered above me. Our breathing mingled, shallow and uneven, as he leaned closer, his lips finding mine again.

Christian pulled back slightly, his gaze locking onto mine. His eyes searched for something—reassurance, permission, maybe both. He sat back on his knees, his hands trembling slightly as he pulled off his t-shirt. The intensity in his expression made my chest tighten, not with anticipation but with a creeping unease I couldn't ignore. He leaned down again, his lips brushing mine, but this time, something shifted. His hands moved to the hem of my sweater, tugging it upward in one smooth motion.

The air felt heavy, the room smaller. My breath hitched as his hands moved under my sweater. The warmth of his touch sent a sharp pang of panic through me, so sudden and overwhelming that it left me frozen.

I told myself to breathe, to focus, to stay grounded. *This is Christian*, I thought. *Christian is safe.* I willed myself to find comfort in his presence, to let go of the tension curling in my chest. He needed me, and I wanted to be here for him. I wanted to let myself fall into this moment, to feel close to him in the way he seemed to need, the way I thought I should be able to give.

But no matter how much I tried to relax, my body wouldn't cooperate. My heart raced for all the wrong reasons, my hands trembling where they rested on his shoulders. I told myself again to stay, to be present, to enjoy this connection. But every soft touch felt like too much.

There was something broken inside of me.

Why couldn't I just… be whole?

The ceiling above me seemed to ripple, my focus narrowing and distorting as I fought to stay present. But the panic clawed its way deeper, dragging me to that dark, disconnected place I'd spent so long trying to escape. My body felt distant, my limbs heavy and unresponsive, as though they belonged to someone else.

No. Not again.

"No," I gasped, the word barely escaping my lips, but he didn't seem to hear it. My hands shot up instinctively, pressing against his chest as hard as I could, trembling as I pushed him away. "Stop," I said, louder this time, my voice cracking under the strain.

He immediately froze, his hands stilling mid-motion as if he'd been struck. The realization hit him like a tidal wave, and he scrambled back, his eyes wide with horror. "Jess…" he whispered, his voice cracking. "I didn't mean to—" he started, then stopped. "God, Jess. I don't even know what I was thinking. I'm such an idiot. I'm so sorry."

His hands trembled as he reached for the shirt he'd tossed aside, fumbling with it like he didn't know what to do with himself. The alcohol-induced bravado melted away, leaving only raw regret and guilt etched across his face. His red-rimmed eyes searched mine, desperate and pleading, but I couldn't meet his gaze.

My chest heaved as I scrambled to sit up, my arms wrapping around myself like a shield. Tears welled up, blurring my vision as I struggled to ground myself in the present. The fear, the helplessness, clung to me like a second skin, and I couldn't stop trembling.

"I didn't mean to—" he started, his voice shaking, but he stopped himself, raking a hand through his hair as he stepped back further, giving me space. "I—I wasn't— I swear I'd never—" He couldn't finish the sentence, and the silence between us stretched heavy and suffocating.

My mind swirled with emotions too tangled to unravel. I wanted to be here for him, to help him through whatever was breaking him apart, but not like this.

"I should go home," I mumbled, my voice shaky as I took a step toward the door. "You need to sleep this off, and I... I need to clear my head."

"Jess, please," he said, his voice cracking again as he moved toward me but stopped himself. "I'm sorry. I—I didn't mean to scare you."

"I know," I said, swallowing hard, my throat tight. I knew he hadn't meant to scare me. But knowing it and feeling safe were two different things.

Christian looked up, his eyes rimmed with regret. "Please don't go," he said quietly, his voice trembling. "I—I just don't want to be alone right now. I promise, Jess. I'll sleep on the floor, I'll keep my distance—whatever you need. Just... stay with me."

I hesitated, the war inside me still raging. But the way he stood there, shoulders slumped, eyes pleading, made it impossible to ignore the weight he carried. "Okay," I whispered, the word barely audible but enough to bring a flicker of relief to his face.

"Okay?" He perked up.

"Yes, okay."

He exhaled, a visible tension leaving his shoulders as he grabbed a blanket and pillow from his bed. "I'll sleep down here," he murmured, settling on the floor beside the bed. He didn't make a show of it or try to argue. He just laid down, pulling the blanket over himself with his back to me.

I climbed onto his twin-size bed, my heart still pounding with residual panic. The room was quiet, save for the occasional sound of his uneven breathing. I stared at the ceiling, the heaviness of the night pressing down on me.

Then, almost without thinking, I reached down, my hand finding his. His fingers twitched slightly before curling around mine, his grip firm but tentative. The contact was grounding, cutting through the swirl of emotions in my chest. Neither of us said a word, but the silence between us felt less lonely, less broken.

Christian

She was gone when I woke up.

The next thing I noticed was the pounding in my head, a relentless throb that made me wince as I sat up on the floor. My back ached from the hard surface, and the blanket I'd pulled over myself sometime during the night was tangled around my legs. The faint light streaming through the window was enough to make me squint, groaning softly as the memories of last night started to surface.

On the bedside table, a glass of water and a couple of Advil waited for me. My chest tightened as I reached for them, realizing she must have left them there before she slipped out. Jessica. The warmth of her touch, the way her hand had lingered in mine as I drifted off—I clung to those fragments, trying to ignore the heavier memories that loomed before it all went wrong.

I glanced around the room, searching for something—anything—that would tell me she hadn't completely pulled away. Her sweater, half-hidden under the tangled sheets on the bed, caught my eye. My heart twisted as I picked it up, the faint scent of soap clinging to the fabric pulling me back to the moment I'd slid it off her. The way she smelled, the way she felt under my hands—it had felt perfect. Right. Until I ruined it.

She said she loved me.

Did she mean it? Or had I imagined it in my drunken haze, twisting something she didn't actually say into something I desperately wanted to hear? The thought made the guilt worse, thick and suffocating. I hadn't just scared her—I'd seen it in her eyes, the panic, the fear. And knowing that I might have been the reason she felt that way made my stomach churn.

I reached under the bed for my phone, my fingers brushing against the cold metal before I pulled it out. Staring at the dark screen, my thumb hovered over the power button. What could I even say to her? Sorry wasn't enough. Words wouldn't fix what I'd broken.

She trusted me, and I'd almost shattered that trust in a single moment.

The glass of water sat untouched on the table as I leaned back against the wall, the phone still heavy in my hand. No amount of Advil could dull the ache that realization left behind.

It was already mid-morning. There was a group thread of texts that I missed. *Meet at Kingston High at 11am. -Tracy*

I groaned, rubbing my face. Tracy desperately wanted revenge on Kingston's band, but all of that seemed so small compared to everything going on at home and with Jessica. I didn't even want to go, but I knew I had to support her and the other seniors who had all agreed to meet there.

I checked my next unread message. It was from Jessica. *Sorry for sneaking away this morning. Had to get back before my mom woke up. Take the Advil and hydrate. I'll talk to you tonight.*

The simple, practical tone of her message shouldn't have hit me so hard, but it did. The fact that she could still think about me—after everything I'd put her through last night—made my chest tighten. I stared at the words "I'll talk to you tonight" for a long moment, feeling a flicker of relief that she hadn't shut me out completely.

I typed out a response, my fingers hovering over the keyboard before I finally hit send. *I don't deserve you.*

I set the phone down and leaned back, staring up at the ceiling, letting the hangover take effect before reaching for the Advil.

After taking a shower and feeling like a new person, I headed downstairs. The house was still empty—no sight of my parents. Grabbing my keys, I got into my truck and started my drive to Kingston.

As I pulled up to the rival high school, the sun was already high in the sky. I found the group of Arcana seniors gathered near the entrance. Tracy, Alex, and Courtney were deep in conversation, their faces set with a mixture of determination and mischief. They glanced up as I approached, and Tracy gave me a tight smile that didn't quite reach her eyes.

"Hey," I greeted them, trying to keep my tone light despite the heaviness in my chest. "What's the plan?"

Alex, with a grin that didn't quite fit the situation, pulled out a knife. "Thought about slashing their tires," he said, flipping it open and showing it off. "You know, an eye for an eye."

The group murmured uneasily, a mix of amusement and hesitation. I grabbed the knife out of his hand before he could make it a bigger deal than it already was. The metal felt cold and wrong in my grip, heavier than I expected. "No way. That's not happening. Let's think of something less... permanent."

I shoved it into my pocket without thinking, my focus already shifting to the rest of the group. "Where's Jessica?" I asked, scanning the group for her face.

No one answered, but the uneasy silence that followed was enough to make my stomach churn. Something wasn't right. Tracy's eyes darted towards the field. "We should just go to their field. They're out rehearsing this morning."

Courtney smirked, almost smug. I frowned. "Why are you all acting weird?"

We started walking toward the field. My heart picked up as I spotted the Kingston band in the distance. They were mid-rehearsal, moving with mechanical precision. But then my eyes locked onto the podium.

She was there.

Jessica.

Wearing their colors. Standing on their podium. Conducting like it was hers.

At first, I thought I was seeing things. It couldn't be her. But it was. The girl who'd held my hand last night, whispered that she loved me—was up there, leading Kingston's band.

The betrayal twisted inside me. Cold. Sharp.

My mind flashed back to the blood oath in the band room. That stupid moment when we made her "prove" herself.

"Relax," she'd said, laughing as she opened her hand, unharmed. *"This is probably the worst cult I've ever been part of."*

We laughed because she got it. Because we trusted her.

I trusted her.

But now? Now I wasn't sure I could trust anything about her.

The realization hit like a freight train. She had been working with Kingston all along, playing a role, working behind the scenes to undermine everything we had built. My chest hollowed out, anger roaring to life in the empty space. I wanted to believe our connection had been real, that she had been genuine. But now it seemed she had been playing us—playing me—all along.

The field blurred for a second as my vision clouded, a mix of rage and confusion. A flicker of hesitation tried to claw its way through, whispering that I could be wrong, that I didn't have the full story. But the anger swallowed it whole, dragging me under.

I clenched my fists, the betrayal coursing through me like poison. Tracy and the others moved closer to the field, but I stayed rooted to the spot, struggling to contain the storm inside me. All I could see was her—her in their colors, standing on their podium, as though everything she'd done to us, to me, meant nothing at all.

"This is a closed rehearsal!" a man yelled from the bottom of the podium, probably the band director. "I'm calling security."

All eyes on the field turned to us, and the Arcana seniors instinctively retreated toward the parking lot. But I couldn't move. I stayed rooted to the spot, my gaze locked on Jessica. My mind was a storm. I needed to be sure it was really her—this was the same girl who had shared a vulnerable moment with me the night before, the same girl who had said she loved me.

Jessica descended from the podium hastily, her eyes wide as she sprinted towards me. My heart felt like it was being squeezed, and I struggled to process the pain. She had been playing both sides, working against us all along, and now the truth was hitting me like the crack of a whip—sharp, sudden, and impossible to ignore.

"Christian," she called out, her voice trembling as she reached for my hand. I yanked it away, feeling a surge of anger I could barely control.

"Don't," I snapped, my voice cold and cutting. I turned my back on her and walked toward the parking lot, each step heavy with rage and disappointment.

"Let me explain!" she pleaded, her voice cracking with desperation.

"You don't have to explain anything, Welling," I bit out. "I've seen enough. You lied to me. To all of us. I went to bat for you, and this is what you were doing the whole time?" I shook my head. "You're nothing but a hypocrite."

The words came out like daggers, each one aimed to hit where it hurt. I could feel the other seniors watching, some looking at me with sympathy, others with judgment. This wasn't just about me—it was about how she'd let all of us down.

Jessica's shoulders tensed, her lips parting like she wanted to argue, but instead, she stepped closer. "Christian," she said, voice trembling, "please, listen to me. Waylan forced me—"

"No, I don't want to hear it."

Before I could back away, her hands reached up, cupping my face, forcing me to meet her eyes. "I didn't mean for you to find out like this," she whispered. "I was going to tell you everything tonight."

For a fleeting second, her touch made me freeze, the warmth of her hands igniting something I didn't want to feel. But then the sting of betrayal surged through me again. With a harsh jerk, I ripped myself out of her grasp, my teeth clenched so tightly it hurt.

"Don't touch me," I snarled, stepping back, the words slicing through the air. My chest heaved as I glared at her and my voice cracked. "I don't believe anything you say anymore. All of this—it was just a game to you, wasn't it? You got what you wanted, and now you're trying to act like you care."

Her betrayal felt personal, like she hadn't just lied but twisted everything between us. She'd wormed her way into my life, got me to trust her, only to turn around and betray me—betray all of us. That realization burned, harder than I wanted to admit. I needed her to feel it, to understand just how deep she'd cut.

"I wish I never let myself care about you."

The words were out before I could stop them, sharp and venomous. A small part of me wondered if I'd gone too far, but the ache in my chest drowned out any second-guessing. She had to feel it, to know what she'd done to me.

Her face fell completely, the impact of my words hitting her like a blow. For a moment, neither of us moved, the weight of everything hanging in the air like a storm about to break.

Then, her voice broke through the silence, barely audible but carrying the weight of everything she couldn't say. "I didn't have a choice."

Her words bled through the quiet, slicing through my anger like a sharp blade. But instead of softening me, it only twisted the knife.

"You always have a choice, Jessica," I snapped. "You just didn't choose us."

Christian

Just as I thought I'd gotten away, someone from Kingston shoved me hard, grabbing my shoulder and spinning me around. I whipped around, glaring at the guy, my vision clouded with pure rage.

"Hey!" he shouted, his face way too close to mine. "I think you owe Jessica an apology."

Her name on his lips was like gasoline on a fire. I stepped closer, my voice low and sharp. "Say her name again, and I'll make sure you regret it."

The guy smirked, his eyes gleaming with provocation. "What's the matter? Can't handle the truth? Everyone knows she played you, Arcana golden boy."

My fists clenched at my sides, my breath coming fast and shallow. All I could see was him—the smirk, the words still hanging in the air like poison. And then it happened.

I swung.

The punch landed hard, the jolt of impact radiating up my arm as the guy staggered back, clutching his jaw. A beat of silence followed, everyone around us frozen in shock, and then chaos erupted. Shouts rang out, bodies lunged forward, and the dam I'd been trying so hard to hold back finally broke.

My heart was pounding like a drumline, breaths ragged as I tried to hold back the surge of violence roaring inside me. But it wasn't just him anymore. His smug face blurred with memories I thought I'd buried: my dad looming over me, the slam of a door that rattled the whole house, his clipped words—"You'll never amount to anything if you can't control yourself."

I couldn't control myself.

The weight of the knife in my pocket felt like my father's anger—cold, always waiting. My mother's absence pressed in, her silence pretending we weren't falling apart. And now, the one person who'd made me feel seen—really seen—had turned out to be just like them.

Trust was a joke. My dad taught me that when he couldn't even stay in the room long enough to hear me out. My mom, when she smiled through her lies and pretended I didn't know she was sneaking off to see someone who wasn't my dad.

Jessica wasn't supposed to be like them. She was supposed to be different. Better. But in the end, she did what they always do—left me with nothing but broken promises.

The crowd recoiled, stumbling back. Their fear hit me like a slap, cutting through the haze. I'd wanted to scare him—but their faces, her face—that wasn't fear of him. It was fear of me.

My hand gripped the knife without realizing. The cold metal grounded me for a second, until I saw her.

Jessica stood in the distance, frozen. Her eyes locked on the blade, then shifted to mine. Not anger. Not confusion.

Fear.

Sirens cut through the moment. The crowd scattered like smoke.

Jessica didn't move. Just stared at me. Her eyes full of something I couldn't bear to name.

I stepped toward her. "Jess—"

She flinched.

The motion was small, almost imperceptible, but it stopped me cold. My chest hollowed out as she turned, her movements stiff, and hurried away. No words, no glance back.

It was the same look my mom gave my dad the night he came home drunk and shouting. I was just a kid, watching her shrink back, knowing no one would step in. Knowing she'd have to save herself.

My grip tightened. Then loosened. The knife hit the pavement with a metallic clatter that rang louder than anything else.

I stood there, surrounded by the chaos I'd created, the truth sharp and cold: I'd become the person I never wanted to be. A stranger with a knife. A fury no one could trust.

✗ ✗ ✗ ✗ ✗

"What the hell were you thinking? A knife?" My dad's voice was a thunderstorm of anger and frustration as we drove home from the police station.

He didn't even ask what happened. Just rattled off a lecture like I was some broken part he didn't have time to fix. And why would he? He hadn't asked in years. I stared out the window, wondering if I'd been wrong to expect anything different. The way I'd looked at Jessica when she tried to explain—it was the same look Dad was giving me now. Like he was already done with me.

"You're almost 18, Christian. If you pull a stunt like that again, you'll end up in prison. I don't know what to do with you anymore. You're going to your mother's, and that's final."

I stared at him, arms crossed tight over my chest, feeling the frustration build. "Just like that? You're passing me off?" I turned to look out the window, desperate for this day to be over.

Hours. I'd been stuck in that holding cell for hours, waiting for him. And he'd waited until he got off work to come pick me up. No rush, no urgency, just another thing on his to-do list.

Somewhere in the back of my mind, I'd hoped he'd at least act like he cared—a hint of worry, maybe even a lecture. But all I got was impatience. That look that said he was ready to be done with me so he could move on to the next thing. I clenched my jaw, trying to ignore the feeling gnawing at my gut.

I gritted my teeth, my fingers clenching around the door handle as we pulled into the driveway. His words echoed in my head, rattling around like loose screws. "I don't know what else to do with you." Like I was a chore, some burden he'd just about had enough of.

"I don't care what you do," I muttered, voice shaking, "just don't leave me with Mom." I yanked the door open, stepped out, and slammed it shut, the echo of it still ringing in my ears. I couldn't even look at him.

Of course he'd just hand me off without a second thought. Dump me at my mom's, who was too wrapped up in herself, in her new boyfriend or whatever he was, to care about me or notice how much this all was screwing me up. They'd probably think sticking me with her was "good enough" parenting.

I glanced back at my dad, who'd already gotten out of the car, fiddling with his keys like he couldn't wait to just get inside and away from me. He didn't know—didn't care—about how much it hurt, knowing about her affair, seeing her bring some stranger into our lives while pretending everything was normal. Neither of them seemed to think about me, about what any of this did to me. I was just a kid caught between two people who were too wrapped up in their own lives to give a damn.

In that moment, I realized, standing alone in that driveway, that I was basically on my own.

I stormed into my room, slamming the door shut with a resounding thud. The familiar buzz of my phone drew me in, and I saw a flood of message alerts from Jessica. The sight of her name only fueled my anger further. Her messages were a stark reminder of everything that had gone wrong, and I couldn't help but feel a surge of frustration as I read through them.

Her messages kept popping up, each one hitting harder than the last, digging right into that raw wound she'd left.

Christian, please call me. I know you're angry, but we need to talk. I'm sorry.

I could practically hear her voice, shaky and desperate. My jaw clenched, and I almost swiped them all away, but the next one stopped me cold.

I didn't mean for things to get so out of hand. I was going to tell you everything tonight.

Everything? I scoffed. Like it mattered now. She'd had her chance.

I saw your dad pick you up at the station. Please call me when you get home.

She'd actually waited around for me? I shook my head, refusing to let that hit. She could stand there all night if she wanted; it didn't change a thing.

I never lied about how I feel about you. I meant what I said last night.

I could still hear her voice whisper in my ear, I do. I love you. Another buzz. Her last message lit up my screen, a mix of hope and desperation bleeding through her words.

I'm in the woods near the school. Come meet me tonight. Please.

She had the nerve to ask me to meet her, like nothing had happened, like she hadn't ripped me apart in front of everyone. I wanted to hurt her, to make her feel even a fraction of the pain she'd inflicted on me.

Before I could think it through, I grabbed my phone and stared at it. Courtney's name sat at the top of my contacts, like a button I could press to make it all go away. My mom had her distractions—her way of forgetting everything that mattered. Maybe this was mine. The thought twisted in my chest, but I hit call anyway.

When she picked up, her voice was light, almost surprised. "Christian? Are you okay?"

I forced a smile into my voice, even though all I felt was pure rage. "Hey, Court. Can you come over?"

The thought of Jessica waiting for me in those woods made my chest ache—her voice, her words, her touch from earlier, all begging me to listen. But the anger drowned it out, suffocating everything else. Pain was easier to drown out when it turned into anger.

And Courtney? She was the perfect excuse not to think about what I'd just done, about who I was turning into—she was the perfect person to not expect me to feel anything.

37 Punishments

Jessica

I was staring at the ceiling when my phone alarm went off. It was already Sunday morning, and I had gotten no sleep.

Christian never showed up last night. I convinced myself that he just needed time. So, I went home and locked myself in my room. My mom had pounded on my door when she realized I'd gotten home extremely past curfew, but I kept it locked—not in the mood for another lecture.

The alarm kept ringing, pulling me out of my thoughts. I shut it off, but the weight of everything that had happened pressed down on me like a heavy blanket I couldn't shake off. I grabbed my phone, hoping for a text or call from Christian, but there was nothing. Just the unanswered messages I'd sent him last night, each one more desperate than the last.

He had to understand. Once I explain everything, he'd see why I did what I did. I wasn't trying to hurt him—or anyone else in the band. I was trying to fix things, to make it all right. But now... now it felt like I'd only made everything worse.

My stomach churned at the thought of seeing him today, but I knew I couldn't avoid it. I had to face him, even if the idea made my heart pound with anxiety. I couldn't let this drag on any longer. We had to talk, even if it meant hearing things I wasn't ready to hear.

I forced myself out of bed and headed to the bathroom. The reflection staring back at me looked as exhausted as I felt. My eyes were puffy, and my hair was a mess, but I didn't have the energy to care. I splashed some water on my face, hoping it would somehow make me feel more awake, more ready to face whatever was coming.

Back in my room, I threw on a pair of jeans and a hoodie— something that felt safe, something I could hide in. *I'll just drive over there*, I thought. *I'll force him to talk to me.*

The drive to Christian's house was a blur, the scenery passing by unnoticed as my mind raced with a thousand possibilities. What would I say? How would I explain myself? I had no idea, but I knew I couldn't let things fester any longer.

As I turned onto his street, I felt a sliver of hope. I saw his truck in its usual spot, but an unfamiliar one next to it. Maybe he just needs to see me, to hear me out in person. I pulled up to the curb, my heart pounding with anticipation and anxiety. I was about to open the car door when I saw movement at the front of the house.

Courtney.

She was walking down the steps, her expression smug as she adjusted her purse on her shoulder. I froze, my hand hovering over the door handle, dread creeping up my spine. *Why is she here?*

Before I could make sense of it, Christian appeared in the doorway. He was just pulling on a shirt. The sight of him made my heart ache with longing and confusion. *What's going on?*

And then, as if to answer the question gnawing at me, Christian stepped closer to Courtney, leaning down to kiss her. It wasn't a quick, friendly kiss. It was slow, intimate—the kind of kiss that left no room for doubt.

My world shattered.

The breath was knocked out of me. I felt numb, like everything around me had just turned into static. My hand fell from the door handle, and I pressed myself back into the seat, wanting to disappear. The tears welled up, blurring my vision, but I refused to let them fall.

The betrayal cut deep, twisting in my chest like a knife. How could he do this? After everything I said that night? I thought he understood me, that we understood each other. I thought what we had was real. And yet, here he was, throwing it all away like it meant nothing.

But maybe it did mean *nothing*. Maybe I didn't deserve for it to mean more.

The thought slithered in, uninvited but relentless, rooting itself in my mind. After everything that had happened—the accident, Aiden's scars, the people I'd hurt to survive—was this just the universe balancing the scales? For all the guilt I carried, maybe this moment was inevitable. A punishment I'd earned.

The way he kissed her... It was deliberate, as if he wanted me to see it. To hurt me. Or maybe I didn't matter enough for him to even notice I was here.

Either way, it worked.

The knife twisted in my chest, sharp and cutting, but the truth was, I had handed it to him. I had placed it in his hands, trusting he wouldn't use it. Trusting that I deserved something more. And now, watching him drive it deeper, I couldn't even blame him.

I wanted to scream, to cry, to pound on the steering wheel until the world made sense again. But all I could do was sit there, frozen, watching as he whispered something in her ear before she finally drove away, a satisfied smirk on her face.

Christian watched her leave, a small, twisted smile playing on his lips. That smile was the final blow. It was like he was proud of what he'd done, proud of hurting me in the worst way possible.

When he turned to go back inside, I finally found the strength to move. I threw the car into reverse and sped away, not caring if he heard the screech of the tires or saw me fleeing. My vision was clouded with tears as I drove. My insides felt empty and still; it made me wonder if my heart was still beating.

The one person I thought I could trust, the one who said he cared—the one who said he wouldn't hurt me—he'd turned on me in the cruelest way. And now, all the hope I'd held onto, all the words I'd planned to say, they meant nothing.

Because Christian had made his choice. And it wasn't me.

✗ ✗ ✗ ✗ ✗ ✗

I barely remembered the drive home. The streets blurred past in streaks of orange and red, headlights and taillights weaving together like the chaos in my chest. I tried to pull the familiar numbness over myself like a blanket, but instead, everything burned hotter, brighter. My heart felt like it was cracking apart, every breath sharp and jagged.

By the time I pulled into the driveway, my hands were trembling, and my face was streaked with dried tears. All I wanted was to crawl into bed and forget—forget him, forget Courtney, forget the way he smiled at her like I hadn't just poured everything I had into trusting him.

Forget everything.

I reached for the door handle, but the light spilling through the living room curtains stopped me cold. Shadows flickered inside—my mom pacing, my dad sitting stiffly. Waiting. My stomach twisted, but I was too drained to care. Whatever it was, I didn't have the energy to face it.

But I dragged myself out of the car anyway, each step toward the house heavier than the last. The door creaked as I pushed it open, and before I could even close it behind me, my mom's voice struck like a whip.

"Where the hell have you been, Jessica?"

I froze, the words slamming into me. Her tone was sharp, angrier than usual, stripped of the practiced critique she liked to pass off as concern. This wasn't measured or polite—it was raw, biting, and relentless.

"You've been gone all day without so much as a text!" she snapped, her voice climbing with every word. "First, you stay out late last night and lock yourself in your room. Now this? I've had enough—the sneaking out, the skipping class—this is the last straw!"

I stared at her, her words landing on the raw wound already festering in my chest. My dad sat on the couch, his gaze darting between us, but he didn't say anything. Of course not. He never did.

"You think you can just come and go as you please?" she continued, her frustration boiling over. "That there are no consequences for your actions? You're acting like a child! Do you even care how your behavior affects this family?"

Something inside me snapped. Her words, the way she threw

this family around like it meant anything, like she cared about anything but appearances—it was too much. Everything was too much.

"A child? Are you serious right now?" My voice cut through hers, sharp and trembling with anger I couldn't hold back anymore. "You want to talk about how I affect this family? What family? The one where you nitpick every single thing I do until I can't even recognize myself? Or the one where Dad sits there like a statue while you tear me apart?"

Her mouth fell open, stunned for a moment, but I didn't stop. I couldn't. The words were spilling out, messy and uncontrolled, but they were mine.

"You act like you care, like you're concerned, but you're not! You just want to control me, to make me fit into whatever perfect little box makes you look good! And you—" I turned to my dad, my voice cracking. "You just sit there and let it happen. You let her rip me to shreds, and you don't say a damn thing. Do you think I haven't noticed? How you handed everything over to her the second you got married? Like, 'thank God, I've got a new wife to raise my daughter—she'll handle it.' Because clearly, stepping up isn't your thing."

"Jessica, that's enough—" my mom barked, her voice rising, but it only fueled the fire burning in my chest.

"No, it's not enough!" I shouted, my voice raw now, shaking. "You're always saying I need to get my act together, that I'm ruining everything. But have you ever—" The words lodged into my throat begging for escape. "—have you ever thought about why?"

But they didn't hear it. They never did. My voice was too loud, too sharp, drowning out the quiet desperation behind the words. I needed them to listen—to really listen—but all they saw was anger. *Just a dumb teenager. A phase.*

"Jessica, stop." My dad's voice boomed, the first real thing I'd heard from him in weeks. He stood up, his expression caught between concern and… guilt, maybe. But it wasn't enough. "You don't get to talk to me or your mom like that."

"My mom?" I let out a hollow, bitter laugh that sounded foreign even to me. "She's not my mom. My mom died, and you let your parenting die with her." I turned on him, the tears spilling over now, hot and unrelenting. "You don't get to 'stop' me now, Dad. Where were you when I needed you? When she made me feel like I wasn't good enough every single day? You were there, but you weren't. You just sat there, like *this* was good enough."

His face fell, and for a second, I thought I saw regret flicker across it. But it didn't matter. I was done.

"I'm tired," I said, my voice breaking, the fire in me flickering into ash. "I'm tired of trying to make this work. Of trying to hold it together while you two tear me apart. You want to know where I've been? I've been trying to figure out how to survive *this*. How to survive *you*."

"You think I don't know what it's like to lose someone and feel like it's your job to hold everything together? That's all I've been trying to do, Jessica. But you don't see it." Her voice cracked, and for the briefest moment, I saw it—the exhaustion, the fear, the weight she carried. But it only made me angrier. How could she expect me to see her when she'd never once seen me?

"Stop acting like the victim." My words cut through.

Then I saw it—the way her eye twitched, like I'd just triggered some unwanted memory. For a split second, her expression shifted, cracking at the edges. It wasn't anger or frustration—it was something deeper, darker.

"I'm not—" she started, but her voice faltered. She closed her mouth, her jaw tightening as she drew in a shaky breath. "You don't know what you're saying."

"Don't I?" I shot back. "You walk around like you're some martyr, like everything you do is for us, but it's not. It's for you. You need to feel like you're in control because you're afraid to deal with your own crap. So don't stand there and pretend you understand what it's like to lose someone… or yourself."

Her hands curled into fists at her sides, her composure slipping. "You think I don't know what loss feels like? You think I don't know what it's like to wake up every day and carry the weight of it?" Her voice was low now, trembling with something I couldn't quite place. "You have no idea what I've been through, Jessica."

"Then tell me," I challenged, my voice rising. "Tell me what's so awful that you get to act like this, like you're the only one hurting!"

Her lips pressed into a thin line, and for a moment, I thought she might actually say something. But then she shook her head, a bitter laugh escaping her lips. "It doesn't matter. You wouldn't understand. You're just a child."

"That's convenient," I snapped. "Because if it doesn't matter, you don't have to say it. If you keep it locked up, then no one can call you out, right? But I'm the one choking in this silence. I can't breathe in this fucking house!"

The room was silent except for the sound of my ragged breathing. She stared at me, stunned into silence, and my dad looked like he wanted to say something but didn't know how.

I turned, heading for the stairs. As I climbed, I heard her call after me, her voice softer now, almost pleading. "Jessica…"

But I didn't stop. I didn't look back. I reached my room, slammed the door shut, and slid to the floor, my back pressed against the wood. The tears came then, hot and heavy, spilling over until I couldn't breathe. It wasn't just sadness or anger—it was release. The walls I'd held up for so long had cracked, and even if the mess spilled everywhere, it was mine.

I tried to claw my way back to the numbness, to that cold, quiet place where nothing could touch me. I'd been there before, safe behind the armor of not feeling. But this time, it was like a dam had broken, and no matter how hard I tried to stop it, the flood just kept coming. The emotions surged, spilling out in waves too big to contain.

It wasn't just the tears; it was everything. A torrent of grief, anger, humiliation, and exhaustion crashing through me all at once. I pressed the heels of my hands to my temples, as if I could turn it all off, but there was no off button, no switch to silence it. It was like a faucet stuck open, the water pouring and pouring until I thought I might drown in it.

I sat there for what felt like hours, the tears finally drying but leaving my chest hollow and raw. My breathing steadied, but the chaos in my mind didn't. The ache in my chest, the weight pressing down on me—it was unbearable. I couldn't do this anymore. I couldn't stay here, in this house, under this roof, with them.

My eyes drifted to the duffel bag shoved under my bed, the one I'd used when we moved down here. Without thinking, I reached for it, dragging it out and yanking the zipper open. My hands moved on autopilot, shoving clothes inside—jeans, hoodies, sneakers. My heart pounded, a mix of adrenaline and fear driving me forward. I didn't have a plan, but I didn't need one. All I knew was that I had to get out.

I yanked open the top drawer of my dresser, pulling out socks and underwear, the haphazard pile spilling onto the floor. My breathing was shallow, quick. If I didn't leave now, I never would. I couldn't stay here, not in this house, not with her.

The thought of staying here, pretending to be okay while everything inside me screamed, was unbearable. I grabbed my wallet from my nightstand, my phone charger, anything I thought I might need. The bag was getting heavy, the zipper straining as I forced it closed, but I didn't care. I just needed to leave.

My eyes darted to the window, the one I'd stared out of a thousand times before, wondering what it might feel like to just... go. The big oak tree outside loomed tall and steady, its branches brushing against the house as if beckoning me. Now, it felt like salvation.

The duffel bag was heavier than it had any right to be, digging into my shoulder as I pulled it closer. My fingers gripped the strap tightly, white-knuckled, as if holding onto the bag was the only thing grounding me in this moment. I yanked the window open, the cool night air rushing in and brushing against my flushed cheeks. The old oak tree outside swayed gently, its branches stretching toward the house like it had been waiting for me.

Freedom was so close.

I slung one leg over the windowsill, my foot dangling just above the sturdy branch that had been my secret escape route ever since we'd moved here. The bark gleamed faintly in the moonlight, rough and familiar. I could already picture it—the crunch of the grass under my sneakers as I landed, the hiss of the car door as I climbed in, the road stretching out in front of me, endless and open.

One more leg, and I'd be gone.

But then I froze. The weight in my chest grew heavier, pressing down until it felt like I couldn't breathe. My mind betrayed me, conjuring an image of Aiden in his wheelchair, staring at the empty space where I should have been.

He'd understand, I told myself, gripping the windowsill so tightly my knuckles ached. He'd have to.

Aiden didn't deserve this. He didn't deserve to wake up and find me gone, to shoulder the inevitable questions and disappointments on his own. He didn't deserve having to fend off his bullies alone. He deserved more than being left behind, even if it felt like I deserved to leave.

I loved my brother. But that love was starting to feel like a chain, one that I'd never be free of.

I tried to shake the guilt, to remind myself that I needed this. I needed out. I needed to breathe again. But the thought of Aiden's quiet, understanding gaze rooted me in place, pulling me back from the edge.

I looked down at the duffel bag slung across my body. It felt like a lifeline, but also an anchor, tethering me to the life I was so desperate to escape. My legs dangled there, one in, one out, stuck between two worlds. Freedom was right there, inches away, but I couldn't move.

With a frustrated groan, I pulled my leg back inside, my movements sharp and jerky. The duffel bag slipped off my shoulder and onto the floor with a thud, and I slammed the window shut, the sound reverberating through the quiet room. I leaned against the windowsill, my forehead pressed to the cool glass as I let out a shaky breath.

I hated myself in that moment. Hated the way I couldn't choose me, couldn't take the steps I so desperately wanted to. The tears came again, hot and relentless, and I swiped at them angrily. I wasn't staying because I wanted to. I was staying because I had to.

A soft knock on the door made me jump, and I turned, my breath hitching.

"Jess?" My dad's voice was quiet, almost hesitant. "Can I come in?"

I wiped at my face hastily, not bothering to hide the redness in my eyes. "Yeah," I croaked, my voice raw.

The door creaked open, and he stepped inside, his eyes flicking to the duffel bag on the floor, then to the window, before finally landing on me. He didn't say anything about either, but his gaze softened, and for the first time in a long time, I felt like he really saw me.

"Let's go grab some breakfast," he said, his voice steady but gentle.

I stared at him, my pulse still racing from the decision I hadn't been able to make. His words hung in the air, simple but offering something I didn't know I needed.

After a long pause, I nodded. "Okay."

He gave me a small, almost tentative smile, and without another word, he turned and headed down the hall. I looked back at the window one last time, the branches of the oak tree swaying gently in the breeze.

Jessica

I stared out the window the entire drive, trying to push down the storm of emotions swirling inside me. I didn't want to think about Christian, about Courtney, about anything. I just wanted it all to go away.

When we pulled into the parking lot, my dad turned off the engine and sat there for a moment, his hands resting on the steering wheel. He didn't say anything, just waited, like he was giving me the space to breathe. But I could feel his eyes on me, watching, waiting for a sign that I was ready to talk.

I wasn't. Not yet. Maybe not ever. So, I unbuckled my seatbelt and got out of the car, my movements robotic, my mind still numb. My dad followed, gently guiding me to the front door with a hand on my back.

The place was quiet and cozy, with warm, buttery smells wafting through the air the moment you walked in. As soon as we stepped inside, memories came rushing back—times when it was just the two of us, back before Claire was in the picture. The cozy booths and familiar scents reminded me of weekend breakfasts with him, when everything felt simpler and we didn't have to tiptoe around anyone else's expectations.

We found a small table by the window, and my dad gestured for me to sit while he went to order. I sank into the chair, pulling my hoodie tighter around me, trying to disappear into its fabric. My reflection stared back at me from the window, pale and exhausted, eyes red from crying. I looked like a stranger—someone I didn't recognize, someone who had been through too much in too little time.

My dad returned a few minutes later with a tray of food. He set down a plate of pancakes in front of me, along with a steaming cup of hot chocolate. The sight of it—the simple gesture of something so familiar—made my throat tighten with emotion. I hadn't realized how much I missed this, missed him.

He took a seat across from me, his own plate of eggs and bacon in front of him, but he didn't start eating right away. Instead, he just looked at me, his expression soft and patient. He wasn't pushing, wasn't demanding that I open up. He was just there, offering me a lifeline in the quietest, gentlest way possible.

"Pancakes used to be your favorite," he said after a moment, his voice low and calm. "Remember when we used to go to that little diner up in Riverview? You'd always ask for extra syrup. Said it tasted like candy."

I managed a small, shaky smile, the memory stirring something inside me. "Yeah," I murmured, my voice barely above a whisper. "I remember."

He nodded, taking a sip of his coffee. "You don't have to talk if you don't want to," he said softly. "But I'm here, Jess."

The way he said it—the way he used to call me 'Jess' like he always did when I was younger—made something inside me crack. I wanted to believe him. I wanted to trust that he'd be there for me this time, that he wouldn't sit in silence while Mom broke me down. But part of me couldn't shake the years of him bystanding, the way he left me to fend for myself when I needed him the most.

"I want to go back," I whispered, my voice trembling as I finally let the words out. "I want to go back to Riverview."

He leaned forward, his eyes full of concern and something else—something like understanding, but tentative, like he wasn't sure he had the right to feel it. "Jessica?" he asked, his voice softer now, almost hesitant. "I didn't see it at the time, not really. After your accident... I thought you just needed space, that you'd bounce back on your own. But looking back..." He exhaled, his gaze dropping for a moment as though the weight of it was too much. "I saw the way you withdrew, the way you shut yourself off. And I... I didn't know what to do with that. I didn't know what to say or how to help, so I... I didn't do anything. And I... I'm sorry, Jess."

His voice wavered slightly, but when he met my gaze again, there was a steadiness there that caught me off guard. "I see it again now. That same look you had after the accident. I remember you sitting on the couch, just staring, like you weren't really there. I... I wanted to ask if you were okay, but I was afraid I'd make it worse. And now... I can't let myself do that again."

He paused, his words hanging in the air like a fragile thread between us. "If this is what you need, I'll do whatever I can to make it happen. But, Jess..." He hesitated, his voice softer now. "I just want to make sure it's what you really need—not just what feels easiest right now."

His hand rested on the edge of the table, steady but tentative, as though grounding himself in the moment. "You don't have to tell me everything—I won't push. If you're serious about going back to Riverview, I'll talk to Cassie's parents and see if they're willing to let you finish your senior year living with them. We'll figure it out."

"Seriously?" I asked. It felt like I was finally coming up for air after drowning for so long.

"Yes, I don't want to lose you again—not like last time."

The words were there on the cusp of escaping my lips—to tell him about what had happened to me at that stupid party. My throat tightened, the confession pressing against the walls I'd built around it, desperate to be let out. He deserved to know, didn't he? Maybe if I told him, he'd understand why I needed to leave so badly. Maybe he'd finally see me—not the girl who held everything together, but the one who was trying desperately to pick up the pieces while standing barefoot on shattered glass.

But then his eyes met mine, steady but cautious, like he was walking a tightrope between wanting to help and being afraid of saying the wrong thing. And suddenly, I froze. What if telling him only made it worse? What if I told him, and he looked at me the way I'd seen others look at Aiden—like a problem to be solved, a broken thing that needed fixing?

Or worse. He'd be disgusted.

He reached for my hand, but I pulled it away before he could touch me.

I swallowed the lump in my throat, forcing it all back into the box where I'd kept it hidden for so long. "Thank you," I said instead, my voice barely above a whisper. It wasn't enough—it wasn't the truth—but it was all I could give him right now.

I picked up the fork, cutting into the stack of pancakes in front of me. The first bite was sweet and warm, comforting in a way I hadn't expected. I took another bite, and then another, the food slowly filling the empty space inside me.

My dad watched me eat, a small, relieved smile on his face. He didn't say anything else, didn't push for answers. He just let me be, let me take my time to process everything, knowing that when I was ready, he'd be there.

As I ate, the sunlight streaming through the window began to feel less harsh, more like a gentle warmth on my skin. The cafe, with its soft hum of background chatter and the clink of dishes, felt like a safe haven, a small bubble of peace in the chaos of everything else.

X X X X X X

As Monday morning came, I only had one task to complete. My dad was waiting for me in the school's parking lot, while I headed for the band room, my steps heavy with the weight of everything that had happened.

The band room was eerily quiet when I entered, the echoes of past rehearsals lingering in the air. Mr. Trust was at his desk, his expression unreadable as he looked up from his paperwork. The disappointment in his eyes was unmistakable, but there was also something else—understanding, perhaps, or maybe just the weariness of someone who had seen too many students struggle with more than just music.

"Jessica," he said, his voice calm but tinged with sadness. "I heard you were coming by. I suppose I know why."

I nodded, swallowing hard. "I'm sorry, Mr. Trust. For everything. I never wanted things to turn out like this."

He sighed, leaning back in his chair. "You're a talented student,

Jessica. You brought a lot to this band, even if it was only for a short time. But are you sure this is what you want? Walking away now... it doesn't feel like you."

I looked down at the drill book in my hands, the same one that had caused so much trouble. My stomach churned. "It's not about what I want," I said quietly. "It's about what's best for everyone else. I've already done enough damage."

The room was quiet for a moment, his steady gaze making me squirm. "Jessica," he said softly, "sometimes, the hardest thing isn't owning up to what we've done—it's staying and proving we can do better. Are you sure leaving is the right choice? Or is it just the easiest one?"

His words tugged at something deep inside me, echoing my dad's plea to stand my ground and fight—to not run away. But the truth was, I didn't have any fight left in me.

Mr. Trust didn't know the whole story, not yet. I wasn't sure I could tell him, but the truth slipped out before I could stop it. "It wasn't just a mistake," I whispered. "It was deliberate. I made a deal with Kingston's director. He blackmailed me into spying for him, threatened my future if I didn't cooperate. I thought I could manage it, that I could make it right somehow. But I couldn't. I let everyone down."

His expression didn't change, but something in his eyes softened. He leaned forward, his hands resting on the desk. "Have you told all of this to Christian?" he asked gently.

"I tried," I said, my voice still in numbness. "He won't listen to me, but it doesn't matter."

He let out a slow breath, his brow furrowing as he chose his words carefully. "Jessica, what you did was wrong. I won't sugarcoat that. But from where I'm sitting, I see someone who made a desperate choice because they felt they didn't have another option. That doesn't make it okay, but it doesn't mean you can't make things right now. Quitting? That's not fixing it. That's running from it."

Tears burned at the edges of my eyes. "I'm not running," I said, but even I didn't believe it. "I'm just... I don't want to be the problem anymore."

"Leaving doesn't erase what happened," he said firmly. "It doesn't give anyone closure—not you, not the band, not Christian.

And it won't give you peace, Jessica. You'll carry this with you wherever you go."

I swallowed hard, my voice barely above a whisper. "I don't want to make it worse. I already have. Staying will only hurt everyone more."

He sighed deeply, his disappointment a tangible weight in the air between us. But there was no anger in his voice—only a steady, quiet resolve. "If this is what you've decided, I won't stop you. But, Jessica, running won't mend what's broken inside of you. One day, you'll have to face it. And when you do, I hope you'll see that it doesn't define you. It's what you choose to do after that will."

I placed the drill book on his desk, followed by the garment bag containing my performance dress. He watched me, his gaze softening as he realized how final this moment was.

Then, I reached into my backpack and pulled out the vinyl record I had bought for Christian. It had seemed like the perfect gift back then, something to show him I really understood him. Now, it was just a painful reminder of everything that had gone wrong.

"Can you give this to Christian for me?" I asked, my voice barely above a whisper.

Mr. Trust took the record from my hands, glancing at it before nodding. "I'll make sure he gets it. I'm sorry it has to end this way, Jessica."

"Me too," I replied, my throat tightening with the effort to keep my emotions in check. "Thank you, Mr. Trust. For everything."

Without another word, I turned and left the band room, the office door closing softly behind me. Before I could exit the band room, the doors swung open. Christian walked in, eyes locking on mine before looking away.

I froze for a moment. My fingers tightened around the strap of my bag as I forced myself to keep walking. I didn't look at him. I couldn't. I just kept my head down and moved past him, pretending the ache in my chest didn't exist.

The parking lot was quiet, the evening air crisp against my skin. I was halfway to my car when his voice reached me.

"Jessica."

I stopped, my breath catching in my throat. I didn't turn at first, afraid to face him, afraid of what I might see—or what I wouldn't.

But then I heard his footsteps, deliberate and steady, growing closer until I had no choice but to turn around.

He stood there, just a few feet away, holding something out toward me. It took me a moment to realize what it was—my sweater.

"Here," he said. "You left this at my place."

I stared at it for a second too long before stepping forward to take it. My fingers brushed his as I grabbed it, and for the briefest moment, I thought he might say something else. But he didn't.

"Thanks," I said, the word barely audible, as if it might shatter the fragile silence between us.

He didn't respond. His eyes flicked over me briefly, but there was nothing behind them—no anger, no hurt, just... nothing. Like I didn't matter anymore. Like we had already become strangers.

I clutched the sweater tightly, its weight heavier than it should've been, and nodded once. That was all I could manage.

Christian turned without another word and walked back toward the building, his figure disappearing into the glow of the lights. He didn't look back.

I stood there for a moment, the sweater in my hands, the finality of it sinking in like a stone. There was nothing left to say, nothing left to salvage.

I walked back to the parking lot, where my dad was waiting. He didn't say anything as I climbed into the car, just gave me a reassuring nod before starting the engine.

As we pulled out of the parking lot and onto the highway, an unshakable numbness settled over me. I pressed my head against the window, watching the familiar buildings of Arcana High disappear, knowing they would become memories I'd never get to rewrite, forcing myself to not look back.

Because I knew he wouldn't.

With every mile that passed, the weight in my chest grew heavier, a reminder that maybe I was the common denominator in all of this. That no matter where I went, tragedy would follow. My mistakes, my choices—they were mine alone, and they'd finally caught up with me. I'd wanted so badly to believe I could be someone different, that this time would be different.

I closed my eyes, trying to shut out the sharp ache that came with knowing I'd hurt people who had trusted me, people I had started to love. And what did I have to show for it? Nothing. Nothing but a shattered sense of self, a reminder that I'd never be enough—never for them, never for him, never even for myself.

I'd always come back to this place—this quiet, hollow silence. Here, no one could hurt me. And I couldn't hurt anyone else.

Christian

The seniors were called into the band room before rehearsal even began. Mr. Trust's fury was waiting for us. The tension in the room was suffocating as we filed in, each of us avoiding eye contact. I already knew what was coming, but knowing didn't make it easier. Mr. Trust stood at the front, arms crossed, his expression a mix of anger and disappointment that made my stomach churn.

"Sit down," he ordered, his voice like a whip. We obeyed, the silence deafening.

He let it stretch, the weight of it pressing down on us until I could feel it in my chest. Finally, he spoke. "What the hell were you thinking?"

No one answered. No one dared to.

"Marching into Kingston High in some misguided attempt at revenge? Do you realize how stupid that was? How reckless?"

I kept my eyes glued to the floor, my jaw clenched so tight it hurt. The others were stealing glances at me—I could feel it—but I didn't look up. I couldn't.

"This band is supposed to be a family," Mr. Trust continued, his voice rising. "But what you did? That's not how family behaves.

You acted like a bunch of children, and now you've put this entire program in jeopardy. We're better than this. I expected more from each and every one of you."

The words cut deep, but I stayed still, swallowing the lump in my throat. My anger simmered beneath the surface—not at Mr. Trust, but at myself. He was right. Every word of it. I'd let my emotions get the better of me, and now everyone was paying the price.

"As of today, every single senior involved in that stunt is suspended for the next competition," he announced, his tone final. "You will not perform, and you will not represent this band until you've earned back the trust you so carelessly threw away."

A murmur of disbelief rippled through the group, but Mr. Trust silenced it with a sharp look. "This isn't up for debate. You wanted to act like children, now you'll face the consequences."

I felt his gaze settle on me, lingering just a fraction longer than the others. When he finally dismissed us, I stayed seated, knowing what was coming next.

"Christian, in my office," Mr. Trust said, his voice calmer now but still heavy with frustration.

I followed him, the walk to his office feeling like miles. Inside, the space felt smaller than usual, like the walls were closing in. Mr. Trust gestured to the chair across from his desk, and I sat down, my hands gripping my knees.

"You've been a leader in this band for a long time," he began, his tone steady but firm. "This? This isn't the example I expected from you."

"I know," I muttered, my voice tight.

Mr. Trust sighed, leaning back in his chair. "Your choices affected everyone—your section, your bandmates, the entire program. You let your emotions get the better of you, and now you've put our season at risk. Is that what you wanted?"

I shook my head, guilt twisting like a knife in my gut. "No. I—" The words stuck in my throat. What could I say? That I was sorry? It felt hollow.

Mr. Trust reached into his desk drawer and pulled out a vinyl record, sliding it across the desk. "She left this for you."

I stared at it, my chest tightening. It was from that record shop

Jessica had disappeared into on our ditch day—a Chet Baker record. She'd remembered.

"She also returned the drill book," Mr. Trust said quietly. "And her uniform. She's gone, Christian. Left this morning. She's moving back to Riverview."

The words should've meant nothing. I should've shrugged and said something snide, something to show I didn't care. Instead, my fingers curled into fists in my lap, my nails digging into my palms. I forced myself to shrug, forcing a flatness into my voice. "Good for her."

Mr. Trust didn't react to my words, but I saw his jaw tighten. "You don't care that your co-drum major just... left?"

"Not really." The words came out cold, detached. I wanted them to sound true. I needed them to sound true—to feel true.

Mr. Trust's expression hardened. "You know, Christian, it's easy to put up walls and pretend you don't care. But I think you'll regret it if you don't take a moment to understand what actually happened.'"

I raised an eyebrow, my pulse quickening despite my attempt to look bored. "What's there to understand? She lied. She betrayed us. End of story."

"She told me everything before she left," he said, his voice sharper now. "About Kingston. About Mr. Waylan."

My stomach dropped, but I didn't let it show. "What about him?"

"Kingston's director threatened her. He found out about her DUI and used it against her. Jessica wasn't trying to hurt you or the band—she thought she didn't have a choice."

"She still had a choice," I said, the bitterness spilling out before I could stop it. "She could've told me. Told someone."

"She tried." Mr. Trust leaned forward, his eyes boring into mine. "But sometimes, people don't listen. Sometimes they're too angry or too hurt to see someone who's desperately trying."

Memories of Jessica's attempts to explain—her panicked eyes, her pleading voice—flashed through my mind. I'd shut her down every time.

"She still made things right in the end," Mr. Trust said, his tone softening. "She returned the drill book. She came clean."

I stared at the record, my vision blurring for a second before I blinked it away. My chest felt heavy, like the air had been sucked out of the room. The forced indifference I'd been holding onto cracked, just a little.

Mr. Trust stood, signaling the end of the conversation. "Take the record, Christian. And take some time to think about what kind of leader you want to be. Because right now, you've got a lot of work to do."

I picked up the vinyl, the smooth surface cool against my fingers. It felt like a goodbye. The weight of it pressed down on me, heavier than anything I'd held before.

"I'll see you at practice later. I'm going to let one of the juniors take on being drum major for the rest of the season."

I nodded numbly, clutching the record as I stood. Without another word, I left his office. The band room was empty now, the silence deafening. I stared down at the vinyl, my mind replaying every mistake I'd made. I'd pushed Jessica to leave. My anger had cost the seniors their spots in the competition.

As I walked down the hallway, Jessica's name echoed in my mind, louder and louder, until it was all I could hear. She was gone. The season was falling apart. And there was no one to blame but me.

✗ ✗ ✗ ✗ ✗

I walked into my room that night, exhausted from a long rehearsal of standing on the sidelines, running the metronome as if that beat could somehow drown out everything else. The junior, the one Mr. Trust had appointed to replace me, was actually good, but it was still a reminder that I had lost my role. But nothing could have prepared me for what was waiting for when I got home.

The sight stopped me cold. My entire room was packed into boxes, stripped bare like some ghost of itself. My shelves, once full of books, trophies, little reminders of the last seventeen years, were all cleared off. Clothes, posters, knick-knacks—everything was crammed away. Even my bedspread was gone, leaving just the mattress, blank and sterile like a stranger's bed in some empty guest room.

I felt the anger simmering right under my skin, hot and wild. Once again, they'd made a decision for me, shoved my whole life into cardboard without even a word. Not a question. Not even a heads-up. Just my parents, moving me around like a pawn, making decisions they thought were "best" without even considering that I might want a say.

I tossed my bag onto the floor and stood there, fists clenched, barely holding it together. My whole life, shoved into these boxes like it was just stuff, like none of it mattered enough to leave it be.

My parents were seated at the kitchen table, their expressions neutral.

"After what happened this past weekend, we both believe you need a new environment," my dad said, his voice tinged with exhaustion. "Now that the divorce is final, we've decided it's best if you move with your mom."

Oh, so now they agree on something?

"Where?" I asked, trying to keep my tone neutral.

My mom took over. "Just outside of the Bay Area—Concord. I found a great job at a hospital there, and the schools are excellent," she said, attempting to sound enthusiastic but failing to mask her desperation. "They have marching bands up there, too."

As if that mattered. It was mid-season; there was no way I could just slot into a new show and drill program on such short notice.

"There's also a drum corps in Concord. I know you're big into that whole thing," she added. "I really think this change will be good for both of us."

I looked at them, sitting there with their carefully rehearsed lines and half-hearted smiles, waiting for me to argue, to fight back like I always did. But what was the point? They'd already packed up my life, boxed it away like it didn't mean anything. And maybe they were right. Maybe this place wasn't worth holding onto anymore— not the band, not the house, not even the town.

"Okay," I said, my voice flat.

The shock on their faces was almost comical. They'd expected a fight, but I didn't have the energy for one. Then a thought struck me, like a faint light breaking through the haze. "How far is Riverview from Concord?"

My parents exchanged confused glances before answering. "I'm not sure… Maybe an hour. Why?"

I didn't respond, my mind already racing with the implications. An hour's drive meant there was a chance—however slim—that I could still see Jessica.

✗ ✗ ✗ ✗ ✗

One Month Later

As I pushed through the crowd at the competition, my eyes darted from face to face, every beat of my heart louder than the chaos around me. The buses lined the lot like sentinels, each one marked with school names that barely registered. Concord High. Riverview High. They were both here. She had to be here.

I weaved between clusters of students, their voices blurring into a dull roar. My chest tightened with every Riverview uniform I passed, my stomach knotting when I didn't find her. This was it—my chance to set things right, or at least try. But with each face I scanned, hope slipped further away, like sand through my fingers.

Finally, I spotted Riverview's group. Smaller, quieter, their warm-ups scattered and unfocused. My pulse quickened as I approached, searching desperately for that one familiar face. The dark hair pulled back, the focused determination that always radiated from her.

She wasn't there.

I froze, standing on the edge of their group, my breath shallow. My eyes swept over them again, refusing to accept what I was seeing—or not seeing. I tried to reason with myself. Maybe she was inside the bus. Maybe she was just running late. Maybe...

A student broke from the group, her expression curious, her gaze flicking to me. "Are you looking for someone?" she asked, her tone polite but hesitant, like she wasn't sure if I belonged here or not.

Probably wondering why some random guy was standing there like he'd lost something he'd never find again.

I swallowed, my throat dry. "Yeah. Is Jessica Welling part of your band?"

Her brows furrowed in confusion. "Jessica? Oh," she said, realization dawning. "She's not in band anymore, but she's in one of my classes. Did you want me to tell her anything?"

I stumbled back a step, shaking my head. "No," I mumbled. "Thanks."

She turned away, but I stayed frozen, staring blankly at the group that no longer felt real. My hands clenched into fists at my sides, my nails digging into my palms as if the pain could steady me. She wasn't here. She wasn't coming.

Worse—she'd quit band.

I tried to picture it—Jessica, without the mace in her hand, without her feet marking time to the rhythm of the drums. But I couldn't. Band had been her world, the place where she found herself and made her mark. And now it was gone, taken away by everything that had happened—by everything I'd done.

I didn't just lose her. I'd helped her lose a piece of herself, too.

I stood there, staring out at them, searching for a face that I now knew wouldn't be there. The crowd's noise sounded muffled and distant, as if from another world. My eyes drifted past the uniforms, the instruments, the energy of it all, until they landed on nothing at all. Just empty space.

The music from Arcana's show, Romeo and Juliet, played in my head again—the way it ended. A single, solitary note, clinging to the silence. It wasn't peaceful. It wasn't a resolution. It was raw, broken, final. It left you questioning everything that had come before.

That was our story too, wasn't it? The clash of everything we couldn't hold together. I hadn't seen it then, but the ending was always written into the score. No matter how much I fought it, the tragedy was inevitable.

I understood what Jessica had meant. About not remembering what it was like to feel anything but the hurt. About how it wasn't just inside you—it became you. I'd been so wrapped up in my own anger, so obsessed with fixing everything, that I didn't see what I was really doing. The weight she'd been carrying—the one I swore I wanted to help with—I'd only made it worse. Every time I shut her down, every time I refused to listen, I'd dumped more of it onto her shoulders. I didn't just fail to take it off her—I pushed her further away, left her to carry all of it by herself.

But the silence wasn't empty. It wasn't really an ending. It was the musical rest before the next movement—a chance to take the broken pieces and build something new. Maybe the tragedy was fated, but it didn't have to be the final chapter of our story.

Jessica and Christian will return in
THE SUMMER TOUR

Afterword

Just like the characters in this book, I took marching band way too seriously. It wasn't just my passion—it was my escape, my lifeline, my home. High school marching band has a special place in my heart, and it carried me through some of my toughest times. The friends I made became family, the field became my refuge, and the band room was where I learned to breathe again.

To all the band geeks out there, you know exactly what I mean. We weren't just a group of kids playing music—we were a team, a community, a safe haven. The band room was our sanctuary, where life's noise faded, and the sound of rehearsal took over. We weren't just musicians; we were a family—each other's support systems, cheerleaders, and lifelines.

Marching band might seem like just another extracurricular to some, but it's saved more lives than most people will ever know. There's a quiet magic in this world of precision and camaraderie—a space where you don't just play music, but where you find yourself. It's about more than perfect notes or clean drill—it's about the late-night bus rides, the laughter between sets, and the way the band becomes a second home. It's about showing up, even when it's hard, and knowing you're part of something bigger.

This story is my love letter to marching band because it was my lifeline. It taught me discipline, gave me purpose, and helped me find my voice. There's a piece of that in every page—a testament to the long hours, the doubts, the victories, and the bonds that will never fade.

To all the band geeks: thank you for reading. Thank you for being part of something that makes this world brighter. Thank you for taking something underestimated and turning it into a force of connection and joy. And to my own band family—the ones who played beside me, pushed me to lead, and became my second home: You gave me a reason to keep marching forward. Thanks for trusting me to be your drum major. I wouldn't exist without you.

Play every note like it's your last, march every step with purpose, and remember this: even when the world feels overwhelming, the band has your back. You're never truly alone out there—and that's a rare and beautiful thing.

Keep Marching Forward,
Gemma Lane

Acknowledgments

To my family:
John, thank you never once believing that writing a book was ever out of my reach. You are the very definition of my soul mate. And to my kids, I hope one day you'll march across a football field in step with a hundred others, feeling that indescribable magic that only marching band can bring. And if you don't? That's okay too. I'll love you no matter what.

To BTL:
You know who you are. Thank you for the accountability, the emotional support, and the endless enthusiasm for this messy, ambitious, heart-heavy story. Most importantly, thank you for your friendship. Who knew some strangers on the internet would become some of my closest friends? Look at us. Who would've thought? Not me.

To my beta and ARC readers:
Thank you for lending me your eyes, your time, and your hearts. Your feedback, excitement, and encouragement helped this story grow stronger with every draft. You made this debut feel a little less terrifying and a lot more joyful.

And to anyone holding this book in your hands:
This is my first novel. The first time I've ever let something this personal out into the world. I'm still learning, still stumbling my way forward, but I'm so glad you're here. Thank you for taking a chance on an incredibly niche debut.

Drum Major: The student conductor and field leader of a marching band. Does not mean they play drums.

Guard / Colorguard: The visual performance group that uses flags, rifles, sabres and dance to enhance the show

Battery / Drumline: The marching percussion section, typically consisting of snares, tenors (quads), bass drums, and cymbals
Mace: a large baton used by drum majors to signal commands in parades

Parade Block: the formation bands use for parades; typically block-shaped and compact

Field Show: around 10 minutes in length, a choreographed performance by the band and guard performed at competitions and at halftime at football games

Band Camp: an intense pre-season training that typically happens in the summer to learn fundamentals, music, and the field show

Drill: The written choreography of a marching band show that includes all positions and movements

Dressing the Line: the act of aligning yourself with others to create a straight line; typically visual and based on peripheral cues

Set: a specific dot or position on the field where a marcher is supposed to be during any point of the show

Eight-to-five: The standard marching stride used in most high school and college bands. It means taking 8 steps to cover 5 yards

Front Sideline: the front is the side facing the audience or press box; the back is the opposite (*backfield or back sideline)

Step-off: The moment when the band begins to march or move as a unit

Salute: the drum major salutes to indicate that a band is ready to perform

About the Author

Gemma Lane is a wife, mother of two, musician, and software engineer. She writes character-driven stories that explore love, identity, and the quiet, complicated ways people change. Whether set in the world of marching arts or beyond, her stories prioritize growth over perfect endings and always leave room for a little hope.